Emperor's Sword

Alex Gough is an author of Roman historical adventures. The Carbo Chronicles, including *Watchmen of Rome* and *Bandits of Rome*, was written as a result of a lifelong obsession with ancient Rome, and the culmination of a lot of research into the underclasses of the time. He has also written a collection of adventures following Carbo and other characters from *Watchmen of Rome*, where you can learn more about their rich lives.

For reviews of Roman fiction, and articles about Roman history go to www.romanfiction.com

Also by Alex Gough

Carbo and the Thief
Who All Die

Carbo of Rome

Watchmen of Rome
Bandits of Rome

The Imperial Assassin

Emperor's Sword
Emperor's Knife
Emperor's Axe
Emperor's Spear

ALEX GOUGH
EMPEROR'S SWORD

San Diego, California

Canelo US
An imprint of Printers Row Publishing Group
9717 Pacific Heights Blvd, San Diego, CA 92121
www.canelobooksus.com

Printers Row Publishing Group is a division of Readerlink Distribution Services, LLC.
Canelo US is a registered trademark of Readerlink Distribution Services, LLC.

This edition originally published in the United Kingdom in 2020 by Canelo.

Published in partnership with Canelo.

Correspondence regarding the content of this book should be sent to Canelo US,
Editorial Department, at the above address. Author inquiries should be sent to Canelo,
Unit 9, 5th Floor, Cargo Works, 1–2 Hatfields, London SE1 9PG, United Kingdom,
www.canelo.co.

Publisher: Peter Norton • Associate Publisher: Ana Parker
Art Director: Charles McStravick
Senior Developmental Editor: April Graham
Production Team: Beno Chan, Julie Greene, Rusty von Dyl

Library of Congress Control Number: 2021953479

ISBN: 978-1-6672-0128-3

Printed in India

26 25 24 23 22   1 2 3 4 5

To Naomi and Abigail for continuing love and support

Chapter One

210 AD

Caledonia

Some fifteen miles from his base, deep in Venicones territory and north of the vallum Antonini, staked out in dense forest, Silus said, 'Fuck.'

Rainwater dribbled out of his forelock and down his nose, dripping off the tip so he felt like he had a streaming cold. He shivered despite the waterproof animal skins, woollen under-shirt and whatever protection the lightly leaved branches that covered him afforded. The light was rapidly failing even though the hour wasn't late. Not surprising given the northerly lati-tude and the typical Caledonian weather: bad all year round, but especially at the end of winter. It was the month of Martius, and the Augusti were planning a second consecutive year of campaigning against the troublesome tribes north of the Empire's most northerly border. Hence why Silus, loyal auxiliary with the rank and role of Explorator, responsible for the exciting and vital role of spying on enemy movements in preparation for the coming of the legions, was stuck out here in the wet and cold, trying not to die of exposure.

He shifted his position to move his weight off a stick that was prodding him dangerously close to his groin, and in doing so he released a small flood of cold water that had been pooling in a pocket of his overcoat down his back. 'Fuck!' he said again, as loudly as he thought was safe. What a dreadful fucking job. His mates would be tucked up in their barracks with the rest of their contubernales, or on a sentry shift, or at the worst, on a short patrol. How had he ended up stuck out here for days on end, freezing his balls off, living off the countryside, alternating between miserable self-pity at the conditions and mind-numbing fear of being caught, tortured and killed?

Where the fuck was he anyway? Somewhere nearby was the hill fort the locals called Dùn Mhèad: his destination. The brass had heard murmurings of some unrest this way, so they had sent muggins out to do what he did best: skulk, hide, spy. Survive.

'One of the best Exploratores in the army,' his centurion had called him. His rigid upbringing by his Roman father had instilled both physical toughness and absolute loyalty to Rome. His half-barbarian heritage made him at home in the wilds of Caledonia. His fluency in the local language allowed him to blend in at will. But could he find the damned place? Fucked if he could.

The light was too poor for further scouting now, so he decided to pack it in for the night. He found a hollow beneath a large oak near a stream from which he filled his waterskin, and set two snares. He retrieved the last of his cheese from his backpack, unwrapped it, and swallowed it in two small bites, followed up with a few gulps of icy water. He relieved himself downstream of his shelter, then settled into the hollow, pulling a few branches over him for protection from the rain and for concealment. He closed his eyes, imagining his arms were wrapped around the warm, soft body of his wife, expecting not to sleep a wink.

He awoke to the sound of movement nearby. His eyes flew open, but he resisted the instinct to jump up and grab his weapons. He probably hadn't been found yet, which meant he

2

still had surprise on his side. His heart pounded. He was fully alert with no somnolent transition from sleep to wakefulness. He noted with amazement that it was dawn and he had slept dreamlessly for the whole night. The sounds of rustling in the leaf litter grew closer. He prepared to spring into action, to take his chances against however many of the enemy were there, and hopefully do enough damage and spread enough chaos to be able to slip away.

A shape emerged from the undergrowth a few feet away: a large boar snuffling through the leaf litter for roots and slugs. Even as Silus let out a breath of relief, his stomach clenched as he thought of spit roast pork, and his mouth watered. He slowly reached towards the knife at his belt, then hesitated. It was a big fellow with sharp tusks, and wouldn't fall easily. Silus had no bow on this mission, and even if he was able to jump on the animal and overcome it man to beast, the racket from the tussle and the screams from the boar – and hopefully not from himself – would carry for miles. He relaxed and waited for the creature to move on, heart sinking as it retreated out of reach. Then he emerged from his hideout, rotated his head in an attempt to remove the crick in his neck which seemed to have become permanent, and walked disconsolately over to his snares.

The first was empty, but to his delight the second contained a squirrel weakly struggling, the wire biting deep into its throat. Silus quickly snapped its neck, and used his knife to skin and gut it. Making a fire was clearly out of the question, both because of the risk of detection and the impossibility of starting a flame in this rainfall. He said a brief prayer to Valetudo, goddess of personal health, that the squirrel was not diseased, then another to Apollo, god of sun and healing, on the off chance he might send a break in the clouds as well as protect

3

him from food poisoning. Then he devoured the raw squirrel flesh, not attempting to savour it, just gulping down the chunks of meat.

Silus remembered the first time he had eaten raw squirrel. It was during a long hunt in the forests with his father, when he had been just five years old, still living with his family and others of the tribe of the Brigantes. The slimy texture had made him vomit it straight up. His father had beaten him, then made him eat what he had just puked. He had kept it down the second time. *Father*, he thought, *you really were a bastard*. Still, the skills his father had taught him were the reason why he was of so much use to the legions, and why he was out here now. *So that's one more thing to hate you for, Father.*

Silus buried the remains of his meal, refilled his water-skin, retrieved his snares, relieved his bladder and bowels, and looked up. He could see through the canopy, as the oaks and birches were not yet even in bud, only the pine trees providing greenery. But the sky was a uniform grey, with no indication of the direction in which the sun might be rising. He turned his attention to the trees. In more open spaces, it was possible to work out which was south from the predominance of the branches growing towards the light, but in this dense wood-land most of the trees just struggled upwards for a glimpse of the sun. The same went for the moss, which he knew grew predominantly on the north, the shadier side of the tree. But here all was shade, and the moss grew wherever it liked.

Silus shrugged, picked a direction he guessed was northerly and set off.

After half a day of tramping through leaf litter that hid treacherous roots and fox holes, the trees abruptly thinned, and within moments he found himself at the edge of the treeline.

And there, ahead and to his right, was the hillfort of Dùn Mhèad.

It had to be Dùn Mhèad; there were no other settlements that big nearby. The hill it topped was broad and towered over the rest of the surrounding hills. The fort itself was nothing like the Roman equivalent. There was not a stone or brick in sight. The settlement itself consisted of a number of thatched roundhouses, a longhouse and some smaller structures and tents. These were surrounded by a wooden palisade made of sharpened stakes, and below these was a series of earthworks – ditches with heaped earth embankments. A well-equipped legion would barely break a sweat carrying a place like this. But first they would have to reach it through miles of enemy territory and hostile terrain. The Caledonians and the Maeatae confederation, of which the Venicones were one of the member tribes, had become masters of guerilla warfare, inflicting far more damage on the Roman invaders by ambush and trap than they ever managed in open battle.

Silus settled himself by the treeline, pulling some green branches over himself, and watched. It was hard to make out details from this distance, around a quarter of a mile away, but he could see plenty of activity, and the sound of hammer on metal rang out over the lowing of the cattle gathered in the fort. From his right, the east he thought, a band of warriors twenty strong climbed the hill. They wore cloaks and trousers but no armour, and carried spears and small round shields. Gates in the palisade swung open to admit them, and Silus was able to glimpse a large number of other men inside, with some milling around, some sitting and drinking and some sparring with their spears. Before the gates swung shut again, he had estimated some four hundred. Few were women, and fewer still were children or elderly.

5

This was a warband. Gathering for a raid.

Silus thought of his mates back at headquarters, and much as he resented the fact that they were probably sitting in their barracks warm and dry and fed, or at worst on a short patrol in a well-defended formation, he would hate to have this lot fall on them without warning.

Or maybe the target wasn't even the fortification. Maybe it was a Roman settlement. Maybe it was a village, like the one where his wife and daughter, Velua and Sergia, lived. His stomach clenched at the thought. He weighed up the benefits of staying longer to gather more intelligence against heading home with his information immediately. The information that this band was gathering with battle clearly in their hearts was as important as anything else he could learn, and the longer he stayed, the greater the risk of discovery. He backed slowly away, deeper into the trees, and when he felt there was sufficient cover, he stood and stretched. He turned his back to the fort and started walking back into the forest.

He had made it barely fifty yards when a sudden noise made him freeze: a crashing through the undergrowth. He placed his hand on his knife and faced the direction of the sound, his heart racing. A large stag zigzagged through the trees, veering away when it saw him, then disappeared into the undergrowth. He remained still, letting his breathing settle and his pulse slow. Then he turned to make his way deeper into the thickness of the trees, away from the danger.

Voices stopped him again. Deep, getting nearer. He slid behind a large oak then peered out. He saw movement, and squinted: two, no, three men in the open just beyond the trees, leading horses on tight reins. He crept closer, feeling with the tips of his toes before transferring his weight to make sure he didn't snap a brittle stick. He crept forward until he could make out the conversation. They were talking in a Veniconian dialect of Gallic and Silus could understand most of it.

One of the men was older than the others, and his voice rang with authority.

'Maglorix, that stag is mine, and I will take it.'

'My Lord Voteporix. We have other duties to attend. We can't waste time here.'

'Can't? Be careful with your words, Maglorix. Son of mine or not, I'll have your head if you don't show me respect.'

Maglorix bowed his head. 'I'm sorry, my Lord. Nevertheless, it is my duty to counsel you. The men will be expecting you back at the camp. For speeches and tales and ale.'

'What are you scared of, Maglorix? Surely not of running into some bandits or a Roman patrol deep in our lands? So what is it? Ghosts and demons?'

Maglorix made a little sign to ward off evil, eliciting a sneer from his father.

'Of course not,' said Maglorix. 'I fear nothing, except the hag, the Aos-sídhe and my Lord.'

Voteporix nodded. 'Good. Buan, look after the horses. Maglorix, follow me.'

Buan, a huge, bald-headed warrior, gathered up the three sets of reins and held the horses dutifully, expression blank.

Silus' mind raced. The names meant nothing, but the son had called his father Lord. This must be the tribal chief, the war leader, with his son, maybe even his heir. What should he do? He could still slip away with his information. But what if he could escape with more? Say the head of a rebellious tribal chief? Not only might he stop the raiders by killing their leader, what rewards might await him when he returned? Money? Promotion? A less shitty job and more time at home with Velua and Sergia?

7

Silus gritted his teeth. He was torn. The sensible thing was to disappear. Get back to safety, get a pat on the back for a job well done, then get sent back out into this shitty country with his shitty salary while his wife and daughter sat at home in their shitty house, wondering where he was and if and when he would be back. Or he could do something extraordinary.

The two men came nearer, and the time for him to escape unseen passed. Indecision had made the decision for him. They were too close now. Silus unsheathed his knife, then as silently as possible removed his snare from his sack.

The two men were moving quietly now, searching for the deer tracks. Silus stayed still and silent, his back flattened against a thick oak trunk, listening intently for the crunch of their feet on the leaf litter. He closed his eyes, picturing their exact position as the larger man, the chief, passed the other side of the tree first, followed by his son. Silus eased out from his cover and crept up behind them. He smelt stale sweat and ale.

Maglorix was tall and lean, and well-toned with long, curled red hair. He tiptoed behind his father, and Silus trod in time with the young man, masking the sound of his own steps. When he was in reach, he took a deep breath, lifted his knife and brought the hilt down hard on the back of Maglorix's skull.

The young man crumpled to the ground instantly without a cry. Silus let the knife drop. Voteporix began to turn but Silus was on him, looping the tough string from the snare around the chief's neck. Voteporix's eyes bulged in surprise and fear, and his fingers grappled for the improvised garrotte. It was hopeless. There was no way for him to relieve the pressure obstructing the air and blood to his head. He struggled, kicked, but Silus' grip was firm. The big man even thrust his head backward, smacking it into Silus' nose, making blood flow and his eyes water in pain. Silus merely gritted his teeth and hung on. The chief's desperate thrashing and writhing became weaker and weaker, until it ceased entirely.

Silus eased the body to the ground, but didn't let up the tension on the string until he was sure there would be no recovery. He glanced at Maglorix, who was lying unmoving, bleeding from his head. He picked up the knife from where it had fallen and grasped Voteporix by the hair. The eyes were wide open and rolled up in to the head. The string had bitten deep into the flesh of the neck. Silus used the ligature mark as a guide, and began to cut, using the edge of his blade in a sawing motion. Blood spurted as he went through the vessels, and froth bubbled out of the windpipe as this was severed. He tilted the neck back, using the point of the blade to sever the tendons holding the neck bones together and disarticulated the head. With one last slice through the remaining skin, the head came free. He lifted it high, staring into the dead face, and a chill came over him as he wondered what he had done.

'Father!'

Silus turned abruptly. Maglorix was propped on one elbow, eyes flicking from side to side crazily, blood smeared down one side of his face. His mouth was open in horror.

'Faaaather!' This time the word was a scream. Involuntarily, Silus turned towards the edge of the forest, and immediately there came the sound of Buan running, snapping branches aside in his haste to reach his lord. Silus stepped forward and kicked Maglorix hard in the face, snapping his head back and knocking him out cold. Then he thrust the bloody head of Lord Voteporix, Chief of the Venicones, into his sack and ran.

He made no attempt at stealth or silence. The scream from Maglorix had made his location obvious and now speed was his only ally. He briefly considered stopping to fight, but Buan looked well built and rough. Silas was not a big man, and though he was a mean fighter with a knife or a garrotte and surprise on his side, in a straight one-to-one fight with someone stronger, the outcome would be much less certain. Besides, his job now was clear: get home with the information. And the head.

He would have a short head start. Buan would no doubt stop in shock at the sight of his decapitated chief, then tend to the unconscious Maglorix. He had no idea how long Maglorix would be out for. He could be round in a short while or he may never wake. Then Buan would have to decide whether to return for help to the hillfort, to tend to Maglorix or to pursue on his own. Silus resolved to put the time to good use.

After some time running straight, breaking branches in his path and making deep footprints in the muddy litter, he back-tracked for a hundred yards, treading in his own steps, then took a deer track that led at right angles off into the deeper forest, carefully easing foliage out of the way to avoid tell-tale damage that could be tracked. He moved swiftly but delicately, making little noise and leaving little evidence of his passing.

Soon he heard sounds of crashing in the woods behind him. He fought the urge to break into a run, trusting his stealth instead. He heard two voices, shouted orders and howls of rage. Maglorix had obviously recovered. Silus' heart raced from fear and exertion. The sound of the voices faded, and he breathed a little easier. Before long though, the voices grew louder again. They had found the end of his trail, and worked out that he had backtracked. At least one of them wasn't dumb. And apparently a good tracker too. Silus could hear them gaining on him, and realised that they had discovered his new, concealed route.

'Fuck it to Hades and back,' he muttered, and ran, no longer caring about noise or clues, just wanting to put distance between himself and his pursuers.

It became a race of endurance. Sprinting through thick undergrowth was an impossibility. Silus was encumbered by his pack and the head. He needed the pack for his supplies for his journey home, and he was damned if he was discarding the head after risking his life to collect it. As the ache in his legs intensified, and his breath came in ragged gasps, the forest seemed to close in on him. He cursed himself over and over for his recklessness, and tried not to think about leaving his wife a widow and his daughter without a father.

But slowly, the sounds of pursuit faded. Either Silus was the fitter man, or Maglorix was too injured to continue a long chase, and Buan would not leave him. Eventually the noise of snapping foliage and heavy feet ceased.

'Rooooman!'

Maglorix's roar was attenuated by the forest, but was still loud when it reached Silus' ears.

'Roooomaaaan! I have seen your face. I will find you! You are mine!'

Silus put his head down and ran.

—

Maglorix leaned against Buan at the southern edge of the forest. On the back of his head was a lump the size of a goose egg which throbbed in time with his pulse. Dried blood caked his moustache and beard where it had flooded out of his nose after the Roman had kicked him in the face. He touched his nose tentatively, fairly certain it was broken. A wave of dizziness swept over him, and he felt blackness closing in for a moment. His legs weakened, but Buan wordlessly took his weight with an arm around his chest, and soon the feeling passed. He gazed over the marshland and hills and woods that his homeland was comprised of and uttered a prayer. He did not raise his voice, just spoke in a matter of fact fashion.

'Cailleach Bhéara, divine hag. By all that I hold dear, know that I will have revenge on the Roman who killed and dishonoured my father. He will suffer as I have suffered. This I promise.'

Buan bowed his head in silent witness to the oath. Maglorix closed his eyes. Two images were seared into his mind's eye. His father's head, held aloft, streaming blood from the severed neck. And the face of the Roman. Even though he had been covered in mud, though the light had been poor, though the time he looked at him before being knocked out was short, he would not forget him. Ever.

Maglorix looked at the ground. The Roman was long gone. Maglorix had tried to keep up, but when the energy from his fury and grief was no longer sufficient to sustain him, he had realised he was not going to catch his prey. He had tried to persuade the uninjured Buan to keep up the chase, but Buan would not leave his struggling ward. Though the Roman was no doubt nearly back to safety, his trail was still fresh.

Maglorix pointed to the muddy tracks made by hob-nailed boots.

'I want to know where he came from. And where he has taken my father's head.'

'My Lord. Your family and your men will be worried. We should return.'

'No!' Maglorix spat the word. 'Maybe I won't have my revenge today. But it will come. I need to know where to find him.' He pushed himself away from the large warrior, and stubbornly trudged south. Buan sighed and followed, staying close to his Lord's shoulder, ready to catch him if he should fall.

They travelled for a whole day, bypassing isolated farm-houses and hamlets, not knowing where their loyalties lie. They lost the trail more than once, but Maglorix had grown up hunting and tracking with his father's best warriors, and he always picked it up again. As the light began to fade, they saw one of the forts that made up the vallum Antonini in the distance. The fort the Romans called Voltanio.

Maglorix spat. The wall of Antoninus and the earthworks, forts and other fortifications stretching from the east to the west coast of Caledonia was like a wound in his own flesh. Construction had begun in the time of Maglorix's grandfather, but soon after it had been completed, the Caledonians had driven the Romans out, all the way down to the vallum Hadriani. But that cursed Roman chieftain Septimius Severus had brought the legions back, restored the wall, and devastated Caledonia.

His grandfather had told him of the great Caledonian chieftain Calgacus, who had resisted the Roman warlord Agricola, but had been defeated at the battle of Mons Graupius.

More than a hundred winters later, Severus and his son had invaded the Highlands. When the Caledonians and their allied tribes, like Maglorix's own Venicones, the Kindred Hounds, had harassed the legionaries and auxiliaries and inflicted heavy losses with guerilla tactics, Severus had responded by waging a campaign of devastation. Tough, battle-hardened warriors had wept around Maglorix's home fire as they had told him tales of elderly parents nailed to trees, sisters gang-raped, children starving to death after the crops had been burnt and the cattle and sheep slaughtered. The proud Caledonians had even sued for peace, fearing for their very survival, but Severus' haughty demands were too severe, and the peace talks had failed. The war continued. Not powerful enough to face the Romans in open battle, the Caledonian allies continued to harass and raid, and back at Dùn Mhèad, Maglorix had nearly half a thousand angry warriors ready to bring down death and destruction on the Roman brutes.

This cursed Roman spy though. Not only had he murdered Maglorix's father and desecrated his body, he had no doubt seen their preparations for a raid, and was probably telling his superiors everything he had learned, even as Maglorix stood here, staring at the impenetrable Roman fortress. Maybe Buan was right. They were wasting time here. They should be summoning the warband to fall on the Romans before they had warning and time to prepare.

'Buan…' he said, then frowned. The Roman's tracks were still visible in the muddy ground. But they didn't lead towards the fort.

Maglorix strode forward, following the trail as it diverged from the path that led towards Voltanio. Buan shadowed him, saying nothing, but nervously scanned his surroundings for patrols, or for locals who may be unsympathetic and may report their presence to the Romans. Maglorix was fixated on the trail, and as night drew in, they crested a hill and found themselves gazing on a small civilian settlement, which the Romans called a vicus. These settlements often grew up near forts to house the civilian hangers-on that always accumulated around the legions. The traders, the craftsmen, the tavern owners, the prostitutes. The families.

Maglorix shook his head, regretted it as pain shot through him, then cursed himself for being so slow on the uptake. He had not understood why the Roman would not go straight to the fort, to report to his superiors, and to deliver his prize, Maglorix's father's head. Now he knew. The Roman had been a long time in enemy territory, in poor conditions, alone. What would he do first, before following his duty? A prostitute? Maybe, but after all that time cold and hungry and lonely, Maglorix felt that sex would not be the top priority. If Maglorix was the one wearing those muddy hob-nailed boots, he would want warm food, a warm bed, and the arms of a loved one. The Roman had gone to see his family.

Maglorix watched the little settlement. There was a score of large buildings – temples, shops, storehouses – and lots of smaller buildings, some brick, some wattle and daub, that he presumed were residences. Dogs, chickens, pigs and children played, pecked and snuffled in the streets between the buildings. A door opened and a large woman yelled something incomprehensible in Latin. Two children reluctantly abandoned a puppy and shuffled inside. The door slammed shut behind them.

Maglorix had seen enough.

'Mark this place well, Buan,' he said. 'This is where we will show the Romans what it feels like to have their own homes made into a wasteland.'

Chapter Two

Silus threw the door of the small hut wide open so it crashed against the stone wall, shaking some thatching from the roof. A young girl, no more than five or six years old, screamed and ran behind her mother, grasping her legs and peering out. Silus realised his appearance must be quite terrifying to a child. Muddied, matted beard, and his brown hair grown long and tangled with twigs and leaves, stinking from the time in the field without a bath, and carrying a heavy bag soaked through with congealed blood.

The mother of the child stared coldly at Silus.

'There is nothing for you here.'

'Nothing?' he said. 'Not even a kiss?'

Instead she stepped forward and slapped him hard across the cheek.

'You said you would only be gone two days!' she yelled at him. 'I thought you were dead!'

'Sweetheart,' he said, in what he hoped was a placating voice. 'Velua, darling wife. The mission takes as long as it takes.'

'Shit on the filthy whore of a mission. What about your family?'

'My love. I am a soldier. I go where I am sent. And the money I make keeps this roof over your head, and food on your table.'

She looked up at the roof, where grey sky could be seen through gaps in need of patching. Then she looked at the table, on which sat a loaf of hard bread and tired looking cheese.

'This roof? This food?'

'Mummy?' said the little girl. 'Is that daddy?'

Silus knelt on one knee and held out his arms. 'Sergia, darling. It's me.'

Sergia screamed, this time in joy not fear, and ran to him, hugging him tight. Then she took a step backwards and wrinkled her nose.

'Daddy, you smell.'

'I know, darling. There were no baths where I have been.'

'Where have you been, daddy?'

'I've been helping keep you and mummy safe from the nasty Caledonians and Maeatae.'

Sergia held her thumb and first two fingers in a circle and spat to warn off evil.

Silus smiled, then was overcome by a wave of fatigue. He closed his eyes and put his hand to his forehead.

Instantly, Velua was by his side, steadying hand on his shoulder. 'My love, is everything alright?'

'Yes, beloved. My mission has been... challenging, and I'm very tired.'

Velua turned to her daughter and snapped, 'Sergia, don't just stand there. Get your father some wine, then get a bowl of water heating over the fire so I can wash this filth and stink off him. Silus, come and lie down.'

Velua led him by the hand to what passed as the bedroom, which was actually just a continuation of the room separated by a curtain. A simple wooden box with a straw mattress served as a bed for all three of them, and curled in the middle was a small, elderly black and white dog. She half opened her eyes, sniffed, considered, then jumped up and started yapping and running in little circles.

'Calm down, Issa, your ladyship,' said Silus, smiling and picking her up. 'You must be getting really deaf now if you didn't hear all the screaming and shouting that welcomed me home.'

He cuddled her close to him, and she licked his muddy face enthusiastically.

'By Christos and all the gods of Olympus I swear you love that dog more than you love me.'

'Of course not, my petal,' he said, continuing to hug the little old bitch close. 'Although, Issa has been in my life longer than you...'

'We should put her in the cooking pot. Then at least she might make some contribution to this family. When was the last time she killed a rat or brought home a squirrel?'

'Don't listen to her,' said Silus. He kissed the dog on the forehead, then put her down and gave her a gentle push out of the bedroom.

'She's retired,' he said to his wife in a tone of reproof. 'She has seen twelve summers.'

'Hmm, well she had better stop pissing in the house if she wants to make it to a thirteenth. Now get those filthy rags off. I'm going to have to boil them, no doubt. Or burn them.'

Velua helped Silus out of his tunic and breeches. Her face softened when she saw the scratches of twigs and brambles criss-crossing his skin, bruises made by impacts from branches and rocks. She said nothing, but her gentle touch belied her stern words.

Sergia pulled the curtain back, holding a cup of watered wine, which she proffered to Silus. He took it gratefully and drank deeply, the liquid quenching his thirst and warming his empty belly. Sergia disappeared and returned with a bowl of lukewarm water. Velua tested it with a fingertip. She nodded.

'Well done, Sergia. Now take this copper coin and go to Senovara's house. Ask for six of her eggs. We will boil them for our dinner.'

Sergia grinned and took the coin, running towards the door.

'Oh, Sergia,' called Silus. Sergia stopped and looked at her father expectantly. 'Ask if you could play with Senovara's puppy for half an hour.' He winked at his wife. 'Actually, make it an hour.'

'Yes, daddy,' said the little girl and was gone.

'You think, after you disappear for more than two weeks, without a word, and then return stinking like a derelict who has slept in a pigsty, that you can just…'

Silus silenced her with a deep, long kiss. She melted into him, arms sliding around him, head tilting to one side as she returned the kiss, her tongue pressing into his mouth and exploring desperately. Silus fell back onto the bed and pulled her with him, so she landed on top of him, laughing.

'Silus,' she said. 'You're filthy.'

'Don't you just know it,' he said. 'You're pretty dirty your-self.'

He kissed her again, hands reaching for her breast, squeezing and kneading. Despite, or maybe because of, the stress and fear of the last days, he was desperately aroused. Velua straddled him, guided him inside her, and rode him fast. Her face and body, showing the first signs of the depredations of time and child-birth, were still as beautiful as a goddess's to him, and he kept his eyes locked on hers through the entire short lovemaking.

After, they lay side by side, holding hands, breathing heavily.

'That was quick,' said Velua.

'It's been a while,' said Silus. He stared at the roof, wondering if the reward for his mission would mean he could afford a decent thatcher. Maybe he could buy his wife some jewellery. Venus knew she deserved it. Velua was from a well-off Romano-British family and had been cut off by her father when she had fallen in love with and married the lowly soldier. Not even a legionary at that, just an auxiliary. But this mission could be the making of him. Promotion, prestige, money.

A scream from the main room made them both sit bolt upright. Velua was faster, out of bed and yanking the curtain aside. She put her hand to her mouth, frozen in shock. Silus was right behind her, guts clenching in fear at what had made his daughter scream for the third time this afternoon.

Sergia had her back against the wall, palms pressed behind her as if feeling for the possibility of further retreat. She screamed continuously, her eyes fixed on a point in the middle of the floor. Silus followed her gaze and his heart sank.

In the middle of the straw-strewn dirt floor, lying at an odd angle where it had rolled out of the bag which moments earlier had been opened by a curious child searching for presents from her newly returned father, was the decapitated head of Voteporix. The dead chief's sightless eyes seemed to be trying to see his own eyebrows. The mouth was pulled back in a snarling rictus, black and rotted teeth visible beneath the lips. The long, grey hair was tangled and matted, and one side of the face was plastered in gelatinous globs of old blood. The neck ended abruptly in a jagged wound through which could be seen protruding the white bone of the spine, blood vessels and the food and air pipes.

'Mother Maria, Venus and Minerva Sulis,' whispered Velua. She turned to Silus. 'What in the name of all the holy goddesses is that?'

Silus stepped past her and swept Sergia up in his arms, turning her around so she was facing away from the horror that had invaded her home. Still she screamed, and he clapped a hand on her mouth, muffling the noise.

'Gods, the neighbours will think I'm murdering you both. They'll be breaking the door down if she carries on.'

Velua stepped forward and tore Sergia from Silus' arms. She rocked her gently, smoothing her hair with one hand, and the screaming slowly ebbed into inarticulate sobs. Velua glared at Silus. 'What', she said quietly and dangerously, 'is that, you stupid cunt?'

'Language, darling,' said Silus, then immediately regretted his attempt at levity when her glare felt like a physical burn. 'I can explain.'

'Maybe you could start by explaining to your daughter that you haven't brought a demon into our house.'

Silus moved behind Velua and tilted his daughter's chin up so she could look at him. 'Honeycake,' he said. 'That was a bad man. A Maeatae. Remember I said I was fighting them to keep you safe? I killed that one, and he can't hurt you any more.'

Sergia gulped a few times, then asked, 'Was he trying to hurt you?'

'Yes,' said Silus. Not strictly true, but he was sure the Veniconian chief would have skewered him if he had had the chance. 'And now he is dead, and Britannia is safer because of it.'

'And you haven't brought his ghost home with you? To kill us while we sleep?'

Silus repressed a shiver at the thought. Gods, he hoped not.

'Of course not, baby. You are completely safe. Daddy will never let anything bad happen to you.'

Velua gave him one more dagger stare, then took Sergia into the bedroom. Silus sighed and bent down. He opened the mouth of the sack, then gave the head a kick with the side of its foot so it rolled back inside. He pulled the retaining string tight, and tossed the head into a corner where it landed with a thump. He saw the eggs that Sergia had gone to fetch, and wondered what were his chances of getting them cooked. Slim, he guessed. He slumped into a corner and put his head in his hands.

Velua was gone long enough for Silus to attempt to construct several excuses for his carelessness, but in the end, he was too tired to come up with anything convincing, so he sighed and steeled himself to tell the truth.

The curtain swished back, and Velua came back in, stepping quietly, but her face was set.

'She's asleep,' she said.

'Good.'

There was a pregnant pause. Velua sat on a stool. Silus wondered if he should begin.

'Well?' she said. Clearly, he should.

When he had finished explaining his mission of the last couple of weeks, Velua looked down at her lap and her clasped hands. Silus waited for her to say something. When the silence stretched, he said, 'You're angry with me.'

'Of course I'm angry with you,' said Velua, though her tone was calm, her voice low and flat.

'I'm sorry,' said Silus. 'I shouldn't have brought that thing here. I should have gone straight to headquarters. I would never do anything to upset Sergia. Or you.'

'You're so fucking stupid.'

'Um. Right.'

'You have no idea why I'm angry do you?'

'Because I've been away?' hazarded Silus. 'Because I brought the head here? Because I'm dirty?'

'No, Silus. Because you could have died.'

'Oh,' he said. 'That.'

'Yes, Silus. That. You took a dumb, unnecessary risk that could have left your daughter without a father, and your wife without a husband.'

'But my love, I took the risk for both of you. Look at this shithole we live in. You deserve so much better. This head could be the making of me. A bonus. A promotion. I could buy you jewellery and make-up, buy Sergia toys and fine clothes.'

'Silus, I left riches behind to be with you. It insults me that you think I love money more than I love you.'

He knew that this was his moment to say something beautiful, something to express what she meant to him, his gratitude for her love. Instead, unexpectedly, tears sprang to his eyes. His head dropped, one hand over his eyes, and he tried not to sob as he was overwhelmed with emotion – fatigue accentuating his feelings.

He felt a hand on his shoulder. Velua was kneeling beside him. He looked up into a mask of concern.

'My darling, what's wrong?'

'I love you,' he choked out, then buried his face in her shoulder and let the tears flow. She cradled him in her arms until he had cried himself dry, then she continued to hold him and he savoured her warmth and the relaxing feel of the rise and fall of her chest against his.

'Mummy, why is daddy crying? Did the demon head hurt him?'

Sergia was looking round the curtain.

'No, baby. Your father is fine. He is just tired.'

'Daddy, mummy and me will look after you. You don't have to worry about anything now you're home.'

Silus dissolved into helpless sobs once more.

'You're so fucking stupid, Silus,' said Geganius, Silus' immediate superior.

Silus stood before the bulky centurion, deflated like a punctured water carrier, expectations and hopes pissing out onto the floor.

'But… but this is the head of Voteporix. The Veniconian chief. Leader of the party that was going to attack us.'

'*Was going to?*' repeated Geganius. 'You think you have prevented the attack?'

'Well, I…'

'If I chopped your father's head off, would you just shrug your shoulders and say, "Oh well, time to head home?"'

There had been many times while Silus was growing up when he had wished someone would chop his father's head off, but he saw the centurion's point.

Geganius shook his head. 'You expected glory and promotion for this, didn't you, Silus?'

'No, sir,' lied Silus. 'I acted purely for the honour and safety of Britannia and Rome.'

'Come on. We'd better go tell the Prefect of your monumental fuck up.'

Geganius led the chastened Silus to the Prefect's office. The Prefect's secretary, a tall, ageing bald-headed freedman who brought to mind the statues of Julius Caesar that Silus had seen, looked down on them over his hooked nose.

'What do you want, Geganius?'

'Please announce us to Prefect Menenius, Pallas.'

'He's busy. Make an appointment,' said Pallas.

'This is urgent.'

'Everything is urgent.'

'Announce us right now,' said Geganius in a threatening voice. 'Or if Menenius finds out you have delayed us from seeing him, he will have your balls.' Geganius looked the freedman up and down. 'If you still have them.'

Pallas tossed his head back contemptuously and disappeared into the office. Silus heard indistinct words being exchanged, then the door opened, and Pallas ushered them in.

Menenius, the Fort Prefect, a grizzled veteran who had risen through the ranks to this prominent position, sat behind a desk covered in scrolls and wax tablets. He looked up at them, clearly annoyed.

'Make it quick, Geganius. What is it?'

'I think Silus here might explain things better than I can.' He nodded to Silus.

Mouth suddenly dry, Silus opened the drawstring on his bag, and pulled out the head by its hair.

Pallas let out a small scream, but Menenius merely narrowed his eyes. He fixed his stare on Geganius. 'What,' he said, 'the fuck is that?'

Geganius prompted Silus with an elbow in the ribs.

'This,' said Silus, trying to keep the tremor out of his voice, 'is… I mean was… Voteporix, a tribal chief of the Venicones.'

Now Menenius' eyes widened.

'Silus,' he said. 'you're so fucking stupid.'

Silus grimaced. That message was starting to sink in.

'Tell me, soldier. What exactly was your mission?'

'Sir, I was told that traders had reported rumours of stirrings in some Maeatean tribes in the region of Dùn Mhèad. I was ordered to scout north of the wall to see if there was any truth to the rumours.'

'And? Was there?'

'Yes, sir. I observed a large warband gathering at the Dùn Mhèad hillfort. Maybe some five hundred warriors.'

Menenius whistled. 'That's enough to cause us some trouble, don't you think, Geganius?'

'If they caught us by surprise, yes, sir, especially with the Emperor and Caracalla still wintering in Eboracum right now. But if forewarned? With patrols recalled, the garrison on alert and some local reinforcements? Maybe less of a problem.'

'Quite right,' said Menenius. 'And knowing how vital it was to warn us of this imminent raid, Silus, you made it your priority to return to us as quickly and safely as was humanly possible, correct?'

'Yes, sir,' said Silus, hoping they didn't find out that he had spent last night in bed with his wife in the vicus before he had reported to the fort for duty this morning.

'Then why in the name of all the gods on Olympus, in the name of Christos and Maria and Mithras and every fucking major and minor deity that exists,' yelled Menenius, standing up and slamming his fist on his desk, 'am I staring at the decapitated head of a Maeatean tribal chieftain?'

'Sir,' said Silus. 'I thought…'

'You thought, soldier? Was any thought really involved here?'

'Yes, sir. The opportunity presented itself, and I thought that killing their chieftain might damage their morale, maybe get them to call off the raid completely.'

'Damage their morale? Let me tell you a story, soldier. When I was a child, my older brother showed me a wasp's nest. He told me not to go near it or the wasps might attack me. So what did I do? As soon as my brother was gone, I stuck a stick into the nest to see what happened. I can tell you now that the effect my stick had on those wasps' morale will be very similar to the

26

effect that you murdering their tribal chief, mutilating the body and stealing the head as a trophy will have on the Maeatae.'

A shiver went down Silus' spine. Slowly it was dawning on him that he had made a huge error of judgement, and the consequences might affect not just his own career.

Menenius sat down and took a deep breath.

'Pallas,' he said, 'send messages to the neighbouring forts either side of us on the wall, warn them there is to be a Maeatae raid, which we believe will be on Voltanio. Ask if they can spare any men to reinforce us, but warn them to be on full alert in case the barbarians decide to attack a different fort. Geganius, ensure the garrison is prepared. Everyone is now armed and armoured round the clock until this danger is over. Make sure all equipment is in good order. Ensure we have enough food, wood, arrows and slingshots for a siege. The barbarians could be here in an hour or a week. It will be no longer than that – they can't hold a group together for that long without them starting to fight each other.'

'Yes, sir,' said Geganius. 'And what about him?' He nodded to Silus.

'Throw him in the cells. He can have some time to reflect on his idiocy before I decide his punishment.'

'Sir!' protested Silus.

'Don't make it worse for yourself,' said the Prefect. 'Geganius, get him out of my sight.'

–

Maglorix looked down on the faces in the expansive round-house that served as the meeting hall for the council. He sat in the highest chair, which was adorned with skulls, both animal and human, while the other council members sat on lower chairs or simple benches made out of thick branches and tree trunks. They were a mix of ages, the very eldest a man of more than sixty winters called Erc. Many had tattoos on their faces, arms and for those who disdained to wear a tunic, on their chests. Many too wore scars of battles, from internecine tribe war as well as fights with the Romans.

Erc regarded Maglorix steadily while masticating a nettle leaf with toothless gums. Maglorix couldn't read the older man's expression, but others were more open, and he could see sympathy, fear, anger, suspicion and contempt. His head still ached, but food and rest had restored his energy, and he felt strong enough now to take his case to the council.

'You all know why my father summoned and gathered you here. For two years, the Romans have been ravaging our country. The Emperor – curse him and his family – could not defeat us, so he resorted to murder, rape, and pillage. We have all lost brothers, cousins, children, even womenfolk, to the brutish invaders. The Emperor's son Caracalla led his armies against our brethren in the far north. We know what he did. We have seen it for ourselves. He burnt crops so our people would starve. He burned villages so our people would freeze to death in the winter. How many Caledonian and Maeatae children died cold and hungry this winter? Their blood is on Caracalla's hands just as much as if he had choked the life out of them himself. He murdered the menfolk. He raped our women, putting his seed in them, so they grow Roman bastards in their bellies. Even the Romans relate the story of our forefather Calgacus when he was defeated at Mons Grapius. Erc, you know what he said.'

Erc spat the leaf out, then mouthed the famous phrase that Tacitus had reported spoken by the Caledonian chief more than a hundred years before, after he had been defeated by the historian's father-in-law. 'They ravage, they slaughter, they

28

steal, and they call this Empire. They make a wasteland, and call it peace.'

Maglorix saw nods of agreement around the hall, but still he saw reluctance and resentment.

'My father wished to bring the fight back to the Romans. To teach them to fear us. To drive them back behind the wall, where they can live with the timid Britons, like the Votadini and Novantae who bent over for the Romans to fuck them so long ago. Now the Romans have murdered him, not in open combat, but in the most cowardly way. And not only this, but they have dishonoured his body and taken his head as a trophy. We cannot let this insult go unavenged. For my father's wishes and for his honour, I will lead you against the Romans, and we will win a great victory that will avenge him and restore our pride.'

There was a murmur of approval, but not from every throat, and not as emphatic as Maglorix had hoped.

Maglorix caught the eye of Lon, the druid. His hair was styled in the typical druidic fashion: a high shaved forehead so his hair line ran over the top of his head from ear to ear with a flowing white mane behind. His nose was long and pointed, his eyes too far apart, and his ears, accentuated by his hairstyle, protruded almost comically outwards from the side of his head. He wore a long scarlet robe with gold embroidery, sported a gold torc around his neck and carried a wooden staff with a bell tied to the end. The tribe's holy man was attempting to keep an air of neutrality about him, as he sat haughtily at the far end of the room. Nevertheless, he returned Maglorix's gaze with a slight inclination of his head, and Maglorix smiled inwardly, pleased he had the support of a man who was both important politically within the tribe and as a conduit to the gods.

'We are too few in number,' called out one elder. 'There is a truce with the Romans at the moment and the Caledonians are licking their wounds from last year's disasters, as are most of the other Maeatae tribes. We can't start a war.'

'I'm not talking about taking on the whole Roman Empire,' said Maglorix. 'This will be a punitive raid, for revenge, for pride, for the honour of my father.'

'This is all irrelevant,' interjected one of the elders, a thin-faced bald man with a long white beard called Muddan. 'You are not our chief.'

'Is that so, Muddan?' said Maglorix, fixing his stare on the old man.

'Yes,' said Muddan, unperturbed. 'It is so. The Venicones do not rule by right of their parenthood. Our leader is elected by the Council of Elders.'

'And here you are. So confirm me as Chief and we will continue.'

'The Chief is chosen after debate, after trials of strength and wisdom prove that he's worthy of leading. Your father was no exception, and nor will his successor be, whoever that is.'

'Whoever that is? I am the new Chief, by right of my birth and the strength in my right arm. We have no time for these games. As you dribbling old fools worry and chatter, the Romans are preparing themselves.'

'Have a care how you speak of those older and wiser than you,' said Muddan, voice low.

Maglorix leapt out of his chair and into the centre of the circle, drawing his sword in one smooth motion and sweeping it in a full arc around the seated council members.

'This sword lends me all the wisdom I need. Is there anyone here that would challenge my right to wield it as leader of the Venicones?' He turned slowly, locking eyes with each face present. Each one dropped his gaze to the floor, until he reached Buan, who had been standing behind Maglorix's high chair. His father's faithful bodyguard smiled at him and gave him a small nod. Maglorix nodded back, then faced the council.

'It is settled then. No one disputes my right to lead. So I command you all to—'

'I dispute your right to lead.'

Maglorix looked towards the sound of the voice. A tall, broad warrior was standing in the doorway, blocking the light, shaggy, matted hair cascading over the wolf skin he wore over his shoulders.

'Tarvos,' said Maglorix and spat. 'You are not on the council. You have no right to challenge me.'

'I heard your speech, Maglorix. Right of birth and a strong arm make a chief today? We share a grandfather, cousin, and I am willing to wager my right arm against yours.'

'You wager your life, cousin,' said Maglorix, eyes narrow, voice dangerous.

'So be it.'

Tarvos strode into the centre of the council circle, sliding out his sword. Maglorix assessed his opponent with narrow eyes. His cousin was half a head taller than Maglorix, and his reach just that little bit longer. But Maglorix was older by two years, and Tarvos had not yet developed the full musculature of a warrior in his prime. Nevertheless, Tarvos' smile was condescending, and although Maglorix had not sparred with him for some time, he knew he had a reputation for ferocity and skill among his peers.

Tarvos stood with his feet planted firmly, one further forward than the other, sword held in a loose grip by his side.

Maglorix had his back to the high chair, resting the tip of his sword against the dirt floor.

'Come on then, Tarvos. I stand before my father's seat. Take the place from me.'

Tarvos took a step forward, but he was cautious. Maglorix had his own reputation as a cunning fighter, and Tarvos was wary of a trap.

'You hesitate, Tarvos. If only your mother had been less impulsive.'

'What are you talking about?' growled Tarvos.

'My father was furious when he found out his sister had opened her legs for a Roman soldier.'

Tarvos whitened. 'That's not true.'

'And nine months later she shat you out. Is that why you are hesitating now? Because deep down you want to fight like a Roman. With men to your left and your right and behind you. Sheltering in one of their tortoises?'

'You go too far, Maglorix,' said Muddan. Maglorix ignored him.

'Your poor cuckold of a father loved your mother too much to do the right thing and flay her alive like the whore deserved. So he raised you as his own, and put up with the mockery and the shame. You look like you didn't know, Tarvos. Surely you suspected? Doesn't your soul cry to live in a city? Aren't your dreams filled with images of bathhouses and reclining on couches being fed grapes by your slaves?'

Tarvos was silent, lips a thin line. His sword quivered.

'Why do you want to be chief of this tribe, Tarvos? So you can surrender to your Roman kin at the first opportunity, just like your whore of a mother did?'

Tarvos roared and charged across the circle at Maglorix, sword held high above his shoulder in a two-handed grip. As

32

he reached Maglorix, he brought the sword down in a blow hard enough to split a skull like it was an apple.

But Maglorix slipped nimbly to the side, raising his sword and using it to deflect the power of the blow. Tarvos' blade slammed into the high chair with such force the back disintegrated into kindling. It bit into the wooden seat, and wedged for a moment.

A moment was all that Maglorix needed. As Tarvos heaved to free his weapon, Maglorix pivoted behind him and thrust his sword straight through his cousin's back. The tip burst out of the front of his chest accompanied by a gout of heart blood. Tarvos slumped backwards, body going rigid, then flaccid. The stench of the corpse's bowels opening flooded the hall.

In the silence that followed, Maglorix took a knife from Buan, and quickly sawed through his cousin's neck. He held the dripping head up for the council, turning in a slow circle so all could see. Then he tossed it onto the dirt, where it rolled across the circle.

'Are there any here, now,' said Maglorix, slowly, 'who dispute my right to lead as Chief?'

At first, there was no reply. Then Lon said gravely, 'Maglorix, you are Chief of the Venicones, by right of blood and by right of arms.'

Murmurs of agreement swelled to cheers and whoops of celebration.

'Buan,' said Maglorix, 'get the head of that half-breed on a spike outside the council hall, and when it has rotted, make sure the skull adorns my new high chair.'

'Yes, my Lord,' said Buan.

'Now,' said Maglorix, addressing the submissive elders. 'These are my orders.'

33

Chapter Three

Silus sat on the mud floor with his head in his hands and wondered where it had all gone wrong. He had lived rough and risked his life for weeks, successfully completed his given reconnaissance mission, and improvised with considerable bravery and skill to decapitate the enemy's leadership, figuratively and literally. Yet here he was, water soaking through his breeches, shivering in the cold gloomy cell he had been locked up in all day, listening to one of his cellmates emitting a snore like a two-handed saw felling an oak, while the other sang a repetitive Christian hymn out of tune.

The barred window showed dusk descending outside, and he wondered how long he would be cooped up with these two. The snoring auxiliary, probably Tungrian or Batavian from his build and features, had been thrown into the cell around noon, staggering and stinking of alcohol, and he had been fast asleep ever since. The hymn-singing fellow, tall and lean, his accent suggestive of Celtiberian origins, had arrived about an hour ago, introduced himself as Atius, and then started to pray silently. A fairly recent recruit or transfer, Silus thought, as he didn't recognise him.

Silus had tried to work out the words of the prayer, as Atius appeared unable to pray without moving his mouth, but Silus wasn't that accomplished a lip reader, especially in the gloom of the cell, and drew a blank. The hymns that Atius sung were impersonal, generic words of praise and forgiveness. The verse currently being repeated went:

> *Blessed be the Messiah*
> *Who has given us a hope*
> *That the dead shall rise again.*

Silus was of course aware of the cult of the Christos, who his followers called the Messiah – had even met some – but to him it was just another Eastern mystery religion, like the cults of Serapis or Isis. Sometimes Rome tolerated it, other times its followers were persecuted. He seemed to recall some trouble a year or so ago down in Verulanium after a Christian was beheaded for sheltering one of their priests. What was his name? Alvan or Alban or something like that. In any case, the outcry had been such that Geta, the co-Emperor himself, had to intercede and halt the campaign against the followers of Christos.

He sighed and gazed out of the window, cursing the injustice. Surely he wouldn't be punished badly for what he had done? Couldn't they recognise the heroism?

The hymn singing stopped abruptly.

'How you doing?' said Atius.

'Um, how do you think?' replied Silus, gesturing at his surroundings.

'This? This is just temporary, like everything in life.'

'Fair enough. So what are you here for?'

'Oh. I fucked Menenius' daughter.'

Silus gaped. Atius inspected his fingernails and scraped some dirt out, acting like the conversation had ended.

'Say that again,' said Silus.

'Say what again?'

'Why are you here?'

35

'I fucked Menenius' daughter. Damn, what a lay. Sadly, Menenius didn't approve.'

'Menenius' daughter? You fucked Menenia? Prissy little Menenia, who weaves and sews and whose mouth has never known a sip of wine or a hard cock?'

'Well, she was called Menenia, but that doesn't sound like the girl I was with. I tell you, the things she could do with her mouth…'

'But…' Silus trailed off. Then he thought of something. 'But aren't you followers of Christos supposed to be celibate or something?'

Atius laughed. 'Screw that. I'm looking forward to my reward in heaven, but I'm not passing up a good time on earth.'

Silus smiled and shook his head.

'What about you? Why did they throw you in here?'

'I cut the head off a barbarian chief. Menenius didn't approve.'

Atius threw his head back and laughed so loud the snoring auxiliary briefly woke up, looked around in confusion, then went back to sleep.

'Well, that does sound a bit rash. And I have to say, my crime seems to have been a bit more enjoyable in the commission than yours.'

'Maybe. But there was a certain satisfaction in messing up those barbarians.'

'No regrets then?'

Silus considered, then shook his head. 'Nah. What's the worst that could happen?'

An alarm bell rang out, clear in the dusk air. Silus looked round sharply, and Atius jumped up and ran to the window. He saw soldiers scurrying across the courtyard, struggling to buckle up helmets and belts on the run, rushing to their appointed

36

stations. Atius yelled, shaking the bars and trying to attract somebody's attention.

'Hey! Hey, you, what's happening?'

Most of the preoccupied men ignored him, but Atius finally managed to accost a scared looking youngster. 'What's going on, soldier?'

'The Maeatae,' he gasped. 'They're attacking us!'

He made to run, but Atius reached through the bars and grabbed him by an arm.

'Where? How many?'

'The centurion says around two hundred. He says they are attacking from all sides, and he thinks they are trying to make it look like there are more of them than there really are. He thinks it's just a raid to rattle us.'

Judging from the boy's white face, it was working.

'What's the Prefect's plan?' asked Atius, but the boy wrenched his arm out of Atius' grip and ran off.

'What's going on?' asked Silus.

'Maeatean raid. Two hundred strong,' said Atius. 'We should be out there fighting.'

'Two hundred?'

'It's not many, is it? To take on a fort. And they must have known we would be forewarned, as you escaped them.'

'I saw about five hundred gathering at Dùn Mhèad. What are the rest doing? Attacking a different fort?'

'That doesn't make any sense. Splitting their forces to attack two well-defended forts instead of concentrating on one is going to lead to a rout. Could they be testing our defences before a bigger attack?'

'No,' mused Silus. 'They need surprise. That has been their tactic since they stopped offering us open battle.'

'A feint then, to occupy the fort, while the real attack is somewhere else, somewhere more vulnerable.'

Silus went cold and his heart seemed to stop.

'The vicus,' he said, his voice a hoarse whisper.

Atius grimaced. 'My favourite whore lives in the vicus.'

'My wife and daughter are there,' said Silus.

Atius stared at him. 'Christos! Silus, we need to warn the Prefect.'

Silus ran to the door and started pounding on it.

'Guard! Guard!' he yelled. There was no reply.

'He must have gone to defend the walls,' said Atius.

Silus kicked at the door in frustration. It was solid oak, and the only outcome was a bruised foot.

'Stand aside,' said Atius.

'It's too thick. We can't break it down.'

Atius drew a small piece of metal, bent at the end, from somewhere inside his tunic. He knelt down before the door, slid the hook into the keyhole and fiddled for a brief moment. There was a click, and with one finger Atius pushed the door open.

Silus stared at him in surprise. Atius merely shrugged. There was no time to question him.

'Go and warn the Prefect,' said Silus. 'I'm going to the vicus.'

They emerged into controlled chaos. Although the air was filled with the sound of shouts and screams, of metal on metal where some of the barbarians had made it onto the wall and were fighting the auxiliaries defending there, every soldier seemed to know his place and his duty. Officers shouted commands which were carried out with alacrity, and the men looked nervous but determined.

Atius ran for the nearest centurion, and Silus looked around. The noise of battle seemed to be coming from the direction of each of the eight winds. Having worked out this was merely a feint though, Atius could tell that in many directions the roars of the Maeatae were thinner and less numerous. He picked a point on the wall that seemed quietest and ran towards it, grabbing a spatha from a pile of weapons as he went. He quickly climbed the stone steps to the battlement, joining two auxiliaries who looked surprised to see him armed but unarmoured. They were quickly distracted by a ladder crashing against the wall, and four barbarians ascending rapidly. Silus grabbed the top of the ladder and pushed, but the weight of the four men stopped it from tumbling backwards.

One of the auxiliaries ran to grab a rock from a nearby stockpile, returned and hurled it down onto the head of the lead barbarian. He tumbled sideways soundlessly, but there was no time to fetch another rock as the second barbarian leapt onto the battlement.

The nearest auxiliary engaged him immediately, and as they faced each other, the second auxiliary ran the barbarian through. In doing so, though, he exposed his back to the third barbarian, who leapt onto the battlement and swung his double-edged longsword into the neck of the second auxiliary. The luckless soldier went down, blood spurting from the gaping wound. The other auxiliary roared in anger and threw himself at the barbarian, pushing him backwards along the wall with furious thrusts and jabs with his sword.

This left space for the fourth barbarian to crest the wall. He turned to face Silus, sword before him, and he grinned, revealing a mouth of gaps and black stumps. Silus felt naked without his armour in a one-to-one battle, but he reminded himself that his scouting work was all carried out unarmoured and he had taken down a barbarian chieftain with just his knife and a snare.

The barbarian moved first. He was tall, broad, with wild matted hair full of leaves and twigs, an appearance as far removed from a civilised Roman as was possible. Silus clamped his fear down and countered the barbarians' heavy two-handed overhead swing, steering the blow to one side with his spatha. The barbarian brought up his sword again, bulging chest and arm muscles straining to bring the heavy weapon back into position. Silus thrust with his lighter spatha, but the barbarian was quick and moved to one side, bringing his sword round in a horizontal arc.

Silus ducked under the blow, and this time was able to connect with a slash across the barbarian's chest. The wound was nowhere near mortal, but Silus saw that the next swing of the heavy sword was slower, the barbarian gritting his teeth against the pain. Silus stepped back, letting the sword pass him, then stepped forward quickly, thrusting his spatha into the barbarian's abdomen.

The barbarian doubled forward, gripping the blade where it penetrated him. Silus stuck out a foot, and pushed him away into the courtyard below, where the body nearly flattened a rushing auxiliary. Silus looked over to the other auxiliary on the battlement near him. The soldier had just administered the final blow to the barbarian who had killed his friend. Silus grabbed the top of the ladder and descended.

'Hey! Where are you going?' yelled the auxiliary, but Silus ignored him, and jumped the last few steps down to the ground.

There were no more barbarians in this area, but through the gloom maybe fifty yards away, Silus saw a man on a horse directing a small party of barbarians to attack. Silus quickly and silently covered the distance between them. The barbarian warriors had their full attention directed towards the fort, and as soon as the foot soldiers started to ascend their ladders, Silus loomed up out of the dark beside their leader's horse. The barbarian turned in surprise, but had no time to even yell as Silus grabbed him and pulled him to the floor. He hit the ground with a crack that suggested a broken limb, but Silus was in no mood for mercy. He moved behind the barbarian, put an arm around his neck, and strangled him until his legs stopped kicking. Then he mounted the horse, turned its head, and rode hard for the vicus.

–

Maglorix, seated on his wiry native pony, listened with satisfaction to the sounds of battle coming from about a mile away. He had committed enough troops to keep the fort occupied, leaving his real target, the vicus at the bottom of the hill, completely undefended. Three hundred men stood behind him, and he felt a shiver of pleasure and anticipation. He was their leader now, no longer disputed, and they would do his bidding to avenge the death of his father. And that would just be the start. Once the tribe had tasted victory, others would heed his war cry, and they would gather an army powerful enough to throw the brutal invader out of their lands forever.

He could sense his men getting restless. They too were eager for battle, to start the rampage and destruction. But he wanted to make sure the Romans were fully committed to the battle at their fort, so there would be no interference with what was about to ensue. This wasn't to be just a quick raid, to grab some chickens and a pretty girl or two and flee into the wilderness. This was going to be a slaughter, revenge for all the atrocities and indignities heaped upon their people. He wanted the men to enjoy every moment.

He waited a little longer, until he judged he could hold them back no longer. Then he turned his pony to face his men and raised his sword high in the air.

'For my father. And for every Maeatae who has been murdered, raped, stolen from and humiliated. Revenge yourselves now. No mercy! No survivors!'

The answering roar hit him like a powerful wave, and he soaked up all the energy. He wheeled his pony back so it was facing downhill, kicked it in the flank, and charged.

The wind rushed through his long wavy hair, and he felt an exhilaration more powerful than anything he had ever felt before. More intense than the first time he had deflowered a virgin, more exciting than the first time he had killed a man. These were his men. This was his battle. This was his moment.

They hit the vicus at a run. The streets between the huts and buildings were quiet, just pigs and chickens foraging or sleeping, and a few older children playing with a ball. Chained up dogs leapt to their feet, and a cacophony of barking added to the yells from the tribesmen. Doors opened, and in most cases rapidly slammed shut again. Some terrified mothers and fathers rushed out to grab their children, who were already bolting for home. Most made it before the Maeatae arrived, but it would make no difference in the end.

A fleeing child, a boy of no more than ten years, ran towards his screaming mother. Maglorix rode him down, thrusting a spear through the boy's back before his mother's eyes. He wheeled sharply, dismounted and drew his sword. The mother had reached her dead son now, and had covered his body with her own, wailing. Maglorix stepped forward and with one huge swing of his hefty blade swiped her head from her shoulders.

He looked round to see his men running riot in the small settlement. Some went straight for the temples and warehouses, seeking gold and lootable goods. Others went for the huts, looking for women. Here and there were pockets of resistance. Some men fought furiously with knives, swords or agricultural tools to protect their families, while others begged for mercy on their knees until they were cut down. Maglorix saw a huge blacksmith wielding his hammer. One warrior lay dead at his feet, skull crushed, and as Maglorix watched, the hammer swatted another's spear away like it was a twig, then swung back and caved in the second warrior's chest. Maglorix frowned and approached the blacksmith with his sword held loose in his hands.

The blacksmith snarled. 'Murderer.'

'Your people, too,' said Maglorix, in his broken, heavily accented Latin.

The blacksmith lifted his hammer over his shoulder and swept it round, faster than Maglorix would have believed possible considering its weight. But still it was a slow weapon, and Maglorix could step out of its reach easily. The blacksmith stepped forward, swinging again and again, but Maglorix simply dodged each blow, grinning at his opponent's frustration.

Soon, even the blacksmith's great strength could not keep it up. One tired attack gave Maglorix the opening he needed. He stepped in and whipped his sword across the blacksmith's abdomen, the sharp blade neatly opening him. The blacksmith looked down in horror as his intestines tumbled out, made a clumsy attempt to grab the slippery tubes, then crumpled to the floor.

Maglorix paid no more attention to the dying man. He saw men breaking down the doors of huts or, in some of the less sturdy dwellings, just shoulder-barging through the wall. The raping had started, and though Maglorix did not approve of his men being distracted before the battle was over, he made no move to impose discipline. The last of the resistance was petering out.

He strode to the nearest hut and kicked the door open. Cowering inside were an old lady and presumably her daughter. He grabbed the young woman by the hair, pulled her head back, and held the blade to her throat.

'The Roman spy,' said Maglorix in faltering, heavily accented Latin. 'The soldier. Which his home? Where his woman?'

The woman was panting in terror, eyes wide. The old lady started babbling, 'No, please, take me instead.'

He drew the blade gently across the skin, so incarnadine liquid trickled down the white skin. The young woman let out a shriek.

'The soldier,' he said firmly. 'The one that spies. Which home?'

'Mother,' pleaded the young woman. The old woman showed confusion amongst her terror.

'I don't know who… Do you mean Silus?'

So he has a name. Silus. 'Show me.'

He dragged the young woman to the door, blade still at her neck, and the mother followed, wringing her hands, tears streaming down her face. She lifted her hand and pointed to an unprepossessing hut at the end of the main street. 'Silus' hut,' she said. 'Please let my daughter go.'

Maglorix sliced the blade deep into the young woman's neck and thrust her aside, already walking purposefully towards Silus' hut, while behind him the woman bled out in gurgling gasps, her mother holding her, screaming as she was drenched in her daughter's blood.

Two of his warriors were approaching the Roman spy's hut, making to break it open. He ordered them to stop, and they reluctantly complied. Some of the buildings were on fire now as the Maeatae threw lit torches onto thatch. Maglorix grabbed a torch from a passing warrior and tossed it onto the roof, then stood back to watch with a satisfied grin.

The dry thatch caught like tinder and in moments the entire roof was alight and beginning to collapse in on itself. Flames licked down the wooden beams, and thick smoke filled the hut. The door flew open, and a woman and a young girl staggered out, hands over stinging eyes, coughing and retching. The girl clutched a small dog in her arms.

'Hold them,' Maglorix ordered his men, and the warriors grabbed the woman and girl, thrusting them to their knees before him. The little dog fell to the floor. She immediately jumped up, yapping at Maglorix, darting forward to attempt to bite his ankles. Maglorix lashed out at her, cursing as the little bitch jumped out of the way, then sunk her teeth into his toes. He kicked hard, and the tiny dog flew through the air, hit a timber with a crunch, and fell to the ground limp.

Maglorix stepped forward, looming over the mother and daughter. The woman tried a defiant expression, but it was thin as a leaf, and he tore through it with a backhand across her face, leaving her sobbing and clutching her daughter.

'You are Roman spy's woman. Yes?'

She looked up at him, blinking through the tears.

'Silus. Roman spy. Your man?'

She said nothing, so he waved his sword in the direction of the little girl.

'Yes, yes,' she cried. 'Please, don't hurt her.'

'Your man. Silus. He kill my father.'

The look that passed over her was a mix of horror and resignation. She knew. Silus must have boasted about it. Maybe even showed her his father's noble head.

'Your man kill my family. Now I have revenge.'

Silus' woman bowed her head, pulling her daughter's face into her shoulders, and her shoulders heaved with sobs. Maglorix gestured to one of his men, who ripped the little girl from her embrace. Both started screaming, and the little girl didn't stop even when Maglorix pointed the tip of his sword at her eyes. He threw his sword down, grabbed the girl, lifted her up and threw her onto the ground. She fell hard, her head crashing into a rock with a sickening crunch. Blood poured through her long hair and soaked into the ground. The child was still.

The woman stared in disbelief, mouth hanging open. Then she threw herself at Maglorix and dragged her sharp nails down his face, just missing his eye, gouging away skin and leaving three bloody stripes down his cheek. He hit her hard with his fist in her temple, and she crumpled, half-stunned. He stepped forward and ripped her tunic in half, exposing her breasts and midriff. She tried to struggle, but he ordered his men to hold her down. Then he lowered his breeches.

-

Silus saw the glow in the distance and his heart fell. He had hoped against hope to be proved wrong. He clung to the horse's neck as it pounded along the military road that ran south of the wall. The 'wall' was actually a turf fortification built on stone foundations with a deep ditch on the northern side, unlike the stone-built wall to the south constructed in the reign of the Emperor Hadrian. As such, it made a decent defensive position, but was easily negotiated in an unopposed crossing, and Silus

46

knew it would have given the Maeatae little trouble while the Romans were being distracted with the feint at the fort. The road, always quiet at night, was now deserted.

Silus had little skill as a rider, but desperation kept him in his seat. As he neared the vicus, he encountered the first fleeing fugitives – a young, unarmed, terrified looking man running away as fast she could, then a mother clutching a baby, stumbling along the cobbled road, tears streaming. He wanted to stop to ask them what was happening, the number of the attackers, their direction, but he could lose no time, and besides, he wasn't sure he was able to stop the horse's headlong gallop.

He crested the hill before the vicus and gaped at the destruction before him. Almost every building was ablaze, and as he got nearer, he could see the damage and the slaughter, the dead bodies, the raping and murdering warriors.

In the full grip of horror and fury, he charged the horse down the hill towards his own hut. He saw his wife and daughter, saw Maglorix throw Sergia to the ground where she lay still, saw the warriors hold Velua down as Maglorix dropped his breeches.

At the last moment, the sound of hoofbeats broke through the cacophony of screams, yells and crackling flames, and Maglorix looked round in surprise. Silus threw himself from the horse and landed on the barbarian chief. Both of them went down, but Silus was more prepared. He rolled and quickly regained his feet, drawing his sword in the same motion. Without a pause, he lunged at Maglorix, sword outstretched.

One of the warriors holding Velua reacted quicker than the other, drawing his own sword in time to parry Silus' thrust. Silus gritted his teeth in frustration as his blow went wide of the stunned Maglorix. The warrior swung at Silus, who jumped backwards then thrust hard. The blade penetrated the warrior's throat and buried itself in his neck. His eyes rolled up into his head and he let out a gurgle, gripping the blade in both hands. Then he fell sideways, keeping a firm grip on Silus' sword and ripping it from his hands.

Maglorix got himself into a seated position, hastily pulled up his breeches and searched for his sword in the flickering light of the burning buildings. The remaining warrior hesitated, unsure whether to attack Silus or to continue to restrain his wife. Velua made his mind up for him, sinking her teeth into his forearm, making him howl. He backhanded her hard on the chin, her jaw clacking as it thudded closed and she slumped backwards, moaning incoherently.

Silus wrenched his sword free from the dead warrior, and hesitated as he chose his target, the unarmed Maglorix or the Maeatean who was now clamping his hands around Velua's throat.

There was no choice.

Silus thrust his sword through the warrior strangling his wife, skewering him from back to front. It was enough time for Maglorix to recover. He regained his feet and with a roar gripped Silus in a bear hug from behind, hoisting him into the air and tossing him to the ground.

Silus broke his fall as best he could with outstretched arms, but still fell hard, the breath whooshing out of his lungs. He pushed himself to his feet, and he and Maglorix confronted each other in mutual loathing.

Other warriors had reached them by now, the dramatic arrival of Silus on horseback and the subsequent fight dragging them reluctantly from the fun they were having. Two drew swords and moved towards Silus, but Maglorix motioned them back.

Silus clenched his fists, watching the barbarian's eyes, willing himself not to look at his naked wife or his daughter's unmoving body.

'My father,' said Maglorix, his voice a growl.

'My daughter,' said Silus, the words catching in his throat.

'Yes. And soon your woman. While you watch.'

Silus searched for something to say, some piece of bravado, but nothing came. Could this really be the end? He couldn't deny it, even as part of him screamed that it must be a nightmare, that soon he would wake up. Sergia dead. Velua raped and murdered next. Then his turn. Unarmed amid a host of barbarians whose chief he had murdered and desecrated. His legs trembled and his bowels tried to loosen.

No! This is not how it would end. Velua would see him go down, fighting for her.

With a howl, he hurled himself at Maglorix. Bigger though the barbarian was, the suddenness and rage caught him by surprise, and he toppled over backwards as Silus tackled him around the chest. Silus landed on him and immediately started raining down blows, punching the barbarian leader in the side of the face, rocking his head from side to side. Blood welled from cuts that opened beneath Silus' fists, a tooth came loose, and Maglorix had to grip Silus tight just to stop the onslaught. He rolled, trying to get on top. But Silus kept the momentum going so they turned full circle, leaving Silus once more uppermost. Maglorix was clearly the stronger, and probably the more experienced in one-to-one sword play, but Silus had learned to fight dirty, growing up with a father who was generous with his fists, and in the barracks, and on his scouting missions.

Silus pinned Maglorix's arms with his knees, and pummelled his face. The barbarian's nose crunched, blood and snot splashing over his cheeks and beard. Maglorix roared and heaved, attempting to throw Silus off. The first time, Silus kept his seat, clinging tight while still punching with all his strength.

But ultimately the barbarian was too big and too strong. He bucked again, then rolled and Silus was tipped sideways, sent sprawling into the dirt face down.

Before Silus could rise, Maglorix was on his back, pinning him. He grabbed Silus' hair, pulled his head up and then slammed it into the ground. If it had been rocks beneath him, the force would have killed him outright. As it was, the damp earth was still firm enough to stun him. Tiny dancing lights flashed in Silus' vision, and blackness crawled inwards from the edge of his field of view. He clung onto consciousness determinedly.

Maglorix slid an arm beneath his throat and applied pressure. Silus' chest heaved as he tried to suck wind through his occluded airway. But the effects of the strangulation made him black out before he could asphyxiate.

He came around again moments later, gasping for air, head spinning, the acrid stench of smoke in the air, and the heat of his burning home scorching one side of his face. He rolled onto his hands and knees, coughed hard like a dog being sick, then looked up.

He might as well never have come. It was as if he had never arrived.

Two more warriors held the naked, half-conscious Velua down. Maglorix was once more sliding down his breeches. He turned to Silus, allowing full view of the erection with which he was about to violate his wife. Silus held up a hand in supplication.

'Please,' he gasped, voice hoarse. 'Don't.'

Maglorix spat on Silus, and the glob of saliva hit him in the eye where it mingled with his tears. Silus wiped the back of his hand across his eyes to clear his blurred vision. Maglorix knelt between Velua's legs, using his knees to pry her thighs apart. She shook her head and struggled weakly.

The blare of a trumpet cut through the cacophony around them. Maglorix paused, looking round in confusion. A younger warrior came running over.

'What is it?' snapped Maglorix.

The young warrior gasped for breath. 'Romans. Hundreds of them.'

'Holy hag. How did they get here so quickly? How did they know?'

For a moment hope soared in Silus' heart.

'How far?' asked Maglorix.

'They will be on us in moments. Horses, with foot soldiers close behind.'

Maglorix looked at Velua, appearing torn. Then he pulled up his breeches. Relief flooded over Silus.

'Your knife,' said Maglorix, holding out his hand.

The warrior slapped the handle of his dagger into Maglorix's palm. Without a word, he plunged it into Velua's heart. She gasped, tried to sit up, eyes wide in shock. The she fell back, shuddered, and was still.

Silus stared, mouth open. The world disappeared around him, his focus narrowed to his wife's blank, pallid face. There was no pain, not yet, just sheer disbelief. How was this possible? He crawled on his hands and knees to Velua, clutched her, tried to sit her up. His falling tears splashed into the pool of her blood.

'No, Velua, my love. I'm sorry. I'm sorry.'

Maglorix let out a throaty laugh. Silus looked up at him in abject misery, which provoked even more hilarity from Maglorix and his men. Deep inside, Silus knew he should be raging, screaming, furiously attacking the barbarian with his nails and teeth and anything he could use to hurt him. But he couldn't move. He just watched as the slayer of his wife licked the blood off the blade, and then with a broad grin, stepped towards Silus.

Then the ground started to tremble, and the thunder of a squadron of cavalry filled the air. Maglorix looked up in annoyance, his face darkening as he saw the charging horses in the distance, but closing rapidly. The other warriors looked to their chief in alarm. Maglorix hesitated, then turned to his men.

'We have done what we set out to do. The Romans will remember to fear us now. Time to go home. Move.'

The other warriors needed no further command, disappearing off the main street and scattering. Still Maglorix hesitated, gauging the distance of the approaching relief force against the time it would take him to kill Silus. Then he stiffened his shoulders.

'This not over, Roman,' he said. 'My revenge not finished.' Then he sheathed his blade and ran towards his mount, which had been waiting for him patiently.

Suddenly Silus leapt into motion. He chased after the barbarian chief, and just as Maglorix vaulted onto his horse, Silus grabbed his leg and pulled. Maglorix tumbled to the ground, cursing. Silus gripped him hard, and Maglorix kicked at him then reached round to pummel him with clenched fists. Silus didn't retaliate, just held tight, riding out the blows, his eyes squeezed shut. His strength started to fade, his head spun with the blows, and he felt his grip loosen.

Abruptly, Maglorix stopped fighting. Silus opened his eyes cautiously, and saw that they were surrounded by Roman auxiliary cavalry, swords pointing menacingly at Maglorix. He let the barbarian go, and sank back to the ground.

A centurion walked his horse over, and Silus looked up to see Geganius looking down, face grim. He turned to his men to bark orders.

'Decurion Artorius. Put this barbarian in chains, and have four men take him back to the fort. Then take your turma and chase the rest down. No quarter.'

The decurion saluted. Four men roughly grasped Maglorix and led him away while he looked back at Silus, hatred burning in his eyes. Then the decurion dug his spurs into his horse's flanks. It leapt forward and his men followed. They were still outnumbered by the barbarians, but the Maeatae were now scattering as individuals, making easy targets for the mounted auxiliaries. The barbarians were rapidly fleeing into the countryside though, and the Romans would be able to catch only a few before they had completely disappeared.

Geganius slid off his horse, landing lightly despite his bulk, and knelt beside Silus. He put a hand on Silus' shoulder and for a moment stayed silent. Silus opened his mouth to speak but no words emerged.

Presently the foot soldiers arrived. Geganius organised them into parties to douse the fires, attend to the wounded and gather the dead. He remained by Silus throughout, and Silus sat with his wife and daughter, shaking uncontrollably.

Atius approached, ashen-faced.

'Silus, I'm so sorry,' he said. 'I tried. I found Geganius, and he went straight to Menenius. Geganius persuaded Menenius to release enough men to relieve the village. Menenius wanted to prioritise the defence of the fort, but Geganius insisted.'

'We got here as quickly as we could,' said Geganius. 'I'm sorry we couldn't...' His voice trailed off, and he glanced at the bodies, then quickly looked away.

Atius crouched by Silus, removed his cloak, a hooded ankle length garment called a caracallus, and draped it around him. Atius and Geganius looked at each other helplessly. Geganius shook his head in despair. Atius closed his eyes and intoned a prayer.

'Lord Christos, holy Maria, please take these children into your care. Bless them, absolve them of all your sins, and let them sit with you in paradise forever more.'

Silus tensed while Atius spoke, but said nothing. Atius finished, and Geganius nodded.

'It's time to let go, soldier.'

Silus clutched his family tighter. Geganius took him by the wrist and tried to pull him away. Silus resisted, and Geganius let go, looking helplessly at Atius.

Silus felt pressure against his leg, light, but insistent. He looked down, and saw Issa pressing her nose against him. The fur on her back was singed, her lower jaw was jutting at an unnatural angle, and her front leg also looked broken. She pushed at him again. Numbly, Silus reached for her, picked her up and cradled her in his arms. She whimpered and tried to lick his face.

Atius helped Silus to his feet, and between them, Atius and Geganius led Silus to a horse. They helped him mount. He kept Issa clutched against his chest.

'We will take care of them,' said Geganius softly. 'And that barbarian cunnus will be executed in the most painful way possible. Atius, take him back to the fort.'

Atius took hold of the reins, and led Silus slowly away.

Chapter Four

Silus sat before Maglorix's cell, regarding the barbarian steadily. The metal-barred cage that held the chieftain was in the open, on display for all in the town to see, and Maglorix was exposed to the elements, his long, curly hair plastered to his skull, soaked through from the rain.

On the orders of the Augustus Caracalla, Maglorix had been brought down to Eboracum. Eboracum was the largest town in the north of Britannia, the headquarters of the legions in Septimius Severus' campaign, the Expeditio Felicissima Britannica, and the Imperial household's base in Britannia. Silus and Atius had been given permission by Menenius to join Geganius and form part of the guard that had conveyed the prisoner from the fort of Voltanio to Eboracum, to be presented to Caracalla for judgement and execution. Even though Maglorix had been transported in a cage on the back of a horse-drawn cart, and everyone else had been on horseback, (including the reluctant horseman Silus, who was now horribly saddle sore), the journey had taken a week. During this time, Silus had visited Maglorix frequently, but had found little to say.

Atius had been a source of comfort during that journey. Whether initially it was his sense of duty instilled by his strange religion or a genuine empathy for Silus' grief, Atius had been there for Silus, making sure he ate even when he didn't feel hungry, giving him beer, enough to dull the pain but not so much to make him unwell and morose, listening when Silus wanted to talk, and accompanying him in silence when he wanted peace. Despite everything, he had even managed to make Silus crack a smile once or twice with his stupid sense of humour. Silus wondered if, without Atius, the journey would have been prematurely ended by the death of either Maglorix or himself.

Now, Maglorix looked back at Silus, a hint of amusement in his expression.

'Is it like an itch?' asked the prisoner, speaking in his Gallic dialect.

Silus didn't reply but tilted his head slightly.

'Or is it more like a fire, burning inside you so hot you just want to rip out your own heart? The desire to kill me, I'm talking about.'

Still Silus said nothing, so Maglorix continued. 'You are such a good little Roman soldier, aren't you, Silus? Obedient to your superiors. When honour demands you should have my blood, all you can do is sit and look at me, impotent. I am not impotent, Roman. Your wife so nearly found that out for herself. You were too weak to stop me. She would have found out what a good solid Maeatae cock feels like, not your tiny, limp Roman dick.'

A muscle tensing in Silus' cheek as his jaw clamped was the only sign that Maglorix's barbs were biting home, but it was enough for Maglorix to continue.

'Or maybe she knew already? You know what it's like with soldiers' wives. All that time while their husbands are away. Especially you, spy. She must have got lonely. No doubt she was spreading her legs for anyone who made her feel wanted. Was that little girl even yours? I think maybe I saw a touch of the Caledonian in her features.'

Silus threw himself at the bars, rattled them furiously, reached through in an attempt to grab the barbarian, hurt him, kill him. Maglorix simply stepped back deeper into the cage. Two auxiliaries ran over to grab Silus and pull him away. When he fought them, one of them thumped him in the kidney with the hilt of his sword. Silus staggered, then threw himself at the cage once more. Maglorix roared with laughter as the soldiers wrestled him to the ground, finally sitting on him to keep him restrained.

A small crowd quickly gathered, enjoying the spectacle of the cursing soldiers trying to subdue the raging Silus.

'What the fuck is going on here?' came a loud voice, ringing with authority.

Geganius, accompanied by Atius, barged his way through the onlookers, and looked down at Silus. Then he turned and snapped, 'Fuck off, you lot.'

Atius shook his head. 'Crap, Silus. Couldn't you have left it?'

This time the crowd did as they were asked, and reluctantly dispersed.

'Mithras' arse, what the fuck am I going to do with you, Silus? I knew it was a bad idea bringing you.' He addressed the auxiliaries. 'Help him to his feet.'

Reluctantly, the soldiers got off him and hauled him upright. Maglorix laughed.

'And you,' said Geganius, addressing the grinning barbarian. 'Have you heard of a man called Vercingetorix? Maybe one called Spartacus? Jugurtha? Proud, noble warriors all. Strangled, crucified, starved to death. I don't think our Augustus Caracalla has such a kind end in mind for you. And tomorrow we will all find out.'

Maglorix kept the mocking smile on his face all the time Geganius spoke, but Silus saw a flicker of uncertainty in his eyes. Taking this crumb of satisfaction, Silus allowed Atius to lead him away.

-

The sky was clear blue, the sun low and climbing lethargically, its heat still insufficient to provide any warmth. Silus stood at attention in full uniform, fighting the urge to shiver. Alongside him were Atius and the rest of the execution party drawn from the auxiliaries that had escorted Maglorix from Voltanio, augmented by legionaries from the Legio VI Victrix based in Eboracum. Geganius stood before them, back stiff. A short distance away, in an open space just outside the city walls, was a large pile of tinder and branches. Protruding from the centre of this was a tall stake, which sported a small platform big enough to stand on just above the wood.

Mounted on a fine black gelding, walking the horse up and down inspecting the men, sat Marcus Aurelius Severus Antoninus Augustus, popularly known as Caracalla after the Gallic style long-hooded tunic called a caracallus that he habitually wore, even, so it was said, to bed.

Caracalla finished his inspection, then turned his horse to face the soldiers. A large crowd of locals had also gathered, both to see the Emperor's son and to enjoy the execution. A significant number had lost friends and family in previous Maeatae and Caledonian raids, especially in the years prior to the arrival of Severus and his army on his Expeditio Felicissima Britannica, when the north of the Roman province of Britannia had been repeatedly ravaged. A massive incursion that had devastated the Romano-British three years previously had forced the governor Lucius Alfenus Senecio to appeal to the

Emperor and the Senate of Rome for aid against the barbarians. The Emperor, Septimius Severus, bored and with two unruly sons to keep occupied, had jumped at the chance of excitement and glory and gathered his legions for war.

Caracalla, the elder son, had grown hard, tempered in the forge of battle. Silus watched him now with fascination, the closest he had ever been to the heir to the empire. Caracalla had short dark tightly-curled hair, a heavy brow and a square, bearded chin which framed a dark-skinned face that seemed to hold a perpetually fierce expression. He was broad and well-muscled, the months and years spent marching with the army having toned him so that no one could doubt that this was a man with the personal strength to back up his imperial authority.

Caracalla addressed the crowd. 'We are at war,' he said, and absolute silence fell the instant he spoke. 'We fight an enemy without honour. One that flees rather than face open battle. That hides like a coward and ambushes like a back-alley cut-throat. That slaughters and rapes and destroys unarmed and undefended civilian settlements, like the vicus near the fort of Voltanio pillaged by the Maeatae, led by a craven barbarian called Maglorix. A man, if he even deserves that name, who dared not attack the brave Roman soldiers in the fort himself, though he was prepared to let some of his men die in a diversion. A man who took delight in ravaging the innocent population: the defenceless tradesmen, the merchants, the labourers who help support the army, and their families, the women and children.'

A low murmur ran through the crowd, and even from some of the soldiers. Geganius turned to glare at his men, who were instantly quiet, though the grumbling from the crowd continued.

'Many were lost in that raid. But many were saved, due to the actions of one man. Gaius Sergius Silus, step forward.'

Silus' heart skipped a beat at the unexpected mention of his name, but he immediately marched forward obediently to stand before the young Augustus. Caracalla regarded him steadily, and Silus looked uncertainly to Geganius for guidance. Geganius inclined his head towards the ground, and Silus swiftly knelt, head bowed.

'This man, despite being in some disgrace for a previous misdemeanour and despite being confined to barracks, anticipated the raid. Not only did he warn the fort of the impending attack, allowing the diversionary raid to be beaten back easily with minimal losses, he was also the first to realise the true target. He sent a warning to his commanding officer and without thought of danger to himself, rode to the rescue of the vicus. His actions, in summoning help and in engaging the enemy until reinforcements arrived, saved many lives that day. Sadly, his own family were not among the lucky ones.'

Silus was glad his head was bowed, so no one could see the tears springing to the corners of his eyes. He clenched his jaw rhythmically, struggling for control.

'I have three boons to bestow upon you,' said Caracalla, placing one hand on Silus' head. 'Firstly, you are pardoned for your transgressions prior to the attack. Secondly, extend your hands.'

Silus looked up and held his hands out. Geganius passed Caracalla a small, engraved silver cup. Caracalla presented it to Silus, who took it wordlessly.

'This cup is presented to one who has slain an enemy in single combat after throwing himself into extraordinary danger,' said Caracalla.

Silus turned it over in his hands, eyes skimming over the intricate depictions of uniformed legionaries overpowering cowering barbarians. He felt numb, as if he was floating above himself and looking down at the scene. Was he really here, kneeling before the son of the Emperor, receiving honours, while Sergia and Velua lay buried in the small cemetery outside the vicus?

Caracalla bent forward, and in a voice lowered so only Silus could hear, he said, 'I am sorry for your loss.'

Straightening again, he addressed the gathering once more.

'For the third gift. Well, bring out the prisoner!'

A small door in one of the gate towers opened, and stripped naked, hands bound before him, Maglorix was led out by two burly auxiliaries. As soon as they caught sight of him, the crowd started jeering and screaming abuse.

'Murderer! Barbarian! Pig-fucking cunt!'

Maglorix scanned his gaze over them all, a sardonic smile playing on his features. One of his guards noticed and gave him a sharp dig in the ribs with an elbow, making the smile falter. It was soon back though, and when he saw the kneeling Silus, the smile broke into a full-faced grin.

Silus slowly rose to his feet, despite the lack of command from Caracalla, and stared at the man who had torn apart his world and ripped out his heart. His fists balled of their own volition, his teeth gritted, and he took a step forward. A hand on his shoulder restrained him. He turned angrily to see that the hand belonged to Caracalla, who was looking on him with compassion.

'Hold, Silus,' he said. 'I have one last gift.' He gestured to the guards. 'Tie him to the stake.' The guards led Maglorix to the pile of wood and ushered him onto the platform. Maglorix did not try to resist, obviously sensing the futility and aiming to retain his pride for as long as possible. The guards swiftly tied his hands behind the stake and looped another rope around his midriff, binding him tight. Caracalla nodded to Geganius, who, while Maglorix was being paraded, had fetched a lit torch. Geganius handed the flame to Silus and stepped back.

'Gaius Sergius Silus. You, who did the most to foil this barbarian. You, who lost as much as man can lose. The honour of lighting the fire that will take his life is yours.'

Silus looked at the torch in his hand, the cloth at the end impregnated with lime and sulphur to hold the flame. Acrid smoke irritated his nostrils, and for a moment he could smell burning houses and burning flesh, hear the screams of the dying, see...

He took a deep breath and let it out slowly.

'Thank you, Augustus,' he said, and walked to the pyre. Maglorix regarded him haughtily, but when Silus stared into his eyes he saw the doubt and fear. What was the man thinking? That he could retain his bravery to the end? Silus knew that would not happen.

'Nice trinket,' said Maglorix, nodding to the cup that hung loose in one of Silus' hands.

'I was awarded it for killing two of your friends. Killing your father was of course its own reward. And killing you, that is purely for pleasure.'

Maglorix stiffened, then put on a smile.

'It's not a very big pile of wood that I'm standing on,' he said. 'Think it's enough? I know you Roman men are used to think little things are sufficient for big jobs, but I assure you, your women don't think the same.'

'It is small because it takes you longer to die,' said Silus matter-of-factly. 'I have been told by people who understand these things that people burned to death in a big fire die quickly

62

from the smoke, sometimes before the flame has even touched them. This fire will build slowly. You will feel it eat away the flesh on your legs, but your heart and lungs will still beat and bellow. It will reach that cock you are so proud of, and shrivel it like an overcooked sausage. Then it will eat into your guts before it kills you. You are going to scream for a long time.'

This time Maglorix had no reply, and Silus saw a little urine had trickled down the inside of the barbarian Chief's thigh.

'Nothing to say now, Chief?' asked Silus. 'No jokes, no last words?'

'My shade will come for you,' whispered Maglorix.

A shiver went down Silus' spine as he locked eyes with the condemned man, and he felt frozen in place.

'Get on with it,' yelled someone from the crowd. Others joined in. 'Do it! Burn the murderer! Kill the barbarian!'

Silus thrust the torch into the dried grass, leaves and twiglets at the base of the pyre, and the kindling caught immediately. Maglorix looked down as the flames leapt into life, small at first like a seedling in spring, but growing rapidly, igniting the branches. Silus stepped back as the heat built, and he watched. Maglorix stared at Silus, exuding hate. He remained stiff and straight as long as he could, then began to writhe as the pain on his feet and lower legs became intense. Finally, able to bear it no longer, he started to scream.

A noise in the crowd and a mumble growing to shouts of surprise caused Silus to turn. Many had taken their eyes away from the execution and were pointing towards a detachment of Praetorian Guards that were marching double-time towards them. As they came on without slowing their pace, even Caracalla turned to stare open-mouthed.

Eight Praetorians and their mounted commander ploughed into the middle of the gathering. The commander, a tall slim man, his hooded cloak drawn tight against the cold, gestured to the fire. Two of the guards ran to the pyre. Using spears and swords, they began to hack at the fire, exposing themselves to the heat and smoke, but doggedly beating the fire out with brave efficiency. After a brief moment of shock, Silus stepped forward to stop them, but two other Praetorians stepped in front of him, hands on half-drawn swords.

'Soldiers, stop what you are doing this instant,' yelled Geganius, face white with anger. 'On whose authority are you interrupting this execution?'

'On mine,' said their commander, pulling his cloak back. Silus stared in disbelief at the dark, smooth-chinned face of Geta, the Emperor's youngest son, easily recognisable from his attire and from the ubiquitous coins and statues of the imperial family throughout the empire.

The fire was subdued enough for one of Geta's men to step through and cut the bonds holding Maglorix. The barbarian chief screamed as the soldiers pulled him out and dumped him on the grass. He lay on his back, coughing and wailing in agony. His feet and lower legs were blistered and black, but Silus could not tell how much damage had been done under the soot and ash.

A bucket of water was produced and dumped over Maglorix's feet, then another over his face, which worsened the coughing but stopped the screams. Silus stared down at the man he had been expecting to see die, stunned.

Caracalla strode up to Geta, his face a mask of fury. Geta looked down on him haughtily.

'Get down, brother,' hissed Caracalla.

Geta considered for a moment, then with insolent slowness dismounted. Standing side by side, the contrast between the two Augusti was marked. Geta was some fifteen years junior to

Caracalla and the difference in age was visually striking. Caracalla's curly beard was full and wiry, his face was broad-boned but leaner, his shoulders wider and his arms more muscled. Caracalla had been campaigning in the field since a much younger age than Geta had. He had been promoted by their father to Augustus twelve years previously and had lived the life of a soldier emperor like his father. Geta by contrast had only been promoted to Augustus in the last year to appease their mother Julia Domna, it was said, and had spent much of his time on bureaucratic and administrative duties, while Caracalla had been commanding legions.

Physical appearance was not the only difference between the brothers that their disparate military experience had engendered in them. Caracalla exuded confidence. Slightly taller, he looked down at Geta with a sneer, hands loose at his side, near but not gripping his spatha.

Geta was not intimidated, and his right hand gripped the hilt of his sword in its scabbard on the left.

'I should have you cut down where you stand,' Caracalla growled, and the civilian and auxiliary onlookers stared in amazement at this public row between the two powerful men.

One of Geta's Praetorians took a step forward, half unsheathing his sword. Instinctively, Silus moved forward too, his own sword half out of its scabbard, chest almost touching his opponent's. They locked eyes, daring, even willing the other to make a move. Silus felt a cold anger deep inside him, ready to be unleashed at the least provocation.

'Stand down,' said Geta and without hesitation his soldier sheathed his weapon and stepped back.

'You too, Silus,' said Caracalla, and reluctantly Silus complied.

Geta smiled. 'No embrace for your brother, Bassianus?' he said, contemptuously using his brother's childhood name, before their father had renamed him for political reasons. Caracalla frowned at this, then gave a contemptuous snarl.

'Start talking, little Publius,' said Caracalla.

'My dear brother,' said Geta. 'You always choose the violent way. War, slaughter, execution. Sometimes there is a better path.'

'Listen, you little prick,' said Caracalla, drawing gasps from the crowd. 'While you have been sat on your round backside, putting your seal on orders for new consignments of writing tablets and socks, I have been out there.' He gestured vaguely to the north. 'Fighting the Maeatae and the Caledonians. Getting bloody.'

'I'm aware that father has seen fit to give you a command,' said Geta tightly. 'And I am aware of how your atrocities have hardened the barbarians against us—'

'Atrocities?' said Caracalla, his voice rising, but Geta continued to speak over the interruption.

'But often there is a bigger picture, and if you weren't so bull-headed, sometimes you might be able to notice it.'

'You have no authority to command me, little brother, or to stop this execution.'

'No, but father does.'

Caracalla's eyes narrowed. 'What are you talking about?'

Geta held out his hand, and one of his men passed a scroll closed with a red wax seal. He handed it to Caracalla, who made a show of examining the seal, then opened it. The older Augustus scanned the contents, then threw the scroll into the sputtering embers of the aborted fire. The dry material quickly ignited and turned to ash. Caracalla gave Geta a hate-filled stare, then turned on his heel and strode away into the fort.

Geganius stood at attention, eyes forward, his example showing his men that they should also remain where they were until ordered otherwise. Silus looked around him with no idea what to say or do. Nearby, lying on his back, Maglorix had stopped coughing. His eyes locked with Silus'. Despite his pain, he managed a mocking smile.

'So, Silus,' he said, voice hoarse. 'Not my day to die after all.' He bent over, coughing uncontrollably again.

'Bring him,' said Geta to his men. Two soldiers gripped him under the arms and hoisted him to his feet, provoking more screams as his blistered soles touched the grass. The soldiers tried to get him to support his own weight, but his knees folded, so they pulled him backwards, his heels dragging, and lifted him unceremoniously over the saddle of one of the horses.

Geta remounted and kicked his spurs into his horse, moving to the front of his retreating men at a canter. The hooves kicked up great clods of dirt, one of which hit Silus in the face. They disappeared inside the fortress walls. Once the sound of hoofbeats faded, all was silence. Then Geganius turned to his men.

'What are you all gawping at? Show's over. Dismissed. Back to work, the lot of you. Civilians, disperse. Now!'

Silus stood still in disbelief as the area emptied. Geganius approached him.

'I'm sorry, soldier,' he said wearily. 'The politics between those two brothers—'

'No,' said Silus, voice low.

'What did you say, auxiliary?' asked Geganius, a warning tone in his voice.

'I said, no.' Louder this time. 'No!' Voice rising. 'I will not let this stand.' Shouting now.

'Control yourself,' snapped Geganius.

'Silus,' said Atius, placing a cautioning hand on his shoulder. Silus shrugged him off.

'How can you allow it?' cried Silus. 'That barbarian murdered innocent civilians. Women and children. My wife and daughter!'

'It is not for us to—'

'I will not let this stand!' screamed Silus, stepping towards the centurion, drawing his sword from his scabbard. Geganius did not flinch as Silus drew the sword back. Fury and grief warred with duty and honour in his heart. His hand gripped the hilt tight till his fingers turned white, and the muscles bunched in his forearms started to tremble. Then he let the sword drop, and collapsed to his knees, head down, sobbing.

Two pairs of strong hands lifted him under the armpits.

'Silus,' whispered Atius, 'what the hell are you doing?'

'What are your orders, sir?' asked the other who held him, a Voltanio auxiliary.

'Lock him up till he cools off,' said Geganius.

'And then?'

'The man has only just been honoured by the Augustus. And he has lost his family. Just… let him go.'

'Yes, sir.' Atius and the auxiliary led the unresisting, sobbing Silus into the fortress and into another cell.

From the shadows of the city walls, Caracalla looked on thoughtfully.

-

Silus was treated with respect by the legionaries, though he was a mere auxiliary. The soldiers had all seen how Caracalla had honoured him, and Caracalla was the military one of the two brothers Augusti, the one who shared their hardships and dangers. Silus was given fresh bread, meat, some well-watered wine and a comfortable mattress.

Atius was one of the two guards stationed at his cell door, but although his friend tried to engage him in conversation, or at least tried to initiate some interaction, Silus refused to reply or even meet his eyes. Instead he lay on his back, staring at the mould on the ceiling, distracting himself from the internal agony and fury by trying to make out pictures in the shapes. That patch in the corner looked a little like a wolf's head. He thought of Issa, who had accompanied him on the journey and was being looked after by one of the slaves in the barracks. The blob in the middle could be an old lady with a long nose and pointy chin, like the aunt who helped raise him after his mother died. Another patch reminded him of a little doll that had belonged to Sergia.

Fuck.

Suddenly he couldn't breathe. He gasped, rolled over onto his side, and curled up like a dormouse, face in his hands, fighting the rising nausea. Shudders racked his body.

'Open the door,' snapped Atius. The other guard fumbled for the key, and Atius snatched it off him. He unlocked the door and threw it open, and in two strides was at Silus' side, kneeling by the mattress. He put his arms around his friend, rolling him over so Silus could weep into his chest.

The sobs lasted an age, and Atius held him the whole time, tears streaming down his own face at his friend's distress and loss.

Finally the well ran dry, and Atius cautiously released his friend. Silus wiped a rough hand across his face and looked up.

'I'm sorry you had to see that,' he said, voice hoarse.

'Don't you dare apologise, you idiot,' said Atius, and pushed him firmly in the shoulder, making Silus rock back.

'It's not fair,' said Silus dully.

'The Lord our God…' began Atius, then stopped and looked down. 'No,' he said. 'It really fucking isn't.'

They sat on the mattress side by side in silence for a while. 'Why?' asked Silus. 'Did anyone tell you why they took him away? Let him go?'

'No one is saying anything,' said Silus.

Silus closed his eyes, then looked out of the barred window into the sunlight. It felt inappropriately bright, with the noise of city life, the carts, the squeals of pigs, yips of dogs and yells of children and merchants making it seem like nothing had changed in the world. Yet Silus knew that the world had been ripped apart, and no one even noticed.

'It's on me,' he said. 'No other fucker is going to sort him out. If I want my family avenged, if I want peace, it's all on me.'

Atius said nothing for a moment, then squeezed his arm. 'I'm with you, friend. I know it's not the same, but I lost someone I cared for in that raid too.'

'I'm sorry, I didn't realise. Who was it?'

'That whore I mentioned. I was really quite fond of her.'

Silus looked up sharply, unsure if he was being cruelly mocked, and was surprised to see his friend's eyes brimming with tears again. He nodded. 'Thank you.'

They sat in silence once more. The guard at the door made no move to extract Atius, leaving them to recover. A slave fetched some water, and the guard passed it through to Atius. He offered it first to Silus, who took a swig, then drank from it himself.

'Are you calm?' asked Atius.

'On the outside, yes, I suppose so.'

Atius nodded. 'I'll go and find the centurion to see if we can get you out of here now.' He rose, but before he reached the door, Geganius appeared and cleared his throat.

'Gaius Sergius Silus,' he said in a booming voice, 'you are summoned to appear before the Augustus.'

Silus and Atius looked at each other. Then Atius cocked his head. 'Which one?' he asked with a half-smile.

Silus wondered for a moment whether the question was unduly impudent, but the centurion simply frowned and said, 'Marcus Aurelius Severus Antoninus Augustus, of course!'

Caracalla. Atius stuck out a hand and hauled Silus to his feet.

'May we change, so we are presentable before the Augustus?' asked Silus.

'No,' said the Geganius. 'You are summoned now.'

Atius patted Silus down, brushing off the worst of the mud and dust and straw, and adjusted his tunic. Geganius opened the door and marched straight to the imperial residence in the city centre with the two auxiliaries. Red cloaked Praetorians barred the way while a slave scurried inside to announce the visitors. He returned quickly, and they were ushered inside, escorted by a Praetorian centurion.

Silus had never been anywhere so opulent. He understood that this was a temporary headquarters for the Imperial family, and so would in no way be the equal of their palaces in Rome, but the ornate columns, the statues, the frescoes, the abundance of slave boys and girls carrying documents and food and wine, and the immaculate Praetorian guards standing at attention still took his breath away. This was as far removed from his experience of draughty huts or army barracks as Olympus or Elysium would be.

Silus could see that Atius and Geganius were looking around them in similar amazement, though Atius was doing his best to keep his cool. The Praetorian guided them to a pair of gold-inlaid bright red doors and knocked loudly. The doors swung open and the Praetorian centurion indicated that the three auxiliaries should enter. They walked into a large chamber at the end of which, flanked by two burly Praetorians, sat on a marble throne, was Caracalla.

Chapter Five

Geganius led Silus and Atius to Caracalla under the watchful eyes of the Praetorians, and knelt at the co-Emperor's feet. Atius and Silus quickly followed suit, dropping to one knee, gazes downcast.

'Centurion Marcus Geganius and auxiliaries Lucius Atius and Gaius Sergius Silus, as commanded, Augustus.'

There was silence. Silus risked a glance up. Caracalla was reading from a wax tablet, his heavy brow furrowed. To one side of him was a balding, grizzled man in his sixties, scars on his face and his still well-muscled arms. To the other side stood a tall, thin noble man, his olive complexion and aquiline nose making him look like a Syrian Julius Caesar. Silus looked back down, waiting, not daring to push his luck. He studied the mosaic beneath him, though only a small portion of the big picture was within his field of vision. A shapely woman's ass and a swan's head. Presumably an illustration of Leda's seduction by Jupiter in the form of a swan. Why a woman would be attracted to a swan he had never been sure, though of course it wasn't as bad as Minos' wife Pasiphae, and all that stuff with the bull. His father had told him some messed up bedtime stories.

The silence stretched. Then Caracalla sighed and tossed the tablet aside, where it clattered onto the floor.

'Maeatae and Caledonians, curse them. Fine, so they live in the worst land in the entire world, with its rain and its cold and its mountains, but it's their home. Why couldn't they have just

73

stayed there, instead of raiding Britannia and dragging me and half the Roman army the length of the Empire to put them back in their place?'

Caracalla seemed to notice the three soldiers kneeling before him for the first time. Silus and Atius exchanged uncertain looks, unsure whether they were supposed to answer.

'Maybe because they had insufficient resources for their needs, and felt their only solution was to steal from those they saw as more affluent in the Roman province...' Atius' voice trailed off, as Caracalla fixed him with a glare that could have crucified him. Then he laughed.

'It was a rhetorical question, soldier, but thank you for your analysis.'

Sweat beaded on Atius' brow, but he still smiled cheekily.

'The pleasure was mine, Augustus.'

Caracalla shook his head, disbelieving the impudence, but seeming entertained by it. Silus could see Geganius clenching his jaw rhythmically, clearly restraining a desperate urge to smack Atius around the side of his head.

'Stand,' said Caracalla, and they rose promptly to their feet. 'Be seated on those couches.' He gestured to a couple of plushily upholstered couches to one side, and they dutifully trooped over, then awkwardly sat, unsure whether to recline in the traditional manner of the Roman banquets they had heard all about but never attended, or whether they should attempt to sit at some sort of attention. They opted for the latter, and Silus had the uncomfortable feeling they looked like they were lined up in the cubicles of a lavatory having a synchronised shit.

Caracalla took a sip of wine from a gold goblet, swilled it round his mouth, then spat.

'British piss,' he said sourly. 'Slave, get me some of that stuff from Gallia Aquitania that I had last night. And tip the entire amphora of this stuff in the sewer.'

The slave bowed deep and took the goblet from the Augustus with trembling hands. Slaves had been tortured for lesser crimes than serving a bad wine, but if Caracalla was that sort of master, he didn't show it today.

'Wait,' said Caracalla, and the slave froze, turning pale. 'Distribute the wine to the soldiers from Voltanio. I'd wager they don't get the chance to drink even wine of this quality with any regularity. Am I right?'

'You are right, Augustus,' confirmed Geganius. 'It's mainly beer. Thank you for your generosity.'

Caracalla nodded. 'See to it, slave. After,' he added, 'you have fetched me a new full cup.'

The slave hurried away, and Caracalla turned his attention to the three soldiers.

'So Silus, I owe you an apology. All of you, really.'

This seemed unlikely to Silus, so he kept his mouth shut. What would the co-Emperor feel the need to apologise to him for? Caracalla supplied the answer.

'It was my intention to have that barbarian prince, Maglorix, suffer for his crimes, and for you, Silus, to be the one to deliver justice upon him. My interfering brother stopped that.'

Silus still said nothing. He was certainly not going to criticise one Augustus to another.

'Politics. Nothing more, nothing less. Geta said he had good reason for what he did, but I think his main motive was simply to humiliate me.'

'What reason?' asked Silus, surprising himself at his own boldness, but angry enough inside not to care.

'A ransom,' said Caracalla. 'A prisoner swap. Some fool favourite of Geta's got himself captured by the Maeatae, and Geta cares enough to trade Maglorix for the idiot's life,' said Caracalla sourly. 'Personally, I don't get it. If someone is useless enough to get themselves captured, they only have themselves to blame.'

Silus thought about how close to getting captured he had been on numerous occasions while spying and suppressed a shudder at the thought of being totally on his own with the barbarians. But he had always been too good for them. So far.

Caracalla sighed. 'Explain, Papinianus.'

So that was who one of the men flanking Caracalla was. Aemilius Papinianus, close friend of Septimius Severus and Prefect of the Praetorian Guard.

The nobleman looked down his nose at the lowly auxiliaries and answered grudgingly. 'He is some sort of official, helps Geta with the bureaucracy. His party was ambushed, and everyone killed, but they thought he might have some value, so they sent a messenger offering to trade him. Negotiations were ongoing to hit upon a sum, but when you captured Maglorix, Geta realised there was a way to get his man back without having to spend a sestertius. He claims that the man is indispensable.'

'I think he is just Geta's favourite fellator,' interjected Caracalla. Papinianus closed his mouth tightly, not speaking.

Silus gritted his teeth to stop himself from speaking out loud. He didn't know who this important official was, and he didn't care. All he wanted was Maglorix dead in the most painful way possible and this useless bureaucrat had prevented that. Silus hated him, whoever he was.

'So Geta negotiated the exchange behind my back and got approval from our father at the last moment. Just a little longer and that barbarian bastard would be charcoal like he deserves.'

Caracalla shook his head before continuing, 'There is little I can do to make it up to you, Silus. Maglorix is gone, released already. He looked lightly grilled to me, but I think he will sadly recover. But what I will say is that your skills and bravery have been noted.'

Silus couldn't resist stealing a sideways glance to Geganius, who had called him fucking stupid when he had brought him the head of Maglorix's father. At least someone appreciated him.

'Oclatinius, what do you make of Silus here?'

Silus' gut clenched. Oclatinius? That's who that old bastard was? Shit!

Oclatinius walked up to Silus and stood in front of him, looking down on him from a height that was still considerable despite the stoop in his upper spine. Silus felt strangely vulnerable, seated, looking up at this man with his fearsome reputation. Images of his father flashed into his mind, towering over him with a stick in his hand.

Oclatinius spoke in a deep, gravelly voice.

'Physically unimpressive. Past the first flush of youth, but not over the hill yet. Naïve. Reckless. Some skill with stealth and tracking.' He turned to Caracalla. 'I would say not completely useless.'

Silus reddened and Caracalla laughed. 'Silus, that's high praise. You should be flattered. Thank you, Oclatinius.'

Oclatinius nodded and resumed his place at Caracalla's side.

Caracalla put his hand on his chin and regarded Silus thoughtfully. Then he waved his hand.

'Centurion Geganius, Lucius Atius, you are dismissed. Return with your men to Voltanio.'

The three soldiers stood promptly, saluted, and turned to leave.

'Silus!' snapped Caracalla. 'Did I dismiss you?'

All three turned, hesitating.

'You two, get out! Oclatinius, find Silus some decent quarters and some decent clothes. He can dine with the Imperial family tonight. Tomorrow you will start training him as one of my Arcani.'

Silus felt his guts tighten as his sphincter relaxed, and he nearly had the embarrassment of voiding himself in front of the co-Emperor of the Roman Empire. Juno's tits, had he ever been this scared?

Geganius and Atius threw him sympathetic looks and trooped out. Atius mouthed, 'I'll look after Issa.'

Oclatinius approached Silus, put a hand between his shoulder blades and propelled him out of the door.

–

The room Oclatinius assigned to Silus in the Imperial headquarters was about the size of Silus' barrack room in Voltanio, which was designed for eight. He looked around in some confusion at the bed with a feather mattress, the decorated chamber pot and the ornate oil lamp.

'Sir, I don't really understand what is happening,' he said.

'I don't think your understanding is really required, soldier,' said Oclatinius.

'No, sir.'

'Listen. Things are complicated around here. It's best if you keep your head down and do as you are told.'

'Yes, sir.'

'What you need to know is this: Caracalla is angry with his brother. Nothing new there. He sees something he likes in your actions. He is a man of action himself, I'm sure you know. And in these times, he wants people like you in his camp. But you are far from the finished product. That's where I come in.'

'You, sir?'

'Yes. You know of me?'

Crap, of course. Who hadn't heard of Oclatinius? Ex-mercenary. Ex-Frumentarius, the messengers and spies of the Emperors. Ex-speculator, darker side of the scouting service, who doubled as couriers, bodyguards and executioners. Now presumed by everyone to be the head of Caracalla's secret police, the Arcani. His exploits were the stuff of legend. And of nightmares.

'Yes, sir.'

'And you know of the Arcani?'

Rumour had it that the Arcani were like a secret cult, fiercely loyal to the Emperors, and ready to do anything that was commanded of them. Execution, assassination, extortion, blackmail, inciting riots, and dealing with any threats to the Imperial court, real or perceived, in any way they liked. The laws did not apply to them, and they operated under the direct command of the Augusti, particularly Caracalla these days. And yet nothing was ever written about them. No one ever discussed them except in hushed whispers. And no one ever – ever – wanted to meet them.

Silus swallowed. 'Yes, sir.'

'Fine. I don't need to waste any time scaring the shit out of you then.'

'No, sir.'

'Caracalla wants me to knock some rough edges off you.'

'Yes, sir.'

Oclatinius looked him up and down. 'Not sure I see it myself. But the Augustus is no fool. I'll give you a chance. If you don't break, you may be of some use. For now, though, get yourself to the bathhouse and get cleaned up, then get yourself into a decent toga and get ready for the banquet.'

'Sir, I don't have a toga.'

Oclatinius sighed. 'Fine, I'll have a slave bring you one. I presume he will need to help you put it on as well?'

Silus nodded, embarrassed.

'Listen, son. You will need to learn some airs and graces for your job, but I don't care if you are low born or a fucking patrician. I'm from a poor family myself. But I do care that you are loyal, obedient, and a fucking good soldier. Understand?'

'Yes, sir.'

'Fine. Be ready.'

Oclatinius walked stiffly out. Silus sat on the soft bed and stared at the wall, head spinning. Images flashed through his mind: Maglorix screaming, then grinning; Caracalla furious during the aborted execution, then laughing in the throne room; Sergia and Velua, dead.

Sergia and Velua. Dead.

He curled up on the mattress and hugged himself.

–

If Silus had been intimidated by the throne room, the banquet hall took it to new heights. He was reclining on a couch at the lowest level while beautiful young slave girls and boys served him fine wine and imported olives. Next to him was a minor official who had not yet deigned to introduce himself. On the next couch, keeping an eye on him, but too far away to whisper too, was Oclatinius. Silus stayed quiet and tried not to spill anything. He resolved to drink heavily to calm his nerves.

On other couches were high ranking army officials, bureaucrats, officials and other Imperial courtiers. On the top couch lay the Imperial family. Silus tried not to stare, but he had never expected to be this close to the cream of the Empire. In the centre was the Emperor, Septimius Severus, his curly grey beard longer than Caracalla's, ageing, his dark skin deeply lined. Beside him lay his wife, Julia Domna. The Syrian Empress was around fifty years of age, the second wife of Severus, and some fifteen years Caracalla's senior. Her dark brown hair was arranged in curly waves, and her fine features were still smooth. Objectively, Silus thought, she was still beautiful, although the idea stirred no emotion. To her right lay Caracalla and to Severus' left lay Geta. The atmosphere was subdued. Most of the guests who weren't on the top couch seemed disinclined to contribute too much to the conversation, maybe for fear of talking over the Imperial family. However, the three Augusti were quiet too. Geta and Caracalla seemed to not be speaking to each other, and Severus seemed out of sorts, picking at his food listlessly. At one point he started to cough uncontrollably, and when the spasm continued despite Julia's slaps between his shoulder blades, the guests started to look at each other nervously and a Praetorian officer stepped forward, uncertain how to deal with this possible threat to their Emperor's life.

The coughing fit passed and the Emperor waved away his wife and the Praetorian.

'I'm fine,' he rasped, and took a deep sip from a cup of water.

Serving slaves brought out another round of drinks and fruits, and after chewing on some apple chunks, Caracalla addressed his brother.

'My fellow Augustus, how's your wine?'

'It passes, Augustus. Straight through, actually.'

A few of the guests chuckled politely at the joke, but Caracalla just nodded.

'Maybe we should try to develop a taste for beer, if we are stuck here longer.'

'Hopefully we can leave this island forsaken by the gods before too long,' said Geta.

'We could leave quicker if we didn't release the important prisoners we catch.' He gestured at Silus. 'This poor soldier lost his entire family to that monster, and not only has justice been denied to him, we have released the murderer back to his people to stir up more trouble.'

Silus stiffened as all eyes turned towards him. So that was what he was doing here: a visual rebuke from Caracalla to Geta. A little piece in a game of *ludus latrunculorum*, and Silus wondered how carelessly Caracalla would sacrifice him for an advantage in this contest between the brothers. When the attention swung back to the top table, he took another long draught of the wine, starting to feel pleasantly warm inside.

'There is a bigger picture here, Marcus. It's not all about cutting throats and slaughtering innocents.'

Caracalla stiffened. 'Don't be naïve, Publius. Just because you managed to pacify some upset Christians by giving them the recognition they wanted doesn't mean you know anything about waging war or governing a rebellious province.'

'I think you will find that your army would grind to a halt pretty damn quickly without me organising the supply chain here.'

'Maybe so. Every army needs those unwilling or unable to fight to help in any way they can.'

Silus saw Geta's fists clench, and he realised he was holding his breath, waiting for an explosion. The explosion that came was from Severus, however, in another coughing fit. After a few deep breaths, he gestured to a slave standing nearby. 'It's like a funeral. Sort some entertainment out.'

'Antoninus,' said Geta to Caracalla, 'maybe you could play us a composition by Mesomedes on your lyre.'

To Silus, the comment seemed superficially well meant, but Caracalla let out a grunt.

'You know well I am a complete beginner, brother. It would be unfair to inflict that on our guests, and I think would do Mesomedes dishonour too. Slave, do as your Emperor bade you.'

The slave rushed to the door, and in moments the centre of the open-ended square of couches was filled with swirling dancing girls and flautists. Silus reflected that Atius would have been disappointed that the girls were clothed. Maybe the entertainment would have been more risqué if the elderly Emperor and his wife had not been present. Silus didn't care. Women held absolutely no interest to him whatsoever. He felt that he would never look at another woman with desire ever again.

Geta, however, showed the young girls a lot of attention as they danced towards him, then tantalisingly twirled away. Caracalla paid them scant heed though, engaging in whispered conversation with the Empress, which made her frown, smile and once even giggle. Severus' eyes closed several times, and his head began to nod. Then suddenly, he fell asleep, his face plunging into a bowl of seafood. He jerked upright and began coughing once more. The dancers stopped mid-twirl and stared. Julia grabbed a cloth from a slave and brusquely wiped the Emperor's face, holding him until the coughing fits passed once more. Then she helped him to his feet.

'Gentleman, my husband has a busy day tomorrow. He will take his leave now.'

The guests rose together to bid their Emperor goodnight. He waved at them, and allowed himself to be led away by his slaves. Silus noticed an odd look pass between Caracalla and Julia Domna, but no one else seemed to pick up on it. Geta was still distracted by the dancing girls, and the others were averting their eyes from the frail Severus, the once omnipotent soldier Emperor. Julia settled herself back down.

The entertainment started again, but Caracalla looked bored, and soon he clapped his hands and ordered them away. Geta grabbed the wrist of the slave that had caught his interest the most, a young Egyptian girl, and whispered in her ear. Her eyes widened in fright, but she nodded, and hurried out after the rest.

'Will you attend the games tomorrow, brother?' asked Caracalla, seeming to Silus like he was making an effort to be polite to his sibling.

'Perhaps,' said Geta. 'But can any gladiatorial contest match the quail fights we used to have when we were children?'

Caracalla grinned, a genuine smile splitting his face as childhood memories came back to him. 'You certainly had a knack picking them. I lost a fair few denarii on those bouts.'

'I have an eye for detail,' said Geta, acknowledging the praise. 'And what about our chariot races?'

Now Caracalla frowned, but Geta continued regardless. 'Brother versus brother in the Circus, you in blue, myself in green, the crowds cheering us on. It was exhilarating.'

'Until you nearly killed me,' said Caracalla, his muscular arms tensing.

Julia put a calming hand on his shoulder. 'My son, there was never any evidence that Geta was responsible for your crash.'

'That crash nearly ended my life. I was lucky to get away with a broken leg.'

Geta smiled smoothly. 'It was merely bad driving on your part, Antoninus. Some of us have natural talent—'

'I was winning that race when the wheel suspiciously came loose.'

'Blame the slaves who maintain your chariot then, and stop being paranoid. Anyway, you are one to talk. After you drew your sword on our father!'

'I have told you, and him, over and over: I had raised my sword to give an order to kill the Caledonians!'

'Who were surrendering!'

'And you trust their word? I still don't understand why father would not let us end them when they were most vulnerable. Instead, we have let them go, free to raise trouble against us once more. Just like you have done, letting the criminal Maglorix go, free to attack us once more.'

'Father believed you were trying to kill him.'

'I have explained, and he knows the truth now. When he told me to ask Papinianus here,' he gestured to the Praetorian Prefect, 'to cut him down, he tested my loyalty, and I was found not wanting. It is not me he needs to be wary of, brother.'

'Meaning what?' said Geta dangerously, rising to his feet.

Caracalla stood too. 'Let's just say my military prowess is not the only reason that father entrusts me with command over his armies, while leaving you in Eboracum to count nails for caligae.'

The guests looked uncomfortable, looking from one Augustus to the other with consternation, and the Praetorians shifted in position, uncertain when or if to intervene. Silus looked to the companion on his couch, but the man had his eyes fixed firmly on the floor.

'Boys,' said Julia Domna, and her voice brooked no argument. 'This is unseemly. Sit down and behave yourselves. Geta, drink your wine. Antoninus, eat.'

The brothers glared at each other. Then Caracalla made an obscene gesture at Geta.

'I have no appetite, mother.' He whirled and strode out.

Geta wore a smug smile as he settled back into the couch and took a glug of wine.

'Geta,' said Domna with a disappointed tone.

'What, mother?' asked Geta with mock innocence.

'You knew mention of the chariot race would rile him.'

'No, mother. He should accept it was just bad luck.'

'You should apologise.'

'And will he apologise to me for questioning my loyalty to father?'

'As you questioned his.'

'He believes he should be sole Augustus, mother, you know that.'

'Geta, that's enough. I will talk to him.' Domna rose, and her personal slave hurried to her side. 'My friends, I am sorry you have witnessed this disagreement. If my husband was not temporarily unwell, I think he might have had some words to say to his sons.'

Geta shot her a sulky look at the public admonishment, but said nothing.

'I will take my leave now. Please stay and enjoy the rest of the banquet and entertainment.'

The guests stood and bowed heads, murmuring goodnights. Domna swept out, a picture of regal elegance and beauty, with all male eyes following her.

Geta called for the dancers and musicians, and they quickly reappeared. The girl that Geta had singled out earlier had smudged make up around her eyes, and Silus wondered what sort of reputation Geta had among the slaves.

Oclatinius appeared at Silus' elbow, making him start. The old veteran leaned forward and murmured in his ear.

'That's enough for you, soldier. Time to leave.'

'How do I take my leave?' whispered Silus, no idea of the etiquette.

'Usually, you stay until the Emperor leaves, but you were Caracalla's guest, not Geta's, and he is distracted now.'

Sure enough, Geta had pulled the slave girl onto his lap now, and he was kissing her hard, hand roaming under her tunic uncomfortably, judging by her pained expression.

'Let's go, stealthy now,' said Oclatinius. Silus eased himself to his feet, and quietly followed Oclatinius out of the chamber, attracting a few envious glances from guests too bored to want to stay but too scared to leave.

When they were out of earshot, Silus let out a breath he hadn't realised he had been holding.

'Fuck me,' he said. 'Is it always like that?'

'Sometimes not so bad. Sometimes worse.'

'Isn't it dangerous being in the middle of all that bad feeling?'

'You have no idea, soldier. You think mixing it up with the Maeatae is bad? The risk in there is higher.'

'Crap. What the fuck have I got dragged into?'

'Time will tell. Just keep your head down, do as you're told, and hope the horse you are backing wins.'

Right now, Silus wished he was out in the Caledonian forests, being hunted by barbarians.

'Go to your chamber, soldier. Report to me at dawn. Your training starts then.'

'Yes, sir. Um, which way is my chamber?'

'Are you serious, soldier? Have we chosen wrong? You're the scout!'

'Yes, sir.'

Oclatinius turned and stiffly marched away. Silus looked around him. He was at an intersection of two corridors, both of which looked identical, differentiated only by the scenes on the frescos. Silus cursed himself. Oclatinius was right. Some scout. He had paid no attention to the route when he had been led to the banquet hall by a slave, overawed by simply being there. And now he was comfortably drunk.

He looked at the floor, but the abstract pattern of the mosaic gave him no clues. The frescoes had various pastoral scenes. Had he come down the corridor with the shepherd boy and the flock of sheep, or the goatherd sitting on a hilltop? He sighed, picked one at random and set off down it.

After half a dozen turns, he was hopelessly lost. He encountered palace staff from time to time who eyed him suspiciously. He squared his shoulders and looked straight forward, hoping he looked like he knew where he was going, too embarrassed to ask directions, sure that he must come out somewhere he recognised soon. How big was this place?

One more turn took him into a blind end with a door at one end. He sighed, and slumped down against the wall, head in hands, feeling the effects of the alcohol. Stopping was a mistake, because the memory of his grief hit him like a club to the back of the head, the emotion heightened by the wine. Tears poured down his cheeks, and he sobbed silently.

Presently he became aware of a noise. He looked up, realising the sound was coming from the other side of the door. A regular knocking noise, like something banging against the wall. And as he listened harder, he heard human noises too. Moans – a man and a woman. He groaned inwardly. Of all the luck, to be mourning his wife right outside the room where a couple were fucking. The room was some sort of store room, so it was probably a guest taking advantage of a slave.

Their moans intensified as the banging rhythm speeded up. Silus wanted to run as far away as he could, but all will had left him. He pressed his eyes into his forearm, and hugged himself. Shortly, the moans crescendoed, then faded as the passion peaked, crested and passed.

For a short while all Silus could hear was the sound of heavy breathing and soft murmuring. He slowly heaved himself to his feet, but feeling momentarily dizzy he fell against the wall with a quiet thud. For a moment he held his breath, wondering if the mystery lovers inside had heard him. There was silence. He tiptoed away in search of his bedchamber.

–

'Antoninus, you are wonderful.'

'As are you, Julia.'

Caracalla paused, head cocked to one side.

'Did you hear a noise?'

Domna listened, but all was silence.

'Nothing, my love.'

Caracalla shook his head. Maybe he was being paranoid, but he hated to think what would happen if spies took news of his relationship with Domna to Geta or Severus. Although Caracalla was the son of Severus' first wife Paccia Marciana, and so Domna and Caracalla were not blood relatives, it would still cause a scandal he would do best to avoid. The age gap alone would raise eyebrows – Caracalla was in his mid-thirties while Domna was around fifty. But worst of all, if news of the affair got out, he would surely lose his father's favour, or even lose his head for treason.

Julia Domna seemed to read the concerns in her lover's eyes and raised her own.

'Antoninus, what are we doing?'

'Whatever we want, my love. I am Augustus of the Roman Emperor, and you are the Empress.'

'You are not the only Augustus, Antoninus. You are one of three and you know it.'

'Father is declining rapidly. And Geta is a little whelp with no experience and no guts. When father goes, the Emperor should belong to me alone.'

'That is not for you to decide, Antoninus. Your father and I both want you to rule together.'

'You're biased, Julia. Just because Geta is your son.'

'And you are my stepson. I love you both.'

'In different ways, I think,' said Caracalla with a laugh, and did something that caused Domna to let out a little shriek, then a giggle. Her voice became serious once more.

'But we must be careful. The damage to your reputation, if we were discovered… even you might not survive it.'

'I can survive anything, my love,' he said with more confidence than he felt. 'The army is mine.'

'The army is fickle. You know that.'

'As long as I march with them, share their hardships, lead them to victory, and pay them well, they will never betray me.'

'Many Emperors have thought that, right before someone they trusted plunged a knife into them. Antoninus, please, try to overlook Geta's foolishness. He is still a child in many ways. He respects you, you know, even as he resents you.'

Caracalla let out a sigh. 'I do love my brother, Julia. Much as he angers me. I hope we can find a way for us to work together when father is no more. But he must acknowledge that I am his senior, in age and experience.'

'Try, Antoninus,' said Domna. 'For me? I hate the thought of my son and my lover fighting, hurting each other, or worse…'

She broke off, gave a sob, controlled herself with an effort. Caracalla put his arms around her, always at his weakest with Domna. He didn't envy her position, her loyalties split three ways between husband, son and stepson-lover. He hoped that he came first, but could any man hope to be put before a woman's son?

'I'll try, Julia. For you, anything.' She smiled at him, and he wiped a tear from the side of her nose.

Then he rose, adjusted his clothing, and went to the door. He opened it a crack, looked through to check no one was around, then took one last look back at Domna. He sighed, then slipped out.

–

Silus lay flat on his front, gasping for air, the heavy rucksack of rocks pressing down on his back not helping his efforts to breathe. His head was pounding and his tongue felt like sand. Oclatinius bent down and said softly in his ear, 'Too much skulking around in forests and not enough route marches, son. On your feet now.'

Silus struggled slowly to his feet, legs trembling. He had managed to report to Oclatinius at dawn, head still muzzy from the night's wine, several cups of water doing little to quench his thirst. Oclatinius had bawled him out for not being ready and waiting for him, then bawled him out some more for being out of shape before sending him on a five-mile run loaded down with the weighted backpack. Oclatinius rode alongside him, giving him instructions every half mile to drop and perform push-ups or squats. Silus hadn't had a workout like it since basic training, and although his fitness was better now than when he was a raw recruit, he was considerably older.

Oclatinius threw a wooden sword onto the ground, then drew his own very real gladius. 'Pick it up,' he said.

Silus shucked off his backpack, bent and picked up the training weapon. Without warning, Oclatinius took a swing at Silus' head. Silus whipped his own sword up just in time to parry. Although his arms were sluggish from the workout, the wooden sword was lighter than the steel one so moved quicker, but the heavier steel gladius swatted his own fake weapon aside easily.

Oclatinius gave him no time to recover, following up with thrust after thrust, making Silus dance and twist to keep from injury. Finally, the old veteran locked blades, gave a twist, and disarmed Silus, his weapon skittering across the ground. Oclatinius slashed a backhand like a striking snake, and Silus clutched at his throat, terror rising in him as he felt warm blood between his fingers.

Oclatinius had barely scratched the skin, so skilfully timed and placed had his stroke been. Silus dabbed the stinging wound, and then stared at the old veteran with anger.

'Keep it in, son. Don't let the anger get the better of you.'

But anger was what he had now. All he had. He looked down at his hand, where blood had navigated along the deep lines and around the calluses, like streams flowing around little hillocks, and something snapped. He put his head down and charged at Oclatinius with a roar.

The old soldier was taken by surprise, struggling briefly to keep to his feet, before toppling over backwards. From on top, Silus rained blow after blow upon him. But as he fatigued, and the anger ebbed with his strength, he realised that Oclatinius wasn't fighting back, nor had any significant blows actually landed as Oclatinius blocked with his forearms.

Oclatinius twisted abruptly, flinging Silus to one side, then he sat up and started laughing, the rumbling chuckle coming from deep in his chest.

Silus frowned, prepared to renew the fight, but Oclatinius held a placating hand up.

'Pax, son. It's good to see the spirit. But we need to channel it.'

Silus panted heavily, not enough breath for words.

'Caracalla sees something in you. I'm not sure. Maybe you carry something of the younger me. You will prove yourself, or you won't. Survive, or die.'

'What do you want from me?' Silus managed to gasp out.

Oclatinius stiffly got to his feet and brushed the dust from his uniform. He held his hand out. Silus looked at it suspiciously for a moment, then took it and let himself be helped to his feet. He touched his wound, which was now a line of damp, clotted blood. Bastard.

'You may have noticed there is a war on,' said Oclatinius.

'Oh, that must explain why those fucking barbarians killed my family. I thought they were just being friendly.'

'Not that war. The one you saw last night.'

Silus thought of the obvious and public conflict between Caracalla and Geta, and then also recalled the odd looks between Caracalla and his stepmother. What was going on there? He frowned.

Oclatinius saw his expression and misunderstood. 'You are right to look distressed. Conflict between rulers never does the rest of us any good. But when it does happen, you have to pick sides. Geta has his courtiers and his lackeys, but Caracalla commands the respect of the army. It's not a hard choice.'

Silus shook his head. 'I don't give a shit about politics. I want to kill the Maeatae and their Caledonian friends. And that fucker Maglorix above all.'

'Of course. But to defeat the barbarians, we need a strong leader. Severus was a magnificent soldier in his day, but now he weakens. And can you imagine Geta leading soldiers? We need Caracalla.'

'So? Where do I come in?'

'Like any ruler, Caracalla has enemies. Maybe they are commanded by Geta, maybe they do what they think Geta would like, maybe they hate Caracalla for their own reasons. We need someone with your skills and drive to weed these people out. Your main job of course will be to fight the Maeatae. But you may be called upon for other tasks from time to time. What do you say?'

'Do I have any choice?'

'There is always a choice, soldier. If you decline the Emperor's offer, you will be allowed to return to your fort.'

'Really?'

'And another one of the Emperor's spies will be dispatched after you to put a knife in you while you sleep. If they know their work, they will probably frame your friend Atius for it.'

'Ah well, in that case, it is an honour to do the Emperor's will.'

'Yes, it is. Now, as it happens, soldier, we do have a job for you. But first we need to knock some rough edges off you. Where did you learn your scouting skills?'

'My father,' said Silus. Oclatinius waited for more information, but Silus was not interested in elaborating, so after a moment Oclatinius nodded.

'Very well. You need to learn how to hide, how to run, how to kill silently, and how to kill from a distance, so you'll need to practise more with a bow. You need to learn how to retrieve information. You need to be able to remain undetected for long periods of time. You need to swim and climb and live off the land, and pretend to be someone you are not. And you must be loyal, and keep your secrets to your grave.'

'I can do all those things already,' said Silus sullenly.

94

'I don't doubt it,' said Oclatinius. 'But how well? If you can't perform them to perfection, it might cost you your life. Or worse, the mission.'

Silus looked sour but said nothing.

'Let's start with getting some of that flab off you. Then we can work on some real training.' Oclatinius looked at the backpack full of rocks. 'Pick it up, son. Let's go again.'

Silus hefted the pack onto his back, though his muscles screamed.

'Five miles. Now! Run, son, run!'

Chapter Six

The mood around the council hall was somber. Maglorix sat in his high chair, regarding the elders. Few would meet his eye. There had been no direct challenge to his rule since he had returned to Dùn Mhèad on the back of a wagon, drifting in and out of stupor in his agony. The healers had chanted to the gods and sacrificed numerous animals on his behalf. When his fever would not break, there were even some mutterings about human sacrifice, but Maglorix was conscious enough to forbid it. Eventually, his breathing and his coughing settled as his smoke-damaged lungs healed, the heat in his head cooled with the damp rags and the herbs, and the poultices and preparations soothed his purulent oozing soles.

He could walk now, though the pain was still intense. He exercised regularly with sword and spear, and he had begun to ride once more, his feet dangling loose at the horse's side. His strength was returning, and soon he would be himself.

He looked over to the man sitting at his right hand.

'Elders, last night we feasted with Taximagulus here, and for one night we forgot our worries. We shared our meat, our beer and our women with him and each other, the way Caledonians and Maeatae have always done, though the Romans sneer at us for our morals. But today, we discuss war. We discuss our response to the Roman outrages. Do we bend over and let them violate us, like some maiden captured in war and thrown

96

to the soldiers? Or do we stand up to those demons, like real men?'

Some of the elders exchanged nervous glances, until one was pushed forward to reply.

'Oh Chief,' said the elder, an innocuous, slender, bent old man with a kind face called Usnach. It would be hard to become angry with Usnach, Malgorix reflected. He had no doubt been selected by his fellows as the least likely to provoke Maglorix into putting a knife in his throat. Tarvos' skull, long on a spike outside the council hall, had now rotted away sufficiently that it could sit on the back of Maglorix's high chair, from where it grinned sightlessly at the council.

Usnach cleared his throat and tried again.

'Oh Chief.' His voice wobbled with anxiety, engendered both by fear of Maglorix and the unaccustomed role of spokesman for the council – under the tolerant rule of Maglorix's father, he had been most noted for falling asleep in meetings. 'There are those among us, not myself you understand, but I have heard murmurings...'

Maglorix regarded him steadily, giving him no assistance. Usnach clutched his walking stick with a tremoring hand, swallowed and continued. 'Those who say that the Romans are too powerful. That we should avoid confrontation until they get tired of our country and leave.'

'I see,' said Maglorix. 'And who are these men who fear the Romans? Or are you talking of women and little children speaking like cowards?'

'They s-say that the Romans are too well armoured, too well equipped. There are too many. But that there are not enough riches here, and that when their emperor has had s-sufficient glory, he will get bored and leave.'

Maglorix said nothing, waiting for Usnach to continue. The elder reddened, and looked over to Muddan, the council member seated next to Usnach, who had opposed Maglorix's rise to Chief. Muddan gave a faint nod, but Maglorix didn't miss it.

'He says – I mean – *they* say that we can never defeat the Romans in open battle, and we should bow to them until they leave.'

Maglorix stood slowly. Pain shot through the soles of his feet, but he didn't allow the expression on his face to change. Buan, his faithful bodyguard, devastated at his own failure to prevent Maglorix's capture, took a step forward and offered his hand. Maglorix waved him off. He walked slowly, stiffly, up to Usnach, who quailed back. Maglorix drew a long knife from his belt, and jabbed the point on his thumb. A drop of blood formed, pooled and dropped to the earth floor, soaking into the ground.

'I would bleed for my people, Usnach. I would die for their right to live free on their own lands. Would you?'

'Of… course, Chief,' stuttered Usnach. Maglorix walked around the back of Usnach's chair, the blade still drawn. He placed a hand on the elder's shoulder, who flinched like he had been stabbed then started to shake uncontrollably. Then with the speed of a striking wildcat, he thrust the blade out sideways. It skewered Muddan's neck from side to side. Muddan staggered upright, his mouth opening wide. Blood spurted from the holes on either side of his neck where the vessels had been neatly severed. He tried to speak, but he had no air to make a sound beyond a formless gurgle. Then blood bubbled from his mouth, and he toppled forward, twitching for a moment before lying still, head twisted to one side, eyes open but unseeing.

'Usnach,' said Maglorix. 'It can be dangerous being the mouthpiece of cowards and snakes. Tell me, is there anyone else in our council or in our tribe who feels we should bow to the Roman devil?'

Usnach could barely speak, but Maglorix squeezed the old man's shoulder painfully until he gasped out, 'N-no, Chief. Muddan was the only one. And he made me...'

Several others of the council were looking openly terrified, and Maglorix knew that Muddan was not the only one muttering discontent. But he felt the point had been made. Muddan was childless and not well-liked. There would be no gain from provoking a blood feud with others in the tribe by slaughtering half the council.

Maglorix returned to his seat, face impassive as stabs of agony shot up his legs. By his side, Taximagulus wore a faint smirk.

'Members of the council.' Maglorix looked down at Muddan's body. 'Remaining members of the council,' he corrected himself. 'It's true that the Romans are formidable. And that they are hard to defeat in open battle. But we proved last year that with our vastly superior knowledge of our land, our ability to hide and ambush, to harry their supply lines, that we can defeat them. Still, Muddan thought that we should bow down and wait until they leave. Maybe others of you think that this is just a raid, a bigger version of some of their raids on our territory since we stirred them up a moon or so ago. Inconveniences that will pass. Elders, listen to the words of Taximagulus, cousin of Ir who is chief of our allies, the Damnonii. Taximagulus, please, tell the elders what you told me last night.'

Taximagulus rose to his feet, and though his face still wore a cheeky smirk, his demeanour was respectful.

'Wise elders, I am honoured to be invited to speak at your council. I bring the greetings and friendship of Ir, and of all our tribes. Elders, the Romans are still on our soil. I bring word of the development of their fortress of Horrea Classis, on the coast, where the rivers Uisge Èireann and Tatha meet. From there, their ships can supply their legions indefinitely. Wise council, this is no brief raid by the Romans. No punitive expedition. They are here to stay.'

Murmurs ran around the circle, accompanied by the shaking of balding heads rimmed in tangled white hair and the tugging of grizzled beards.

'Tell us what you have witnessed in the north, Taximagulus.'

Taximagulus shook his head, and the smirk vanished. 'We have all known hardship and loss since the Roman invasion last year. I know that you have known battle, loss of supplies, hunger over the winter. But what I have seen...'

Taximagulus tailed off, looking into the distance, staring at nothing. One or two of the elders looked round to see what had attracted his attention. Most understood that he was remembering horrors.

Taximagulus' voice was thick when he spoke again. 'The Romans defeated us on the field, but then they discovered they couldn't find us if we didn't want to be found. So they turned on our homes. On the defenceless.

'Elders, they tried to exterminate us. They burnt our crops. Cut down our sacred groves. They raided our villages and killed every single old man, woman and child. If you have seen the population of an entire village murdered... women with legs spread and throats cut, babies with brains bashed out against trees, old men clubbed to death with hands clasped for mercy...'

Taximagulus stopped, and the council hall was silent except for the wheezy breathing of old men. Maglorix waited, letting the moment drag out. Then he put a hand on the Damnonian and guided him to be seated.

'Council,' said Maglorix, 'the Romans are going nowhere, unless we make them. Our small tribe alone can do nothing. But if the whole of the Maeatae joins the whole of the Caledonians and we fight wisely, we can chase the Romans out of the north of this island, and who knows, maybe even the subdued tribes of northern Britannia will rediscover their courage. Together, we may end Roman rule on the whole island of Britannia!'

The council, so cowed just moments before, broke into cheers, the body of Muddan forgotten as it cooled on the chamber floor.

'Taximagulus, can we rely on the support of the Damnonii?'

'I cannot speak for all, Chief. But I know my cousin Ir was dismayed by the murder of your father, and of your near execution at the hands of the demons. When the council of the chieftains meets, he will be calling for a resumption of the war.'

'As will I.'

Taximagulus reached out his hand, and Maglorix grasped it firmly.

'The Romans will regret the moment they set foot on our lands.'

Maglorix waved towards Muddan.

'Buan,' Maglorix said, and the bodyguard was before him in an instant, 'you know what to do with my enemies. Head on a spike till he rots. Then he can join young Tarvos here to adorn my furniture.'

Buan nodded, drew his sword and without ceremony began to saw off Muddan's head.

–

The splash of leather shoes on the cobbled streets of Eboracum became louder as Silus' mark drew nearer. He tried to calm his breathing and willed his heart to slow so that his grip on his dagger would be firm and without a tremor. The overhang of the gutter above him afforded some protection from the persistent drizzle, but nevertheless he was as cold and wet lurking on this street corner as he ever was out in the field in Caledonia. The main difference was that he was only a short distance from the caldarium of a bathhouse where he could sweat the cold and dirt out of his pores.

The footsteps drew nearer, almost upon him. He pictured his target walking down the street deserted because of the hour, mentally focusing on his exact location from the sound of his tread. As the tips of the man's toes appeared around the corner, Silus was already in motion. Smoothly he wrapped one hand around the victim's mouth, jerking the surprised man backwards. In almost the same action, his knife hand was moving, seeking the heart via the liver under the ribs.

But the man was quick. He twisted in Silus' grip, so swift that the knife merely glanced off the outside of his ribs. With his left hand the man gripped Silus' right wrist, the one holding the knife, and drove his right elbow back into Silus' midriff. Air escaped from Silus' lungs with an 'oof' but he hung on to his knife and let the hand around the man's mouth slip to his shoulder so his arm was tight around his neck. He squeezed with all the strength in his arm, even as his victim elbowed him twice more in the guts and tightened his grip on Silus' wrist till he thought bones would break. But as the pressure built on the man's windpipe, he was forced to let go of Silus and grasp the strangling arm. Silus drew his knife back to attempt again to plunge it into his victim's chest, but suddenly the man, gripping the arm Silus had around his neck with both hands, jerked himself forward and down. Silus flew over the man's shoulders and landed on his back on the cobbles.

In the time it took Silus to recover his momentarily stunned wits, the man had drawn a knife of his own, and was bringing it down in an overhead thrust towards Silus' supine form. Silus rolled to one side, the knife slamming into the cobblestones where his chest had been a fraction of a heartbeat before. The knife came up, ready to descend again, but Silus reached out both arms above his head to grasp the man's ankles, and jerked hard. He crashed down onto his back, and Silus spun, rolled and sat on the man's upper chest, pinning his arms to his side. He placed his knife against the man's throat and pressed.

He felt two taps of the man's hand against his leg, and elation buzzed through him. He rolled to one side, breathing hard, looking up at the starless sky. The man beside him sat up stiffly, rubbing his neck, gasping for air. His voice was hoarse. 'Fuck me, Silus. That was rough, even with a wooden knife.'

'Thought you had me for a moment there, Oclatinius.'

'Thought I had you, too. You've definitely learned a trick or two.'

Silus got stiffly to his feet and held a hand out to Oclatinius. The old veteran took it and allowed himself to be hauled upright.

'So? Am I ready?' asked Silus.

Oclatinius smiled. He was spattered in mud, the drizzle forming mucky rivulets down the creases of his face.

'You've been ready since I met you.'

'What? Then what the fuck has all this shit been about?'

'Just honing an already sharp knife. You want to work for Caracalla, you need to be the best.'

Silus looked at him in dismay. 'All the marches with rocks on my back, all the gymnasium exercises with stone weights,

103

all the boxing fights and practice bouts with wooden swords and knives, the trap-setting and hiding and ambushing, I didn't need any of it?'

Oclatinius' hand shot out, the old man's reflexes still sharp as a striking viper, and gripped Silus' neck, taking him by surprise.

'You listen to me, boy. When you are hiding from a barbarian army or being chased through the mountains by naked madmen, you will want to get down on your knees and suck my cock in gratitude for the skills I have given you.'

Silus grasped Oclatinius' wrist and tried to prise it away. For a moment, Oclatinius held tight. Then he let his hand drop away. Silus rubbed his throat, his face sour. 'You're a prick, Oclatinius.'

'Maybe. But a prick that might have just given you the skills that will save your life.'

'Fine, fine. So, what now?'

'Now, boy, we get some beer.'

-

It was well past the time when the taverns threw the last of their customers out on the street to stagger home, collapse in a back alley, or be mugged and left for dead. But Oclatinius had his mind set on a drink, and Silus felt he could do with something to quench his thirst and steady his nerves. They came upon a doorway just off the main street, with the sign of a blue boar painted on the wall.

'This will do,' said Oclatinius.

'It doesn't look very open,' said Silus.

Oclatinius smashed the door open with one hard kick.

'It is now.'

He walked in, casting a glance at the splintered doorjamb, muttering about shoddy workmanship, and walked into the tavern. It was small, one of dozens in the city that catered to a handful of people at a time, serving beer, wine and basic food.

'Service,' yelled Oclatinius at the top of his voice. Moments later, an elderly man entered the room from a back door, holding a candlestick with a stinking sputtering tallow candle which threw a little light.

The room held half a dozen tables, with dirty cups and plates on most. Oclatinius wrinkled his nose. 'Your slaves deserve a good beating, leaving the place like this.'

'Who… who are you? What do you want?' stuttered the old man.

'Just a drink.'

'I've sent a slave to call the night watch.'

'No, you haven't,' said Oclatinius, taking a seat and putting his feet up on the table, kicking the dirty crockery to the floor. 'Place like this, you probably have one slave, likely too young or feeble to be safe out at night. Besides, do you think the night watch would rouse themselves for you? A scummy little tavern keeper?'

'I don't have much money,' said the tavern keeper. 'I had a big shipment of good quality beer. It used up all my funds.'

'Perfect,' said Oclatinius. 'Get your slave up and get them to bring us both a beer. And a pie. Silus, sit.'

Silus sat next to Oclatinius, shaking his head, bemused.

A young slave boy, no more than twelve years old, underfed and with a black eye, peered around the side of the back door. He had blonde hair and freckles, and Silus figured him for a Caledonian captive, which was confirmed by his accent when he spoke.

'Master, what's happening?'

'Get these men a beer and a meat pie,' said the tavern keeper.

'No piss, mind you,' said Oclatinius.

The tavern keeper sighed. 'From the new shipment, boy.'

The slave was efficient despite being bleary-eyed, and soon returned with two cups of frothy beer and two small crusty pies. When he had deposited them on the table, Oclatinius waved him away.

'How much do we owe you?' he asked.

'Owe?' asked the tavern keeper, eyebrows raised in surprise.

'Yes,' said Oclatinius testily. 'For the food and drink. What do you think we are, bandits or robbers?'

'No, sirs, of course not. Two copper asses, please, sirs.'

'And for the door?'

'Sir?'

'How much to repair the door?'

The tavern keeper looked bewildered, but said tentatively, 'One sestertius?'

'Take a silver denarius for the food and the door,' said Oclatinius, 'and make sure you get it repaired properly this time. A good stout oak bar inside, and reinforced hinges. A door like yours, you might as well have a curtain. Anyone could walk in. You are lucky it happened to be us.'

Oclatinius flipped him a denarius, and the tavern keeper fumbled it, and had to drop to his knees to retrieve it from the grimy floor.

'Yes, sir. Thank you, sir.'

'Now leave us until we call for more beer. My friend here and I have some drinking, eating and talking to do.'

The tavern keeper retreated, bowing obsequiously as he left.

Silus picked up his beer and took a deep drink. The tavern keeper hadn't lied – it was decent quality. Not the best he had tasted, but certainly passable, and good to quench the thirst he had worked up with his exertions. It had a bitter taste, flavoured with mugwort, unless he missed his guess. Oclatinius took a deep draught too, wiped his mouth and sat back. He looked at Silus, a thoughtful expression on his face.

'What?' said Silus, his tone a little aggressive.

'I think you won't be half bad at this, you know.'

'Well, thank you very much. I've been doing fine on my scouting missions before I ever saw your ugly old face.'

'"Ugly old face, *sir*," to you, boy,' said Oclatinius, with a flinty stare.

Silus dropped his gaze. He didn't know whether he liked or hated this old veteran, but he certainly respected him.

'Sorry, sir.'

'Forget it. Tonight, call me whatever you like.'

'Yes, sir, you old cocksucker.'

Oclatinius grinned.

'So where did you learn your shit? As I said, you were decent before I took hold of you. You had skills you don't learn humping it around with the legionaries.'

Silus took a sip of beer, then said simply, 'My father.'

'Go on,' said Oclatinius.

Silus pursed his lips, and was silent for a moment. 'Fine. My father was a Frumentarius.'

Now Oclatinius raised his eyebrows. 'Really? Maybe we met each other, back in the day. What was his name?'

'Gnaeus Sergius Silus, but he went by the name of Sergius.'

'Sergius. Sergius,' said Oclatinius, searching his memory. 'Not Sergius the barbarian fucker?'

Silus' jaw clenched, but he regarded him steadily. 'My mother was Maeatae.'

In other company, the silence that followed would have been uncomfortable. But Oclatinius looked anything but uncomfortable as he sat back and took a drink, his stare probing Silus as if he was looking all the way into his heart.

Silus blinked first, looking down at his hands and worrying out a suddenly irritating piece of dirt from beneath his finger-nails.

When Silus didn't expand any further, Oclatinius let out a belch and said, 'You know a few years ago, I was procurator of this shitty island.'

Silus did know that. Procurator was an important post with responsibility for the province's financial affairs, such as collecting taxes and rents and managing the mines. At one point, Oclatinius was second only to the governor in terms of power within the province, and his rise to that position was the talk of the legions. Everyone knew Oclatinius had started as a raw legionary and worked his way up slowly through the ranks. If he could do it, every soldier reasoned, why couldn't they? But Oclatinius was an exception, almost unique in his ascendancy from his humble background.

'The Emperor has had his sights set on this place for at least seven years, if not more. And Severus is a clever man. He learns from his mistakes.'

'Mistakes?'

'Yes. Maybe it isn't sensible to discuss the mistakes of an Emperor, but fuck it, even if that terrified tavern keeper had the temerity to be listening to our conversation, I don't think he will be running off to the palace to report it. Anyway, mistakes. When Severus invaded Parthia, he captured the city of Ctesiphon. An amazing feat. It's even recorded on his arch in the forum in Rome. The trouble is, once he had taken it, he had no idea how to hold it. He knew nothing about the countryside. He didn't know where the Parthian king, Vologaesus, had retreated to, and he didn't even know where he could obtain supplies to keep his army provisioned. Such a waste of a magnificent victory and of all the soldiers' lives that were lost to achieve it.

'So when he set his sights on Caledonia, he knew he wanted more intelligence about the region, so his victories could be obtained more easily and his gains secured. And so he sent me.'

'I've heard so many stories about you. You were a legionary, then a centurion, then a camp-commander, then joined the Speculatores and became a public executioner, then a centurion in the Frumentarii.'

'I'm an old man,' said Oclatinius. 'I've been around. But at your age, I was still a legionary. Even for a man with my skills, it can take a long time to overcome a poor background. Your mother was a Maeatean. So what? I see some of myself in you. You could go places. Besides, your heritage could come in handy for some of the missions I have in mind for you.'

Missions? Despite his weariness and the beer warming him, Silus' heart accelerated. At last, he was going to be used to strike back at those barbarian bastards.

'Tell me about your mother,' said Oclatinius.

Silus blinked at the sudden shift in the direction of the conversation.

'No,' said Silus, glaring at his superior.

'Fine. The whole thing is off. You will set off in the morning for your fort on the wall, and you will return to your life as an auxiliary.'

Silus' jaw dropped open.

'What?' he managed to gasp. All the work of the past weeks, all his hate and anger channelled into his training to be a dagger in the heart of the man who slaughtered his family, for nothing? Without this, how would he have vengeance? How could he even go on?

Oclatinius leaned forward. 'Silus. You are going to take on secret and dangerous missions for the Augusti, and you will be privy to important information. Yet now, I find out that your father was Sergius the barbarian fucker, and that your mother was a Maeatean. If you want my trust, you had better tell me your past.'

Silus shook his head. 'I can't...'

Oclatinius stood, his chair scraping backwards across the stone floor.

'Report to me in the morning. There are some messages I need conveyed to your commander at Voltanio. Goodnight, Silus.' He marched out through the broken door, leaving Silus to stare at his back in disbelief.

–

The two brothers were drunk. Even the drinking had been competitive, downing bitter-tasting local beer, one jug after another, challenging each other to back down. Equally matched and aware that, if they continued, they would both fall unconscious in front of their supporters, they had agreed a different contest – a race around the fortress walls.

Eboracum had been a Roman fortress since a couple of decades after the initial invasion of Britannia under Claudius, and although a walled town had grown up around the fortification, the fortress walls, rebuilt and fortified when Severus arrived, were taller and thicker than the town walls and interspersed with gatehouses and defensive towers.

Now, Severus' sons, Caracalla and Geta, cheered on by equally drunk young nobles, disapproving elders, and a motley collection of bemused townsfolk, stood at the bottom of one of the staircases leading up onto the walls, ready to race the best part of a mile of treacherous footing under a typically cloudy night sky that spun whenever they looked up.

The nominated starter and adjudicator slurred a few words. 'This is to be a fair race, with no punching, biting or kicking. The race will be one lap of the fortress walls, the winner being the first to return to this spot. Both of the contestants have pledged a favoured slave as the prize. Are the contestants ready?'

Caracalla raised a hand to indicate his readiness, and Geta did likewise.

'Go!'

Geta gave Caracalla a sideways barge in the shoulder, the slighter man angling his shove just enough to force his brother to collide face first into the wall. Then Geta was off, taking the steps two at a time despite his inebriation. Caracalla cursed and chased after him.

His initial confidence was immediately dented. He had thought that with all his military experience, marching and training with the legions, that he should be the fittest of the two of them. But his brother had obviously kept up an exercise regime despite his desk-bound job, and being lighter, he was able to accelerate faster up the steep steps. Besides, Geta was significantly younger, something that in the past had always been to Caracalla's advantage.

Caracalla counted around thirty steps to the top of the walls, and when he got there, his brother was already a few yards ahead, sprinting along the narrow walkway. Caracalla put his head down and ran, arms and legs pistoning. Although he started to gain on his brother, soon his legs and chest were burning. A sustained sprint was unaccustomed exercise for him. He was used to long marches, or short bursts of activity during sword practice or wrestling. He struggled for air, but his head cleared marginally with the energetic workout.

Geta reached the first of the eight watchtowers first, pausing to throw open the door, then slamming it shut behind him. Caracalla grabbed the iron handle and wrenched it open, pulling on it to propel himself forward. Inside, two guards looked up guiltily from their game of knucklebones, torn between reaching for weapons and hiding the evidence of their illicit gambling while on duty. Before they could do either, the two brothers had exited the tower on the other side.

Caracalla felt a stitch stab his side. Sprinting on a stomach full of meat and beer was beginning to feel ill-advised in the extreme, and he wondered if he would have to stop to throw up over the side of the ramparts. What a humiliating way to lose the bet.

The thought spurred him on, and when they reached the second gate, he was close enough to Geta to reach out and stop him from slamming the door in his face. Two more sentries looked up in surprise, even more so when Geta reached down for a three-legged stool, picked it up with one hand and threw it at his brother.

Caracalla dodged sideways, but it struck his shoulder painfully. His balance impaired by the beer, he stumbled into one of the legionaries, who tumbled over backwards, Caracalla landing on top of him. The soldier cushioned Caracalla's fall, and though it knocked the wind out of the unfortunate legionary, Caracalla was able to briskly pick himself up and continue, cursing to himself as Geta's mocking laugh echoed back to him.

It took him three more gate towers to get within touching distance of his brother once more. But he was tiring now, only just past halfway around the course. The effort of having to catch up from behind, not once but twice, was beginning to show, as was his greater age and bulk. Geta started to draw away from him again, and by the time they had gone through two more towers and a number of shocked guards in a variety of states of alertness, wakefulness and drunkenness, Geta had managed a decent lead of around thirty feet.

Calf and thigh muscles screaming, abdomen feeling like a spike had been driven through it, feeling like he couldn't get enough air despite his heaving chest, Caracalla began to despair.

And then, as Geta reached the final gate tower and opened the door, his ankle twisted on an uneven cobblestone. Just as drunk as Caracalla, he failed to stay upright, and fell headlong into the guardroom. Caracalla closed the distance before Geta had regained his feet, and feeling a renewed burst of hope and energy, he hurdled over the prostrate form of his rival sibling.

Geta reached up and grabbed Caracalla's ankle as he was in mid-leap. Without the energy or unimpeded reflexes he would have needed to break free and remain upright, Caracalla crashed heavily on the stone floor, where he lay winded for a moment. Geta pushed himself upright, and slower now, made for the door at the far end of the guard room and swung it open.

Caracalla grabbed his leg and held on tight. Geta pulled himself out of the watchtower, and the crowd of onlookers were treated to the sight of one of the three Augusti being dragged along the stone walkway by another, while both of them yelled curses at each other.

Geta reached down to pry Caracalla's arms away, but the elder brother was by far the stronger. He tried to kick him, but drunk and with one leg pinned, this just led to him toppling awkwardly over. They began to wrestle, tearing at each other's clothes, punching and biting, as the first drops of rain began to fall.

Caracalla landed a hefty blow on the side of Geta's head, briefly stunning him. Geta tried to keep a grip on Caracalla, but the elder brother was able to push him away and stand, slowly and stiffly. Every part of him now aching, Caracalla made his way to the top of the steps. Swaying, he paused to look down, no longer sure of his footing. He took a tentative step forward.

From behind him came a roar. His brother barrelled into him from behind, clutching him around the waist, and the co-Augusti tumbled down the staircase end over end. Caracalla felt every bump and crunch as they bounced off the steps and the adjacent wall, until, with maybe six feet left, they fell off the edge. They landed together, heavily, and lay on their backs, groaning and panting, as it started to pour, the rain quickly drenching them through.

'I declare… a draw!' announced the adjudicator, and the watching courtiers and crowd burst into a roar of approval. Supporters of each Augustus came over to offer congratulations and commiserations on the result, and to help them to their feet. Mud-spattered and bruised, Caracalla looked at his brother with barely suppressed resentment.

'That was no draw,' said Caracalla. 'He cheated, like he always cheats. Like when he nearly killed me in that chariot race.'

'You were lucky,' said Geta. 'You would have been a clear loser, if I hadn't tripped at the end.'

'You tripped through your own clumsiness. I fell because you are a cheat.'

Geta stepped towards him angrily, and Caracalla felt a thrill at the thought of teaching his brother a lesson in a fair, unarmed, one-on-one fight.

A sudden silence fell over the crowd. Caracalla looked around to see what had disturbed them. The onlookers parted, heads bowed, as a lavishly-decorated red-curtained litter, carried on the shoulders of eight hefty slaves, came through. When the slaves reached the two Augusti, the curtains opened.

Inside sat the Emperor Severus and the Empress Julia Domna. Severus looked pale and thin. His chest was heaving with a noisy wheeze, but the fury in his expression was unmistakable.

'I brought you here,' he said, voice low but clear through the stillness, 'to stop your dissolute behaviour. To give you responsibilities in the service of your Empire. And look how you humiliate yourselves. Drunkenness, brawling, gambling. Are either of you fit to rule when I am no longer here?'

Caracalla blanched, but he felt his own anger rise.

'Father, I am your heir. The right to rule Rome is mine alone when you are dead.'

Geta protested. 'We are co-Augusti, father. You have decreed we will rule Rome together.'

'Enough!' and Severus' voice carried through the still night air. 'You will succeed me at my will, not by right of birth. And if you continue to disappoint me, I would rather appoint a freedman in my place than one of you.'

Caracalla opened his mouth to say more, but closed it again, aware that he was in no position to put forward a good defence. He bowed his head.

'I am sorry, father.' He would make it up to him on the battlefield, and show his father who should rule.

Geta gave him a sidelong glance, seemingly trying to work out whether his apology was a ploy, but then he too bowed his head and said, 'I am sorry too, father. I vow to live up to your ideals and be a worthy successor.'

Caracalla ground his teeth at this, but kept his retort inside. He looked up and saw his father at least partly mollified, while next to him his father's wife regarded him with concern and disappointment. He looked straight into her eyes, and only she knew that he was asking her a question. She gave a slight nod, then looked down.

Severus started to cough, and then spat into a cloth. Caracalla thought he saw some flecks of blood, but in the gloom he couldn't be sure.

'Go home,' said Severus hoarsely. 'Slaves, take me back to the palace.' He let the curtain drop, and the litter was borne away.

Caracalla stood in the pouring rain, angry, frustrated, tired and sore. But also elated, because he had an appointment to keep later.

–

Julia Domna's bedchamber was lit by gold oil lamps and scented with light fragrances. She had never been one of these matrons who shared her bed with her husband all night every night, nor would he have wanted her to. It would have been impossible for him to bed all the slave girls and free women he wanted if she was there. Not that he partook of that activity any more, with her or with others. He was an old man now, and too infirm to be interested in carnal pleasures.

When Caracalla entered the bedchamber, his stepmother was reclining, sipping from a bronze goblet. Scent filled the air – subtle, not overwhelming. The room was pleasantly warm from the underfloor heating. A trusted slave girl standing in a corner played a lyre, the gentle music floating through the air. Domna was in full make-up, face whitened with lead, eyes heavily made up with kohl, and her hair was pinned up in an elaborate style. Despite the late hour, she had clearly not been preparing to sleep.

She looked up at him through long lashes and narrowed eyelids. He closed the door behind him and shrugged off his thick woollen cloak, the caracallus that gave him his nickname. Underneath, his tunic was plain and functional, remarkable only for its expensive purple dye. Domna dropped her gaze to his sandals, then slowly rose, taking in his hairy, powerfully muscled legs, slim hips and waist, broad chest, thick neck, and up to his stern handsome face framed by a dense curly beard and hair. She parted her lips, breath coming faster, and she ran a hand down her thigh, smoothing the red stola.

Caracalla took two swift steps to the bed and was on her, pushing her onto her back. She let out a gasp, which was muffled as Caracalla's lips sought hers. His tongue probed into her mouth, and she wrapped her arms around him, kissing him back hard. Their hands explored each other hungrily, roughly. He reached for her breast, squeezed, pleased to hear her let out a moan.

He pulled back from her, then took the hem of her stola, lifting it up and over her head as she wriggled to help him get her out of it. He stepped back, and she lay before him, naked, one knee up, biting her finger and smiling coquettishly. Domna was fifty years old, Caracalla thirty-six, but the age difference meant nothing to him. Her face was rounded, her nose a little too long, but turned up sweetly at the tip. Lines at the corners of her mouth and eyes showed through the lead foundation. Her body was slim and curved, but no longer taut, and there were faint stretch marks down the side of her abdomen from when she had borne his brother twenty-one years before.

He thought she was stunning. He tugged his tunic off and cast it aside, then fell on her once more. She encircled him with her legs and arms as he entered her, her mouth forming an O, her eyes half closed. Despite the heat and urgency and passion, the love-making seemed to last an age, all time suspended, though in fact the lyre player, eyes politely averted, only had time to finish one song before the climax.

They lay side by side, Domna stroking her fingertips through his chest hair, both of them covered in a sheen of sweat, breathing hard.

'I love you,' said Caracalla.

Domna put a fingertip to his lips. 'Don't say it.'

'Why not?' he protested. 'No one else can hear.'

The lyre player could hear of course, but slaves didn't count, mainly because she knew she would be horrifically tortured and executed if she whispered a word of what she had seen to anyone else.

'I know it,' said Domna. 'That's enough.'

He sighed and put his head on her breast.

'Do you ever think of someone younger when we make love? Your wife for example?'

Caracalla shook his head. 'Never.'

'Do you think of her at other times then?'

Caracalla rolled onto his back, wiping the sweat from his eyes with the back of his hand.

'We were married because my father wished it, and she is exiled on his whim.'

Domna's lips pursed at the mention of Severus.

'You know he had to. He couldn't let the family of that traitor Plautianus go unpunished.'

'I'm not complaining. You know I have no love for Plautilla. But I resent the decision being taken out of my hands. When he is gone, I will make my own choices.'

'Don't wish your father dead, Antoninus,' said Domna. 'I already carry enough guilt for what we do without your comments risking calling down the god's fate on him before time.'

'Well, you did decide you wanted me tonight.'

She slapped him playfully on the arm. 'Oh, so it was me seducing you, was it? Whose bedchamber are we in, remind me?'

'I know full well what that look you gave me from the litter meant.'

'Am I so transparent?'

'Shall I be generous and say diaphanous?'

'That was almost poetic, my dear. So unlike your boorish behaviour of this evening. What were you thinking?'

Caracalla's grin disappeared abruptly.

'Your son provokes me,' he said sourly.

'That is his intent,' agreed Domna. 'But you are the elder. You should rise above it.'

'He tests me all the time. He wishes to be co-Emperor when father is gone.'

'That is my husband's wish as well, I believe.'

'It's not fair!' Caracalla cried out, thumping the feather mattress, startling the lyre-player into missing a note. 'I am the eldest. I have commanded legions and won victories in battle. Father has always placed military prowess above all else and has always promised I will be his successor.'

'And so you will,' said Domna, her voice placating, stroking his arm.

'Not sole successor, though. Not since he promoted Geta to co-Augustus last year. And what has he ever done except hear the complaints of whining petty officials and minor local noblemen, and sign off requisitions for *caligae* and shovels?'

'Well, he did manage to pacify that local revolt in Verula-nium early last year. I think that may have been the factor that made the Emperor believe he was ready for more responsibility.'

'Pacify the revolt? He caused it! He ordered that follower of Christos... what was his name... Alban, to be executed simply for sheltering one of their priests, and the locals rioted! He had to make concessions and promises to stop persecuting the Christians just to restore the status quo.'

'I know you hate my son...'

'I don't hate him, Julia. He is my brother as well as your son. He just frustrates me so.'

Domna stroked Caracalla's hair, and he tensed then relaxed back into her.

'Please try to keep the peace with him, Antoninus. For your father, and for me.'

Caracalla let out a wearied sigh. 'For you, Julia. Just for you.'

Chapter Seven

Silus slept fitfully. There was a cold draught, and though he pulled his blanket tight around him, he still shivered. He thought ruefully that he had made warmer bivouacs in the forests of Caledonia than this barrack room.

Every time he closed his eyes and started to drift off to sleep, he dreamed of Velua and Sergia, as he always did. The dreams had two main themes. In the first, he was aware they were in some unknown peril, and he was trying to get to them before something terrible happened, but he was wading through mud or trying to climb an endless ladder, and they always remained out of his reach. They'd look back at him with reproach in their eyes. In the second, he returned home to his hut with a sense of foreboding, only to throw open the door and find Sergia and Velua playing with Sergia's rag doll or fussing over Issa. The sensation of finding them safe was always overwhelming, and they would laugh at him and call him silly as he gathered them up in his arms, crying in relief.

It was this latter dream that he was in the midst of when a loud cock crow woke him fully. The sensation of well-being and happiness lasted for a dozen heartbeats before realisation and reality came crashing down. He jerked upright, gasping for breath, pulse racing, sweat breaking out on his forehead.

He pushed his fingers hard against his closed eyes, the external pressure somehow relieving the internal one that was building. He swung his legs out of the bed, stood, and took a deep drink of water. He would never be happy again, he knew that. How could happiness even be possible?

His eyes drifted to his knife, the real iron one sitting on the table where he had left it, not the wooden blade he had used on Oclatinius the night before. He picked it up, testing the edge against his thumb. He placed the point against his heart, blade angled so it would pass easily between his ribs, and gave it an experimental push. The skin indented, parted, so a dribble of blood flowed down his chest.

It would be so easy. And who would care? Not the shades of his wife and daughter, nor the lemures of his father and mother. Not Atius, not Oclatinius. The only one who would give a shit would be the slave who had to clean up his lifeblood.

And Maglorix. He would care. Because he would be laughing himself sick if the news ever reached him.

Silus opened his fingers and let the knife fall to the ground. Then, slowly, he dressed himself in full uniform, washed his face in a bowl of water and walked to the latrines. He sat, emptying bowels and bladder in silence. Some of his fellow latrine users, auxiliaries and legionaries alike, tried to engage him in conversation, but he ignored them, and they speculated among themselves on what was wrong with the moody bastard. He used the sponge stick, cleaned it in the flowing water beneath the seat, adjusted his dress, and reported to Oclatinius.

The old veteran didn't look up when Silus entered his office. He was reading a report engraved into wooden leaves, occasionally making a note with a stylus onto a wax tablet. Silus stood silently at attention.

Eventually, Oclatinius put his work down, pushed his chair back, and looked steadily at Silus. Then he passed him some parchment scrolls.

'These are for Prefect Menenius. Take a horse from the stables, say you are acting under my orders, and make sure you are in Voltanio within six days. Now get out.' He returned to his administrative work.

'My mother was the niece of a Maeatae chieftain.'

Oclatinius looked up sharply, his eyes narrowing.

'You know of my father. A very skilled spy. Trained by the Brigantes. His family had been badly treated in the past by Brigantian nobles, while Rome had treated them well, so the loyalty to Rome had been passed down through generations.'

Silus paused.

'Go on,' said Oclatinius, voice neutral.

'He was an accomplished liar. He pretended to be a Brigantian rebel, fleeing from Rome, and the tribe took him in. He gave them bits of information about Rome that they found helpful, even took part in raids against Roman soldiers. Killed more than one. The end result was that he gained their trust so thoroughly that the Chief let him bed his niece, a young woman called Donella. As you know, the Maeatae share their best women among the most powerful men, but for the important few months, my mother lay only with my father.

'Then one day, he was discovered engraving reports with the tip of his knife onto bark.'

'Careless,' tutted Oclatinius. 'The Maeatae are illiterate. They wouldn't have been able to read what he had written, but they would have known he wouldn't have been writing to anyone in Caledonia. And eventually they would have been able to find someone who could read his words.'

'He admitted he had become complacent,' agreed Silus. 'I think he had found the whole thing too easy. Or maybe he had found out my mother was pregnant, and consciously or

123

subconsciously he wanted an excuse to leave. He never said whether he knew my mother was expecting me before he fled.'

'So your mother found herself pregnant by a Roman spy? And they let her live?'

'It was a close thing, but her cousin Ardra, the Chief's daughter, would not let them touch her, and the Chief was fond of his daughter in a pretty unbarbarian way. My mother raised me as one of them. I learned their ways; I learned their tongue; I *was* a son of the Maeatae.

'Then my mother died.'

Silus scrutinised Oclatinius' expression, but the veteran didn't twitch a muscle.

Silus looked down. 'I would have had a brother fathered by one of the Chief's best warriors. But he and my mother died in childbirth. And suddenly, I was alone, motherless, son of a Roman spy. I was old enough to realise my precarious position even through the devastation of my loss. I saw people talking, then throwing me sidelong glances. I heard shouted arguments between Ardra and her father and brothers. My childhood friends were pulled away from me when I tried to play with them.'

'And yet you are alive,' said Oclatinius. 'Ardra?'

Silus nodded. 'She came to me in my mother's roundhouse where I was being tended by my mother's Votadini slave, Glenna, and told me without honey-coating it that the council had voted to drown me at noon the next day. I was too old to be abandoned in the wilds because I might survive, so they were going to have to execute me to get rid of me. Ardra had begged and pleaded and threatened to no avail.

'But she was brave and headstrong and she had loved my mother, and loved me. So she fled the tribe with me in the middle of the night, taking Glenna with us, who likely would have been killed for letting me escape.'

Silus paused. Why was he giving this prick his life story? Laying open to him the terrors and humiliations of his earliest memories? The easy answer was that working for Oclatinius would give Silus the best chance of having his revenge on Maglorix. Yet in his heart, he wondered if this was his entire motivation. Was he really trying to win sympathy and approval from the old bastard? As he realised where his story was heading, he grudgingly admitted to himself that that was probably true.

'I'm listening,' said Oclatinius, his tone still neutral, his features giving nothing away.

Silus took a deep breath. 'Ardra found my father. I don't know how. I don't know what she had to do to reach him, what dangers she faced escaping through her own territory, suddenly hostile to her, and then in Roman Britannia, which was already her enemy. I don't know what price she paid for my survival.'

That was a lie. He remembered terrified nights shivering in forests and peat bogs. He remembered them being caught by a Selgovian farmer when Ardra was trying to steal a chicken for us to eat, and how he locked Silus in a room for the night, then the next morning let them all go. He remembered how Glenna had a black eye and Ardra walked stiffly, and neither of them spoke or looked at each other for the rest of the day. But he still remembered how sweet the chicken had tasted once Glenna had plucked and eviscerated it and cooked it over a small fire.

And then he remembered reaching the vallum Hadriani, being stunned by its scale, and terrified by the number of people crammed into the towns and villages and forts, while Ardra enquired and begged and pleaded for any information anyone had about Sergius. After a pause, he continued, 'Spies aren't always easy to find.'

'That is a professional prerequisite, I believe.'

'But eventually, word reached the Frumentarii that a barbarian woman was asking indiscreet questions about one of their best men. We were grabbed off the street, blindfolded, tied up, bundled into a cart, and found ourselves in a cell being questioned forcefully by two big men. One talked kindly to us and gave us food and drink; the other screamed and shouted and threatened to kill us. Classic interrogation, but wasted. We had nothing to hide. Ardra told them the truth. She was bringing Sergius his son.

'They kept us imprisoned for a nundinae. Then one day, the cell door opened, and a man stood framed in the doorway, and Ardra cried out "Sergius" at the same time Glenna called out "Master". I looked at my father for the first time. And he looked at me and said, "Oh fuck."'

Finally, Oclatinius' reserve broke down. He tipped his head back and roared with laughter.

'Oh, poor Sergius. Spies in the field never expect their past to come back and haunt them like that. I wonder how many sons and daughters I have left behind in Germania and Parthia.'

Silus pursed his lips, biting back a terse reply. The laughter died down, but Silus still didn't speak. Oclatinius controlled himself with an effort.

'And then?'

Silus said nothing.

'Demons taken your tongue? Or nothing more to add?'

'What else is there to know?' said Silus sullenly.

'Silus, don't sulk. Tell me what your father did.'

'He acknowledged me. He took me into his household. His wife had already died, and she had been barren, so I had

126

no brothers or sisters to compete with. Glenna he kept as his personal slave and night-time companion. At first, she hated him, but I think eventually she grew to love him in her own way.'

'And Ardra?'

'My father offered to shelter her, though I was never clear whether he planned to keep her as a slave or freewoman. But she wouldn't consider it. Though she knew she had defied her tribe, she made it clear that she was of the Maeatae and it was to them she would return. She came to my room the first night we stayed with my father, kissed me, and was gone when I woke in the morning.'

'Did you ever find out what happened to her?'

Silus looked down. 'I went to look for her when I first became a man and found my old tribe. Ardra's father was dead, but I learned that when Ardra had returned, her three brothers had whipped her and buried her alive while her father stood and did nothing.'

'What did you do?'

'Her father's fate was already in the hands of the gods, but I killed each of her brothers with my own hands.'

Oclatinius nodded sombrely and was quiet for a respectful moment.

'And did Sergius raise you well?'

Silus shrugged. 'When he wasn't away on missions, he beat me regularly. He took me out on hunting trips and pushed me to the limits of my endurance. He taught me to survive, to forage, to hunt and to kill prey, four- and two-legged. I hated him at first, but I came to love him in the end. When his body was returned to me after his last mission, I wept, and I buried him with all the sacrifices and libations I could afford. I vowed to enter the army and serve Rome to the best of my ability to honour his memory.'

Silus fell silent, hoping that Oclatinius had heard enough. Oclatinius clasped his hands together in front of his face, his index fingers extended upwards and backwards, touching lightly against his lips. The silence stretched. Then Oclatinius stood and walked round to stand in front of Silus.

'Silus, you are an excellent scout. And you have a ruthless streak to you. Not many would have taken the opportunity you did when you killed Maglorix's father. It may have been stupid in hindsight, but it was brave and it was well executed, pardon the pun.'

He put a hand on his shoulders and pushed him to his knees. Silus was level with the old man's crotch and for a moment he thought the old bastard was going to make him blow him. Instead, Oclatinius drew out a knife, pricked his thumb until it drew blood. He rubbed the warm, red liquid into Silus' forehead. Then he placed both hands on Silus' head and intoned, 'Diana, triple goddess of the hunt, accept this man Gaius Sergius Silus into the secret order of the Arcani. Let him never breach our trust of confidence, on pain of death and eternal damnation.

'Gaius Sergius Silus, swear your allegiance to the Emperor and to the order of the Arcani.'

'I swear my allegiance to the Emperor and the order of the Arcani.'

Oclatinius held the pose for a moment, then walked back around his desk and sat down.

'Is that it?' asked Silus.

'Yep,' said Oclatinius. 'I'm not a big one for elaborate ceremony.'

He reached for a wax tablet on the edge of his desk, and threw it to Silus. Silus read it was inscribed with a single name. Nectovelius Filius Vindicis.

'What's this?'

'Your first target.'

Silus frowned. 'My what?'

'Memorise the name, erase the tablet, then kill him.'

'What? Why?'

'None of your business, soldier. You are an *occulta speculator* now. An Arcanus. Do as you are told and don't ask questions.'

'But... at least tell me how to find him.'

Oclatinius sighed. 'Fine, but only because you are a rookie. Nectovelius is a Frumentarius who has been feeding us information about the Caledonians. He has been well rewarded, and lives in luxury in Isurium Brigantum. Unfortunately, he has been rewarded twice – by us *and* the Caledonians.'

'Greedy,' said Silus.

'Stupid,' said Oclatinius. 'Find him, find out what he knows, then kill him. And kill his slaves.'

'His slaves?'

Oclatinius nodded. 'He is known to keep Caledonian slaves. Who knows what secrets he has passed to them? They need to be silenced so they can't flee back to Caledonia with important military information.' Oclatinius looked into Silus' eyes. 'Are you having doubts?'

'I've never killed innocents before,' said Silus.

'There are no innocents, Silus. When you live as long as I have, and have seen as much as I have, you will understand that.'

Silus hesitated, and Oclatinius picked up the parchments with the messages for Voltanio. He proffered them with one hand, while his other still held the wax tablet with the single name. Silus looked from one hand to the other. He closed his eyes, and images of Sergia and Velua swam behind his eyelids. He opened his eyes again, and snatched the tablet from Oclatinius.

'I don't need his head, mind you! He wears a cygnet ring with a wolf emblem on his little finger. Bring me that. Dismissed.'

Oclatinius returned to reading his reports. Silus looked down at the name on the wax tablet, erased it, tossed it down onto Olcatinius' desk, and turned to leave.

–

Maglorix clenched his fist tight as the elder from the Epidii tribe droned on. Located in the far west, they had been relatively untouched by last year's invasion, and yet to hear them you would think that they had been enslaved or slaughtered to a man, woman, child and dog. As he spoke, his Chief beside him nodding in agreement, Maglorix felt his face grow hot and he was on the verge of jumping out of his chair. Taximagulus stood behind the chair of his cousin, Ir, and noticing Maglorix's temper inscribed on his face, rolled his eyes comically. Maglorix smiled in spite of himself.

'We have seen the Roman's depravity, mercilessness and overwhelming might. But the onset of winter brought peace, a peace we so desperately need to recover.'

'The Romans are preparing for war this spring, regardless of what we wish for,' yelled Ir. Ir ruled the Damnonii, a tribe affiliated with the Maeatae, the confederation to which Maglorix's own Venicones also belonged. The conference of chiefs at the Caledonian stronghold overlooking Loch Nis was split between the Maeatae and the Caledonian confederacies. Looking around the circle of tribal chiefs and their top advisors, Maglorix could see the Caledonians were represented by the dominant Caledonii tribe, together with Carnonacae, Caereni, Cateni, Cornovii, Creones, Decantae, Lugi and Smertae, as well as the cowardly bore from the Epidii who was currently speaking. Argentocoxus, broad and bearded with tangled long red hair, led the Caledonians, and he watched the proceedings with narrow eyes and tightly closed lips.

Maglorix's Venicones dominated the Maeatae confederacy, which was also represented by the Taexali and Damnonii, and Maglorix had been elected Maeatae war chief without opposition or dissent. Their territory was more southerly and easterly than that of the Caledonian tribes, and having suffered more in this current war and in the past than their northern neighbours, they were consequently more bellicose.

The Epidii elder squinted myopically at the Damnonii chief, then said calmly, 'Then we must sue for peace. If war resumes, the Caledonian and Maeatae peoples will be annihilated.'

An uproar broke out around the circle, the Maeatae calling the Caledonians traitors and the Caledonians jumping to their feet to defend their honour. Fortunately, no arms had been allowed in the long hall, or blood might already have been shed. The ancient high priest who nominally oversaw the council seemed powerless to restore order. Maglorix wondered whether he should intervene, but the Selgovian chief's voice broke through the clamour.

The Selgovae tribe was one of four stuck between the two great walls built by the Emperors Hadrian and Antoninus, and were consequently under the Roman yoke already. The Romans had been inconstant in their willingness to rule the region between the two walls, the more northerly vallum Antonini having been abandoned about fifty years ago, only a couple of decades after it had been completed. But the Romans had kept a close control over the region, and another tribe that lived between the walls, the Votadini, were Roman allies and had not been invited to this council of war. The other two tribes in the region had sent representatives but not their chiefs: the south-westerly based Novantes and the Brigantes. Their territory spanned both sides of the vallum Hadriani, and so had been conquered and suppressed in the main since soon after the Romans first invaded the island nearly two hundred years previous, but they still had elements outside Roman control and had retained an angry rebellious streak.

'We have watched the Romans for generations,' said Sellic, the Selgovian chief, and the council reluctantly quieted down to listen. 'My great-great-grandfather fought and died during the massacre of Mons Graupius, where he was proud to be part of the Caledonian confederacy led by the gods-blessed Calgacus. My tribe has known crushing defeat at the hands of the Romans, and it has known victories. It has known oppression, and it has known freedom.

'But we have learned. Sometimes directly under Roman rule, sometimes outside it. We have tested their defences; we have tested the mettle of their soldiers. We have tasted servitude and liberty. We have been enslaved, and we have freed ourselves. We know the Romans. And we know this.

'They cannot be defeated.'

Shouts broke out again, and Maglorix was on his feet, hurling insults along with others from both confederacies. But the Selgovian chief held up his hand and waited patiently for silence.

'Hear me. They are better armoured, better organised, better trained and, I'm sorry to say, better led. They have control of the seas and can bring in supplies and reinforcements to the east coast at will. I say again, they cannot be defeated.

But' – his sharp voice forestalled further protests – 'but, they can be made to want to leave.'

Some of the chiefs and their advisors exchanged glances before returning their attention to the Selgovian.

'The Romans hate it here. The weather last year was worse than usual, and they can't stand the rain and the cold. They hate marching through our dense woodlands and marshes. Their engineers have had to cut down forests, fill in valleys and build bridges in order to get their armies and supplies into our territory. But when we offer them battle, they annihilate us. Too many times last year, our brave warriors hurled themselves all but naked against the Roman shields and spears, and died in droves.

'Have we learned nothing? The Romans have shown us time and time again, since even before Mons Graupius, that they are too strong for us in open battle.

'But we have advantages. When the Romans march in full battle armour, bogged down in marshes, we move lightly without breastplate or helmet, just with spear and shield. When the Romans are lost in our forests, we move freely along secret paths and animal tracks. When the Romans hunt us, we hide underwater in lakes and breathe through reeds.

'We can let them pass us and ambush them in the rear, then melt away. We can set traps. We can harass their supply lines. We could even raid into their territory and threaten what they hold dear. We can make them pay for every foul onion breath they expire in our air, for every time they take a shit in our sacred homelands, until all they will want is to scamper back home like beaten curs.'

Roars broke out again now, the Maeatae in full approval, and even some of the reluctant Caledonians applauding the rhetoric. Maglorix felt the time was right to hammer the point home, and he waved his hand to be heard. The Selgovian sat, and the high priest indicated that Maglorix should speak.

'Friends, kindred and neighbours. Last year was a disaster. We had plenty of time to prepare. We knew they were gathering in the north of their province since the year before. We knew the size of their force. We even had spies telling us where they were likely to attack. And they just walked over us.

'They marched their legions into Caledonia, put a bridge across Abhainn Dubh, and then the gods-cursed Caracalla took two-thirds of their forces like a spear through the heart of our lands, laying down his marching camps on the way, while his father attacked the valley of the middle lands and the fleet sealed off the coast.

'Granted, we didn't make it easy for them, but we lacked leadership and organisation. When we offered open battle, our numbers were too small, and we were crushed. When we ambushed and harried, we were ineffectual. We put cattle and sheep in their way to slow them down. We picked off stragglers. We sprang traps on them from the forests and marshes. The Romans took losses but shrugged them off, and Severus was carried on a litter all the way to Uisge Bhiorbhaigh to look north across the sea.

'The territories of the Venicones and the other tribes of the Maeatae took the worst of their brutality. We returned home to burned villages and burned crops, slaughtered livestock, our wives and children enslaved. To many of you here, the insult was to your honour. To us, the insult was to our lives and the lives of our families.

'And what did we do? With winter approaching and with the Romans ready to retreat at a time of year when they would have been most vulnerable, we sued for peace. You all know I was at the council last year and I witnessed the terms being agreed, even though my father argued against the peace treaty. But most of you were in favour, saying the Romans had had their revenge for our raids of recent years and they would now leave us alone.'

'They will,' yelled a Cornovian. 'They don't want our land. They just want us to stop attacking their province.'

Murmurs of agreement ran around the chamber.

'These people massacred us! Fucked our arses like we were slave-whores. And you Caledonians are lifting your tunics to let them do it again!'

Argentocoxus slowly rose to his feet, and the gathering fell silent. The chief of the Caledonian confederacy was an imposing figure, tall and broad, but lean despite his advancing age. His face was pale, and there was a subtle tremor in his clenched fist.

'Have a care, Maglorix. We have been enemies more than we have been allies. Don't push us apart when we need unity more than anything.'

Maglorix opened his mouth to retort, then closed it again and took a deep breath.

'Chief, I am sorry if my passion and anger led to insult. Please accept my apology.'

Argentocoxus inclined his head in acceptance.

'But my argument remains.' Maglorix swept his gaze around the council. 'You say they don't want our land. Then tell me: why are they building a legionary fortress at the confluence of the rivers Uisge Èireann and Tatha, with a huge granary for their fleet to bring in supplies for their army? A fortress not of timber and turf, but of stone. One that is meant to last.'

No one spoke. Maglorix stood, back straight, breathing deeply, milking the silence. Each member of the council he looked at either dropped their gaze to the floor or stared back defiantly. But nobody contradicted him.

'We must vote, friends, for war. For if we don't unite to throw the invaders from our lands, then our lands will no longer be our own, and we will become just another enslaved people in their Empire.'

He slowly sat back down, and the silence lengthened. The high priest stood arthritically and held up his staff.

'I call for a vote of the chiefs of the northern tribes. All those in favour of war, raise their hands now.'

Maglorix lifted his hand promptly. The Taexali and Damnonii chiefs exchanged glances and raised their hands. Taximagulus smiled at Maglorix. But when Maglorix looked around the rest of the meeting, he was met by expressionless faces. Argentocoxus regarded Maglorix steadily, motionless. The other Caledonian chieftains looked to him for guidance, taking their cue from him.

The tableau held. Then the high priest spoke in his reedy voice. 'There is no mandate for war. The terms of the peace treaty that Chief Argentocoxus brokered with the Romans last year remain firm.'

Maglorix stared around him in disbelief. Then he jumped to his feet, and rushed over to where Argentocoxus sat, quiet and sombre. He pointed his finger into the Caledonian chief's face and roared, 'You fool. There will be war. And destruction. And death such as you have never imagined. If we do not fight together, we will die separately.'

Argentocoxus did not flinch at the tirade, holding up a hand when his allies stepped forward to restrain Maglorix.

'You are the fool, Maglorix. You are turning your mission of revenge for your father's death into a conflagration that will engulf all of Caledonia. The vote is for peace. This council is now at an end.'

Taximagulus moved beside Maglorix and put a restraining hand on his chest, pressing firmly so Maglorix was forced to take a step back and away from the confrontation. Maglorix let himself be led towards the doorway. But on the threshold, he spat into the hall, drawing gasps from the gathered nobles.

'There will be war,' he said again, and then allowed Taximagulus to lead him away.

-

Nectovelius Filius Vindicis. The name was engraved in Silus' mind. He suspected it always would be, never worn away by the weathering of time. He was unlikely to forget his first assassination.

He made immediate progress in tracking his target down. Seated in a barber shop, as the barber snipped away at his beard and chattered inanely, Silus reflected that usually when a barber asked how he would like his hair cut, he replied with the old joke, 'In silence.' Today, though, the barber's jabber was just what he needed.

'So you don't live in Isurium Brigantum, sir?'

'No, I'm an auxiliary. I was carrying a message from Voltanio on the vallum Antonini. I need to head back soon, but I made good time getting here, so I thought they will never know if I spend a day or two in the bathhouses and whorehouses before I set off.'

'Very true, sir. Make the most of what Isurium has to offer before you go back to the frontier. A few of my customers have told me about a slave called Veneria who works at the brothel with the sign of Pan, down by the river Isura. Apparently, she can suck you off while doing a handstand. And another called

137

Fortunata who works out of the sign of the flying phallus on the main street and will take it up the arse if you tip her extra and use plenty of olive oil.'

Silus grimaced inwardly. He couldn't imagine being interested in another woman ever again. But his new job involved playing a role, so he forced a grin.

'Sounds good. I might pay them both a visit. And where is the best place for beer?'

'Ah, you're a beer man, not wine. Good. I always think wine is a drink for southern pansies and posh nobs. Give me a strong, bitter ale any day. You should check out the Eagle tavern. Lots of veterans hang out there. It will be right up your alley. Oh, sorry sir.'

Silus winced as the barber nicked his cheek with the tip of the scissors and then dabbed at the wound with a dirty blood-stained towel.

'Talking of veterans, an old friend of mine lives in Isurium Brigantum. Nectovelius Filius Vindicis. Do you know him?'

'Indeed I do, sir. Regular customer of mine. How do you know him?'

It seemed that Oclatinius had deliberately made his job harder by giving only sparse details about Nectovelius, so Silus kept it vague.

'From the army.'

'Of course. Nectovelius told me he is a veteran of the legions.'

'And what does he do since he retired?'

'Oh, he is a merchant, sir. Often away on business trips, but he is very well to do, so must make a good success of it.'

'Good for Nectovelius. Nice to hear him doing well for himself. Where might I find him?'

'Well, he was boasting to me that he had bought himself a new home. A nice town house, atrium, triclinium, the lot. Next door to the Crow's Foot tavern.'

'Sounds nice. I might pay him a visit.' Silus suddenly realised that he had no idea what Nectovelius looked like. 'Tell me, does he still have that beard?'

'Nectovelius had a beard? I never knew that. Always clean shaven as long as I have known him. Very smooth skin, so I guess he likes to show it off. It's a shame though. I imagine he could grow a big bush, knowing how thick and curly his head of hair is.'

'It was a sight to see,' agreed Silus.

'I think I'm done, sir,' said the barber, brushing the beard hair from Silus' shoulders. 'Are you sure I can't press you to have a haircut?'

'Maybe when the weather improves. It's keeping me nicely warm for now.'

'Yes, sir.'

Silus paid a denarius with a sestertius tip and bid the barber a good day. It was late afternoon and the town was bustling. Silus noted how oblivious the townspeople seemed to be to the war that had been raging just a few days ride to the north. They were all busy going about their daily business: buying market vegetables and bread, taking their clothing to the fullers, visiting the bathhouse, and eating hot snacks from street side stalls.

Silus asked the way to the Crow's Foot from a one-legged beggar sheltering in a temple doorway, and tipped him a couple of copper asses. He followed the grateful cripple's directions and seated himself at a table on the street under the canopy of the tavern. He ordered a beer and a hunk of cheese from the serving slave, and settled down to watch.

The beer was heavily watered and tasted flat, but he didn't object – he wasn't drinking for pleasure but for disguise. The cheese was too hard, but he wasn't hungry anyway. His stomach felt tight, and despite the noise from the street – the copper-smiths and potters and fullers crying for customers, the laden carts and donkeys, the children playing ball games and the adults yelling at them for getting in the way – he could sense his blood pulsing in his ears and forehead. He took a deep breath to settle himself, inhaling notes of fish sauce, dog shit and charcoal burners.

He was on his second beer when he saw a slave leave Nectovelius' house. He considered. Should he keep watching for his target before he made his move? If he didn't confirm that Nectovelius was in residence before he entered the house, he risked tipping him off. At the moment, he believed that Nectovelius had no idea of the danger he was in. If he became alarmed, he would be harder to surprise and might even flee.

Yet, how long might Silus have to wait before seeing the man himself? It could be days. Oclatinius hadn't given him a time limit on his mission, but he was sure that there would be trouble if he wasn't prompt. He made up his mind, took a last sip of his beer and got to his feet.

The slave was a young boy, just old enough to have some fluff on his face, but not old enough to be shaving it. As he walked, his shoulders were slumped, and he kicked at chickens and dogs that got under his feet. He seemed unhappy with his errand, and Silus thought about himself at that age, shivering and half-dead with cold on one of his father's hunting or fishing trips, or being sent across country to deliver messages or fetch goods his father wanted. Slave the boy may be, but he had it easy.

Silus took up an ataxic, drunken gait as he followed the boy. Once he had got well out of sight of the house, he sped up, and at the entrance to a quiet side alley he grabbed the boy from behind and pivoted him against a wall just off the main street. Few noticed, and those that did threw sidelong looks and hurried on, not wanting to get involved.

'I've just got a few copper coins,' gasped the boy. 'I was only sent out for bread. Please don't take them, or I will be beaten when I return empty-handed.'

That was the worst he was worried about? A beating?

'Is your master at home?'

The boy looked confused. 'What? Why?'

Silus pressed his forearm up against the boy's throat, choking him momentarily, then releasing the pressure. 'Answer me.'

'Yes, yes!'

'Which room was he in when you left?'

'The garden room.'

'How many others in the house?'

'Three.'

'Who? Where?'

'The porter, in the vestibule. The cook, in the kitchen. The steward in the tablinum.'

That was as much useful information as Silus could extract quickly from the boy, without taking him to a dark soundproof room and using something sharp. He considered, what next?

The boy was snivelling, tears streaming and snot running from his nose down his upper lip.

'Please, sir, let me go. I won't say anything.'

Silus wasn't particularly bothered about being identified after the act. He was on official business after all, although he imagined that Oclatinius would prefer it if it wasn't made too obvious that this was an Imperial assassination. But if he let the boy go now, he might raise the alarm before Silus was finished, and if he was going to dispatch four with a minimum of fuss and tumult, then he needed time. Surely this young lad was not one of the slaves privy to Nectovelius' scheming though, and did not need to be killed.

'Turn round,' he hissed.

'Please, sir,' begged the boy, even as he complied.

Silus reached down for a loose cobblestone. He weighed it in his hand, then brought it hard against the back of the boy's skull. He went down like a bull being stunned at sacrifice. Silus looked at where the boy lay flaccid and frowned. He had meant to knock him out cold, but the pool of blood rapidly spreading out around the boy's head and the lack of breath showed Silus that the blow had been harder than he had intended. He cursed, tossed the stone aside, and dragged the dead slave deeper into the shadows of the alley, covering the body with some discarded wheat sacks.

He checked himself for blood spatters, then emerged back onto the main street with a purposeful stride which attracted no attention. He made straight for the front door of Nectovelius' house. On either side of the doorway was a shop facing the street: one selling cutlery and metal tools; the other a pharmacist with a variety of multi-coloured, multi-scented herbs, powders and potions on display in little glass jars and clay pots. Both shop owners called for his attention, but he avoided eye contact and knocked firmly on the stout wooden door.

Silus felt as if eyes were boring into him from all sides as he stood in the street, exposed and vulnerable. The door creaked open, and a tall, muscular man with long red hair stood in the gap.

'What do you want?' he said in an unmistakable Caledonian accent.

Silus let his blade slip down his sleeve into his hand. His other hand reached up to the porter's shoulder in a friendly open gesture.

'Just here to see my old mate, Necto,' said Silus, and as the porter looked at the hand on his shoulder with narrowing eyes, Silus plunged the blade into his throat, pushing him backwards and kicking the door closed behind him. The porter's eyes rolled up into his head and he scrabbled at Silus, weakly and ineffectually.

Silus supported him as the strength left his legs, and waited until the soft gurgling had stopped before putting the heavy wooden bar in place across the door. Then he moved quietly down the narrow vestibule into the atrium.

He quickly took his bearings. No two townhouses were identical, varying with the original owner's preferences, the architect's stylistic whims, and the available space, but they often adhered to a standard format. The doors to either side of the atrium would lead to bedrooms, and the door at the far end was almost always the tablinum. The peristylium would be at the back of the house, furthest away from the street. As for the kitchen, well, he would have to follow his nose.

The mosaic floor of the atrium was composed of concentric squares made up of varied abstract geometric designs, with the centre an eight-pointed star. He wondered briefly whether the sign had any mystical meaning for Nectovelius, and whether he was about to raise the ire of some deity or powerful demon. Without a carved phallus to hand, he cupped his genitals to ward off evil, simultaneously laughing at his own superstition and feeling reassured.

He wore soft leather sandals with no nails in the soles, so he was able to slip silently around the impluvium and up to the door of the tablinum, which was slightly ajar. He heard the clink of coins being counted from within. The story of a merchant was a good one, Silus reflected. Long absences and surprising riches could be explained away easily.

Silus intended to ease the door open gently to see if he could surprise the steward, but as he pushed, the unoiled hinge let out a squeal. Silus threw the door open and took two strides across the room to the desk, from behind which the elderly steward was starting to rise in surprise. Silus hurdled the desk, placing one hand across the old man's mouth, muffling the incipient cry for help and plunged the dagger precisely between the eighth and ninth ribs on the left of his chest. He felt the throb of the heartbeat transmit into the handle before the blood spurted out from around the blade.

Only the steward's eyes could express his shock and terror as he stared at Silus before slumping to the ground. Silus stepped back but was too slow to avoid the blood lapping around his sandals. He cursed. Sloppy. Still, he was nearly done. It shouldn't matter now.

Dark red footprints trailed him to the kitchen, from where the scents of roasting pork meat and baking bread were wafting. The sounds of hammering reached him. Tenderising? It left him in no doubt where the kitchen was though: the first door off the peristylium, behind the triclinium. The door was wide open – cooking and baking was hot work even in the northern British springtime. Silus palmed his blade and walked boldly into the kitchen as if he was bringing an instruction to the cook.

The cook, middle-aged and plump, another Caledonian by her appearance, was not stupid. She quickly took in the stranger's appearance, noticing the fine blood spatters across his face and the incarnadine footprints. She was holding a meat tenderiser, a vicious-looking hammer with short spikes protruding from one side of the head, and immediately rushed at Silus.

The first swing would have caved in his skull if he hadn't recovered quickly enough to duck. Instead it thumped into the wall, knocking chunks of plaster out of the centre of a rural fresco. Silus dodged sideways as the hammer came back again, smashing an amphora of olive oil, which flowed across the kitchen floor.

Silus brandished his knife, but it was little defence against the heavy lump of iron, and instead he had to sway out of reach a third time as the hammer came back. This time though, he was able to return a thrust. The cook tried to throw herself backwards, but she lost her footing on the oil-slick floor. Her feet flew out from under her, and with her prodigious weight behind her fall, she cracked her head against the granite work surface. She lay still, legs and arms splayed, the tenderiser falling from her grip.

Silus knelt and checked for a pulse in her flabby neck. It was still there and strong. He looked down at the red-haired woman, wondering at her story. Another Caledonian, he was sure, and maybe one enslaved as an adult. Her martial prowess with a kitchen implement certainly spoke of one who had been raised among warrior tribes, not in domestic servitude.

'Gitta?' came a voice from the peristylium. 'Have you broken something? Struan? Get out here and find out what she is up to.'

Silus sighed and reluctantly cut the cook's throat. Then he emerged from the kitchen into the peristylium to come face to face with Nectovelius.

Nectovelius, son of Vindicus, was clearly of strong native stock, broad-shouldered and barrel-chested. But he had let himself run to fat as he had aged, so his jowls drooped and his belly sagged over the belt of his tunic. He still had a full head of curly hair, shot through with grey as if he had been seasoned with salt, and his clean-shaven face was smooth and free from pocks, so Silus had no doubt that this was his target.

'Who the fuck are you?' said Nectovelius in alarm, taking a step backward. He was holding a glass of dark wine in one hand and a handful of nuts in the other.

'Nectovelius Filius Vindicis?'

'I asked who you are. And what the fuck are you doing in my house?'

Silus held the knife up. 'Are you Nectovelius Filius Vindicis?'

'Yes, yes. What do you want?'

'I was sent by Oclatinius.'

The glass tumbled to the ground and smashed into a thousand fragments, but Nectovelius didn't take his wide eyes off Silus.

'No.' His voice was a whisper. 'I haven't… I didn't…'

Silus shook his head. 'There is nothing you can say to me. I'm not your judge or your jury.'

'Then you are my…' Nectovelius couldn't finish the sentence. Then suddenly he cried out 'Struan! Acco!'

Silus waited patiently. Understanding slowly dawned on Nectovelius' face.

'You killed them all?'

'Orders,' said Silus simply, and took a step forward.

'Help! Help! Murder!' yelled Nectovelius at the top of his voice. Silus wasn't perturbed. The peristylium was the furthest part of the house from the street, purposefully situated away from the noise of the hustle and bustle of town life. But that worked two ways, and sounds from within the villa would be inaudible to passers-by. Maybe someone in a neighbouring

146

garden would hear and raise the alarm, but Silus would be long gone by then. He took another step forward.

Nectovelius dropped to his knees.

'Please. I have money. Name your price. Take it all.'

'My price can't be counted in coins,' said Silus. He noticed a pool of ammoniacal yellow liquid trickle down the inside of Nectovelius' thighs.

'I beg you.'

Silus wondered if he should say something. Should there be some profound words? Maybe he should have considered this before getting to this point. Prepare to meet your doom? I carry out the will of the Emperor?

Instead, he stepped forward and plunged his dagger down into the space between the man's collarbone and neck. When Nectovelius had stopped twitching, he reached down and cut the ring off the smallest finger. He turned it over in his hand. A wolf's head. Silus slipped the ring onto his own little finger.

How was he supposed to feel right now? This was different from when he had killed Maglorix's father. That was in battle, in enemy territory. As more blood splashed onto his clothes and feet and skin, he simply felt like a murderer. That he had done what he had done because he had been commanded did not lessen the cold bilious feeling rising in his throat.

Then he thought of Sergia and Velua. Just ashes now in their funerary urns. A small stone stele, as elaborate as he could afford, paid for with all his savings and the help of the funeral club which he had contributed to, along with his comrades, on the assumption that the money would be for his own burial expenses, not his family's.

The words on the stele, as many as he could fit on, were in the standard form.

> To the sacred spirits of the dead,
>
> *Velua of the Otadini tribe, wife of G. Sergius Silus,*
> *murdered by barbarians aged thirty-two years,*
>
> *And Sergia, daughter of G. Sergius Silus, murdered by*
> *barbarians aged five years,*
>
> *This stone was dedicated by their husband and father,*
> *G. Sergius Silus, who will avenge their deaths.*

His tears had soaked the earth more thoroughly than the wine and milk libations he had poured on their graves.

True, Nectovelius had not killed Sergia and Velua with his own hands. But he had been complicit with the enemy. A traitor to his own people. Who knew if the information he had passed hadn't aided or enabled the raid and massacre that Maglorix had led? And more practically, if Silus was to achieve the vengeance he had sworn over his dead family's gravestone, to have a hope of being able to confront Maglorix and bring him to justice, he needed to gain the trust and aid of Oclatinius.

A hammering at the front door broke his reverie, and he looked round sharply. Faint shouts came from beyond the thick door, yelling for Nectovelius, worried enquiries for his wellbeing. Silus cursed. Someone must have found the slave boy already and recognised him as one of Nectovelius' familia. That the murder was to be discovered was of no matter to Silus. People would speculate as to the reason, but they would see that this was no robbery, and that Nectovelius had no doubt upset someone high up with some duplicity and been punished for it. Nevertheless, it would do Silus no good, nor the mysterious reputation of the Arcani, if he was caught. He could even be executed before Oclatinius was able to use his influence to have him released.

An axe crashed against the door, and wood splintered as the head was pulled out before descending once again.

The townhouse had only one entrance and exit, and no windows facing onto the street, for security. At first this had seemed like a boon to Silus – once he was inside, there would have been no way for Nectovelius to escape. Now he felt like a fox in a trap.

Silus' father had once killed a fox with a single arrow. An elderly, skinny animal that had been sneaking around stealing chickens at night. Looking over the still warm body with his son, Sergius had pointed out the missing foot on one of the forelegs.

'That's where he chewed his own foot off to escape a snare. It saved his life, though he had to resort to stealing to eat afterwards, like a crippled veteran from the army. Still, that's guts right there, boy. That's the animal instinct to survive.'

Sergius looked around him desperately as the axe descended again. No way out to the front. An enclosed garden, with ten-foot walls and scant handholds, surrounded by a roofed colonnade. But the garden had some furnishings and decorations: a statue of a half-naked nymph, a water trough, and two wooden benches.

Hastily he dragged the benches to the edge of the overhanging roof, throwing one on top of the other. He vaulted onto the uppermost bench, put his hands out to retain his balance as the two pieces of furniture unnaturally mounted one atop the other wobbled dangerously. Then he leapt, grabbing the edge of the overhanging roof. A tile came loose in his right hand and smashed on the cobbled path beneath, but he gripped tight with his left and managed to get his right hand up to hold the wooden beam that had been revealed beneath the lost tile.

He had seen acrobats perform amazing stunts with their own body strength, pulling themselves up poles with only their arms, hanging from ropes with arms stretched at right angles to their bodies. Silus was no weakling, but he was no acrobat. Neither his grip nor his upper body strength was enough to simply haul himself onto the roof.

The sound of the door crashing down after one last axe blow reached his ears, and he realised that he was simply dangling from the roof of the garden colonnade like a crucified criminal. Desperately, he started to swing from side to side, until his momentum allowed him to hook his heel onto the edge of the roof.

'Stop!' came a voice from below.

Two auxiliaries burst into the peristylium, one bearing an axe, the other with his sword drawn. Silus clawed at the roof, scrabbling up the tiles. Behind him, one of the auxiliaries sprinted across the garden, leapt onto the piled benches and grabbed Silus' foot. Silus kicked out hard, catching the auxiliary in the face. The soldier held on tight, and Silus felt himself sliding back down the roof. The shouts of more auxiliaries entering the peristylium reached him, and he lashed out again desperately. The soldier's grip slid from Silus' ankle to his sandal. The leather straps stretched, then snapped, and the soldier plummeted backwards with a yelp. Silus thanked the gods for cheap leatherwork, and scrambled back up onto the roof.

He looked down into the peristylium at half a dozen soldiers. One appeared to be taking command, organising the others to pile up more furniture to make a stairway to the roof. Silus turned and worked his way up to the apex of the roof, dislodging tiles as he went. The roof was a flimsy construction, and at one point he put his foot straight

150

through, grunting in pain as jagged tile edges scraped bloody grooves in his shin.

At the top, Silus looked around him. He was some way from the street. Other houses backed onto this one, and directly behind it was another, smaller peristylium. He slid down the tiled canopy into this garden, landed with a painful bump, and then sprinted into the house. Past the kitchen, through the corridor by the tablinum and into the atrium where a middle-aged man and a young slave were kissing on a bench.

The slave looked up, but by the time she had drawn breath, Silus was past, and the scream echoed down the vestibule behind him. The porter turned in surprise, not expecting to guard against a threat from within. The front door was ajar, and Silus shouldered him aside and burst out onto the street.

More shouts came from within the townhouse – the more athletic soldiers had obviously followed him over the roof and into the garden. More soldiers were charging down the street towards him as well. Fuck! Oclatinius would be shaking his head at this mess.

Silus sprinted through the crowded street, hurdling dogs and pigs and shoving aside slow-moving slaves laden with shopping. His foot caught on the outstretched leg of a one-armed beggar, who cursed him to the local gods and to the Christos.

A narrow alleyway appeared on his right, and he cut down it, then jogged again behind two houses. He was breathing hard now, heart racing. He probably had the endurance to outrun these soldiers, but he didn't have the local knowledge. He selected a flimsy looking doorway of a small, run-down house and kicked it open. An elderly man was squatting over a chamber pot, while a cat purred around his ankles.

Silus looked around and saw a ragged but clean hooded tunic lying on one side, and some scuffed leather sandals. He sloughed his bloodied clothing and dragged the tunic over his head, while shoving his feet into the sandals. The old man watched him wordlessly, mouth hanging open.

'Thanks, grandfather,' said Silus and rushed back out.

The sounds of pursuit were coming nearer, although they had clearly lost his exact path, judging by the questioning shouts. Silus rounded another two corners, and found himself back on the main street. He slowed his pace and his breathing, pretending to browse a jewellery store.

Hob-nailed boots clashed against the cobbles as half a dozen auxiliaries charged past him.

Silus took a long deep breath, and then headed slowly along the road out of Isurium Brigantum, fingering the new ring he wore.

Chapter Eight

This time it wasn't a feint. This time it wasn't a punitive raid, dashing in and doing some damage before the Romans could collect themselves. This time it was war.

Maglorix sat on the back of his wiry highland pony, with Buan to his left and Taximagulus to his right. The main gates to the fort had been breached by a combination of fire and an improvised battering ram, and his men were already pouring through. Taximagulus and Maglorix had drawn together around a thousand warriors, and this time had concentrated their forces on one stronghold: Voltanio.

The choice of point of attack had been fiercely debated by the elders and warriors, with some suggesting that Maglorix wanted to attack Voltanio for a second time because he had a personal score to settle. Maybe that was true, but the thought of finding Silus within and executing him slowly was merely a bonus. Maglorix wanted Voltanio because his men already knew the ground, and had seen that the enemy was beatable. Furthermore, they had killed a number of Romans the last time they were here, and though the manpower supply at the disposal of the Empire was vast, it may be that not all the casualties had yet been replaced.

The Romans fought fiercely at the breach, but they were gravely outnumbered. Maeatae warriors carrying only spear and shield clashed against the interlocked shields of the auxiliaries and were mostly rebuffed. But enough thrusts sneaked

153

through a careless gap to start thinning the Roman ranks, and Maglorix knew it would only be a matter of time before the resistance collapsed.

'Do you think this message is strong enough?' asked Taximagulus, grinning.

Maglorix smiled back. 'I think this will provoke the Romans to anger and the Caledonians will have to respond, if only to defend themselves. They will have to cast aside the whining puppies opposing war, and let the wolves have their way.'

A mounted warrior skirted the edge of the fort wall, the rider peppering arrows at the defenders. But as Maglorix watched, a slingshot from the battlements shattered one of the pony's forelegs. The mount went down hard, tipping its rider head first. The rider lay stunned for the briefest of moments, but even as he tried to rise, half a dozen more slingshots rained down on him, and he lay back, still.

Taximagulus looked across at Maglorix to gauge his reaction.

Maglorix shrugged. Though the rider was a Veniconian noble, Maglorix displayed no emotion. 'There will be losses,' he said. 'This is just the start. If we want to defy the invaders, if we want our peoples to have a future, to survive, then this land must be engulfed in a fog of death like it has never experienced before.'

Taximagulus chewed a dried piece of meat thoughtfully, and watched the battle unfold.

–

'It's hopeless,' Atius yelled at Geganius. The centurion was staring grimly at the splintered gates which moments before had looked so impenetrable. Three ranks of auxiliaries held the breach, mostly Batavians and Thracians with a sprinkling of exotic and local ethnic flavour. They held firm for now, but the numbers assailing them were truly frightening. Atius had seen the extent of the warriors' strength from the battlements and had hurried to warn Geganius, but the old veteran seemed stunned.

'Sir, what are your orders?' cried Atius.

Flames licked around the gateway, creating ominous shadows against the walls and eating away at the supports of the main tower. The ramparts themselves were layered clay with earth piled behind to reinforce it, but there was no need to breach the walls when the gate was so vulnerable. Two brave auxiliaries poured a cauldron of heated oil down on the attackers. This exposed them to missile fire though, and the burning gates illuminated them against the night sky. One of the men took an arrow that skewered him from cheek to cheek and shattered his upper jaw. He let out a muffled cry and toppled down into the attackers, who finished him off quickly with spear thrusts.

'What is there to do?' asked Geganius helplessly. 'We stand and fight.'

'Sir, there are too many!'

'What would you have me do, soldier?' snapped Geganius. 'Pray to the Unconquered Son to appear and smite our enemies? Or maybe pray to Christos, and then ask them for mercy and forgiveness while we kneel before them?'

Atius winced. His faith in the Christos was being sorely tested at that moment, and he didn't need his usually unflappable centurion mocking the risen saviour.

The Maeatae drew back briefly, then charged, the momentum rocking back the three defending lines of auxiliaries, and leaving a dozen gaps in the first rank and half a dozen in the second. The auxiliaries dutifully closed the gaps, but the line was looking threadbare now. With a resigned sigh, Geganius drew his sword.

'Go and find Menenius and report to him what you have seen. If he has orders for me, come back here. If he wishes you for something else…' Geganius trailed off and looked at the scores of barbarian warriors thrusting and howling and vying to be the first inside the fort. 'Well, your god be with you, soldier.' He clapped Atius on the back, squared his shoulders, and marched into the back of the defensive line, waving his sword and yelling encouragement to the auxiliaries.

Atius watched him for a moment, then looked around to find Menenius. The prefect was observing from the centre of the courtyard, deep in conversation with his second-in-command, and flanked by four tough auxiliaries who were fidgeting and fingering the hilts of their swords while watching the developing battle.

Atius ran over to him, and two of the auxiliaries barred his way with outstretched palms and half drawn swords. Menenius saw him and motioned for him to be allowed through.

Menenius' second-in-command, a veteran centurion from Thrace named Damanais, was arguing, face red behind his grizzled beard. He stopped speaking and glared at Atius.

'Report, soldier,' he snapped.

'Sirs, I come from the battlements. Centurion Geganius told me to report to you. I have seen the enemy numbers and their movements.'

'Speak. Be quick.'

'I estimate fifty score warriors. Most are concentrated at the main gate, but detachments are circling around in both directions to mount an attack from the rear. They have ladders with them.'

Damanais turned to Menenius. 'Sir, we must strip the walls and gather everyone for a counter-attack, before these others get into position. The line can't hold as it is, and if they get behind us, we are done.'

Menenius shook his head. 'They have ladders. If they see the walls undefended, they will be free to launch their assault on the ramparts. They will be in and among us before we know it. It will be slaughter.'

'Then what? We just hold for reinforcements?'

Menenius looked grim. 'Damanais, you know as well as I do that our messenger was killed before he was out of arrow shot. Before anyone knows this battle has even started, it will be long finished. Still we must hold.'

'What's the point?' muttered Damanais. 'Just to die with honour?'

'No. We need to hold, to give this man time to get a message out.'

'Me?' yelped Atius in surprise.

'Him?' grunted Damanais.

'Yes, Atius, you. I haven't forgotten the bravery you and Silus showed in the last raid, nor the good sense. Take my cygnet ring and escape this fort. Find the first waystation and requisition two horses in my name. Leave word of what has happened here, so the other forts can be alerted, but make all haste to Eboracum to tell the command what has happened. We will buy you as much time as we can, but it will be with our blood, so spend that time wisely.'

Atius stared in disbelief. First Geganius and now Menenius had given up. It was fine for a foot soldier such as himself to despair, but these were the men who were supposed to tell him everything was going to turn out for the best.

'Two horses?' enquired Damanais.

Menenius looked sheepish for a moment, then he said, 'Take my daughter with you, Atius. For the sake of all the gods, please spare her this.' He looked defiantly at Damanais, who stared back, angry for a moment that Menenius could be so selfish when everyone else was going to die. Then he relented, and gave a harsh nod.

Menenius twisted the tight-fitting ring off his finger and slapped it into Atius' hand. 'She is in my quarters. Show her the ring and get her out of here.' The pleading in Menenius' eyes nearly broke Atius' heart. 'I know you have used her as a plaything. But she is the most precious thing in the world to me. Please, Atius.'

Atius grasped Menenius' hand. 'I will protect her with my life, sir.'

Menenius held the grip for the briefest of moments, then in a gruff voice, said, 'Go.'

Atius sprinted to the Camp Prefect's praetorium, his house in the centre of the fort. A flight of stone steps led to the entrance, and he hammered loudly on the door. When there was no instant reply, he tried the handle and found it was unlocked.

Atius had visited three times before, twice when reporting for punishment for minor misdemeanours, and once when he had slipped in for his liaison with Menenia. This time though, the place was deserted. He ran through the atrium, up some more steps to the peristylium, and on to the cubiculum that he knew was Menenia's bedroom. The door was locked, and with no time to waste, he barged the door open with his shoulder.

The girl inside, who was clutching a small dog against her chest, screamed the moment he burst in. He hesitated, holding a hand out, palm up, scanning the room for threats. The screaming continued, and Atius realised that looking grimy and

158

blood-spattered and having just knocked her door down was doing nothing to calm the situation.

'Menenia, darling, it's me, Atius.'

Menenia hesitated, then placed the dog down and rushed forward, threw her arms around him and placed desperate little kisses over his face. He gave himself a moment to enjoy it, then took her wrists and slowly pulled her away.

'Menenia, listen. Your father sent me. He wants me to get you to safety.'

Menenia looked confused, and Atius' heart skipped a beat as he looked into her eyes. She really was very beautiful.

'Safety? But we are in the fort. Surely this is the safest place?'

Atius pursed his lips. The forts could hold off a small attack for a limited time, but there were plenty of times in the recent past when barbarian assaults had overwhelmed the local forces and garrisons had been massacred. Atius knew that garrison duty meant long periods of mind-numbing tedium interspersed with moments of bowel-loosening terror. He couldn't ignore the cold sweat and creeping skin, the senses heightened so every bang and crash made him jump. But he also understood that, dangerous as escaping from the fort would be, he stood more of a chance than the poor grunts in the defence line below, trying to hold on as long as they could before being overwhelmed and killed on the spot, or taken into captivity and tortured to death.

'There's no time to explain. Come with me.'

Menenia backed off, shaking her head. 'No, my father would never...' She stopped when she saw Atius holding Menenius' ring out to her in the palm of his hand. She put a hand to her open mouth. 'Is he...?'

'He lives,' said Atius. 'I left him organising the defence. But he ordered me to take you away. Now, come. Please.' Atius held out a hand, and after a moment more of hesitation, she took it. Atius gripped it tight and pulled, but she reached down to scoop up the dog. Atius realised it was Silus' dog, Issa. After promising his friend he would look after her, he had given the old little bitch to Menenia's safekeeping, and she had been delighted. He was glad he had the chance to save the last remnant of his friend's family, as well as his commanding officer's daughter.

From the top of the stairs at the front of the praetorium, Menenia was able to see the perilous state of the defences. The defensive line had been forced back even further in the short time since Atius had left Menenius. Bodies littered the courtyard – gore-covered faces, heads split open, limbs torn like cuts of meat, guts like a gorgon's head bursting from midriffs. Menenia froze, face white, mouth a perfect circle of shock. Atius tugged at her hand, yelled her name, but she was as immovable as a statue. He considered throwing her over his shoulder, but that would slow him down considerably.

Instead he slapped her hard across the face.

She flinched back and stared at him accusingly, hand pressed to her cheek.

'If you want to live, we need to run. Now!'

The spell broke and Menenia followed Atius down the steps, clutching Issa tightly. At the bottom Atius looked left and right, assessing where the fighting was at its most intense. Then he pulled her towards the south-east corner of the fort.

'Where are we going?' hissed Menenia. 'There is no way out in this direction.'

Atius ignored her, rushing for the building in the corner. At the doorway, a foul smell hit them and Menenia pulled back.

'You think to hide in the latrine?' gasped Menenia. 'We should be trying to climb over the wall.'

Atius grabbed her shoulders and looked into her eyes. 'I will say this only once: you will do everything I tell you, without question or hesitation. Do you fucking understand?' He yelled the last words. Menenia blanched, but nodded mutely.

'Good.' He kissed her impulsively on the lips, then dragged her into the latrine.

The construction was standard, a long wooden bench-like structure along the length of two walls with holes in the top and the front. A small stream ran down the centre, for the men to rinse their sponge sticks in, or more commonly given the rarity of sponges in northern Britannia, to discard used leaves and moss.

More importantly, though, a stream ran underneath the seats themselves, to wash away the solid matter out of the fort and into the nearby watercourse.

Atius grabbed the wooden seat nearest the external wall of the fort and heaved. It resisted for a moment, then the nails ripped out and he staggered backwards as it came loose. He looked down into the dark channel below. At springtime in rainy Britannia, the stream was in full flow, which meant the smell wasn't as bad as it would have been at the height of the summer. Nonetheless, decades of intermittent use had stained the walls with faecal matter, and mushrooms and ferns grew in the dank conditions.

'I'll go first,' said Atius. 'With Issa. You need to be right behind me.' She stared at him in horror, and he knew she was thinking about the delicate stola she wore and the expensive jewellery hanging from her neck, ears and wrists. But to her credit, she didn't argue.

Atius swallowed, took the dog, then stepped into the hole he had created. Even though Atius was not a particularly bulky individual, the space available was tight. He got flat onto his front and wiggled along the narrow channel like an earthworm, holding Issa in front of him. At the end, the stream disappeared under the wall. Atius sent up a brief prayer to Christos and the God of the Jews that he would not get stuck, then took a deep breath, and ducked under.

The water was freezing cold on his face, and he squeezed his eyes and mouth tight shut as he reached forward, using any handhold he could find him to drag himself beneath the wall. He was aware on a purely factual level how wide the wall was, but as he struggled forwards, holding his breath, feeling the sides of the channel grazing him on all sides, he fought the rising panic down. Issa, panicking too, struggled out of his grip, and he prayed she was swimming ahead of him. He kicked hard with his legs, aware that with his exertions he was using up his breath faster than he should, but not caring.

After moments that seemed like hours, he emerged into a small sewer that was just big enough for him to get onto his hands and knees and turn round. It was completely black, and he could only tell where he was by touch. Issa was splashing in the water, and he reached down and grabbed her. He felt the edge of the fortress wall, waiting anxiously for Menenia to emerge.

Too much time was passing. She had been right behind him. Had she balked? Had she got stuck? His heart sank at the prospect of going back for her.

Then there was a splashing noise, and Menenia emerged, gasping and floundering, a flailing limb catching Atius painfully in the nose. He grasped her hands, and whispered calming words. When her panic subsided and her breathing stabilised, he said, 'I think the sewer runs about a hundred yards before it empties. Follow me. The worst is over.'

Maybe that was true for them, he thought, but the worst was just about to start for the poor defenders fighting for their lives in the fort behind them.

They crawled in a silence broken only by the sounds of their hands and knees splashing in the fast-flowing water that accompanied them, and by the snuffling of Issa just ahead. Time stretched again, with no way of judging distance in a darkness that was so complete he may have been blind. But then a dim light emerged from the black, and Atius could make out the end of the sewer. As they neared, he saw that the exit was covered by an iron grill. Water flowed through it and over the edge, and various bits of detritus from the fort's inhabitants had been caught in the metalwork: a worn boot, a mouldy scarf, pieces of broken pottery.

Atius grabbed the grill and gave it an experimental shake. Anxiety arose at how immovable it seemed. He wriggled around so he was feet first, and then kicked it. At first, there was no discernible result except for painful shock waves radiating up his legs. But by concentrating on one corner, he was able to see the concrete holding the grill in place starting to crack. One final two-footed kick sent the whole piece of metal spinning out to land in the stream below with a splash.

Atius wriggled forward and looked out. The drop was about ten feet. He turned, dangled his legs over the lip and then slowly lowered himself down. He had intended to hang from the edge before letting himself fall the last part, but the grip was slimy with algae and shit, and he tumbled backwards.

The stream was a couple of feet deep, enough to break his fall as he landed on his back and disappeared under the surface for a few moments, before finding his feet and emerging, spitting out ice cold water.

Above him, he could just make out Menenia's face peering down at him.

'Jump,' he called out, in a voice he hoped was low enough not to carry. 'I'll catch you.'

Menenia seemed to have passed beyond resistance now. She sat on the edge of the outlet, Issa in her arms, and then simply let herself tumble forward. Atius put his arms out to grab her, but he had not accounted for her velocity or the fact that she had done nothing to break her own fall, so she hit him like a falling sack of wheat, and once again he disappeared under water, this time with the weight of a young lady on top of him. After some more undignified flailing, he managed to get to his feet, and grabbing Menenia's arm, hauled her upright too.

She coughed for a few moments, then looked at him with eyes full of wretchedness. Her hair was tangled with fern leaves and slime coated her face and bare arms. Her necklace and one earring were gone, and her stola was streaming dirty water from the hem. He stepped forward and took her in his arms, hugging her. Out of her depth, Issa was paddling. She swam to the bank and dragged herself out, then shook the water out of her fur.

Shouts came from nearby, then the clash of weapons and a scream. Atius grabbed Menenia's hand and helped her out of the stream.

'We need to get moving,' he whispered. 'Can you run?'

Menenia nodded.

'Fine, let's go. The waystation is about five miles south of here. We can be there before dawn.'

Atius started them off at a slow jog through the boggy terrain, Issa leaping between tufts of grass sticking up above the surface water. Behind them, the fort glowed as flames reached for the starless night sky.

Menenius, Geganius and Damanais knelt before Maglorix, hands tied behind their backs, ankles tied together. Geganius was being held upright by two warriors. He was bleeding profusely from a head wound and was barely conscious. There were only a handful of other survivors from the garrison. Menenius had debated whether to surrender, and some of the auxiliaries had thrown down their weapons of their own accord. In the end, he had commanded his men to fight to the last. He could guess what sort of fate awaited them if they were captured.

Menenius, Geganius and Damanais had all tried to fight to the death, but Maglorix had clearly decided he wanted the officers taken alive. The three had formed a circle back to back, but the Maeatae warriors had parried their sword thrusts with their shields, and used the blunt end of their spears to knock the Romans to their knees. Geganius had been the last to go down, and it had taken an axe blow to his helmet to finally fell him.

Now Maglorix drank deep from a cup of ale, letting it overflow down his face. He filled his mouth with the liquid, then spat it over Menenius. Menenius didn't flinch, just kept his eyes fixed tightly ahead.

'How does it feel, mighty Roman?' said Maglorix. Behind him, Taximagulus smirked. Both warriors wore soot- and blood-stained visages that looked terrifying in the light of the dancing flames from the burning fort. 'To kneel before better men?'

Menenius said nothing. There was nothing to be gained from conversation.

His silence angered Maglorix though. Maglorix gestured to one of the Romans who had surrendered. Two warriors

dragged him over and thrust him into the dirt. He was a burly Batavian, but his face ran with tears. Menenius racked his mind for the man's name, struggling to recall it through weariness and fear. Brinno. That was it.

Maglorix drew a curved knife from his belt, and Brinno flinched back, the whites of his eyes showing.

'Brinno,' said Menenius. 'Courage.'

Brinno looked Menenius straight in the face and said, 'Fuck you! And fuck Rome!'

Maglorix laughed aloud and dragged the blade across Brinno's neck, cutting deep. Blood fountained, and as Brinno's eyes rolled up into his head, Maglorix shoved him aside where he twitched and gurgled for a short time before lying still. Menenius closed his eyes. But Brinno had probably been lucky. He suspected Maglorix had far worse in store for him.

'Well,' said Maglorix, 'he didn't seem too happy. I wonder how many of these foreign mercenaries that you drag over here to fight for your Empire really love their Emperor and would die for him and his sons? Still no answer? Shall I kill another of your men before your eyes?'

'What do you want from me?' said Menenius. 'I will tell you no secrets.'

'We don't need secrets. We have our spies. You trust too many who come from the tribes of northern Britannia. Do you really think that every one of the Brigantes and Votadini who you call allies have forgotten their freedom?'

'Then what?'

'I just want your realisation, Roman, that your days in the north are nearly at an end. I want to see defeat in your eyes before you die.'

'You won this battle, barbarian. But you have no idea the destruction you have unleashed on your people.'

Taximagulus gave a mocking smile, but Maglorix wore an expression of fury. He grasped a spear from one of the standing warriors, and thrust it through Geganius' eye. The point burst out the back of the veteran centurion's skull, carrying blood and brain with it. Geganius went rigid and his limbs spasmed. The warriors supporting him stepped back and let him fall.

Damanais roared in anger and threw himself at Maglorix, but the chief simply stepped backwards as the bound Thracian fell on his face. Maglorix kicked him hard in the head and Taximagulus laughed.

'We are wasting time here,' said Maglorix to Taximagulus. 'Nail the survivors up on trees and burn them. Tell the men they can loot, eat and rape whatever they can find, but be quick about it. We will be gathering soon to take the next fort. The Romans will be enraged, and the Caledonians will have to join us to defend against their retaliation. This is the year the invaders will be thrown from our lands in despair.'

The warriors near enough to hear let out a cheer, and his words were passed to those further away.

Menenius felt his bladder loosen as he was dragged to his feet and marched towards the nearby woods. He prayed he would have the courage to die like a Roman. But he prayed even harder that Atius had got his daughter to safety.

–

From behind his desk, Oclatinius regarded with narrow eyes the two auxiliaries who stood before him. Silus stood at attention, while Atius, still grimy and dishevelled from the road, slumped wearily. Atius had delivered his report succinctly. Oclatinius' initial suspicion that Atius had deserted was quickly allayed by the Prefect's ring.

'And you rescued the Prefect's daughter, you say?'

'Menenia, yes. She is in Silus' quarters now.'

Little more than an hour had passed since Silus had opened his door in amazement at finding Atius and Menenia, with little Issa jumping up to his knees and yapping excitedly. Atius had been unsure who to report to or what to do with Menenia and Issa, so had asked around about where to find Silus and eventually had been directed by a friendly soldier to Silus' quarters. After hearing an outline of Atius' tale in distress, he had taken him straight to Oclatinius, to whom Atius gave the full story.

'Do you believe there were any survivors?'

Atius shook his head. 'At the time of my escape, I believe it was Menenius' intention to fight to the death. There was no hope of victory or rescue. And if he surrendered or was captured...' The sentence didn't need finishing. They had all witnessed the mutilated corpses of Romans captured after the previous year's campaigning.

'And your numbers are accurate?'

'My best estimate, sir.'

Oclatinius stroked his chin. 'That's no raid. And it's more than enough to take one fort.'

'They must be going for more,' said Atius. 'Other forts, or a full-scale incursion into Britannia.'

'Or it's a provocation. But the motivation is irrelevant. It's a definite breach of last year's peace treaties, and it must be answered. I need to see the Emperor. And you two are coming with me.'

–

The throne room of Imperator Caesar Lucius Septimius Severus Pertinax Augustus Parthicus Britannicus, father of his country, conqueror of the Parthians in Arabia and Assyria,

Pontifex Maximus, was even bigger and more opulent than Caracalla's. But the sight of Severus seated on the throne, with Caracalla to his right, Domna to his left, and Geta to her left, terrified Silus too much to consider examining the colourful frescoes and exquisite statuary decorating the room.

The three of them, Oclatinius flanked by Atius and Silus, knelt before the three Augusti and the Augusta, heads bowed. Severus gestured impatiently for them to stand.

'What is it, Oclatinius?'

'Augustus, this soldier, an auxiliary from the fort of Voltanio, is the sole survivor of the massacre of the garrison by a large force of Maeatae.'

Silus saw Caracalla lean forward, hands gripping the armrests of his throne. Domna looked from Caracalla to Severus. Severus' eyebrows drew together in anger. Geta's face was unreadable.

'They dare to break the peace treaty? Not just a raid, but a full-scale assault.' Severus' voice was quiet, weak, but held an unmistakable threat.

'So it would seem, Augustus.'

'You, soldier, tell me what happened. But be brief.'

'Sir... um... Augustus, the fort was assaulted in the middle of the night by around a thousand warriors of the Maeatae tribes. I saw different banners and shield decorations, and I believe...'

Atius trailed off, suddenly aware he was reporting opinion rather than fact.

'Continue, soldier,' said Severus. 'What do you believe?'

'I believe that it was an alliance of tribes, sir, I mean, Augustus.'

'An alliance. You hear that, Antoninus? They dare to form an alliance against us?'

'I hear, father,' said Caracalla. 'The war must resume.'

'I thought we had finished this war last year when they surrendered to us,' said Geta petulantly. 'All we had to do was consolidate our territorial gains, and we could return to Rome in triumph.'

'I'm sorry these barbarians have upset your travel plans, brother,' said Caracalla.

Before Geta could reply, Severus asked another question.

'Do you know who led these barbarians, soldier?'

Atius swallowed nervously. 'I… I can't be sure.'

'But?' prompted Severus impatiently. 'Come on, do I have to have it beaten out of you?'

'He was some distance away, and it was night, but once the fort started burning, I got a look at the face of their chief. I think… I believe it was Maglorix. Sir. Augustus.'

Silus turned to stare at Atius, mouth hanging open. He had not mentioned that little detail before. Caracalla in turn was staring in fury at his brother.

'Would this be the same Maglorix,' asked Caracalla through tight lips, 'who recently massacred a vicus, including Silus' family, was captured and was about to be executed on my orders, only for those orders to be countermanded by you, Geta, and the murderer set free?'

'It was an exchange of prisoners,' said Geta defensively. 'Besides, executing him would have been a provocation, and father agreed with me.'

'A provocation?' roared Caracalla, leaping to his feet. 'And what do you think this is? A tickling contest?'

Geta stood too, face red, but Severus held a hand up and barked, 'Sit down, both of you.' The Emperor then started coughing, drawing breath between spasms in strident gasps.

Geta and Caracalla reluctantly retook their seats and waited for the coughing fit to pass.

Severus took some deep, wheezy breaths, then spoke slowly, enunciating each word carefully.

'When Menelaus fought before the walls of Ilium, he captured Adrestus, who begged for mercy and ransom. And Menelaus was of a mind to agree. Then Agamemnon came to him and said, "Has your house fared so well at the hands of the Trojans? Let us not spare a single one of them from sheer destruction – not even the child unborn in its mother's womb; let not a man of them be left alive, but let all in Ilium perish, unheeded and forgotten."'

Severus looked slowly around the room, at his family, the soldiers trying not to tremble before him, the courtiers lining the walls.

'So shall it be with the barbarians. Antoninus, ready the men for war.'

Chapter Nine

Caracalla's face was thunderous as he strode up and down his office. Oclatinius, Silus and Atius stood in a row, eyes front, backs straight, barely daring to breathe.

'The fucking idiot! Playing at being emperor and just fucking everything up. We had won! We had victory! Now we have to do it all over again. Just because my cretinous half-brother and, for some bizarre reason, co-Augustus valued the life of one of his favourites more than the peace and security of the province and the whole fucking empire. What if, while we are pissing around in this gods-cursed country, the Parthians break the truce and attack in the east? What if the Germans invade Gaul? What if one of our loyal governors in Syria or Africa decides they would make a better Emperor, and take the opportunity, while my father is here at the arse-end of the world, to take their legions and march on Rome?'

None of the soldiers gave reply. Silus presumed the questions were all rhetorical, until Caracalla whirled and jabbed a finger at him. 'Well?'

Silus' bowels turned to water. 'Well,' he stuttered, 'I think the loyalty of the Empire to the Augusti is solid as rock.'

'Rock can be shattered with a pick aimed at the right weakness. You!' Caracalla now pointed at Atius. 'What if the east is invaded?'

'I'm just a humble auxiliary,' said Atius, and Silus breathed a sigh of relief that his friend hadn't said anything stupid. But he had relaxed too soon.

'But as you asked for my opinion,' continued Atius, 'I think in the event of a Parthian or German incursion, you would have to withdraw some of the legions from Caledonia, and march swiftly to meet the threat. If it was a major invasion, the presence of at least one of the Augusti in the expeditionary force would be required to reassure Rome and bolster the morale of the troops. The local forces would hopefully be able to hold for long enough for you to reinforce them. I would suggest taking the vexillations from the Rhine and Danube legions back with you, and since the legio VI Victrix has put down roots in Eboracum for so long, I would recommend that vexillations from this legion were left behind to form the basis of a garrison, together with a stripped down legio II Augusta and legio XX Valeria Victrix, maybe using the vallum Hadriani as the frontier since it is nearer the supply lines from the province. Your father seems unwell, so he could travel to Rome to secure your family's position, while you lead the counter-invasion force, given you have already proven yourself as an able commander in the field. But I would suggest you leave your cretinous half-brother behind to sort out the logistics, since he got us into this mess in the first place.'

Caracalla stared at Atius open-mouthed while he delivered his monologue. Silus closed his eyes, waiting for the furious response. Then Caracalla burst out laughing and clapped Atius on the back so hard he staggered forward a step.

'Oclatinius, where did you find this one?'

'One of the local recruits to the auxiliaries, I believe, Augustus. Seems to have a good head on his shoulders, but a big cakehole in his face.'

'And will these two do?'

'I think they stand as much chance as anyone. A fine arcanus and a decent speculator. And they are both motivated. Maglorix killed Silus' family, and slaughtered Atius' comrades.'

Silus' jaw clenched at the mention of his family, but he remained still.

'Fine,' said Caracalla. 'I'll trust your judgement. Soldiers, I don't like this Maglorix. He is becoming a pebble in my boot, annoying me wherever I go. As Oclatinius says, neither of you have any love for him either. He has escaped punishment once. I want him dead.

'It will take time to get the legions ready to march again. But when we do, there will be a slaughter such as the people of this land have never dreamed. Maglorix seems to be a rallying figure, and an instigator. No doubt he is a hero among the barbarians right now. I want him out of the way. If we have to fight him, so be it, but without him the resistance will be weaker, and many legionary and auxiliary lives will be saved. You two are going to go into enemy territory, locate Maglorix and kill him.

'Understand, though, that this is not an official mission. My brother would no doubt come up with a reason to delay or prevent this, just to spite me, and father is not the risk taker he was in his younger days and might take his side. So, keep your heads down, and get it done.'

'Yes, Augustus,' said Atius. 'I accept.'

Caracalla looked at him curiously. 'Oclatinius, do you recall me asking for volunteers for this mission?'

'I do not, Augustus.'

'Soldiers, you have your orders. Dismissed.'

-

'There is a big part of me hoping you idiots never come back,' said Oclatinius, when he had them both in his office. 'What were you trying to do to me back there?'

'To you, sir?' asked Atius innocently. 'I was just answering the Augustus' question.'

Oclatinius shook his head. 'On another day you would have been thrown to the beasts in the arena for that sort of insolence. You are lucky his anger was directed elsewhere. Anyway, here we are. You have your mission. Atius, I am admitting you to the ranks of the Speculatores. But let me make one thing clear: Silus is in the Arcani. He is in charge. I don't trust your reckless attitude. Is that clear?'

'Yes, sir,' they both said.

'Fine. Get what kit you need from the quartermaster. Atius, say goodbye to your girl. Silus, say goodbye to your dog. Go out and get drunk, or go to bed early, whatever you want tonight. Tomorrow, you depart for Caledonia.'

Atius and Silus saluted and retreated hastily.

'Fuck, mate,' said Silus once they were out of earshot. 'I don't know about Oclatinius, but you nearly killed me in there!'

'I don't see what the fuss is all about,' said Atius sulkily.

'Forget it. So, are you going to spend the night with Menenia?'

'The whole night?' Atius looked shocked. 'What would I do for a whole night?'

'Maybe comfort her? She has been through a big trauma and lost her father.'

'Well, I'll certainly give her a bit of comfort. Then after that, let's go out on the town.'

Silus grimaced, but he felt too keyed up to get an early night, so he nodded. 'Meet me at the tavern with the Blue Boar sign two hours before midnight. We can drink to departed spirits.'

'I'll drink to whatever you tell me to, sir,' said Atius with a wink.

'Don't start that crap with me. I'm no one's sir.'

'Whatever you say, sir.'

'Piss off. Go and kit up, give your girlfriend a five minute fuck, then meet me for a drink.'

—

Silus visited the quartermaster to stock up on basic provisions for the journey, but in truth he needed little. His weapons – dagger, garrotte, short sword – were his own, and he would not be wearing armour on this sort of mission. The main supplies he needed were nutritional. He took some cheese and salted beef, and a new canteen. They would supplement their supplies in the field – foraging, hunting and stealing should be sufficient for their needs. Silus was keen to travel as lightly and as quickly as possible, both to track Maglorix down and to escape after they had finished him. He spent the rest of his day in the gymnasium and baths, performing some light exercise with weights, and relaxing in the tepidarium, alternating with visits to the frigidarium and caldarium. The coldness of the frigidarium took him back to freezing nights in the outdoors, both as a child and a soldier, and while his heart told him to enjoy the hotter rooms while he was able to, his head cautioned him to tolerate the cold as long as he could to help him acclimatise.

After a massage and oiling from a bathhouse slave, he went on to the Blue Boar. The tavern keeper recognised Silus instantly, and his eyes darted around to see if he was accompanied by Oclatinius. When he saw that Silus was alone, he greeted him suspiciously.

'What do you want?'

The tavern was more than half full, and a few of the clientele looked up in surprise at the sound of their usually friendly tavern keeper greeting a customer so impolitely.

'No trouble,' said Silus. 'Just food.'

The tavern keeper nodded grudgingly.

'Nice new door by the way,' said Silus. 'Looks solid.'

The tavern keeper looked at him uncertainly, not sure if he was teasing him, but he apparently decided to take it as a compliment. 'Good workmanship, that's for sure. Should stop any more unexpected visitors.'

The other customers quickly lost interest and returned to drinking, laughing and games of dice and knucklebones.

Silus ordered lamb stew and ate slowly, blowing on the hot food before putting the spoon in his mouth. Though he tried to keep his mind clear, his thoughts oscillated between past and future, from loss to vengeance. His emotions followed his thoughts, swinging from grief to anger, from eyes welling with tears to clenched fists and clenched teeth. He decided he needed a drink and ordered a large beer.

He was on his second when Atius came in, a cheeky grin on his face. Silus marvelled at how the younger man was able to put aside the grief and fear that he had so recently experienced. But maybe he was simply able to push it down deeper than Silus. He grabbed a stool from a man who had just stood and announced he was going outside for a piss. His two friends protested that their comrade would be back, but Atius pretended not to hear and thumped the stool down at Silus' table.

'Looks good. What are you eating? I'm famished.'

'Just stew. Not too tough though.'

Atius ordered the stew and a beer together with a small loaf of bread. The tavern keeper ladled it from one of the large containers at the bar counter into a bowl, and passed it over with a cup of beer.

Atius placed the meal on the table, then picked up the bread and broke it in half. He bowed his head, closed his eyes and said quietly, 'This is my body broken for you. Do this in remembrance of me.'

Silus looked at him curiously. Atius noticed the odd look on Silus' face, and just muttered, 'Fuck off, Silus. You wouldn't understand.'

Silus shrugged, and they ate and drank together. Silus asked, 'How was Menenia?'

'Fucking incredible,' said Atius. 'She was all over me. Didn't want to stop.'

'I meant, how was she in herself?'

'Oh. Well, she did cry a bit afterwards.'

'And you left her to it?'

'Well, she was cuddling Issa. I think she'll be fine.'

'Atius, you're an asshole.'

Atius looked offended, then noticed a young female slave carrying some jugs of beer over to another table, and he whistled.

'Would you look at the tits on that. Fuck me, if I wasn't already tapped out, I wouldn't mind a go on that. What about you, Silus?'

Silus' dagger glare made Atius shrink back.

'Sorry, mate, I wasn't thinking. Still too soon?'

'It will be too soon for the rest of my life.'

Atius looked down into his beer, swirling it around the cup, the noise of the busy tavern covering an awkward silence.

The man who had gone for a piss returned and looked for his stool. Over Atius' shoulder, Silus saw his friends pointing in their direction. The man was early middle-aged, bulky with a combination of muscle and fat, and long red hair. He walked up behind Atius. When he spoke, his accent was typical of the local Brigantes, and he spoke in the Brigantian dialect of common Brittonic.

'Hey. Did you nick my chair?'

Atius didn't even turn. He took a sip of his beer as if no one had spoken. Silus wasn't sure whether Atius understood any of the words spoken in the Brittonic dialect of the Celtic language, but it was clear that the Brigantian was talking to him. Silus tensed, ready for trouble.

The Brigantian put a hand on Silus' shoulder. 'I said, did you—'

Atius grabbed the hand, rose, whirled and twisted at the same time, one hand pressing into the back of the Brigantian's shoulder as he pivoted forwards. The man's face slammed into the table with the crunch of breaking nose cartilage, and blood spurted from his nostrils.

Atius put his face close to the man's ear, and whispered in Latin, 'Don't ever touch me again.' Then he spun the man round and threw him to the floor. The Brigantian crashed into his three friends, who had only just got to their feet at the sight of their drinking partner being assaulted. They all fell backwards into their table – drinks, food and dice flying into the air.

Atius turned to face them as they all regained their feet. Silus groaned and stood up. His knife was at his belt, but he left it sheathed. Hopefully this could be sorted out without death, but it was nice to know it was there.

The others in the tavern either exited quickly or stepped back to make space for the two groups of men squaring up. One enterprising lad near the back said he would take bets on the two newcomers against the locals, and he had some immediate take-up.

The tavern keeper came hurrying over.

'Please, not again,' he said, interposing himself between Silus and Atius and the Brigantians. The broken-nosed man hurled him aside, then threw himself at Atius. Atius turned his body to absorb the momentum and with an extended thigh threw his attacker down. But the man hung on, taking Atius down with him, and straightaway the two were trading blows in the sticky straw of the tavern floor.

The other three Brigantians stepped forward to help their friend. Silus took a step forward, blocking their path. They turned to each other, and a look of agreement passed between them. Then, as one, they charged at Silus.

There wasn't much space, and the three men got in each other's way, breaking their momentum. Silus targeted the one to his left. Accepting the outstretched hands grasping towards him, he pulled and stepped further to his left. The man charged head first into a pillar and slumped to the floor unconscious.

Silus didn't pause, but moved on the central attacker with a two-handed blow to the side of the head. When he rocked sideways into the right-hand attacker, Silus kicked out, the edge of his foot smashing into the side of the man's knee, caving it inwards with an audible snapping sound. Even as he was falling, Silus was upon the last man standing, two punches to his midriff and one to his throat.

Once he had made sure none of the three was rising, he turned to watch Atius. His friend clearly needed no help. He was sitting astride the Brigantian, raining blows into him, knocking his head from side to side. After a few moments to let Atius work out the last of his fury, Silus stepped in, grabbed him under the shoulders and lifted him up. Atius rounded on Silus furiously, fist back to strike.

Then recognition came back into his face. He dropped his hands, looked around him at the carnage, then tipped his head back and laughed.

The young lad at the back collected his winnings from the begrudging gamblers, and the tavern keeper returned to berate Silus.

'Look at the damage. The table is destroyed. My customers have fled.'

'Only a couple of the more cowardly ones,' said Atius. 'I think the rest loved the entertainment. Didn't you?' The onlookers cheered.

'Here's the money for the table. And a drink for everyone here, on me. And a copper coin for a lad to fetch some slaves to clear away these deadbeats.'

More cheering, and soon the beer was flowing. The conscious and semi-conscious Brigantians were dragged away, and Atius and Silus mingled with the locals, other Brigantians, some Votadini and some retired auxiliary Batavians and Tungrians. For a brief while, Silus forgot about his grief and anger and desperate desire for revenge, and just drank and laughed.

It didn't last. Later in the evening, Atius came over to him with a Brigantian girl under one arm and a Votadini girl under the other. Both were obviously about as drunk as Atius and were laughing and smiling coquettishly at him.

'Mate,' said Atius. 'These two are well up for it. I sung your praises for your talents in the sack, so they agreed you could have your pick first. Which one do you prefer?'

Silus looked from the redheaded Brigantian to the blonde Votadini, and everything came crashing back down on him. His wife and daughter. His mission. Maglorix.

He leant forward and vomited loudly onto the floor.

'Oh, for fuck's sake,' said Atius. 'Fine. Sorry girls. Another night. Mate, let's get you home.'

Atius put a hand under Silus' shoulder, helped him to his feet, and after blowing two kisses over his shoulder, he helped Silus out of the tavern.

-

The constant bounce in the saddle felt like some sort of torture. The muscles in Silus' calves ached, his inner thighs were chafed raw, and the bones at the base of his pelvis felt like he had been bent over and repetitively kicked in the arse. The journey along a Roman road that led north from Eboracum to Segedunum at the eastern end of the vallum Hadrian should have taken four or five days at a normal pace on horseback, but by swapping horses at the auxiliary cavalry forts along the road and riding twelve hours a day, they had made the journey in just three days.

As they approached the south gate of the fort, Silus recognised one of the sentries, Suadurix, a Nervian from the lands of the Belgae. The VI Nervian cohort had previously manned Segedunum but were then subsequently transferred to one of the forts on the vallum Antonini. Segedundum was now garrisoned by the IV Lingonian cohort. However, personnel were often transferred between the sites. Silus had met Suadurix more than once, when their forts had taken place on joint manoeuvres, and when Silus' scouting missions had left him nearer Suadurix's barracks than his own and he needed a roof for the night.

Suadurix's colleague presented his spear as the two riders neared, but Suadurix stepped forward.

'Silus, it been a long time.' His Latin was heavily accented with Gallic.

Silus swung himself off his saddle with a groan, steadied himself against the horse's flank, then reached out to shake Suadurix's hand briskly.

'Dark times,' said Silus gravely and Suadurix nodded.

'What brings you here?'

'I can't really say.'

'Still doing those secret scouting missions, eh? You need report to prefect? I think he in his praetoria.'

Silus shook his head. 'No, we are just keeping our heads down. Please don't go spreading it around that we are here.'

'Anything you say,' said Suadurix. 'I owe you. You save me that time I fell asleep on sentry duty. I be dead now if you not heard the centurion out for my blood, and come find me.'

'You would have done the same for me, I'm sure. Listen, we could do with some news. What have you heard about the barbarian movements?'

'Bits. I off duty in one hour. We get beer and food and talk about bastard officers?'

'That sounds good. We'll stable the horses and come to meet you. Where is good?'

'Come my barracks, last one of north-western block. Our contubernium is two men down, so you bunk with us, yes? You don't mind snoring?'

Silus laughed and looked to Atius. Atius nodded and dismounted. Suadurix exchanged words with his colleague in a Belgic form of Celtic that Silus half understood, and the other auxiliary stepped back to let them past. Hobbling, Silus and Atius led their horses into the fort.

The barrack room of the contubernium was newly built in stone, which was part of the reinforcement and repair work done to the vallum Hadriani by Severus when he had first arrived in Britannia. This had improved the quality of life of the auxiliaries who lived in the fort and no longer had to sleep in wooden structures with their draughts and leaks.

Silus and Atius sat on the lower level of one of four bunk beds that lined the walls of the room. Suadurix was the decanus of the contubernium, the leader of the small squad of eight, although as he had explained to them, they currently numbered only six after two of their comrades had fallen to a Maeatae ambush while on patrol at the end of the previous year's campaign and had not yet been replaced.

Suadurix passed Silus and Atius a bowl each of hot pulmentum, a wheat porridge that provided basic nutrition and was easy to cook from the daily rations the contubernium received from the granary. Atius mumbled a quiet prayer before eating, and Suadurix gave Silus a questioning look. Silus mouthed the word Christian, and Suadurix nodded his understanding.

As they had guests, Suadurix broke out some of the squad's other supplies, and he surprised Silus by cooking up a decent myma – offal and blood with herbs and goat's cheese – on their charcoal stove. The meal smelled delicious after a couple of days of eating hard tack on the road, and the bronze cooking pot was steaming by the time they had finished their pulmentum.

Once the meal was over, the spoons licked clean, and the youngest of the squad detailed to do the washing up, Silus kicked his boots off and sat with his back against the wall and his feet dangling over the side of the bed.

'I hear about your family,' said Suadurix. 'I'm very sorry.'

Silus nodded his acknowledgement.

'Things are bad,' said Suadurix.

'We know,' said Silus. 'Atius was in Voltanio.'

All the members of the contubernium froze and stared at Atius. Atius straightened his back, challenging them to look him in the eyes.

'You are the one that escaped?' Suadurix voice held awe.

Atius' expression was still defiant. 'I left on the orders of the prefect to bring word to the Emperor. And to save his daughter. Both of which I accomplished.'

'We heard news of your fort three days after it happened. A boat of Classis Britannica came and centurion told us be ready for war.'

'What else did you hear?' asked Silus.

'They told us there could be an attack any day. Told us we were on our own until the legions from Eboracum came. But, no attack.'

'What have the barbarians been doing then?'

'Destroying,' said Suadurix glumly. 'Fleeing soldiers and civilians reached us. Not many. They tell us stories. Bad stories.'

Silus and Atius waited, and even the other members of the contubernium looked to their leader to enthral them with horror stories.

'Voltanio was just the first,' said Suadurix. 'All along the vallum Antonini, the Maeatae attacked. Some garrisons made a fighting withdrawal. Most were massacred. A few men escaped. They say that the Maeatae torture and burn their prisoners. And when they finish the forts, they turn to the vici.'

Silus felt suddenly cold, as unbidden memories crowded in on him. He bit the inside of his cheek hard to distract himself, and concentrated on Suadurix.

'Yesterday a woman arrive with a baby in her arms. It was not her baby. She had been caught by the Maeatae fleeing with her sister, the mother's baby. The woman herself was pregnant. I heard that she said that the Maeatae raped her, and then raped her sister. She fled while they were occupied with her sister, but she look back, and saw them killing her; they continued even after she was dead.

'The day before, an old man appeared seeking help. He had burns on his hands and face and couldn't breathe well. He kept crying that he couldn't save his wife when the Maeatae burnt their house. He died yesterday.'

'Is it purely revenge?' asked Atius.

'Of course,' said Suadurix. 'They hate us for our invasion. They want bring death to us, like we have to them.'

'It's more than that,' said Silus. 'They want to provoke Caracalla into marching deep into their territory so they can ambush him. And when the other barbarian tribes see Caracalla on the march, they will have no choice but to resist.'

The squad were pale-faced, sipping their beer and watered wine morosely, finding nothing to say.

'But you, Silus. You will save us all, right?' Suadurix laughed and clapped Silus hard on the shoulder. Silus gave a half-hearted smile.

'Or die trying, friend.'

Chapter Ten

The stout wooden gates were blackened and splintered. The upper hinge had broken on one of them, causing it to lean at an awkward angle. Every wooden structure was charred or reduced to ashes. Every stone building and structure that had wooden supports had collapsed.

The ground was littered with bodies. The earthly remains of a garrison that had fought to the death. A couple of foxes looked up as Atius and Silus approached on horseback, gore hanging from their mouths. They watched the men approach resentfully, then turned tail and ran away, trailing ropes of guts behind them. A horde of crows tore at flesh – there was so much death that even this long after the battle, the carrion feeders had plenty to choose from. The air was heavy with the stench of wood smoke and rotting corpses.

Atius made the sign of the cross and muttered spiritual words to himself as the two of them dismounted and wandered disconsolately around. This had been their home, and these had been their friends. Most were hard to recognise now, and all distinctive jewellery had been looted, but Silus knew these men like family. Atius was a more recent recruit to the garrison, but his face was white with the horror of the scene and the realisation that it could so easily have been his corpse being pecked at.

Silus knelt by a body that lay face down, extremities ravaged, and turned it over. Maggots and worms spilled from the mouth and eye sockets, and he recoiled. The bald head and hooked nose were intact enough for Silus to recognise Pallas, Menenius' secretary. Though he was unarmoured, he still clutched a short sword in his stiffened grip. Even the ageing freedman had joined the battle in the end.

Nearby he found a corpse wearing armour he recognised as belonging to Geganius, and next to him was a man whose neck had been partially severed, who Silus thought might have been Brinno.

Not only Romans were dead. As they walked towards the gate, Atius pointed to where the garrison had made its final stand, but it was unnecessary. The press of corpses was at its densest here, with Roman bodies piled on top of each other facing mounds of unarmoured, long-haired warriors. The barbarians, without armour to protect them from the scavengers, had been picked much cleaner and were mainly bone and gristle, but their long red or blonde hair still outlined their skulls.

Silus didn't feel nauseous. He had seen enough death and decay both in the army and during his upbringing. He didn't particularly feel anger, not yet, though he knew it would come. His main emotion was awe at the scale of the destruction. The fort, so strong and impregnable and manned by invincible Romans had been reduced to so much ash, rubble and bone.

The stench was overwhelming as they picked their way out of the fort and through the breached gates. A short walk out of the fort led them to the nearby woods. From a distance they could make out a handful of skeletal figures nailed to the trees that faced the fort. Crows grudgingly dispersed as they approached.

Only half a dozen had survived the battle to be tortured and crucified. Silus presumed the two rotting corpses at the front were Menenius and Damanais. They had been stripped naked, so they couldn't be identified by brooches, insignia or armour, and their facial features were gone. But the build and hair were right. Silus made a sign against evil and directed a curse on the barbarians to Antenociticus and Nemesis. Atius dropped to his knees, raised his hands to the skies and sang out a hymn of mourning. Silus waited respectfully for him to finish.

When Atius stood, Silus looked around, and saw they were being watched. A young boy stood at the edge of the woods, some twenty yards away, regarding them with sorrow-filled eyes. Silus called to him, but as soon as the boy realised he had been noticed, he turned and hared off into the depths of the wood.

Silus swore and chased after him, Atius close on his heels. The boy, maybe around ten years old, was nimble, darting around trees and leaping over streams, and the older men tired even as they gained ground. Through a break in the trees ahead, Silus saw a rock face that the boy was heading straight for. He signalled for Atius to circle round, and he kept chasing.

The boy hit the base of the cliff at full speed and leaped, grabbing handholds and footholds and ascending vertically like a squirrel up an oak tree. Silus reached the rocks and started to climb. He was a decent climber himself but didn't have the advantage of the boy's slightness, and he panted hard as he heaved himself laboriously from hold to hold. Slowly the boy pulled away from him, and grit and dirt fell down into Silus' mouth and eyes as the boy scrabbled his way upwards.

When the boy was nearly at the top, he paused to look down at the struggling man beneath him and spat. Silus saw the glob falling towards him and turned his face, so it hit him in the cheek.

'Fuck you, barbarian,' yelled the boy in a high voice that was attenuated by the wind.

'I'm not a fucking barbarian,' yelled back Silus, aware that his lack of armour made him appear unlike a Roman soldier. The boy threw a rock at Silus' head, and even though he ducked out of the way, the fist-sized chunk hit him painfully in the shoulder.

'Stay there, you little brat,' yelled Silus, but the boy just made an obscene gesture, then disappeared over the top of the cliff.

Silus reached the top of the cliff with a bruised shoulder, scraped knuckles and one skinned knee. As he hauled himself over the top, he rolled onto his back, looking up at the grey sky and gasping to recover his breath.

Atius let out a low chuckle. 'Is this what you were looking for?'

Silus' friend held the boy's long unruly hair in his fist. The boy struggled and spat and swore, while Atius just held him at arm's length wearing an indulgent smile.

'Damn, that little shit can move,' said Silus. 'Trust you to take the easy option.'

'Well, the path around the side of the cliff was certainly a little less onerous,' said Atius.

Silus stood and took the boy's chin in a tight grip, forcing him to look into his eyes.

'Listen, boy. We aren't barbarians.'

'Where are your shields then? Where's your armour?'

'We're travelling light. Listen to our accents. Look at my hair. Look at his skin. Do we look like Maeatae or Caledonians?'

The boy looked from Silus to Atius, then went limp. Atius loosened his grip, and the boy fell to the ground and started sobbing. Atius squatted next to him and waited. After a few moments, the boy wiped his eyes roughly and looked up at them. Where there had been fear, then grief, now there was anger.

'Where were you?'

'What? When?'

'If you are Roman soldiers, where were you during the attack?'

Atius opened his mouth to answer, but could think of nothing to say.

'Where were you when the barbarians came to the vicus and killed everyone still alive after the last attack? Why aren't you dead in the fort, like all the other soldiers? Like my father!'

The boy threw himself at Atius, knocking him onto his back. He sat astride him and started pummelling him. Atius caught his wrists, kicked him off, and threw him away. The boy fell to the ground and started crying again.

Silus and Atius stood and looked down at him.

'He lived in the vicus?' said Silus.

'His father was a soldier?' said Atius.

'Oh, crap. Boy, are you Brinno's son?'

'Don't you say his name, you coward. You aren't fit to speak it.'

Silus searched his memory. The little time he had spent in the vicus had been with his own family, and Sergia was too young to have been playing with a boy this age, but he had a memory of Brinno talking proudly about his boy's first hunting trip.

'Fulco? You're Fulco, aren't you?'

The boy's eyes brimmed with defiance, but he nodded reluctantly.

'Fulco, listen to me. I wasn't in the fort at the time of the attack. I was performing a mission for the emperor in Eboracum. Atius here was in the fort, but he was ordered to report the attack to the emperor, and to save the prefect's daughter.'

'He didn't save my mother, did he?'

Silus noticed now that the boy was thin and pale with hollow cheekbones.

'What have you been living on since the attack?' asked Silus gently.

'I can look after myself,' said the boy.

Silus drew some hard tack from his pack and handed it to the boy. Fulco stared at it suspiciously for a moment, then wolfed it down.

'Fulco, we need to know what happened after Atius left.'

The boy held his hand out for more food. Silus sighed, broke a biscuit in half and gave it to him. 'You get the rest after you tell us everything.'

—

Atius made a fire, while Silus brought down a pigeon and a couple of crows, using his belt as a sling and some smooth pebbles as shots. Fulco watched with grudging admiration, and while Atius gutted and plucked the birds, Silus showed Fulco the technique, just as his father had shown him. It involved having a belt of the right thickness, length and pliability, but when Silus was in the field, he made sure everything he carried or wore had at least two functions. For a short moment, Fulco forgot his grief as Silus showed him how his waterskin could double as a flotation device to help him cross a fast flowing river or a wide lake when filled with air, how his snare could be used as a garrotte, how his cloak could be used as the roof of a bivouac, and the myriad uses to which a sharp knife with a stout handle could be put.

Contrary to what they had told Fulco, they let him eat while he told his story. The cooked bird flesh set all their mouths watering long before it was ready, and although the boy had claimed he could look after himself, he still gulped down the meat he was given like a small dog bolting a found carcass before the bigger pack members arrived.

'Tell us what happened,' said Atius gently.

Fulco paused mid-bite into a pigeon leg. He looked up at them both over the drumstick, then tore off a chunk and swallowed it whole. Atius and Silus waited expectantly.

'What do you think happened?' said Fulco sullenly.

'We want to hear it from you.'

Fulco took another bite, swallowed, then threw the leg away angrily, though strands of meat still clung to it. The survivalist in Silus cringed at the waste, but he bit his tongue.

'Fine. They slaughtered everyone. Is that good enough for you?'

'Where were you? What did you see?'

Fulco's eyes darted from side to side, suddenly looking like a frightened little boy.

'I was in the fort. I had sneaked in to see my father. The guards turned a blind eye to let me do that every so often, especially if he hadn't had any leave for a while. I would hang out with his contubernium, playing dice and knucklebones, or talking about battles and girls. Sometimes they would let me drink some of their beer. I didn't like it much.'

The boy's gaze was far away now, and Silus and Atius were silent, unwilling to break his reverie.

'When the alarm sounded, it was late, but they were all still drinking and gambling. Not drunk, you understand. They grabbed their weapons and armour and ran for their stations.

My father was the last one out. He gave me a hug and told me to hide.

'At first all I could hear was the auxiliaries preparing for battle. Shouts of orders. Clattering boots. I hid under my father's bed. He had a box with letters carved on little wooden leaves. I looked at them while I waited. I can't read very well, but I could see my mother's name at the bottom of most of them.

'Then I heard the sounds of battle. Screams. Swords clashing. Then a massive crash. I don't know if it was because I was being brave or because I was scared, but after a while I didn't want to be alone any more. I crawled out from under the bed, and went to the window to look out. I could see the main gate burst open and in flames, the Romans in a half circle trying to hold back the enemy. I watched them fight until they were almost all dead.

'In the end, there were just a few left. A few surrendered.' Fulco looked sharply at the two men. 'But not my father. Nor the commander and his deputy, or that centurion Geganius. I don't know their names. You need to know that. They fought until they were overpowered.

'I watched the officers kneeling. Two barbarian chiefs were talking. I couldn't hear what they were saying. Then they dragged my father over and… and…'

Fulco swallowed, and his eyes glistened. 'They killed him. Then they killed Geganius. Then they dragged the rest of the survivors off towards the woods. All the barbarians went along to watch, and for a moment the fort was deserted. I took my chance and ran.'

Fulco raised his head defiantly. 'I wanted to kill them all. The murderers… but… there was only me. I had no choice.'

Silus put a hand on Fulco's shoulder. 'You did right, boy. It's what your father would have wanted.' Atius was looking down, and Silus wondered if he too was feeling the guilt of being the survivor.

'Did you see anything else?'

Fulco shook his head. 'A little. Once I was out of the fort, I found a hiding place amongst some rocks, and I... I watched. I saw them start to nail them up to the trees. At the front they had the commander's deputy and another centurion. They made the commander watch while they crucified them. When all the men were nailed up, screaming and begging, they left with the commander tied over the saddle of one of their horses.'

'What?' Silus' voice was harsher than he meant, and it made the boy start.

'What?' repeated Fulco.

'Menenius survived?'

'Is he the commander? Yes, he did. Or, he was alive when I last saw him.'

'Gods,' whispered Silus. 'Poor bastard.'

'Silus,' said Atius. 'We have to rescue him. Christos alone knows what tortures they are inflicting on him.'

'That's not the mission.'

'Fuck the mission. He is our commander. We owe him our loyalty.'

The two men glared at each other. Then Fulco spoke again.

'Then I went back to the vicus. Everyone was dead.'

Atius and Silus focused back on Fulco.

'Everyone?'

'Not a single thing left alive. Man. Woman. Child. Dog, pig, chicken.'

'Your mother?' asked Atius tentatively.

Fulco shook his head. 'She wasn't there.'

Taken as a slave, Silus thought. Her fate would probably be worse than Menenius'. He kept that to himself, though he knew Atius was thinking the same thing. At least his own family had been spared that.

They all sat in silence, then. In each other's company, but alone with their thoughts of guilt and loss and anger and despair.

The fire burnt lower, and with an effort Silus shook himself out of his despondency.

'Atius,' he said. 'It's getting late. Let's prepare a camp and settle down. We can make an early start. Boy, you can stay with us for the night. In the morning we ride north, into danger, and you can't come with us.'

Fulco nodded.

'Go and find us some wood for the fire then. Good lad.' Fulco stood and shuffled away, picking up sticks and branches unenthusiastically. Atius and Silus started gathering the material for a bivouac. The fort was only a short distance away, with stone walls and at least some remaining roofs intact. But though it was unspoken between them, they knew that none of them would want to spend the night amongst the corpses and lemures of their departed comrades.

It started to rain.

—

'Do you think he will make it?' asked Atius for the tenth time.

Silus shook his head in exasperation. 'We gave him supplies. We pointed him in the right direction. He is a sharp kid, he'll be fine.'

'He's lost everything, and he has no one. Even if he makes it back to Roman lines, what future does he have? Living on the streets, or taken into slavery.'

Silus pulled on the reins of his horse sharply, causing his mount to stop abruptly with a whinny of protest.

'What did you expect me to do, Atius? Escort him home and set him up with a nice noble family, so that one day he will become a senator?'

'There's no need to be like that.'

They rode in silence for a while.

'Do you think Menenius is still alive?'

Silus rolled his eyes. Again, it was at least the tenth time he had asked.

'I am no wiser than the last time you asked, Atius. Though I pray for his sake that he is dead. We both know what the barbarians do to their prisoners.'

'I still think we should be looking for him. He should be our priority.'

'Look, we have a job to do. And that job happens to be to find the bastard who killed my family. Nothing and no one is going to get in the way of that. Do you understand?'

Without waiting for a reply, Silus goaded his mount into a canter and pulled away from Atius, settling back into a walk when he was a hundred yards or so ahead. The terrain was scrubby. A little elevated above the marshland they had ridden through for most of the day, the horses squelched morosely through the mud that came up to their fetlocks. Now they could make better time on the firmer ground, and there was better grazing for the horses when they stopped for breaks. Well beyond the vallum Hadriani now, they were fully in barbarian territory. The maritime supply base of Horrea Classis lay far to their east, and there was no hope of reinforcements, shelter or resupply from Roman forces. The horses' energy needed to be conserved as they could not exchange them at the mansiones that dotted the Roman roads in Britannia, and if one broke a leg, they would be on foot from there onwards.

A light drizzle reduced visibility, but up ahead on a small hill, Silus saw a palisade appearing from out of the gloom. He pulled up and waited for Atius to reach him. He gave his friend what he hoped was an apologetic shrug, and they continued forward.

As they neared, they saw the wooden palisade was torn down and burnt in many places. They rode through one of the gaps into the barbarian hill fort. Like many hill forts, this was clearly primarily a civilian settlement, more akin to a Roman vicus than a fort. There were a number of roundhouses arranged in a circle inside the palisade around a central open area. The roundhouses had steep conical thatched roofs supported by wooden timbers, and walls of wattle reeds daubed with clay and insulated with grass and heather. Or at least, enough of some of the houses remained for Silus to see how they should have looked. Most of them were charred, the roofs collapsed inwards, and the walls fallen or ripped down.

They dismounted, tied up their horses, and wandered slowly around. There were no carrion feeders here. No hordes of crows, or scavenging foxes. The skeletons had long ago been picked clean and washed by the rain. Silus crouched by one collection of bones, still recognisably human despite a missing leg that may have been dragged away to be feasted on by a fox's young in its den. The bones were too small to belong to an adult. A child then, though he couldn't tell what sex. He picked up the skull, looked into the eye sockets, then rotated it in his hands and saw the catastrophic split in the top of the cranium, long and wide. A heavy two-handed sword blow, he thought. He let the skull roll out of his fingers, and looked over to Atius.

Silus' friend stuck his head into one of the roundhouses, then pulled it out again abruptly, grimacing. Silus went over to investigate what had upset his friend. Atius shook his head, but Silus looked inside anyway.

The smell was still overpowering, retained by the house's largely intact roof and walls. The dwelling, as with most, was a single open room, with beds and storage jars around the periphery, animal skin rugs on the floor and a central fire. The cooking pot was overturned and had long since been licked dry.

On one of the beds were two adult skeletons, one atop the other, facing each other. A legionary pilus still skewered them together, like a spit with pieces of meat on for roasting. Some desiccated sinew and flesh still hung off them, especially where the two were pressed together and the scavengers had found it hard to reach. Another child's skeleton lay partially in the central fire, the bones charred. The skull was disarticulated from the neck, but Silus didn't know whether that was from wild animals or the Roman soldiers who had massacred these villagers.

He came back out, and walked over to Atius, who was standing and staring into the distance, face pale. Atius was mouthing a silent prayer, and Silus let him finish, waiting beside him patiently.

'Was it necessary?' asked Atius when he was done.

'That's not our job to decide.'

They were quiet for a moment. 'Once, some parents brought their children to the Christos for him to pray over and lay his hands on them. The disciples of the Christos were angry and told them to go away. But the Christos said to let the children come to him. For, he said, the kingdom of heaven belongs to such as these. Silus, they killed the children.'

'Have you forgotten who you are talking to?' Silus' tone was low and full of warning.

'Of course not. But these children did not kill your family.'

'Their kin killed my kin. They deserve every punishment that the Augusti and the gods throw at them.' Silus turned towards the hut and spat in its direction. Atius' face hardened for a moment. Then his head dropped. He put a hand on Silus' shoulder, and Silus grasped it briefly.

'It's going to get worse, you know that, don't you,' said Silus. 'Last year was brutal, a lightning thrust right through Caledonia, destroying anything that stood in the way of the legions. But its aim was to cow the barbarians into submission with a show of power. This year is different. This year, Severus means to eliminate them. When he is done, there will barely be anyone left alive of the tribes of the Maeatae and the Caledonians. Maybe you should be thankful you are with me, trying to track down the man who broke the treaties and is bringing this destruction down on his people, rather than with the auxilia and legions who will be slaughtering these so-called innocents.'

Atius didn't answer. After a moment more, Silus sighed. 'There is nothing for us here, no supplies and no survivors to question. It's getting late. There should be a temporary marching camp maybe two hours' ride to the north, abandoned after last year's campaign. Let's get there to shelter for the night.'

–

The camp was further than Silus remembered or maybe the going had been slower than expected, as night had fallen by the time they reached the southern bank of the river the locals called Uisge Theamhich. He had scouted this way before, had actually been the one to report the suitability of the site. The northern bank of the river had been a good place for a marching army to set up for the night – easily defended and with fresh water. Roman doctrine through the centuries had always been to make a fortified camp every night when marching in enemy territory, and between them the soldiers carried all the tools and materials to dig ditches and make palisades. Though hugely time consuming, and always a massive pain in the backside for the legionaries and auxiliaries at the end of a long day's march, it had been an immutable part of the Roman routine since the time of Julius Caesar and before. Not only did it protect the army for the night, but it also provided a defensive position to the rear should the advance be checked by superior numbers, and further, it created a series of stepping stones that allowed smaller forces to hold the territory that had been taken.

The river wasn't particularly wide, and at the ford that Silus had scouted previously the depth was only waist high, but it was fast flowing. They led their horses across the river rather than ride them and risk being thrown if their mounts lost their footing, and by walking downstream of the horses, they were partly sheltered from the buffeting of the cold water. Nevertheless, they were shivering and soaked when they pulled themselves up the northern bank. The camp lay about a hundred yards further north.

The marching camps of Severus and Caracalla, although varying to some extent with the vagaries of the terrain, followed a common pattern of a v-shaped ditch, an earth rampart and a palisade of sharpened stakes. There were no gateways as such, just gaps in the defences, with ditch, rampart and palisades set a few yards further forward, to break the charge of an enemy. The stakes had been taken away by the departing soldiers to build the next camp, but the ditch and rampart remained.

Silus and Atius remained dismounted and approached warily. The camps had been abandoned at the end of the last campaigning season, and so could be occupied by anyone who fancied a pre-constructed place for defence and shelter, either for the night or more permanently.

And indeed, as they neared, Silus and Atius smelled the smoke from a wood fire and heard voices from within the boundaries.

'Do we go round?' asked Atius.

Silus considered. He was cold and wet, and had been looking forward to a place to rest for the night and get warm and dry. He didn't relish journeying onwards in the dark for however long was needed to find another place to stop, and then having to construct a shelter before getting rest. On the other hand, he wasn't supposed to be taking unnecessary risks.

'Let's check it out,' he said.

They tied the horses to a small tree and crept towards the camp. The square structure was big, enclosing around sixty acres, which meant that each side was around five hundred yards long – enough to contain a legion of five thousand men. But the locals were scared enough of the Romans returning to avoid settling in the camp, despite its advantages. The voices from within had to be of travellers or maybe a barbarian war party large enough to be unafraid of a Roman return.

There were four entrances across the ditch at each point of the compass. Silus and Atius approached the boundary about a third of the way along from its south-west corner, slithered down the muddy bank into the ditch, then kept low and inched towards the entrance. The intermittent rain was back in force, sending rivulets down Silus' neck. But the discomfort was offset by the advantage from the reduced visibility. As they neared the entrance, Silus saw a sentry, wrapped tight in a cloak, leaning on a spear for support, head down in a vain attempt to exclude the weather.

Silus signalled Atius to stop, then drew his knife and approached silently. At the last moment, the sentry sensed Silus' presence and looked up, eyes wide. He was way too slow. Silus' knife punched into the sentry's voice box, and the man went down, clutching his throat and gurgling quietly. Silus beckoned Atius over, and they took an ankle each and pulled the man into the deep shadows of the encircling ditch. With the sentry disposed of, Atius and Silus slipped through the entrance into the camp.

The internal plan of marching camps was also formulaic. The spaces for the tents were arranged so that every contubernium knew exactly where they would pitch for the night, and there was a large open area between the ramparts and the tents known as the intervallum. This distance from rampart to tent ensured that the soldiers were out of reach of missiles sent from beyond the rampart, ensured that the soldiers could easily access the ramparts for defence, and also acted as a parade ground on which the units could form up into battle order, ready for deployment.

It was in this intervallum region that the barbarian interlopers sat, huddled together. An empty marching camp was an eerie place, and one didn't need much of a superstitious mind to be made nervous about occupying one of the semi-permanent buildings that had been constructed.

There were four men, the flickering light from the flames illuminating long hair, the red colour bleached out by the orange glow from the flames. The fire hissed and spat as the raindrops landed and evaporated. Smoke and steam rose into the black sky.

The men talked in low voices, grumbling about the weather and cursing the Romans, their own leaders, and the gods, that they should be out in this cursed place. Silus heard enough to make out that, like himself, they were a group of scouts, on the lookout for Roman incursions. He beckoned to Atius, and they retreated back to the palisade, out of earshot.

In a low voice, Silus said, 'What do you think?'

'They look tired and their lack of alertness is negligent. We can take two before they know we are on them, which then leaves us two on two with the advantage of surprise. I like the odds. But why? Just for a place to rest for the night?'

'We are on an intelligence mission, remember? These are Maglorix's men, Maeatae, I'm sure of it from their accents. If we take one alive, we can find out where that bastard is.'

Atius considered for a moment then nodded. They quickly sketched a brief plan of attack, then advanced towards the men, their knives drawn.

The barbarians were blinded by the fire, all of them facing inwards to get the most comfort from the heat and light. They clearly had great confidence in their sentry or felt that they were not in dangerous territory. Silus and Atius were able to approach the small party from behind without the slightest warning. In unison the two Romans stepped forward. They each grabbed the hair of their pre-selected victims, jerked their heads back to expose pale necks, and sliced their throats. Crimson liquid fountained outwards, spurting onto the fire, and a smell like blood sausage filled the air.

Silus and Atius hurled the men to one side, ignoring their dying efforts to stem the catastrophic haemorrhage. They drew their short swords as one, and threw themselves at the remaining two barbarians, while the shocked warriors were still coming to terms with what had happened.

Atius' target ducked sideways, just avoiding an impaling thrust, and grabbed his spear from where he had left it, butt end buried in the ground. Atius gave his opponent no time to prepare, ducking inside the spear's reach to thrust again for the man's chest. The barbarian twisted, the sword slicing across the muscles of his unarmoured chest, but not penetrating. He grabbed Atius' wrist, then abandoned his spear to grip Atius' sword hand with both his hands.

Silus' target was the one they had selected to live. The smallest of the four, they had figured he would be the easiest to overpower. But it turned out he was also the quickest. Reacting as soon as the two Romans had made their appearance, he turned and ran for the nearest exit.

Silus started to pursue, then realised immediately that this light young warrior would leave him standing. But he couldn't let him go: who knew how far away the nearest reinforcements were?

Silus grabbed the spear the warrior had abandoned, hefted it to gauge the weight, then lined it up. He would only get one chance at this, then the warrior would be gone, and their lives would be in danger. He threw.

The spear sailed true through the air and implanted itself cleanly between the warrior's shoulder blades. He pitched forward with a cry, and was still.

Silus turned to where Atius was wrestling with the sole surviving barbarian. The warrior had Atius' sword arm pinned tight, but the Roman's other hand was free. Silus saw his friend draw back, the knife clutched tight. As the blow came forward, Silus cast his weapons aside and barrelled into the barbarian, knocking him sideways and saving his life.

'Christos, Silus. What the fuck are you doing?'

The barbarian was winded, but as Silus straddled him, pinning him to the ground, he started to struggle. Silus grabbed the man's wrists, but he was strong and lithe, and Silus couldn't hold him.

'Mine's dead,' gasped Silus. 'Fucking help me! I want this one alive!'

The barbarian's grasping hands closed around Silus' discarded knife, forcing it upwards despite Silus' efforts.

'Atius!'

Atius took two steps forward and stamped on the hand holding the knife. Bones crunched and the barbarian howled. Atius pressed the point of his sword into the warrior's throat, and the struggles ceased.

Silus got slowly to his feet, taking deep gulps of air into his lungs. The Maeatae warrior lay on his back, holding his broken wrist gingerly with his other hand, looking up at the two auxiliaries with a furious glare. The tip of Atius' gladius still indented the skin over the barbarian's larynx, and he held himself still, aware that any sudden movements could lead to a hole in his windpipe.

'What's your name?' said Silus in perfectly accented Brittonic Celtic.

The Maeatae warrior's eyes widened.

'You are one of us?' he hissed. 'Traitor.'

Silus' face remained impassive. 'I'm not one of you, barbarian pig. I'm a soldier in the Roman army, and you are going to be a dead barbarian pig if you don't answer my questions.'

'Ask me what you like. I won't tell you a thing.'

'We'll see.'

Silus retrieved the tough string from his snare and used it to tie the barbarian's ankles together, the material biting deep into the skin and cutting off the blood supply to his feet. He then did the same with his wrists, and though the barbarian gritted his teeth, he couldn't fully suppress a cry of pain when his crushed bones ground against each other as the bonds tightened.

When he was safely trussed, Silus took a step back, then kicked him hard in the ribs. The barbarian groaned, squeezed his eyes shut, then opened them to continue his defiant stare.

'Your name,' said Silus.

'Laeg,' he said. 'Now tell me yours, so I can look for you in the next life.'

'I am Gaius Sergius Silus. Come and find me. This is Atius, but he believes he will end up somewhere else, so he might be harder to track down.'

'What are you saying?' asked Atius, able only to pick out his name from the barbarian words.

'Just making introductions so far,' said Silus. 'Help me get him upright.'

Atius and Silus pulled Laeg to his feet and Silus looped the bonds of his wrists over the top of one of the few remaining spiked stakes that had made up the palisade. The pain in his broken wrist was obvious, but though he hissed air through gritted teeth, he made no protest.

'So, let's have a talk,' said Silus. 'I only want to know one thing: where is Maglorix?'

Laeg's face remained expressionless.

'You must know how this will go,' said Silus. 'We are going to kill you. Do you want to die in terrible pain, or do you want it to be swift and easy?'

'It doesn't matter to me, traitor. As long as I keep my honour, Belenus will come in his chariot to take me to the Otherworld.'

'My friend here believes his god, Christos, could kick your god Belenus' ass. Tell me where I can find that piece of shit, Maglorix.'

Atius looked sternly at Silus when he heard the name of his god, with warning in his eyes, but he said nothing.

'If his god is as weak as he looks, I think that is unlikely. But have a care: you are not fit to speak the sun god's name, traitor.'

'Me? I don't give a fuck about the gods. What good are they to me if they can't save innocent women and children? So fuck Belenus and fuck you.'

Laeg lunged at Silus, but the bonds held tight, and he screwed his eyes up at the pain. Then he started to laugh.

'I think you have experienced loss, traitor. Your wife? Your children? Was it Maglorix? Is that why you ask me where he is, not where the warband is or where the Caledonians are?'

Silus punched him with his right hand straight in the ribs with a follow up from his left into his midriff. As the breath whooshed out of him, head coming down, Silus punched him with an uppercut to the jaw and then a straight jab to the nose. Cartilage crunched, bone broke, blood ran down Laeg's moustache and soaked into his beard. Silus drew his fist back for another blow, and found it caught and held fast by Atius. He rounded angrily on his friend.

'Silus,' said Atius gently. 'I don't know what he is saying to you, but it looks like he getting to you. He is winning.'

Silus stayed defiant for a moment, then nodded and took a breath. Atius was right. He was letting his emotions get away from him. Laeg was probably trying to provoke him into killing him before the barbarian could be tortured into revealing any secrets. What would Oclatinius say if he could see him now? His mentor had taught him how to extract information from a prisoner, with techniques learnt over many decades of experience. For Silus, this would be a first, but now the anger inside him was like ice, not fire, and he felt fully in control.

Slowly and with purpose, he drew his knife from his belt. He held it up and tested the edge with his thumb. Laeg was breathing heavily through his mouth, nose bubbling with blood, but he kept a fascinated gaze on the knife.

'Silus?' said Atius uncertainly. 'What are you doing?'

'What Oclatinius trained me to do. If you don't have the stomach to watch, turn your back.'

Laeg was still wearing the cloak that had been sheltering him from the cold and rain, and Silus used the blade to cut the straps holding it in place, so it fell to the ground. Beneath, Laeg wore breeches and a tunic. As Silus cut the tunic away, he spoke in a conversational tone.

'Tell me about the Otherworld. When Belenus takes you there, are you made whole again? Will your wrist be mended? Your jaw?' Silus cut the cord that kept Laeg's breeches up, and they fell around his ankles. Silus looked pointedly at the barbarian's manhood, shrivelled from fear and pain, and shook his head.

'What about your prick? Will that grow back? Not that it looks of much use to any woman.'

Laeg's lips worked, and he whispered, 'No.' Silus took hold of his cock and laid the blade against the base.

'Silus,' whispered Atius. 'Sweet Maria.' But he made no attempt to stop him.

'Tell me where to find Maglorix.'

'Please,' said Laeg, tears springing to his eyes. 'Don't do it.'

'I am going to cut off your cock and balls and feed them to the crows. I wonder how you will enjoy the afterlife without them. This is the last time I will ask. Where is Maglorix?'

'Tell him,' yelled Atius, understanding the threat without knowing the words, and not caring that Laeg would not understand him.

There was a moment's silence, then Silus sighed and shook his head.

'Wait,' said Laeg. 'I'll tell you. Belenus, forgive me.'

Silus didn't withdraw the blade, just waited expectantly.

'Maglorix is with his warband.' The words were muffled and nasal. 'He is gathering more Maeatae tribes for the war, and persuading the Caledonians to join him.'

'Where?'

Laeg sighed. 'Inchtuthil,' he said, and dropped his head.

Atius looked at Silus. 'Did he say…?'

'Inchtuthil,' confirmed Silus. 'Pinnata Castra. That's bold.'

'But…' said Atius, 'isn't it haunted?'

Silus' attempt at a brave laugh came out weak and strained. Pinnata Castra was a Roman legionary fortress built in the early stages of the invasion of Britain, when the Romans were subduing the Caledonians over a hundred years before. Agricola, the governor at the time, built the fortress after his mighty victory at Mons Graupius, a defeat for the Caledonians that still rankled with the barbarians as much as Alesia for the Gauls, or indeed Cannae for the Romans. Taking around three years to construct, the fortress was of a size to rival the great legionary fortresses at Eboracum, Deva Victrix and Isca Silurum. But after being occupied for only six years, the Legio II, Adiutrix, which called it home, was withdrawn to Moesia to deal with a Dacian invasion. Jealous of the Governor's victories, the Emperor Domitian recalled Agricola to Rome.

With typical Roman attention to detail, the soldiers had taken everything they could carry with them, and destroyed or buried everything they couldn't. Every piece of pottery was smashed into pieces no bigger than the tip of a man's finger. The timber from all the houses was removed and the wattle burned. There was even a rumour that the soldiers had carefully buried nearly a million nails that were too heavy to carry to deny them to the locals. Inchtuthil remained in enemy territory, beyond both the walls of Hadrianus and Antoninus, deserted and useless, but nevertheless a constant reminder to the locals of the awesome power that Rome could bring to bear if it was so minded.

Silus had seen the fortress from a distance once when scouting far to the north. The earth and timber curtain walls, once faced with stone, had collapsed. Through the gaps, he could see inside, and where once there had been barracks and drill halls, mess halls and headquarters and workshops, there was now just debris.

An empty legionary fortress is a chilling sight. Five thousand Romans had marched from that place to the battle of Mons Graupius, from which thousands of Caledonians and hundreds of Romans had never returned. In the dusky gloom, as Silus had watched the fort, he swore he could see the lemures of long dead soldiers patrolling where once there had been ramparts. There was no sign of local tribesmen though, no doubt as scared of the haunted fortress as he was himself. Silus had given the place a wide berth, and found a good reason to scout well away from the cursed place.

And now Maglorix had set up camp here.

'It's a pretty big statement to his men,' said Silus. 'He is showing them he isn't afraid of Rome, or the afterlife. Not like Laeg here, who doesn't want to go to the next world without his prick.'

Laeg didn't understand the Latin, but his eyes were still wide with fear, not least because Silus still hadn't taken the blade away from his genitals. Silus looked down at his knife as if only just realising he still held it. He took a step back, letting go of the warrior's fear-shrivelled parts.

'So,' said Silus. 'It looks like we are going to Pinnata Castra.'

Atius didn't look pleased at the prospect, and spat to ward off evil. 'What about him?' he asked, nodding at Laeg.

Silus thought for a moment, then plunged the knife through Laeg's ribs and into his heart. Laeg spasmed, opened his mouth, and blood poured out. His head lolled to the side and he sagged limp in his bonds.

Atius pursed his lips, then said, 'After all that, I hope he gets to use his cock in his afterlife.'

Silus gave him a steady glare, then shook his head. 'Let's make camp.'

Chapter Eleven

They approached the old fortress under an overcast starless night sky, accompanied by a light drizzle that somehow made its way past every waterproof barrier to soak the skin. The crumbling fortifications loomed out of the gloom, and the shiver that ran through Silus' spine had nothing to do with the cold rain.

This structure was very different from the abandoned marching camp they had recently spent the night in. The fortress was vast – fifteen hundred feet along each side. A twenty-foot-wide and six-foot-deep ditch surrounded the five-foot-thick walls which topped a turf rampart. If the Romans had not destroyed the fort themselves, it was hard to imagine an enemy doing so.

When they were close enough to make out details, they paused and took stock. Silus estimated it was not yet midnight, and firelight and song from within the walls told him that the camp was very much awake. The timber gateways that had once hung between two stone towers were long gone, either removed or burnt by the Romans, looted by locals, or decayed. In multiple places, the stone walls were breached, initially pulled down by the Romans to make the fortress useless to the enemy. The destruction had been augmented over time by the elements and by the plundering of the stone at the hands of the locals to use in their domestic building projects.

The ditch was easily deep enough to break the charge of infantry or cavalry, but no real barrier to two men moving slowly, and the remains of the walls provided decent cover for an approach. But unlike with the handful of scouts at the temporary marching camp, the sentries here were numerous and vigilant, pacing out patrol paths with diligence despite the weather.

'What do you think?' whispered Atius. 'Shall we just go in there and take them all out?'

'Very funny,' said Silus. 'Let me think.'

Silus watched the tracks of the patrols, squinted through the drizzle at the defences and the positions of cover, and pursed his lips.

'There is no way we are going to sneak in there. There are too many of them, and the fires and torches aren't leaving enough shadows to hide in. Besides, we don't know where Maglorix is exactly, and if we spend time searching for him, we will definitely be caught. I think we need a more open approach.'

Atius frowned. 'I don't think I'm liking the sound of this.'

'First we need to get some of their clothes. Look how most of them are wearing Gallic cloaks with the hoods pulled up. This may be the first time I have thanked the Gods for the Caledonian weather.'

'Where do we buy those cloaks then?'

Silus tutted his disapproval. 'See these two? They are patrolling further out than the others, but still on a set path. We can take them down without raising the alarm and take their clothes. They are about our size.'

'Hmm, they look a little skinny. Are you sure you can squeeze into their outfits, fatty?'

Silus shook his head. He didn't carry an ounce of fat on him, but he was bulkier than his Celtiberian friend, who was all sinew and bone. He tried not to show annoyance at Atius' levity. Although his friend always played the joker, Silus knew that his comments now were to hide his fear. Silus too could feel his heart pounding inside his ribs; the tension that comes before action. But his fear felt muted. Ever since he had lost his family, every sensation had been the same. Food tasted blander, beer tasted insipid, perfumes had no scent. Sometimes he felt he was living in a dream, and that he would suddenly wake up; Velua would be lying next to him and Sergia would be curled at their feet with Issa. But that thinking could get him killed, and then who would avenge his wife and daughter?

They crawled through the rough grass to hide behind two thick tree trunks close to the path the barbarians were patrolling, and waited, hidden from sight. Silus needed to pee. He wondered whether to ignore the sensation or just let it go.

Then they heard the sound of low disgruntled voices accompanying the squelch of feet in the boggy ground. They waited, barely breathing, until the footsteps passed them. Silus gave Atius a nod and they stepped out from cover as one, drawing their knives with the soft sound of polished metal on leather. With perfect co-ordination, they each clamped a hand across their victims' mouths and sliced their throats. They held tight, making sure the blood jetted away from them, and waited for the convulsive struggles to cease before laying the bodies on the ground.

They undressed the bodies, pulling off the cloaks and breeches, though not without difficulty. Then they took off their own Roman-style attire and, shivering in the cold drizzle, dressed themselves as Maeatae warriors. They possessed no tattoos and their hair was not long and blonde or ginger, but their hooded cloaks hid these details.

They pulled the dead bodies into the undergrowth, pulled some foliage over them and over their packs and clothes and weapons, then grabbed their victims' spears and walked on as if continuing the patrol. Two Maeatae warriors approached in the other direction.

'Don't say a word,' whispered Silus.

'I couldn't if I wanted to.'

Silus kept his eyes on the ground. The hood pulled up around his face seemed to intensify the sound of his heart pounding in his ears. He willed them to walk on, but as they drew level, the other two scouts stopped.

'Fuck this weather,' said one, in Brittonic Celtic.

Silus nodded.

'Got anything to eat?' asked the other.

Silus thought about the food in his pack. Would it be so Romano-British in flavour that it would give them away? It was irrelevant now anyway. Much as he would like to have given these barbarians something to get them on their way, the food in his pack might as well have been in Eboracum.

'Not a thing,' said Silus, keeping his reply brief in case they questioned his accent.

The second barbarian spat on the ground. 'There is precious little to go around this year. Even for the warriors.'

'Fucking Romans,' said the first. 'They are starving us.'

'Well, we'll be in their province soon, eating their grapes and drinking their posh wine and fucking their stuck-up women,' said the second. 'Isn't that right, brother?' He addressed Atius, and frowned when Atius didn't reply.

'What's wrong with him?'

If they pressed Atius to speak, his lack of Britonnic Celtic would give them away in an instant. They could probably kill both the warriors before they had a chance to react, but they were too close to the encampment to avoid the noise raising the alarm. Silus improvised.

'The Roman scum cut out his tongue when he was a boy. He was their slave before he was released in a raid.'

The two Maeatae scouts looked at him with pity. 'Poor bastard. The Romans have a lot to answer for.'

'We will make them pay, brother,' said Silus. 'Gods be with you.'

'And with you.'

The Maeatae guards walked on, and Silus heaved a sigh of relief.

'What were they saying?' breathed Atius.

'It doesn't matter. Oh, and don't say another word. You had your tongue cut out when you were a boy.'

Atius looked at him in confusion, then stuck his tongue out.

'In the name of all the gods, Atius, be serious for once in your life. We are nearly into the camp. When we are in, keep your head down and your mouth closed. We'll find out where Maglorix is, kill him and get out.'

'What could go wrong?'

Silus shot him a dagger glare, but they were now too close to the fortress to continue talking in Latin. They approached the nearest entrance. Two guards leaning on spears barely acknowledged them as they entered. Silus reflected thankfully how the barbarians' lack of discipline was in such a stark contrast to the Roman mindset. To enter a Roman fortress, a password would have to be given, and a visitor who didn't know the password would be searched and conveyed to a centurion for questioning about the purpose of their visit and their credentials. The Maeatae may have been residing in a Roman fortress, but any similarity with a Roman camp ended there.

As Silus and Atius entered, they looked around in amazement. They could see the patterns in the dirt marking the locations of the buildings of Pinnata Castra. Barracks, workshops, store rooms, granaries, a hospital, the command house. All straight lines and right angles, orderly, everything in its place and a place for everything.

The Maeatae were sprawled across it as if there had never been anything there. Tents, camp fires, stone blocks torn down from the walls for makeshift seating, all higgledy-piggledy across the site. But despite the lack of organisation, Silus couldn't help but be impressed by the size of the host gathered. Although spread out much less densely than the legion occupying the fortress would have been, there had to be several thousand warriors there. More than enough to do some serious damage to whichever part of the province of Britannia they wanted to take on. Even to take on a legion, if surprise was on their side. And this was just a part of the Maeatae confederation. Somewhere out there, more Maeatae tribes were gathering, and further north, the far more numerous Caledonians were being stirred into action.

Silus had no doubt that once Caracalla brought the legions north, the Maeatae would shrink from an open fight. The barbarians had been defeated too many times, and had learned their lessons. Caracalla, operating under Severus' orders, would make sure that the Maeatae regretted their rebellion.

But that wasn't enough for Silus. Defeat of the Maeatae would not give him the satisfaction he needed to unclench the spasm in his guts that never went away. For that, he needed Maglorix dead. And somewhere in this camp, the demon who had killed his wife and daughter was drinking beer and laughing and planning to make more widows of Roman wives and to slaughter more women and children.

Silus realised his fist and jaw were clenched and he had to will himself to relax to avoid his anger being noticed. Atius put a reassuring hand on his shoulder. Silus nodded to his friend to let him know he was under control.

The lack of organisation in the encampment, although working in their favour when it came to infiltration, was against them now when it came to finding Maglorix. In a Roman fortress, the camp prefect or praetor would be housed in the praetorium, the headquarters building situated in the middle of the central region of the camp, the principia. But here there was no indication where the Chief might be. Some of the tents were bigger than others, presumably belonging to nobles and their retinues, but no single tent stood out.

Silus indicated a nearby campfire with several warriors warming themselves. The two Romans seated themselves on a large vacant stone block, put their hands out to soak up the warmth of the fire, and listened to the conversation.

A broad warrior with a thick red beard and a flattened misshapen nose was talking in loud slurred words, emphasising his points by gesticulating with his clay mug, sloshing beer over the sides.

'And I tell you again, Kian, the Votadini are cowards and traitors, and will never turn against the Romans.'

'You are wrong, Gebann,' said Kian, an older warrior, balding on top but with long grey hair straggling down his neck. 'When the Votadini sees which way the wind is blowing, they will join us. They may be cowards, but they will fear loss of territory when the Romans are driven out. If they don't join the confederation of the tribes, the Caledonians and Maeatae will turn against them and enslave them for their cowardice.'

Gebann threw his hands in the air, all but emptying his mug. 'They have balls of butter and spines of soup. They were a proud race once, but no more.' Gebann gestured at Atius. 'You, what say you?'

Atius saw that he was being addressed, and looked helplessly at Silus.

'Well?' demanded Gebann. 'Someone cut your tongue out?'

'Actually yes,' said Silus. 'The Romans.'

Gebann narrowed his eyes, not sure if he was the butt of a joke. But Atius' expression was suitably mournful and Silus looked suitably serious. After looking from Atius to Silus and back, Gebann said, 'Well, may the gods strike down those she-pigs that did you such wrong. You then, the tongueless one's companion. What do you think of the Votadini?'

'I think when we are finished with the Romans, it will be their turn next,' said Silus.

'You see,' exclaimed Gebann, backhanding Kian. 'This man knows what he is talking about.'

Kian cocked his head on one side, and stroked his beard as he regarded Silus.

'I can't place your accent, brother. Which is your name and your tribe?'

Oclatinius had taught Silus that a lie was most believable when it was as close to the truth as possible. Then again, he wasn't sure how famous his father's exploits were. Should he mention his Brigantian parentage?

'I am Syagris,' he said, using the name of one of his child-hood playmates who had died of a wasting disease. 'I was born into the Damnonii, but my father was a Brigantian traveller.'

Kian turned to another of the warriors who had been staring into the fire, largely oblivious to the argument going on around him.

'Sittan, you are of the Damnonii. Do you know this man, who calls himself Syagris?'

Sittan shrugged. 'No. Still. It's a common enough name. And we are a far-flung tribe. Why would I know him?'

'Stop being so suspicious, Kian. He is sitting in the middle of a Maeatae war gathering, speaking our language and warming himself at our fire. What? Do you think he is a Roman spy?' Gebann laughed uproariously at the idea. Silus smiled while fighting down the bile rising in his throat.

Kian hesitated then handed Silus and Atius a chunk of lamb they had been roasting on the fire. 'Apologies, brothers. I am greyer in the mane than most of these youngsters, and suspicion comes more easily as you age. Please, eat with us.'

Silus and Atius accepted and ate gratefully, Atius covering his mouth with his hand to disguise the presence of a tongue. The meat was hot and juicy, and much preferable to their travelling rations.

'Have you travelled far to get here?' asked Gebann.

'Many days,' said Silus. 'But we heard of the great Maglorix and how he is uniting the Maeatae. We wanted to join him in the fight against the invaders.'

The warriors around the fire nodded agreement.

'He is a great man, for certain,' said Kian. 'His father was a strong man, but after Voteporix's cowardly murder, Maglorix has become far more than the old man ever was.'

'I need to see him and pledge him my spear. Where is his tent?'

Kian gestured to the middle of the fortress. 'The big red one with two bodyguards on the door. You can't miss it. But I doubt he will be taking visitors. He is said to be spending time alone with the gods tonight.'

'Maybe he will see me. My uncle's cousin once hunted with the Venicones and became a friend of Maglorix. He bade me pass his greetings.'

Kian spat into the fire, the spittle turning to steam with a transient hiss. 'I doubt it, but it's not up to me to stop you from trying.'

'Let us go to pay our respects then,' said Silus to Atius. Atius didn't understand a word, but a slight nod from Silus as he stood indicated it was time for them to leave.

'Good hunting on the battlefields, brothers,' said Gebann.

'And to you,' said Silus, and they took their leave.

Few paid them much attention as they walked between the clusters of warriors, over piles of supplies – grain, beer, tallow for torches, piles of wood for the carpenters to make spears and arrows – and in one secluded area they had to pass by a warrior rutting with a whore-slave tied to the back of a cart. As they passed her, the girl, her features suggesting Romano-British origin, turned her head and locked her gaze on Silus. For a moment he stared into her dead eyes as she was rocked aggressively backwards and forwards by the barbarian using her, and images of Maglorix preparing to violate his wife flooded through him. He took a step forward.

Atius took his elbow and tried to guide his friend away. Silus looked back, and saw the girl was now staring into the middle distance, expressionless. He gritted his teeth, and turned to face forwards, trying to concentrate on what was before him, to focus on the mission.

He couldn't do it. Before Atius could intervene, Silus had taken two strides forwards, gripped the busy warrior's head and twisted sharply. There was a crack as the neck snapped, and the warrior slid to the ground.

'For Christos' sake, Silus,' said Atius. 'What are you doing?'

'If things had turned out differently during Maglorix's first assault on Voltanio, that could have been Velua. Or even Sergia.'

Atius shook his head, grabbed the dead warrior's ankles and pulled him into the shadows. Silus cut the slave girl's bonds. 'Get out of here.'

She made no move, didn't even attempt to cover herself up. He wondered how much abuse she had endured in her young life. He picked up the cloak that the warrior had discarded nearby, and covered her with it. She looked at him, eyes unblinking.

'I'm sorry I can't do more. Flee from here if you can.'

Atius returned and tugged at Silus, and they continued towards Maglorix's tent. When Silus looked back, the girl was sitting up and looking around her like she had just woken from a bizarre dream.

Maglorix's red tent was now visible, maybe fifty yards away, standing higher than those surrounding it. They worked their way towards it and Silus felt his gut clench as they neared their target.

Something in the corner of his eye nudged his subconscious. He turned to see what had distracted him. At first the scene seemed innocuous enough: a warrior with his breeches pulled halfway down, his hairy white backside shining at Silus in the firelight, urinating against a post.

But Silus could make out something tied to the post. Someone. He took a couple more steps forward, so he could get a better line of sight. A man on his knees, tied by his wrists to a stake, grey hair and beard long and matted, his face swollen with fresh blue bruises and older yellowing ones. His chin was resting on his chest, and he made no protest as the urine splashed onto him.

Silus squinted. Something familiar about those features. Atius stopped in confusion as Silus walked slowly towards the captive.

The warrior shook the last drops away, pulled up his breeches, and as he turned, he saw Silus staring.

'Hey,' said the warrior. 'Whatever you do to him, don't kill him. Maglorix would go berserk. He has plans for this one.'

He walked off, and Silus at last had an unimpeded view of the miserable wretch. There could be no doubt. It was Menenius.

–

Caracalla groaned, staring up into the half-closed eyes of his stepmother as she rode him. Her hand was behind her fondling him, and he groaned again, trying not to finish, knowing this would be the last time for a long time.

Julia sank down deep onto him and let out a long wail, and it pushed him over the edge. She fell forward, and they clutched each other as they rode their peaks, then stayed embraced as they breathed hard, both sheened in sweat.

Caracalla rolled onto his back and stared at the painted ceiling, an extension of the wall frescoes. The whole room had been painted to create a panoramic view of a beautiful Roman garden with artistic topiary and ornamental bushes, small creatures hiding behind greenery, and blue sky overhead, with white clouds and Italian birds. It made Caracalla feel homesick, and he thought about the campaign ahead in this dreary country. Even though it was heading for summer, and the sun occasionally made an appearance at this time of year, it was still winter compared to the glorious heat of May in the villa of Hadrianus in Tibur.

'I remember the day you married my father. How old was I? Fourteen? You were the most beautiful thing I had ever seen. I watched the ceremony in awe, proud that father had caught someone as powerful and stunning as you, and seething with jealousy too.'

'You sound like a certain tragic hero.'

Caracalla frowned. 'You are not my mother. You are not Jocasta, and I am not Oedipus. We aren't even Agrippina and Nero.'

'Maybe Phaedra and Hippolytus?'

'No!' said Caracalla vehemently. 'Hippolytus rejected Phaedra. I would never do that.'

Julia smiled, then her brow furrowed. 'Society would still condemn us. And if your father ever found out…'

'Father was an Alexander in his time, but now he is a weak old man. He should have died at his peak like Alexander, not decayed like this. I can't believe you still let him touch you.'

'He is my husband, and I love him,' said Julia reprovingly. 'But don't be jealous. It is rare that we share the bed to do anything but sleep these days.'

Caracalla let out a growl, but said nothing. Julia leaned over to him, and kissed him on the forehead.

'He is failing, Antoninus. Let the gods have their way with him, and don't interfere with their plans. For me?'

Caracalla nodded. 'He is my father and I love him too, but sometimes I…' He sighed. 'For you, my love.'

Julia stroked the wiry curls of hair on Caracalla's muscular chest.

'How long will you be gone?'

'Who can say? I don't anticipate it being a hard fight, but the land is so vast and desolate that pinning them down to a battle can be demoralising and time consuming.'

'You will return, won't you?'

Caracalla pulled Julia to him and kissed her deeply, arms encircling and trapping her. Then he released her, and stood, pulling on his tunic and sitting on the edge of the bed to pull on his boots. When he was dressed, he kissed her, his eyes drifting over her naked body hungrily one last time.

'How could I not return to you?'

Julia smiled, but he could easily see the worry she tried to hide. He ran his fingertips over her cheek.

'A Roman Emperor has never been killed in battle,' he said, hoping his tone was reassuring.

'But Roman generals have. Like Marcellus. Or Varus. What if this Maglorix character is playing the part of Arminius, luring you into a massive trap?'

Her eyes were wide, breathing quickening.

'Calm yourself, Augusta,' said Caracalla, holding both her shoulders in a firm grip. 'Think of your dignitas and gravitas. Besides, Arminius was pretending to be a friend to the Romans. Maglorix makes no such pretence.'

Julia took a deep breath in, let it out slowly through pursed lips so the wind whistled past her teeth, then nodded.

'I'm sorry, Antoninus. It's just… I know I will lose Septimius soon. I can't lose you too.'

'Father is an ox. He will go on for ever.'

'You know that isn't true. You see his health declining. And look at the omens. That dream he had about his deification. The statue that fell over in Horrea Classis during his victory celebration games. The time he tried to make a sacrifice on his return to Eboracum and all the victims were black-furred or - feathered, and when he refused to sacrifice them, they followed him to the palace.'

'Omens and superstitions are for the weak-minded.'

'Antoninus, you are talking to the daughter of the high priest of Elagabal. You disrespect my father and your own.

Remember, Septimius travelled to Emesa because of a horoscope that foretold he would meet his wife there, and he found me.'

Caracalla opened his mouth to argue about coincidence and self-fulfilling prophecy, but saw the iron glint in Julia's eyes and thought better of it. It surprised him how deeply rooted her beliefs were, even more so as she was such a learned student and patron of philosophy and the arts. But she was far from alone, and she was right: his own father was a slave to the seers and prophets and astrologers. Even himself, though sceptical that everything they were asked to believe could be true, because of occasional bouts of illness, made sure he paid a healthy respect to Serapis, the eastern god of healing and fertility, and to Aesculapius, the god of medicine. He had no desire to die young and ignominiously from a simple fever, like his hero, Alexander. He put his arms around her and kissed her hard, and he felt her relax.

'I will come back to you, my love,' he whispered in her ear.

'Make sure you do, or I will be very cross,' she whispered back.

-

Caracalla sat astride his immaculately groomed chalk-white mount, back straight, armour gleaming. Behind him was an enormous force drawn from the Rhine and Danube armies, and the legions based in Britannia – the Legio II Augusta, the Legio VI Victrix and the Legio XX Valeria Victrix, as well as a vast number of auxiliaries. They were similarly scrubbed and polished to within an inch of their lives, and the soldiers' predominantly young faces shone with enthusiasm and excitement. Facing Caracalla and seated on a temporary throne was Severus. He looked tired, slumped, his chest rising and falling deeper than it should. His face spasmed intermittently with pain from his gouty legs. Still, his stare was hard, uncompromising.

To Severus' right was Domna, her face now set in an expression of benign passivity. To his left stood Geta, tight-lipped, jaw clenched. Caracalla could imagine the resentment seething inside him, seeing his elder brother at the head of a mighty army, marching off to glory on the field of battle. It gave him a warm glow of satisfaction deep inside, and he shot Geta a broad grin that he realised must appear incredibly smug. Geta tilted his head in acknowledgement, returning a superficial smile, while his eyes spoke of red-hot coals and sharp knives.

Severus spoke, his voice hoarse and weak. It would not carry beyond the front line, but Caracalla knew that the message would be passed with a reducing level of accuracy back through the ranks. The speech was short and reprised the one he had given in his private chambers.

'The barbarians have broken faith with us. They have torn up the peace treaties we made with them in good faith last year. They have attacked and slaughtered our men, our women and our children. They will know the consequences of their actions. As Agamemnon said, let us not spare a single one. Not a man left alive, not a woman, not a child, not even the unborn in its mother's womb. The barbarians will rue the day they raised weapons against the power of Rome.'

Led by the centurions and optiones, the soldiers roared their approval and clashed their swords on their shields.

'Father,' said Caracalla, 'we will not let you down. We will take your fire and your righteous anger to the oath breakers of the north. They will never again challenge your power, nor the power of Rome.'

The soldiers roared again, the volume resonating throughout him like his body had become a drum that the men were beating. He luxuriated in the feeling, then held up his sword for silence.

'Men. We go to war.' He wheeled his horse, and with Caracalla at its head, the bulk of the Roman army in Britannia began its march for the north.

–

Atius' eyes widened as, a few moments after Silus, he recognised their camp commander. He took a step forward, but Silus put a strong arm around his shoulder and steered him away.

'Silus,' Atius protested. 'What are you doing? That's Menenius!'

'Keep your voice down. You aren't supposed to be able to speak, let alone speak Latin.'

'But...'

'Listen, we have a mission: Maglorix dead. That's it. No side-tracking.'

'Silus, be serious. He was our commanding officer. Look at him. He is being tortured. Humiliated. We can't leave him like this.'

'We can and we will. He would be the first man to tell us to do our duty.'

'You just risked the mission for a whore you have never even met!'

'That was no risk. It was in a quiet area – no one could see – and I didn't try to smuggle her out past five thousand armed warriors. Menenius is in a public space, in full view. We can't get to him; let alone get him out. That's all there is to it.'

A couple of warriors sitting outside a small tent nearby looked over at them curiously, and Silus became aware that he was raising his voice. He grabbed Atius' elbow and pulled him away, out of earshot of any warriors.

'Atius, look at these barbarians around us. Thousands of them. All here because Maglorix summoned them. Last year they were beaten, humiliated, suing for peace. Now they have a new confidence. And that's because they have a new leader. If we can stop Maglorix, this whole alliance may fall apart. And if we don't, then just think about what destruction will be rained down on the province of Britannia. Think of our brothers in arms who will fall to barbarian spears, of the civilian families in the vici, of the women and children.' He gripped Atius' arm tightly and pulled him so their faces were inches apart. 'Like my family, Atius.'

Atius pulled away angrily. 'You're letting your personal feelings affect your judgement. We were never told that we couldn't perform a rescue if the situation arose, just that Maglorix was our primary mission.'

'Our *only* mission. Let me remind you, I am in charge here. Oclatinius was very clear about that.'

'Well, fuck you, sir! What are you going to do about it? Want to start a fight with me here in the middle of an enemy camp? I'm not leaving our commander to Christos alone knows what kind of miserable fate.'

They glared at each other, totally at odds, completely needing each other. But Silus saw that there would be no swaying his friend. He took a deep breath.

'The chances of us getting him out of here with any of us alive are tiny.'

'I know. I'm fine with that.'

'And Maglorix is still our main mission?'

'Of course.'

Silus looked at his feet. 'We need a new plan.'

'We had an old one?' Atius grinned and Silus smiled in spite of himself.

'Fuck you. Right, this is how it will go. I'll create some sort of diversion. When you hear it, get to Menenius and free him. Then he is on his own. You meet me at Maglorix's tent, we take out the guards, kill Maglorix and then run for our fucking lives.'

'Genius,' said Atius, and as usual Silus couldn't tell whether he was being sarcastic.

'Well, I haven't exactly had much time for preparation. Now go. And remember: no tongue!'

'Damn, I hope I don't meet any hot girls.'

'Fuck off.'

Silus left him in the shadows and wandered back into the main encampment. He saw Maglorix's tent, large, red, two bored-looking bodyguards at the entrance, just as described. He looked around him for inspiration. What could cause a big enough distraction? He supposed he could set fire to something, but it would be hard to get the flame to take in this drizzle, and the tents were far enough apart that it was unlikely the fire would spread. A couple of buckets of water and some cursing would be the extent of the disturbance.

Nearby, a group of warriors were sitting around a campfire, throwing knucklebones. The gambling didn't seem good-natured. They were playing for items of jewellery – iron torcs, amber necklaces and even some gold rings. Silus noticed with interest that the markings of dye on their faces were quite distinct from each other, and he realised that these were men of different tribes. He couldn't recall which tribe was which – it had been many years since he had belonged among these men – but that probably didn't matter for what he suddenly had in mind.

He sat down with them, watching the rolls of the bones, seeing the valuables change hands back and forth, sampling the mood. These were fighting men, united by their hatred of Romans, but with all the grievances and prejudices that neighbours always bore for each other. Whether it was the man next door whose grandfather had stolen your grandfather's pig, or the next village who had stolen your winter stores when they had failed to save enough themselves, or whether it was the next tribe with whom you had had border disputes for centuries, it was human nature to hate those who were close but separate, even more than those a long distance away, no matter how strange their fashions and mores.

One man with a Taexali accent swore loudly as his Veniconian opponent threw a winning roll. Silus wasn't entirely sure of the rules – he had been too young to participate when he had belonged to the Damnonii – but it seemed similar to the knucklebones games beloved of Roman gamblers throughout the empire. The Veniconian raised his hands in triumph, and the other Veniconians around the fire cheered, while the Taexali and Damnonii looked disgruntled.

Silus leaned into the Taexali gambler and whispered in his ear. 'Those bones look weighted to me.'

The Veniconian reached down to pick up his prize, a dagger with an ornately jewelled handle, but as he did so, the Taexali reached out and clamped his hand on top of his opponent's. The Veniconian looked up in surprise. 'What are you doing, brother?'

'I want to see those bones,' said the Taexali in a low, threatening voice.

'What are you talking about?'

'Afraid to show me, brother?' He snarled the last word.

'Are you calling me a cheat?' challenged the Veniconian, his voice rising in shocked anger. 'Are you questioning my honour?'

'There will be no question if you show me those bones and I can check they roll true.'

'You do not challenge the honour of a Veniconian warrior lightly,' said another Veniconian. 'You might need to back up your words with a sharp edge or a hard point.'

'You do not cheat a Taexali without risking much,' said another Taexali.

'I am no cheat,' yelled the Veniconian, grabbing at the prize knife. As quick as a striking snake, the Taexali stabbed his own knife into the top of the Veniconian's hand. Small bones crunched and blood spurted around the blade, and the Veniconian screamed in outrage and pain. The other Veniconian who had spoken roared and threw himself at the Taexali warrior. In a few heartbeats, all the warriors around the fire were brawling.

Silus slipped away as the commotion drew attention. Warriors from nearby groups came over, perhaps intending to break up the brawl, but actually getting drawn into it. The fight spread faster than a forest fire. Silus stood close to Maglorix's tent, watching for an opportunity. The two bodyguards looked at each other nervously but didn't move. Silus cursed. He couldn't take them both on without warning Maglorix. Damn Atius and his nobility. Together they could have silenced the guards, entered the tent unseen, killed Maglorix and been away while the fight outside still raged. He looked around him for inspiration, but he couldn't imagine a bigger distraction than what was already happening.

Then Maglorix stuck his head out of the tent. Silus stared at the man he hated more than he thought was possible, then shrank back even further into the shadows. Maglorix didn't turn towards Silus though. He took one look at the fight, and said to his bodyguards, 'Go and break some heads.'

The two bodyguards were huge, even by Maeatae standards. They grasped their spears first and waded into the fight, thrusting left and right with the spears' butts anywhere someone didn't obey their commands for order quickly enough. Warriors went down stunned, or maybe dead. Slowly, order began to be restored.

Silus stared at Maglorix's tent. The entrance was unguarded. He took a deep breath, let it out slowly, then strode purposefully towards the tent.

He expected a hand on his shoulder or a spear in his back with each step he took, but he reached the tent flap with no challenge. His distraction had worked well. He pulled back the tent flap and slipped inside.

A small log fire illuminated the inside of the tent, the smoke disappearing up through a central hole in the roof. The air was warm, and thick with the scents of smoke and sweat. After sending his guards off, Maglorix had returned to the business at hand, which was two naked slaves, one who looked Caledonian, while the other looked Romano-British, maybe Brigantian. He was naked too, lying on his front and enjoying them massaging his muscles. Silus could see the scars on his lower legs from the flames that had so nearly delivered justice.

Silus drew his knife. The slaves turned to him wide-eyed and drew breath, but Silus pointed his blade at them and put his fingers to his lips, and the girls were astute and composed enough not to scream. He took two steps forward, and touched his knife to the side of Maglorix's neck.

Maglorix froze. He started to turn his head, but Silus dug the knife in deeper.

'Silence,' hissed Silus. 'You girls, stand where I can see you and don't make a sound.'

The two girls moved away from Maglorix, covering their nakedness as best they could. Silus had eyes only for the barbarian chief.

'May I sit up?' asked Maglorix. 'It's hard to talk when I'm face down.'

'We have nothing to discuss, you savage. I am here to kill you.'

'You don't even want to tell me who you are and why you want to kill me? Have the satisfaction of goading me first? I'm guessing you are a Roman spy, though you speak Brittonic well.'

'You should know why I'm here.'

'To stop the uprising? It's unstoppable. If I fall, they will rally around another leader.'

'Damaging the uprising is just a bonus. This is about justice for my family.'

Now Maglorix did turn. The knife dug in, penetrated the skin so red pooled trickled from the point, but the chief kept turning his head until he was looking into Silus' eyes. His expression showed more resignation than surprise. He knew that he could not bargain for his life with someone whose wife and daughter he had killed.

'Get it over with.'

Silus' heart thumped in his chest, and his wind caught in his throat. This moment that he had dreamed of, that he had had denied to him in Eboracum, that he had worked so hard to bring about was finally here. Yet he hesitated. What would happen next? Not the difficulty of escape, but his very being. When he had destroyed his nemesis, expunged his hate, what would remain of him? He feared the answer.

But his life, his well-being, was unimportant. He needed to appease the lemures of Velua and Sergia before all else. He took a breath and gripped the knife tight.

The tent entrance flew open and one of the bodyguards burst in. Silus turned automatically. The burly warrior – Silus recognised him as Buan, who he had first met at the start of all this mess – held a struggling Atius in an armlock.

'Chief, we caught a spy attempting to free the Roman officer.'

Silus hesitated for only a heartbeat, but it was too long. Maglorix twisted sideways and grabbed Silus's wrist, heaving the blade away from his neck.

Silus was uppermost, and used his superior position to his advantage. He rolled on top of Maglorix and leaned all his weight on the downward pointing blade. With gritted teeth and straining muscles, Maglorix fought to keep the point out of his chest. But the knife continued to press down, inexorable as a boulder gathering speed as it rolled down a mountainside. Maglorix's eyes widened and he cried out in desperation.

A spear butt to the side of Silus' head sent him sprawling across the floor. Blackness seeped into his peripheral vision, and small bright lights danced before him. He pulled himself to his hands and knees, still somehow clutching the knife. The tent was rotating around him like it was attached to a chariot wheel. He got himself upright, only to receive another blow from the spear butt into his midriff. He doubled up, vomiting, desperately tightening his fingers around his weapon. But the spear cracked down on his knuckles, and his grip flew open, the knife falling to the floor.

He stood, swaying like a boxer who had taken one punch too many. Maglorix appeared before him. They looked into each other's eyes for a moment. Then Maglorix punched him hard in the jaw. Silus dropped and Maglorix laid into him, roaring in rage as he kicked him hard in ribs and kidneys, until he was exhausted, and Silus was a sack of tenderised flesh and bruised bones.

'Take them both away,' Silus heard Maglorix say, 'And guard them well. Tomorrow you can all witness their fate.'

Chapter Twelve

'This is a reversal of fortune,' said Maglorix.

Silus squinted up at him through eyes that were closing up with swelling bruises. They were tied up in Maglorix's tent, Atius and Silus bound hand and foot with constricting ropes. Menenius had been brought in too, but though he was also bound, this seemed redundant as he showed no evidence of having any fight in him.

The first rays of dawn were illuminating the animal skin tent. Some sun at last, suggesting that finer weather was finally coming to this miserable land. Silus regarded Maglorix balefully.

'Why are we still alive?'

'Silus, my people are embarking on a great campaign. We will punish the Romans for their depredations and atrocities. Their occupation of our lands, the burning of our crops, the slaughter of our tribes. We march in a few days. It will be glorious.'

'You were slaughtered last year,' said Silus. 'Why do you think it will be different this time?'

'Because you Romans always think the same. Severus or one of his sons will react to my provocation by dispatching a powerful force north. My scouts will track its path – there will be no hiding the march of an army of that size. In a week, it will be deep in Caledonia, being harried by small bands of warriors. And we will bypass it. While your legions chase their tales in the north, looking for a fight, my men will move south

238

and destroy everything in our way, all the way down to the Emperor's palace in Eboracum.'

Silus' heart beat faster. If Severus or Caracalla led the legions deep into Caledonia, then Eboracum would be all but defenceless. Yes, there would be a garrison, but the size of the Maeatae force that Maglorix had gathered around him, not to mention the Caledonians, would be unstoppable without the legions. It would be a massacre.

'That still doesn't explain why you haven't killed us yet,' said Silus.

'I would not have so much pride as to embark on a campaign such as this without a blessing from the gods. And what better way to ensure their blessing than by offering them the blood and flesh of our enemies?'

Silus went cold. Human sacrifice was not common among the Celtic tribes, but it was certainly not unheard of in times of strife or war. Sometimes the victims were criminals. Sometimes they were the diseased and infirm. And sometimes they were enemies and prisoners. So this was why Menenius had been kept alive, and why Silus and Atius were spared.

'This is Lon, my tribe's Chief druid,' said Maglorix. 'He can explain more. I think your sacrifice will be so much sweeter if you have some time to anticipate it.'

Silus looked at the man standing behind Maglorix's right shoulder, taking in his druidic hairstyle. Lon wore a long scarlet robe with gold embroidery and a gold torc around his neck and carried a wooden staff with a bell tied to the end. He looked down at the three prisoners gravely.

'Tonight will be the full moon. We had meant to sacrifice this one' – he indicated Menenius – 'to Teutates, the god of the tribe. But now the Aos-sídhe have seen fit to provide us with a more powerful sacrifice for the war gods. At midnight, the three of you will undergo the triple sacrifice to Teutates the Tribe, Esus the Lord and Taranis the god of Thunder.'

'Have you heard of the triple sacrifice, Roman?' asked Maglorix. 'It is a very powerful magic. Three men – criminals, prisoners, enemies – are sacrificed, one to each of the three high war gods, each in a different way. To Teutates, the chief of your fort here will be made a sacrifice by drowning. To Esus, your odd-looking friend here will give his life by burning. And you, Roman, slayer of my father, betrayer of the natives of this land, you will be hanged from a tree and the skin delicately sliced from your body.'

Silus' bowels and bladder loosened, but he was too terrified of the awful punishment to feel shame. Being flayed alive was surely one of the most terrible ways to die.

'Just kill us,' said Silus. 'Please.' Now the shame came. What would Velua and Sergia say now if they saw him, bound, soiled, begging for a merciful end? But he couldn't help it. Courage failed him completely now.

Maglorix laughed. 'Tonight, Lon will command his Vates to perform the sacrifices while he performs the rituals, and my men will see the proud, invincible Romans for the weaklings they really are, and the bards will sing across the land that the end of the Romans is near. I wish we could begin the fight tomorrow, but we are still waiting for the Caledonians to arrive. Just one more week, and we march!' He turned and walked out, Lon following close behind him.

'What did he say?' asked Atius, his voice high with desperation.

They were alone except for a single guard, a young, serious-looking warrior who seemed honoured to be chosen for the task. A couple more guards stood outside at the entrance to the tent. That was all. Why waste more guards on these three pathetic men?

Silus tested his bonds but they were secure, and they were tied to stakes planted deep into the soil, far enough apart so they couldn't reach each other's ropes. They were in the middle of an enemy camp, friendless and alone. No hope of rescue. Every man sympathetic to their cause within a score of miles was tied up helpless on the floor of this tent.

'Tell me,' pressed Atius. Should he burden his friend with knowledge of their fate? They had a whole day to contemplate it. Atius surely knew he was going to die. How would telling him the time and manner help him?

Silus told Atius about Maglorix's plan to attack Eboracum.

Atius looked grave, but wasn't satisfied.

"What else?"

'It was just taunting,' said Silus. 'Nothing of substance.'

'Quiet,' said the guard, in Brittonic, looking unsettled that he didn't understand their Latin. Atius ignored him.

'Don't lie to me, Silus. I have never seen such terror in your eyes.'

Silus looked away, unable to meet his friend's accusatory stare.

'Silus? Is that you?'

Silus looked around in surprise to see Menenius with his eyes open, squinting in his direction.

'Prefect?'

Menenius blinked, then noticed Atius.

'Atius. My daughter.' His voice cracked. His mouth worked, and he swallowed twice. 'Menenia is safe?'

Atius nodded. 'Safe in Eboracum, Prefect.'

Menenius let out a sigh of relief. 'I never hoped… to have news. I thank you, more than you could ever know.'

241

Menenius tested his bonds weakly. There was not the slightest give. 'So, it is to be…' He took a breath. 'It is to be the tripartite death.'

'How do you know that?' snapped Silus.

'You don't serve on the northern border of Britannia for thirty years without picking up a little of the local vocabulary.'

'What is the tripartite death?' demanded Atius.

Silus looked at Menenius uncertainly.

'He has a right to know what awaits him.'

Silus wasn't so sure, but Menenius had opened the draw-strings, so he had no choice now but to empty the bag.

'It's a ritual. A different death for each of us. Menenius will be drowned and you will be burned.'

Atius paled, and was silent for a moment. Then he said, 'And you?'

'It doesn't matter. It can't be changed.'

'I'll pray—'

'Spare me,' spat Silus. 'There will be no miracle rescue.'

'That wasn't what I was going to pray for. I was going to pray for courage in the face of death.'

Silus glared at him, then let his head droop and he stared at the earth floor.

Failure. Torture. Death. His family dead. His comrades, even his Emperor, under threat of being wiped out. What good had he done in his life? He thought of the woman whose rape he had interrupted, whose rapist he had killed, just hours ago. Maybe saving her balanced the scales in his favour, just a little.

The entrance to the tent was swept open. The guard stood to one side, his spear rigidly vertical. Lon entered and announced, 'You are all to be fed and watered. To be a worthy sacrifice, you must go to the gods in good health. Enid, come.' He held the flap aside and a woman entered with a tray of bread and water.

Silus, still looking downwards, noticed she was walking stiffly. He looked up and his heart fell. It was the woman whose rapist he had killed. The one he had thought he had saved. The only good thing he thought was going to come out of this disastrous mission.

She was still enslaved.

-

Lon and the guard watched attentively as Enid got to her knees before Menenius, and offered him water from a clay cup. She was slight, freckled, with long red hair. Her face was blank, just as it had been when Silus had first seen her the previous night. Menenius took a small sip, swallowed, coughed, then took a deeper draught. When he had emptied the cup, she fed him some bread and nuts, taking care to give him time to chew and swallow. Then she moved to Atius and, after refilling the cup from a jug, did the same. He drank the water, but refused the food, no doubt too nauseous with terror to contemplate eating.

When she knelt before Silus and held the cup for him to drink, he paused and searched her green eyes. He couldn't say anything, not with Lon watching. If the druid realised she was involved in the death of one of the warriors, even involuntarily, her punishment would be at least as bad as the one in store for him.

She was quiet as well, but her eyes held something he couldn't read. Compassion? Regret? Or something else? She proffered the cup to Silus again, and he drank. Like Atius, he had no stomach for the food, and turned his head when she offered it. But he fixed his eyes on hers again, and she held his gaze with an intensity he couldn't read. Then she stood, and Lon ushered her out of the tent, following after her without a backward glance. The guard took up his position again near the tent entrance.

The three condemned men sat in their bonds in silence, each alone with his own fears. Silus' tried to focus on Sergia and Velua, but try as he would, he couldn't suppress images of himself suspended by the neck, trying to draw breath to scream as they sliced his skin and peeled it back, exposing his raw flesh to the chill air. Panic was beginning to overwhelm him, and to stop himself from screaming and struggling madly and pointlessly at his ropes, he spoke to Menenius.

'Prefect,' he said, trying to keep his voice even. 'What happened to you?'

Menenius looked off into the distance, but his eyes were unfocused. For some time he said nothing, and Silus was about to return to contemplating his own fate.

'Atius, you saw it was hopeless,' said the Prefect. 'That there was nothing more we could do?'

Atius nodded. 'You did everything in your power to hold the fort, Prefect. Even now, I feel guilty that you sent me away.'

'You saved my daughter, Atius. You made sure something precious survived the destruction.'

Atius bowed his head, and Silus saw glistening in the corner of his eyes.

'We saw the fort, on our way north,' said Silus. 'We could see where you made the last stand. And we found some bodies in the nearby woods, stripped and nailed up. We thought that you and Damanais were among them. The crows had made it... hard to be sure.'

'I watched them nail Damanais up. I could still hear him cursing them as they rode away, taking me with them. Maglorix told me he had me marked for a more useful death.'

'Sacrifice,' said Atius glumly.

'He never said. Many times over the last weeks he has threatened to kill me. Had me on the back of a pony beneath a tree with a rope around my neck. Had me held under water until I was sure I would drown. He once tied me to a broad tree trunk and had his warriors see how close they could fire their arrows at me without hitting me. Some failed. Once he even let me go, for his warriors to hunt me down. I was so weak by then I must have lasted less than an hour before their dogs found me. They savaged me before the warriors arrived... to save me.' He gave a mirthless laugh. Then something seemed to occur to him.

'Why are you here? You thought I was dead, so it wasn't to save me.'

Silus looked to the tent entrance and lowered his voice.

'We have orders from Caracalla himself. To kill Maglorix.'

'Oh, what went wrong?'

Silus looked over at Atius, unwilling to blame his friend. Atius spoke instead.

'It's my fault. I was... distracted from the mission.'

'I have... not been myself,' said Menenius distantly. 'I think they broke something inside me. But I remember... I remember you, Atius. You... killed my captor. You cut my bonds. You urged me to flee.'

Atius said nothing but looked distraught.

'And I didn't move, did I? I sat there like a bull stunned with a hammer before a sacrifice.'

'I tried,' said Atius. 'I did everything I could to get you moving. I even told you Menenia was waiting for you.'

'I'm seeing it now as if looking through fog. You pulled, you cajoled, you swore. And then... oh gods, then I cried for help, didn't I?'

Atius stared down, and tears dropped to the ground.

'Forgive me,' said Menenius, his voice a hoarse whisper. 'I brought the warriors down on your head. And they took Atius straight to Maglorix, and caught you too, Silus. Am I right?'

Silus nodded, not trusting himself to speak.

'Fortuna. What have I done?'

–

The day passed in a strange combination of boredom and terror. It was his last day alive, and Silus felt they should be having profound conversations about lives well lived, and the after-life. But he could not bring himself to speak, and the others clearly felt the same. Each retreated into his own inner world to confront or hide from what awaited them that night.

The day was punctuated with two more visitations for food and drink. None of them ate, though they all drank, especially as the tent was becoming warm in the late spring sun. The drinks were brought each time by a different slave unaccompanied, just watched by the bored guard. Silus was relieved none of them were Enid; he didn't want to be continually confronted with such a stark reminder of his failure. The guard remained silent throughout their captivity. Silus had expected taunting and mockery, but the young warrior was seemingly respectful of the status of the sacrificial victims.

The light leaking through the diaphanous tent walls brightened to a peak, then faded, until eventually darkness fell.

'Three hours from sundown to midnight at this time of year,' said Menenius.

'I wonder when they will come for us,' said Atius.

Silus remained silent. Menenius' breathing was stertorous, and beyond, he could dimly make out the sounds of war songs and chants, laughter and cries of anger. All the usual sounds of a large gathering of warriors, killing time before the proper killing started.

The tent flap opened again, and a slave came through bearing drinks on a tray. This time it was Enid. Silus sighed. He didn't want to see her. The guard looked at her with little interest, and then turned away, maybe lost in thoughts of the battle soon to come. Enid knelt before Silus, and he saw her draw something metallic from the folds of her tunic. Silus looked at the knife, then at her in surprise. In one smooth motion she rose, turned, and plunged the blade into the guard's throat. She clamped her hand over his mouth to cover his gurgling cry. Silus feigned a loud coughing fit to cover up the sound, although there was plenty of noise from the revelling barbarians outside. The guard slid to the floor in a pool of blood.

Enid slipped over to Silus and disappeared behind him. He felt a sawing between his wrists, and then the ropes parted. Blood rushed back into his hands, and he was immediately gripped by a spasm of agonising little stabs in his fingers as the circulation returned. He flexed his fingers as she worked on the ropes at his legs.

The agony hit his feet just as Enid knelt before him and offered him the knife.

'Enid,' he gasped. 'It's too risky.' She put a finger to her lips and held the knife out to him again. He rubbed his hands and gestured to Atius and Menenius, and she scurried over to free them too. When she returned, Silus stood, stiffly and uncertainly. She put a hand out to steady him.

'Since the barbarians captured me,' she whispered, 'I have been less than an animal to them. You are the only one who has shown me concern.'

'We are so grateful to you, Enid,' said Silus. 'I just wish you had run when you had the chance.'

'Where would I run to? I could never get back to my own lands, a woman alone. But with you…'

Silus understood. She was freeing them not only out of undoubtedly genuine gratitude, but also to obtain her freedom.

'It will be dangerous,' said Silus. 'But if you don't slow us down, you can come with us, south. We are going to warn the Emperor so he can meet the threat. If we fail, the province will be at the mercy of the barbarians.'

'I won't slow you down,' said Enid firmly. As Atius and Menenius gingerly got to their feet, Silus looked to his two comrades in silent consultation. They both nodded, their faces bearing a grim set.

'Very well.'

'We don't have much time,' said Enid. 'They said they were going to come for you around an hour before midnight, to prepare you.'

'So we have maybe a two hour head start,' said Silus. 'But they have horses and dogs.'

'And we are in poor shape,' said Atius, purposefully not looking at Menenius.

'We can only try,' said Silus. 'But let's agree one thing: not one of us will be taken alive, right?'

He looked in turn at each of the other three, and they all gave him a firm nod back.

'Come then,' she said. 'Make a hole in the back of the tent. There are no guards there.'

Silus slit the canvas with the knife. Enid slipped out through the tear and into the night. The three Romans followed her.

Enid clearly knew her way around the camp, and leaving turned out to be an easier task than entering. This time they were not trying to find out Maglorix's whereabouts or to kill him. The patrols, such as they were, were designed to detect people trying to enter, not leave, and the great holes in the fortress walls made it simple to find an unguarded exit.

Silus wondered briefly if he should return to his mission, and attempt to kill Maglorix. He rationalised that the information that he had about the attack was vital and getting back to Eboracum to warn the Emperor was now more important than killing the barbarian war leader. Deep down, though, he knew that Atius could complete that mission on his own, while Silus made an attempt on Maglorix. But he couldn't take his mind off the hanging and flaying that awaited him if he was captured again. He burned with shame as they left the ruined great fortress behind, but that didn't stop his legs wobbling with sheer relief.

Once they were a short distance from Inchtuthil, Silus took the lead from Enid. She may have known the camp, but these environs were as foreign to her as they were to the rest of them, and it was Silus' job to find their way. First, he led them to where their packs were buried. They hastily clothed themselves and retrieved their knives and rations. Silus handed out some hard biscuits, but made it clear that they were to eat on the move.

The clear sky was a boon to navigation, though when he looked up to orient himself, he shivered at seeing the full moon glaring balefully down on them. Still, the light allowed them to move faster, and for now it was a blessing, although it may become a curse once the barbarians were closer on their tails.

Silus took them first to the nearest stream, then made them all walk downstream. The icy water numbed their feet, and they stumbled along the uneven, rocky bed, stubbing toes and stabbing their soles onto sharp points. Enid grumbled incessantly at the discomfort, but Silus was more worried about Menenius. Though he was silent and plodded forward with a fixed face and gritted teeth, Silus walked near him, offering a supporting arm whenever needed, which was often. Despite this, Menenius still managed to catch his foot on a submerged root, falling headlong into the water. Silus and Atius hauled him quickly upright, but he was now soaked to the skin and soon shivering uncontrollably.

Before long, both Silus and Atius were supporting him, one on either side with a hand under each elbow, guiding him like a blind man. Atius looked over at Silus, and Silus grimaced and gave a little shake of his head.

'How long must we stay in this freezing water?' asked Enid. 'I can't feel my feet any more.'

Silus considered. They had managed about a quarter of a mile and were now in thick woods. Although the stream would be doing a good job of masking their scent from the dogs and disguising their trail from the trackers, progress was slow, and they had no idea how long it would be until their absence was discovered and the hunt began.

'It's enough,' he said. 'It's time to start getting some miles between us and the barbarians.'

Enid quickly scrambled out of the south-easterly facing bank and removed her shoes. She rubbed her feet hard, whimpering as the returning circulation stung. Atius climbed out next and took Menenius' hand. With Atius pulling and Silus pushing, they indelicately manhandled the prefect out of the water. When he got to the bank, he sank to his knees, then rolled onto his back, breathing heavily.

'We need to get moving,' said Silus. 'Atius, take the other two due east for a mile, then head due south. I'm going to smooth over the first part of your trail, then double back and lay a false trail along the bank to the south-west. I'll catch up with you. Or I'll try. If for any reason I don't meet you, you must get to Segedunum, and from there get a message to the Emperor about the Maeatae attack. That mission takes precedence over everything else.' Silus looked pointedly at Enid and Menenius. 'Everything. Do you understand?'

Atius hesitated then nodded reluctantly. Menenius made no sign of having heard, but Enid, though not comprehending the exchange in Latin, glared at Atius and Silus suspiciously.

Atius and Silus helped Menenius to his feet, then Silus took a twiggy branch from a tree and began to scrape away the muddy tracks of their exit from the river, and to conceal the flattened area of ground where Menenius had been lying.

'I hate them, too,' said Enid suddenly.

Atius looked to Silus for a translation, but Silus said nothing, just faced her with squared shoulders.

'They killed my family. Took me from my home. They have used me as a house slave and a whore. Treated me as less than their dogs. I want to return home. But first, I will help you, if helping you hurts them.'

'Thank you,' said Silus. 'For all you have done. If you want to hurt the barbarians, then help Atius and Menenius reach Roman lines. Then you can go back to your people knowing you will have damaged the Maeatae beyond all imagination.'

Enid nodded, then turned to Atius. 'Come.' She beckoned, and he placed an arm under Menenius' shoulder and together they moved into the undergrowth of the trees. Silus followed behind for a few hundred yards, carefully erasing their trail as they went. When he felt he had done enough, he clapped Atius on the shoulder, and without a word headed back the way they had come.

He moved quickly but carefully, ensuring the signs of his passing were minimised. From his own internal clock and the position of the moon, he estimated they had been gone an hour. They had maybe one more hour until their absence was discovered, if they were lucky. Then it would be down to Fortuna's will. When the hunters found the stream, they would have a straight toss-of-a-coin chance as to which way the fugitives will have gone. But if Maglorix allocated sufficient resources — and he would, as both pride and the success of his surprise attack were at stake — they could split and track in both directions. Hopefully, they would then follow Silus' false trail, but when that ran out, they would either return to the stream, where they may pick up the subtle signs of passage that Silus couldn't completely remove, or failing that, they would institute a thorough search pattern that would find them, given enough time.

So once Silus' initial subterfuges were completed, it would all come down to speed. And that meant horses. As Silus reached the stream, then went about setting a more obvious trail, endeavouring to make it appear that four people had passed through rather than just one, he thought hard about where they could find mounts.

He couldn't rely on there being any Roman forts along the vallum Antonini that were occupied by friendly forces since the latest Maeatae excursion, so they would have to make their way all the way down to the vallum Hadriani, a journey of many days even if they could find horses somewhere in this sparsely populated barbarian country. He pictured the region in his mind, imagining it as a drawing on a cloth, dotted throughout with landmarks joined by lines with the length proportional to the distance of the journey between each point. The vallum Hadriani and the province of Britannia seemed hopelessly far away. He populated the image with villages and minor dwellings he had come across in his scouting missions, and noted a few along their route from where they might be able to steal some ponies. He thought of the line of the vallum Antonini, an unknown number of its forts sacked and destroyed. Then, as he extended his mental picture outwards to the coast, he suddenly thought of Horrea Classis.

As a purely land-based soldier, he had never been to Horrea Classis, the port that served as headquarters for the British fleet, the Classis Britannica, since the start of Severus' Caledonian invasion. But he knew it was a significant fortress, full of granaries to supply the legions, and as it could be supplied by sea, it could hold out against a siege indefinitely. Its vital importance to the Roman campaign as a route of supplies meant it was heavily defended. Maybe Maglorix had surprised it and sacked it already. The port sat deep in Veniconian territory, and it would be a major victory to the Maeatae, and to Maglorix personally, if he removed that insult to his people from his land. On the other hand, the effort and time he would need to take Horrea Classis wasn't consistent with Maglorix's plans to make a swift and devastating raid into Britannia with his full strength.

The more Silus mulled over the options, the more he became convinced that they must try for Horrea Classis. Yes, it was in the heart of Maglorix's homeland, and yes, it may have been already overrun. But it was only two days' ride from Inchtuthil, and it possessed boats that could swiftly send a message down the coast to Eboracum. It was their best chance.

When he decided he had gone far enough, he backtracked half a mile, then headed east, once again being careful to minimise his trail while hoping he would find the others quickly. Now that he had decided on a plan, his thoughts could wander, while he automatically picked his way through the woods. Inevitably, Sergia and Velua came to mind. Their sudden appearance in his mind's eye still had the power to make him gasp and the air stick in his throat, and to make him feel like he couldn't breathe. He tried to distract himself by concentrating on childhood memories: his earliest days with the Maeatae, the games he played with his barbarian cousins in the marshes and streams and woods – climbing trees and playing tag, whittling spears and wrestling in the mud – before returning home to a scolding from their mothers. He tried to think about his time with his father, his tough upbringing on wilderness treks and hunts. But always his wife and daughter forced themselves to the forefront. In the end, the only way he could take his mind off them and take away the pain in his chest and the weakness in his legs was to focus on Maglorix and what he would do to the cunnus if he ever got him alone again.

He judged it was around midnight when he picked up the trail of the others, and soon afterwards he caught up with them. Although they were now clear of the woods and in open marshy fields, they had made frustratingly slow progress, especially as he knew that the hunt would be well and truly on by now. Menenius was looking dead on his feet, shivering and pale, leaning heavily on Atius, who seemed exhausted with the effort of supporting the prefect. Enid looked impatient to be going, but wouldn't move ahead on her own.

Silus clapped Atius on the back, embraced Menenius, then spoke to Enid.

'We need horses. I think there is a village nearby. Do you know it?'

Enid thought for a moment.

'I don't know this area well. It is not the land of my birth. But the tribes did pass this way.' She looked around, eyes narrowed, focussing on the landmarks she could recognise in the moonlight. 'I think you are right. Beyond those hills. A few roundhouses, some sheep and cattle.'

Silus relayed the information to Atius.

'This near to the war gathering, though,' Atius said, 'won't they have requisitioned any horses already?'

'Maybe,' said Silus. 'You know as well as I, though, how good people are at hiding their valuables from foraging armies. And as a bonus, their young men will likely have been drafted into the war gathering too, so they shouldn't put up much of a fight.'

Atius looked at Menenius. 'I'm not sure we will either.'

Chapter Thirteen

The village consisted of half a dozen roundhouses at the top of a hill, and they could soon smell the burning wood and peat and see the smoke drifting out from the central holes that were situated in the roof directly above the firepits. There was no palisade, and no sign of activity beyond a few cows grazing in the nearby fields. Silus instructed Menenius and Enid to stay out of sight, and he and Atius approached. He reflected as they left the other two behind that he was giving orders to his former commander, who obeyed like a beaten dog. Those barbarians really had broken his spirit.

As they neared, they could make out a few outbuildings. One looked like a store, while the others seemed more likely to be stables. They quietly approached one, and Silus eased the door open. It was pitch black inside, but the lactic faecal smell suggested it housed milking cows. A high-pitched bleat and a low confirmed that at least one nursing cow was inside. Silus quietly closed the door, hoping that the bovine sounds were sufficiently innocuous not to alert any of the villagers.

They made their way over to the next stable, and this time Fortuna seemed to be on their side. When their eyes had adjusted to make out the occupants, in the moonlight shining through the high window on the opposite wall they could see two decent-sized horses and two smaller ponies tied to posts. Silus eased inside, extending a hand to the first. They snickered and shifted nervously from foot to foot, but these rides were properly broken. They put up little protest as Silus and Atius retrieved their saddles and bridles from their hooks on the walls and got them ready.

Once they were all saddled up, they untied them, opened the doors wide, and led them out of the stables. That was when they realised Fortuna had not been quite so generous. One of the horses was limping badly, ducking its head down every time it put weight on its front left leg. Silus felt down its leg and found the foot above the coffin joint was swollen, and there was an odour of pus.

'Fuck,' he said. 'He has an abscess. We can't take this one.'

'There's a stable we haven't checked,' said Atius. 'Maybe we should try in there.'

One of the horses, maybe perturbed by the break in its routine or the unfamiliar people handling it, let out a loud neigh. A long-limbed, shaggy dog which had been asleep in front of a nearby roundhouse lifted its head, spotted the strangers, leapt to its feet and started barking loudly. Other dogs joined in and a chorus of barks and howls began. Voices came, sleepy, questioning.

'Time's up,' said Silus. 'Let's go.'

They mounted two of the horses, and led the other sound one at a canter out of the village. Behind them, doors slammed open, and shouts and curses followed them as they fled.

Menenius and Enid were waiting where they had been left. Enid stood when they approached, her face a broad smile. She frowned though when she counted the horses.

'Only three?'

'Beggars can't be choosers,' said Silus.

'You're a thief, not a beggar.'

'Menenius and Atius are the heaviest. They get a pony each. You and I will share a horse.'

Enid looked like she would protest, but realised there was no point and shrugged.

'Come on, mount up. If Maglorix's men come here, they will know for sure it is us and be straight on our arses. Let's get going.'

Atius helped Menenius up, then mounted himself. Silus grasped the saddle and heaved himself up and over, then reached down to help lift Enid up behind him. She was light, undernourished, and he hoisted her easily up. She settled behind him, hesitated, then put her arms around his waist. He suddenly became acutely aware of the young woman's body pressed against him and was glad for the darkness that hid the flush of his face from his companions. He kicked the horse into motion, and they cantered away into the dark, leaving the shouts of the outraged villagers far behind.

—

They rode through the night, sticking to deer trails and badger tracks, avoiding any paths that looked like they were frequented by men. The terrain changed from rugged hills to marshy lowlands to dense woods, and they picked their way through with as much speed as they dared without endangering their mounts. Every time his pony stumbled, Silus felt his stomach lurch. A foot caught in a badger hole could easily snap a leg, greatly reducing their chances of reaching safety.

But the mounts stayed sound until dawn. In the east, Silus watched the dark sky lighten, turn cerulean, then a vivid orange. The low-hanging scattered clouds glowed with a fire that brought unbidden images of burning thatch to Silus' mind. He shook his head to rid himself of the distraction. Behind him, Enid still clung to him, her cheek pressed to his back. He thought she had slept for some of the ride, and he had found himself occasionally nodding off as well. Atius had remained alert throughout the night though, watching out both for his own path and keeping an eye on Menenius, who at times seemed to be struggling to stay in the saddle.

The track they were following intersected with a wider path, with parallel grooves in the stone-speckled mud suggesting it was a route used by carts and wagons. Silus pulled his horse up and waited for Atius to pull alongside him.

'I guess we are about a half day's ride from Horrea Classis,' said Silus. 'That is if we only stop to give the horses enough time to rest. Should we push on and try to make safety as soon as possible, or should we stop?'

Atius looked around to see Menenius bring his horse slowly to a halt behind them. He swayed in his saddle, looked about to fall, then caught himself, and with great effort sat upright. He gave Atius and Silus a weak smile. Behind Silus, Enid was fast asleep.

Atius shrugged. 'My head says we should carry on. My heart says we need to rest. So does my arse.'

'If only we knew how far behind us they are. Or even if they have picked up our trail at all.'

'We have to assume they have at least a few warriors following. There are so many of them that they can search many trails at once. And with the shape we are in, a few warriors would be enough to finish us.'

Silus nodded. 'Speed is our best chance. Our only chance. But what will get us to safety quickest? Pushing the horses and ourselves beyond endurance, or resting now hoping we'll make up the time?'

'If it was just the two of us, I would say we keep on. But look at the others. They need to rest.'

Silus looked behind him, squinting into the darkness to the north-west. He half expected to see a host of barbarians burst out of the gloom, screaming their war cries as they descended on them. But all was quiet. Before him, the cart track stretched out, beckoning him to safe haven.

He sighed. Atius was right. Menenius couldn't go on, not without a short respite. Silus pointed to a nearby copse.

'Let's rest up there for a couple of hours, then get moving.'

'You don't think we should wait for night again?' asked Atius.

'No, if they are following us with dogs, darkness will not save us.'

They rode together up to the copse, then dismounted and led the horses into cover. Once the horses were hitched to trees, they settled into the hollow made by the roots of an elderly yew tree. Silus passed out some bread and water from his pack and they ate and drank eagerly. Then Menenius slumped against the trunk and immediately passed into a fitful slumber. His eyes twitched from side to side behind closed eyelids, and his body jerked intermittently as if he was being kicked in the ribs. Silus made himself comfy in the leaf litter, leaning against a protruding loop of root.

Enid came over and sat next to him. She slid her arms around him and put her head against his chest. He stiffened. She looked up at him, puzzled. He turned, putting his back to her. After a moment she got up and sat next to Atius. When Silus looked over, Atius was cradling her in his arms. Silus gave him a warning glance, and Atius feigned innocence.

'I'll take watch,' said Silus, standing up abruptly. He walked to the edge of the copse, looking out as the terrain became more and more visible under the lightening sky. He wondered if he would ever feel comfortable in the presence of a woman again.

—

Atius was snoring loudly, arms wrapped tightly around Enid, when Silus booted him in the backside. He woke with a jerk, which made Enid awake and emit a cry. Atius gave Silus a filthy look, then extricated himself from Enid.

'Time to get moving,' said Silus. Menenius still slept, face pale, head lolling, mouth open. Silus knelt down and put a gentle hand on his shoulder. Menenius' eyes flew open, and he grabbed Silus' wrist in sudden terror.

'Calm, sir,' said Silus gently. 'You are safe. But we need to be on our way.'

Menenius gathered himself, then nodded. 'Of course.' Silus helped him to his feet. He wondered how much of Menenius' damage was physical and how much was to his soul. Clearly both his mind and body were badly hurt. Atius and Silus helped Menenius onto his pony again, and then the rest of them mounted up.

They rejoined the cart track which led east, and pushed their rides to a gentle trot. Silus tried to estimate how far they had come, how far they had to go and how much longer it would take at this pace, but he soon gave up. There were so many guesses that it was just unknowable. He wasn't even sure he was on the most direct route to Horrea Classis, in any case. It was entirely possible that they weren't going to intersect the great fortress port on this path.

Still, he knew that Horrea Classis lay on the south bank of the Tatha, at its confluence with the Uisge Èireann. The Tatha was a vast river, so if they continued south-east, they would hit its northern bank, and could then find a boat that would take them to their safe haven.

The sun rose and they encountered occasional travellers in both directions: drovers of livestock, merchants, itinerant craftsmen. All looked at them curiously; some greeted them with friendliness or suspicion. Some seemed inclined to conversation, but Silus didn't engage them. There was nothing of use they could discover, and the more they spoke, the more the fact that they didn't belong there may become apparent.

The path wound around the foot of a hill. Silus looked behind them, but there was still no sign of pursuit. Surely they must be getting closer to their destination now. A treacherous hope began to arise deep within him.

They rounded a corner, and ahead of them, coming in their direction, some fifty yards distant, were two riders. Silus' stomach lurched. He prayed that they were just locals, riding from one hillfort to the next, but he knew in his heart that they were discovered.

The riders pulled up and sat, watching them. Silus raised a hand in greeting and urged his horse forward, hoping to reach them or at least close the gap. The riders conferred briefly, then wheeled their horses around and sped away.

Silus swore and kicked the mount into a gallop, Atius accelerating at his side.

The riders were too fast. Silus' horse was weighed down by two riders, and Atius' pony was too small for his bulk. The distance opened up between them and Silus despaired. Then one of the fleeing horses stumbled and pulled up lame. Its rider cursed, tried to get it moving, but the horse was going nowhere. The rider's companion looked back at his friend, then rode on, taking a left fork in the path that curved to the east. The rider with the crippled horse shouted at him angrily, then dismounted, pulling his spear from his saddle bag, and turned to face his pursuers.

Silus and Atius drew near and circled the man, clearly a Maeatae warrior. He spat at them.

'The traitor, the Roman scum and the slave whore,' he said. 'And the broken prisoner, back there. Your time is short. We are nearly on you.'

'Where are the rest of your men? How far away?'

'Close,' said the warrior. 'Very close. Your punishment for denying the gods will be so brutal, you will wish you had died last night.'

Silus blocked out the words, though they chilled him. He would not be taken alive, nor allow the same for any of his companions. He was aware that Enid was still behind him, vulnerable, and still holding him, restricting his movements. He slowly dismounted, and Atius did the same behind the warrior. The man could only point his spear in one direction, and it was an unwieldly weapon for close quarters combat. He feinted at first at Atius and then at Silus, but without conviction.

'Tell us where your brothers are and you will live. Your friend has escaped already, so there is no benefit to killing you.'

'I would rather die,' said the warrior.

The tip of Atius' sword burst through his chest accompanied by a gout of blood. The warrior coughed a stream of red, then fell forward.

Silus stared at Atius open-mouthed.

'We don't have time for this. His friend has escaped and will be bringing a storm down on our heads at any moment.'

'It wasn't your decision to make,' growled Silus. Atius shrugged and mounted up. Silus looked down at the corpse lying in the blood-stained mud and shook his head. He got back in the saddle and beckoned to Menenius, who had been making his way to them slowly. When he reached them, he dismounted slowly, gingerly. He bent down to pick up the warrior's discarded spear, then remounted. He looked at Silus steadily, but said nothing. Silus simply nodded and said, 'We ride hard now. We need to make the river and find transport before they catch us. Is everyone ready?'

When he had their assent, he tugged on the reins to orient his horse along the path and kicked hard. They rode at a brisk canter, taking the right fork that led south. Every part of him screamed to increase the pace, to put the horse into a gallop, to put as much distance between him and any pursuit as quickly as possible. But though he wasn't a skilled rider, even he knew that a horse could only sustain a gallop for a mile or two before fatiguing.

The sun rose higher in the sky, warming them, and riders and horses alike began to sweat. This damned country seemed to go on forever. His father had once shown him a map of the world in a book by a man named Ptolemy, who had tried to gather the knowledge of the geography of the world in one place. Silus remembered marvelling at discovering places on the far side of the world like Sinae and Taprobane, places so far beyond the boundaries of the empire that all that was told of them was legend and myth. But when he had examined the area around Britannia and Caledonia, he had been disappointed. He knew that the end of the island of Britannia was far to the north, not deviated at a right angle, as the map showed, so that the tip was to the east, and he knew that the Tatha flowed west to east not north to south. If he had been using the map instead of his knowledge of the country, they would have had no chance of finding Horrea Classis. Still, the map did give a sense of scale, of the vastness of this land beyond the empire. Silus fought down a rising panicked feeling of hopelessness.

Then at last, as the sun was descending towards the horizon, they crested a hill and saw, some two miles away, the wide river Tatha. The path they were on led down the course of a tributary, dry at this time of year, but with a damp bed and the type of vegetation that suggested it seasonally carried water. The banks were steep, the path narrow, but the footing seemed firm. Silus pulled up, waiting for Menenius and Atius to draw level.

'There,' he said. 'We'll find a boat to take us to Horrea Classis, and we are home safe.'

Behind them a dog barked. Then another. Silus looked back. Ascending the slope of the hill they had just climbed were half a dozen Maeatae warriors, their mounts eating up the ground, throwing clods of mud behind them as they laboured up the incline. It was hard going, but their horses looked like tough native breeds, and fresh. They would be on them in moments.

'Ride!' yelled Silus. He urged his horse into flight, kicking it and screaming in its ear to encourage it to full speed. The frightened mount charged down the river bed, skittering and skidding on slippery rocks. Silus hung on to its neck and Enid clutched him tight. He could hear her breathing heavily, but she said nothing, just trusted to his riding and to the natural instincts of the horse. Atius yelped as his own pony lost its footing momentarily, nearly tossing him off, then cursed, 'Christos, that was close,' as mount and rider recovered.

The track was too narrow to ride side by side, but Silus could hear Atius right on his tail. The hounds were baying excitedly, and the shouts of the warriors became clearer as they neared. Silus was desperate to look back, to see how near the pursuit was, to gauge whether they were going to make it, but he knew it would make no difference to their chances, except to risk a fall, which would be swiftly fatal.

Atius had no such compunction.

'What the fuck is Menenius doing?' he yelled.

Silus turned now and swore loudly. 'Oh Mithras and Mars. Menenius, no.'

Their superior officer had fallen behind. He must have realised he would not outrun the pursuit, so he had turned his pony, and was standing, his spear tucked under his arm, waiting for the warriors to reach him.

'We have to go back,' cried Atius, tugging on the reins to pull his horse to a halt. Silus stopped too, staring in horror.

'We can't. Atius, it's too late, and they are too many. He is buying us time to escape. With his life.'

'Silus, help me. We can still save him. But I can't do it on my own.'

'No, Atius. We must reach Horrea Classis. We need to get news of Maglorix's raid to the Emperor. It's more important than any one of us.'

'Damn you, Silus. He is our commanding officer!'

'I am your superior. Follow me now. That's an order!'

Without waiting for an answer, Silus kicked his horse into flight once more. A few moments later, he heard Atius behind him, the pony breathing hard, hooves clattering on the rocks. He looked back, past his stony-faced friend. The warriors reached Menenius, but the width of the path allowed them to confront him only one at a time. They pulled up and conferred, then one launched his spear at Menenius. The old Roman ducked in time, the missile skimming over his shoulder.

The leading warrior was passed another spear, and this time he trotted forward. As soon as he was in range, he thrust out. Menenius tugged on the reins with one hand, and the pony stepped sideways as he parried the thrust with his own spear. The warrior cursed and drew back to stab again.

Menenius yanked the reins in the other direction, and his pony reared and spun on its hind legs, so he was side on to his attacker. Silus marvelled – he hadn't known that the Prefect was such an accomplished horseman. The man who so recently had seemed finished had come alive in battle.

Menenius roared and thrust out with all his failing strength. His spear went straight through his attacker's mouth and out the back of his skull. Without a cry, the warrior toppled off his horse and hit the ground heavily, taking Menenius' spear with him.

There was a moment of silence. Then two warriors dismounted, skirted their comrade's horse, and grabbed Menenius, dragging him to the ground. The prefect was obscured from Silus' view, but he could see the Maeatae spears thrusting down into his body over and over again in blind fury.

Silus blinked tears from his eyes, and faced front, concentrating on his own escape, praying to every god he could think of that Menenius' sacrifice had been sufficient.

The distance to the river reduced rapidly, but soon the sounds of pursuit reached them again, getting louder. The tributary widened as it reached the river, and they clambered up its sides to find a wide path that ran along the north bank of the Tatha. Now they needed a boat.

But there was none. Silus wondered for a moment what he had expected. That the river would be thronged with barges and ferries, all waiting to transport some desperate fugitives to safety? They rode along the river bank, eastwards, heads down, galloping full speed. Their mounts were wide-eyed and they frothed profusely, and there were speckles of blood in the foam. Their breathing was hoarse and laboured, and Silus felt them tiring. Behind them the pursuers yelled curses. To the left was dense forest, to the right the fast-flowing river. They rounded a bend.

A boat!

A rowing boat to be precise, a hazel and ox-hide construction with two wooden oars. It was lying against the bank, and sitting in it was a boy eating an apple, while a trout caught in a net flapped in the bottom of the boat. He looked up in fright at the sound of the galloping hooves, then dropped his apple and grabbed his oars.

Silus reached him in an instant, leapt from his horse and grabbed the boat before the boy could row away.

'Leave me alone,' cried the boy.

'Get in,' yelled Silus to Atius and Enid, ignoring the young fisherman.

He held the boat steady and used his other hand to help Enid in, then Atius got on board, stepping carefully so as not to tip the craft over. The boat was meant for only one or two people, and with three on board it sat dangerously low in the water. If Silus got in, it would sink. He turned to see the warriors bearing down on them, a scant hundred yards away. He drew his knife, and prepared to face them, to sacrifice himself as Menenius had to buy time for Atius to get the all-important message to Horrea Classis.

A cry and a splash made him turn. Atius had unceremoniously upended the fisherman into the water where he flapped and spluttered in indignation.

'Get in,' urged Atius. 'Now.'

Silus stepped into the boat, watched it sink deeper into the water, then settle, the sides just protruding above the waterline. Only then did he give a hefty shove to push the little craft out into the faster flowing water of the river. He grabbed an oar, and Atius did likewise, and clumsily, they rowed with all their strength. A gap opened between the bank and the boat. One yard, two, three. The first of their pursuers reached the bank. He leapt from the back of his horse towards the boat. He fell short, but for a moment Silus thought the wave he produced would flood the boat. They held on as the boat rocked. The warrior started to swim towards them, but Atius lifted his oar and brought it hard down on the swimmer's head. He disappeared beneath the water and didn't come back up.

The four remaining warriors lined up on the bank, yelling insults. Silus and Atius rowed hard, and the gap with the bank increased even further. There was no way the barbarians could reach them now. They were safe.

The warriors hefted their spears, drew their arms back, and as one, loosed them towards the boat. Four missiles arced through the air towards them.

One fell short and disappeared into the water.

One sailed over their heads.

One grazed Atius' upper arm.

One buried itself in Enid's chest.

She fell backwards into Silus' arms.

Silus dropped the oar, which fell to the bottom of the boat. He stared down in to Enid's wide eyes. He grabbed the spear shaft, tried to pull it but she screamed and gripped his hand, and he let it go. Blood oozed around the entry wound, but it wasn't the profuse gush of a heart wound. It wasn't a clean kill.

Silus looked at Atius helplessly. His friend said nothing, and continued to use his oar to steer them into the faster-flowing water in the centre of the river. From the bank, the mounted warriors watched them escape.

'I'm sorry,' said Silus. 'I tried…'

'It… hurts,' said Enid. 'Can't breathe.'

'We'll get to Horrea Classis. Find a medicus. Just be brave…'

'Tired,' said Enid. 'Wish I was... home.'

Her body went rigid, back arched, mouth pulled back in a rictus. Then she went limp, and her last breath left her in a long drawn-out sigh.

The river carried them downstream towards the fortress of Horrea Classis.

Chapter Fourteen

Silus felt as tired as a mine slave. Was that the right comparison, he wondered? He was on horseback again, Atius plodding along by his side. The horses were fresh, but his body certainly wasn't. But then, neither was his mind, nor his spirit. Tired as a mine slave who had lost his family, watched friends die, and had to work on. Maybe that was closer to reality.

They had had precious little rest at Horrea Classis and no time to mourn their losses. After the initial suspicion from the fortress guards, they had been taken to the camp Prefect, who had listened to their story with rising alarm. He had summoned his senior officers into a conference and dispatched a messenger by boat down the coast to Eboracum to warn the Emperor. But by the time the message arrived, and the Emperor had then sent word to his son in the field, it would be too late for Caracalla to do anything about the invasion. It was clear that a message had to be dispatched direct from Horrea Classis by land into the Caledonian interior where Caracalla was laying waste to the undefended land.

And guess which poor fucker got that job, Silus reflected bitterly. The prefect gave him perfectly good reasons why it had to be Silus, of course. No one else had the experience. No one else knew the land as well as he did. He was already acting under Caracalla's personal command. All completely reasonable.

The complete cunt.

He looked over at Atius. His friend was lost in his thoughts, or maybe just as exhausted as he was. Caracalla's army would not be hard to find. They had ridden south-west from Horrea Classis, hoping to intersect the trail as far south as possible. They had reached the vallum Antonini, where Caracalla had left a small garrison to start the rebuilding task. The first fort they reached, one to the west of Voltanio, had been similarly sacked and razed to the ground. The auxiliaries freshly arrived there had only made the barest of beginnings – pulling down the timbers that were too charred to be salvageable, putting up temporary gates, collecting the Roman dead for cremation and tossing the dead barbarian warriors into a mass burial pit.

The centurion who had been left in charge had grown pale when they had told him their mission and what they knew of Maglorix's plans. He had actually asked Silus what his orders were, and Silus had had to gently point out that the centurion was actually superior in rank to him. They had left the poor man in a quandary as to whether to continue to obey his orders and repair the fort, or to retreat in light of the new information. Silus suspected he would continue to follow his orders to the letter, dig in, and be massacred by Maglorix's invasion like a good little Roman.

They were half a day's ride north-west of that fort now. Up until now, the countryside had largely been abandoned by the natives. Decades of skirmishes along the border had always made it a dangerous place to be for either side, but the invasions and raids of the last couple of years had devastated crops, herds and dwelling places. Caracalla's force had scoured the land to supplement their supplies as they marched. A large body of men deep in enemy territory always ran the risk of running out of food, even though each of them would be carrying a decent supply in his backpack. So it was no surprise to find piles of butchered cattle and sheep, the valuable meat expertly stripped from the bones by the legion's butchers.

Nor was it a surprise when they got further into barbarian territory, into the region more populated by the barbarians who thought themselves far enough away from routine Roman patrols to settle safely, to see a pall of smoke on the horizon. Atius and Silus exchanged grim glances, but said nothing as they rode closer.

The settlement was in an area of flat, well-drained farmland. Fertile land. But everywhere they looked was devastation: herds of cattle and sheep slaughtered and taken for supplies as they had seen elsewhere, but also the crops in the fields, the turnips, barley and oats, had been hacked down and trampled. It was hard to scorch the earth in this cold, marshy land, but the principle was clearly being applied in the best way possible.

The huts were on a low hill, with no palisade. Not a hillfort, just a collection of people who lived together for protection, company and to trade goods and skills with each other and with other villages.

Every single roundhouse had been set ablaze. They continued to smoulder now, though Silus estimated it was maybe a day since the army had passed through. Silus led the way up the gentle slope into the village. The scent of roasted meats and woodsmoke hung in the air. Crows cawed but otherwise the village was silent. No dogs barked, no chickens clucked and there were no howls from fighting cats. There were no sounds of industry or the normal noises of a community. No sawing wood, or hammered iron, no laughter, no arguments. No children playing.

Silus swallowed and steeled himself for what was ahead. He had seen everything, he thought; he could harden his heart against anything.

He was wrong.

They rode into the centre of the village and pulled their horses up. They both stared in stunned silence. The colour had drained from Atius' face, and Silus was sure he looked the same. They didn't move, didn't speak, barely breathed.

Every roundhouse was burned and the remains pulled down. Every outbuilding, barn and stable was similarly destroyed. And every inhabitant of the village – man, woman, child, domestic animal – had been killed.

A few feet from where Silus sat on his gently breathing mount, there was the body of a youthful boy with a gaping wound in his neck. Nearby was an old man, with a hole in his skull that showed the grey matter beneath. Not far from him was a young woman, clothing torn, no obvious injuries apart from dark bruises around her neck that were the width of a man's fingers. Beside her was a small blood-soaked bundle of rags. As Silus watched, he saw the cloth move, twitch. He kicked his mount forward, reached down to move the cloth aside with the tip of his spear. Wrapped in the swaddling was a baby, probably only weeks old. A wide hole in the infant's abdomen showed the fatal wound. The body twitched again, and for a moment Silus thought that, impossibly, the baby still lived. Then a rat's head emerged from the wound, covered in gore. Silus flinched back with a cry. The rat stared at Silus for a moment, then scurried off in search of more dead flesh.

They had seen the aftermath of slaughter before, but that had been sanitised by weather and the completed work of the carrion eaters. Bones and long-abandoned dwellings were sobering enough. But this was so fresh it felt like they had participated in the massacre. He looked around further, not needing to explore to see the devastation. A hunting dog impaled on a spear; a litter of piglets crushed and stabbed; a young boy face down in the mud with a sword wound in his back; an old lady hanged from a tree. He turned his back, and saw a young woman, heavily pregnant. The spear that had run her through had been left in place, fixing her to the ground, right through her gravid belly. *Not even the unborn child in its mother's womb.* Those were the orders of Severus, and his soldiers had obeyed them to the letter.

He pulled on his reins, kicked his horse's flanks, and rode out of the village at a gallop, giving the horse its head. It was unsettled by the sights and smells, and took the opportunity to run off its fear.

The savagery, in its scale and ferocity, was worse than Silus had ever imagined. He hated the barbarians for what they had done to his family and his colleagues. He detested Maglorix with all his might. He wished the chief dead and his people defeated.

But.

Was this what he wanted? Was this what vengeance looked like? He tried to picture Sergia and Velua, but their images would not come to mind. If he closed his eyes, he still saw the pregnant woman, womb and foetus impaled, not his own family.

The horse came to a halt, blowing heavily. He sat, and stared into space. Soon, Atius caught up with him.

They sat in silence, each lost in his own thoughts. Then he clenched his jaw, and whispered to himself, 'For you, my girls. All for you.' He nodded to Atius, and they kicked their horses into a trot and continued north.

–

They tried to skirt any further sites of massacre. They were obvious from a long way off, the repeated pattern of slaughtered herds and smoking dwellings. Sometimes, though, the path took them unavoidably past or through the butchery. As they closed the distance to Caracalla's marauding army, the slaughter became fresher. Fires still burned. Pools of blood were sticky and damp. In one small collection of dwellings, they found a dog dragging itself helplessly around by its front legs. Both hind legs were crushed and broken. As they passed it, Atius bent down and thrust his spear through its chest, his mouth a thin line as he ended the creature's misery.

They camped overnight in the open countryside, well away from any habitation, not admitting it to each other, but both knowing they were scared to face the ghosts of the freshly dead at night-time. Normally while scouting in barbarian territory, Silus would go to great pains to hole up in a discrete, easily defensible area. But with any enemies – or even merely unfriendly locals – dead or fled, and a mood as dark as the gloomy Caledonian forests, they simply pitched a tent in the open, made a fire, and cooked a tasteless but filling stew.

Still, they took it in turns to keep watch, and Atius woke Silus from a dream that he couldn't quite remember but left him feeling shaken and unsettled. It was four hours till dawn, judging by the position of the constellations of the Great Bear in relation to the Little Bear. Atius was asleep and snoring in moments, leaving Silus to stare into the flames of the fire, the heat on his face contrasting with the chill wind on his neck. Long stretches of time on watch at night were boring and terrifying in equal measures, and although Silus had no real fear of ambush, apart from perhaps a lonely and desperate deserter, he still started and his heart raced whenever he heard the noise of small creatures snuffling in the leaf litter, the snap of a twig broken by a prowling predator, or the unexpectedly loud hoot of an owl.

He watched the horizon lighten with impatience, and as soon as he felt it was fair, he woke Silus. Having his friend conscious again and the dawn slowly breaking helped calm his anxieties, but he was keen for them to be on their way as soon as possible. They packed up camp, ate some hard tack, drank some water and refilled their bottles from a nearby stream, pissed and shat, fed the horses, then mounted up.

After passing uncomfortably close to two more sites of devastation, they found themselves following a trail along a pass between two steep hills that took them straight through a large village. This one was of course in ruins like the others they had seen, but unlike those, this village had life in it. As they drew close, they found a small detachment of half a dozen light cavalry auxiliaries still in residence.

The auxiliaries watched the approaching riders with suspicion, forming into a five-wide rank, spears forward. Their leader, a sesquiplicarius, third in line to the decurion in a cavalry turmae, sat mounted before them, one hand on the hilt of his sword, the other held up, palm facing them.

When they were close enough to be heard, Silus hailed the sesquiplicarius.

'We are auxiliaries on special assignment,' shouted Silus, 'carrying a vital message for the Emperor Antoninus.'

'One of you stay there,' the sesquiplicarius called back. 'The other approach with empty hands.'

Silus trotted forward, one hand holding the reins, the other out and well away from his side. When he was six feet away, the sesquiplicarius barked at him.

'Stop there. State your name and the name of your commanding officer.'

'My name is Gaius Sergius Silus, formerly under the command of Prefect Menenius of Voltanio.'

'Formerly?'

'Menenius is dead, and Voltanio destroyed.'

The sesquiplicarius pursed his lips. 'I heard that. And what are your orders? Why are you here in barbarian lands in civilian clothing? Are you a spy?'

'My orders are none of your concern. And I am a member of the Arcani, acting at the direction of Oclatinius Adventus and the Emperor Antoninus himself!'

The auxiliaries muttered among themselves at the mention of Oclatinius, and Silus smiled inwardly. The old bastard invoked terror wherever his name was mentioned, as did the Arcani he commanded.

'I need to see your orders to let you pass,' said the sesquiplicarius, less sure of himself now, but trying to save face in front of his men.

'I have no papers, sesquiplicarius. Are you stupid? Would a spy carry papers that would identify him as a spy when he was in enemy lands?'

'Of course not. But how do I know you are who you say you are?'

'Listen. If you let me through, and I am not who I say, then all you have done is let two lightly armed men loose on an army of thousands. But if you don't let me through, and I am who I say, then you will have done your Emperor immeasurable harm and will have incurred the wrath of Oclatinius.'

The sesquiplicarius' eyes widened at this thought. Then he nodded.

'You may pass. I will escort you. Make way, men.'

Silus beckoned to Atius, who trotted forward. They followed the sesquiplicarius through the gap the cavalry men had made and through the village. Although he had expected it, the sight of the bodies – the decapitated and mutilated women, children and old men – strewn around like dolls thrown by a child in a tantrum still turned his stomach. They rode out of the village, leaving the slaughter behind.

'What are you doing here?' asked Silus.

'Mopping up,' said the sesquiplicarius. 'Our orders were to make sure no one was left alive and nothing of value was left behind. No food, no shelter.'

Silus nodded his understanding, mixed emotions churning inside.

'What's your name?' asked Silus.

'Valentius.'

Silus took in his long, light hair, his broad build and his height, which Silus could tell was lofty even though he was on horseback.

'Are you a Gaul?'

Valentius shook his head. 'I'm from Galatia. My ancestors were Celts who lived in Asia Minor before the Romans.'

'So you are cousin to the people of this country. How do you feel about what you have to do here?'

Valentius gave him a look as if he was mad. 'These people aren't my cousins. My land has been part of the Roman Empire for centuries, and my loyalty is to Rome. These barbarians hate civilisation and make war on law and culture. They don't read or write. They fuck each other's wives, sacrifice babies to their evil gods, and enslave and torture Roman women for fun. They are vermin, and they need to be exterminated, like you would if your house was infested with rats.'

Silus bit his lip, unsure how to respond. The Maeatae and Caledonians were his cousins, closer than the distant relationship that Valentius' ancestors had with the Celtic inhabitants of Caledonia. He shared blood with these people. Was it his upbringing that meant that he was not vermin? If the circumstances of his childhood had been different, would it have been him and his family being exterminated by the Romans? And yet, these barbarians had killed his own precious daughter and wife.

Atius was obviously having his own doubts as well.

'Do the women and children deserve to die as well?'

Valentius rolled his eyes. 'Obviously. You don't wipe out an infestation just by killing the adult males. Or the women will turn the young into adults and they will breed new pests, and before you know it, we will be back in the same situation. Besides, they had their chance for peace. They chose war and have to live with the consequences of that.' He looked at Atius and Silus suspiciously. 'What's wrong with you two? Are you really Romans? You sound like you secretly love these scum.'

'No!' said Silus, louder than he intended. 'These maggots killed my family. I hate them.' He paused, looked away. 'It's just... so much death.'

'This is war. It's not about sneaking around, bumping off unsuspecting victims in the dark, like you lot do. This is in your face – bloody, dirty, scary, painful. This is real soldier work.'

Silus thought back to the dead villagers, and wondered how much real soldier work it had taken to butcher them. But he said nothing, and they rode on at a brisk trot.

—

They passed through three more sites of massacres, two villages and a small hill fort, before they reached Caracalla's army. The repeated sights of dead Caledonians with livid faces and bloodied throats and torsos, the devastating wounds, the piteous tableaux of dead parents frozen in the act of trying to protect dead children, eventually had a numbing effect on Silus, and he rode on with eyes set straight ahead.

By the time they reached the sentries of Caracalla's marching camp, it was late in the day. He was tired, saddle sore, and his eyes and throat stung from the repeated exposure to the smoke of burning settlements. Valentius gave the sentries the password, vouched for Atius and Silus, and escorted them into the camp. He took them first to his commanding officer, a grumpy decurion, who in turn took them to the co-prefect of the Praetorian Guard, Aemilianus Papinianus.

Papinianus, thin-faced and narrow-eyed with a dark Syrian complexion, looked at the two travel-grimed spies down his beaked nose. But his demeanour changed rapidly from disdain to alarm as Silus related his message, and he sent a centurion to request an urgent audience with Caracalla. While they waited for the reply, Silus and Atius were given meat and water, and they rested on stools outside the legate's quarters, backsides and inner thighs burning from the long rapid ride.

Camp life buzzed around them. The Roman marching camp, a tradition and tactic in use for centuries, was a place that was never still. Romans in enemy territory would not rest unless surrounded by fortifications, and so after every day's marching they constructed a fortification consisting of a ditch, an earth rampart, and a fence on top. Every legion carried with it the tools and supplies needed to make the fortresses, and as the legionaries assigned to construction swiftly raised the camp, the rest stood guard in case of ambush.

Now it was dusk, the perimeter was complete, and the tents were being pitched – accommodation for legionaries and cavalry, stables, quarter master's tent, headquarters. Silus watched as four senior centurions presented themselves to the legate and were each given a small wooden tablet on which was inscribed the new camp password for the night. These would be passed to other officers in turn until the password was known by all who needed it. Guards patrolled the streets between the rows of tents, looking for signs of trouble, internal or external. Sitting in front of other tents, legionaries polished armour and sharpened swords, made fires to cook stews, and ate from small wooden bowls using spoons.

Almost everything the soldiers needed to survive they had carried here on their backs, although pack animals and carts helped transport some of the bulkier supplies. Silus reflected on the enormous contrast between the perfect planning and execution of the Roman encampment compared to the chaotic and haphazard approach to camping that the barbarians employed. This, as much as anything else, showed Silus clearly the complete futility of the Maeatae rebellion. The power of Rome was projected from that far off capital of the Empire all the way into Caledonia, and was surely invincible to any full-blown assault.

That, of course, was the biggest headache that the Romans faced. The previous year, the Maeatae and Caledonians had avoided a head-on confrontation, and harried and ambushed instead, inflicting serious losses which, while never enough to make a Roman defeat likely, were sufficient to mean that victory was bought dearly.

And now there was this new change of tactic by Maglorix, with the provocation followed by a major assault into the depth of the Roman province of Britannia while the army was chasing its tail in the middle of Caledonia. Again, there was no chance of a barbarian victory in the end. But in the short term, what damage could be done, how much death could be dealt to his comrades in the army, to the Roman civilians and native peoples of Britannia, and even to the Emperor Severus and his family?

Silus was still finishing his joint of lamb when Papinianus' centurion returned and saluted.

'The Emperor wishes to see you immediately, legate. You are to bring the arcanus and his friend with you.'

Papinianus sprung to his feet, snapped his fingers to indicate Silus and Atius should follow, and marched the short distance from his own tent to the Praetorium where Caracalla was headquartered. The Praetorians who guarded the entrance to Caracalla's tent immediately escorted them inside.

The bearded co-Emperor was standing behind a trestle table, examining some drawings inscribed on a wax tablet. A military tribune, a primus pilus and two other centurions stood with him, discussing their route for the next day's march.

'Augustus,' said Papinianus saluting, and Silus and Atius did likewise.

Caracalla looked up. 'Papinianus, thank you for attending so promptly.' He looked Silus and Atius up and down, and wrinkled his nose at their odour. 'You haven't been offered a chance to clean up, I take it?'

'We judged the message was too urgent for such niceties,' said Papinianus, sounding a little aggrieved.

'Indeed,' said Caracalla. 'So let's hear it from the horse's mouth. You have been busy I hear, Silus. There will be time later for you to relate all your adventures. Now, tell me what I need to know.'

Silus took a deep breath, then spoke, brisk and economic. That he was addressing the co-Emperor should have awed him, part of him realised, but he was too weary and soul-sick to care right now.

'We located Maglorix, Augustus. Our intention was to kill him. Unfortunately, we were captured. Maglorix intended to sacrifice us to his gods. The tripartite death, the offering was called, I believe.'

'Tripartite? There were three of you?'

'Yes,' said Silus. 'We found Menenius was being held prisoner as well.'

'Menenius? He lives?'

Silus shook his head. 'He gave his life so that we could escape, Augustus.'

'Ah,' said Caracalla. 'He was a good man.'

'Yes, Augustus.'

'Continue.'

'Maglorix did not believe we would escape, and I think he wanted to humiliate me as much as possible before my death. So he told me his plan. He provoked you with the initial attack on the vallum Antonini, then waited for you to respond by sending your forces north to deal with him. He has gathered a large force and will bypass you. He is marching south. To Eboracum.'

Caracalla's aides, the tribune and centurions, gasped.

'You're sure?'

'Yes, Augustus. He mentioned the Emperor's palace.'

'He thinks he will defeat us by cutting the head off the snake, Augustus,' said Papinianus.

Caracalla banged the table with his fist. 'He will find a hydra,' he said emphatically. 'Where is Maglorix now? Is he already on the march?'

'He was camped at Pinata Castra, Augustus.'

'Really?' said Caracalla. 'Another insult. Did he say when he would depart?'

'He just said a few days. I would guess he was waiting for more men to arrive. Maybe the Caledonians.'

'That makes sense. Even against the small garrisons left behind on the walls and in Eboracum, he will need great numbers to overcome the defences.'

'I don't think it will take much to get through the walls, Augustus,' said Papinianus. 'The defences are not yet repaired. But I agree Eboracum will be a tougher nut to crack.'

'So we march for Eboracum?' asked Papinianus. 'Or Pinata Castra?'

Caracalla frowned, his brow crinkling. 'If we catch them at Pinata Castra, we can fight them on enemy territory and save the garrisons on the vallum Antonini and vallum Hadriani. But if we arrive there too late, we will have lost time. They will be able to move quickly; they know the land, and they are lightly armoured and have many horses. We might not reach them before they get to Eboracum.'

'They will want to skirt Horrea Classis, so they are not seen or challenged by the forces there. They will travel inland, heading directly south,' said Papinianus. 'We should march south-east to intercept them at the vallum Antonini.'

'What you say has wisdom, Papinianus,' said Caracalla.

'Shall I give the order to prepare to march back towards Eboracum at first light?'

'No,' said Caracalla.

'Augustus?' said Papinianus, surprised.

'We march to Pinata Castra. It gives us our best chance of saving the garrisons manning the walls.'

'You gamble with the lives of your father and brother, Augustus,' said Papinianus, voice low.

'War is a gamble,' said Caracalla. 'Now leave me, all of you. I want some time to think.'

'Augustus.' Papinianus, the officers, and Silus and Atius saluted and turned to leave.

'Silus.' Caracalla's voice was firm. 'Stay.'

Silus looked at Atius, who shrugged, and across to Papinianus, who was frowning.

'Of course, Augustus,' said Silus, and stood at attention while the others filed out.

When they were alone, Caracalla gestured to a foldable wooden chair with a leather seat.

'Help yourself to wine, then sit.'

A small flagon of wine and an empty cup lay on the desk, so Silus poured himself a generous measure and sat where he was directed. For a while, Caracalla said nothing, pacing the tent and stroking his curly beard. Silus sipped his wine nervously, not tasting it, wondering what he was doing here.

Eventually, Caracalla settled himself into a chair opposite Silus. He took a small sip from his own wine, then looked at Silus curiously.

'What drives you, Silus?'

'I... don't understand, Augustus.'

'What makes you get up in the morning, go out into enemy lands, risk your life?'

Silus took a moment to formulate his words. These were deep questions, and ones that he asked himself all the time. With his family dead, what was the point of anything? It always came back to one thing.

'Revenge.'

Caracalla nodded and looked down into his wine, swirling it, seeming to look for inspiration or prognostication in the small vortex.

'It's good to have a purpose. I wonder, what is mine?'

'Augustus?' Silus wasn't sure if it was a rhetorical question.

'My father is old and sick. One day he will no longer be here. Then my brother and I will be co-Emperors. Is my purpose to keep the Empire safe and intact? To expand its borders and increase its glory? Or is my purpose solely to augment my own dignitas and auctoritas?'

Silus kept his mouth closed. He suspected that his opinion was not strictly necessary.

'It's nearly twenty years since my father became Emperor. He didn't need to. Rome had an Emperor already.' Caracalla looked up at Silus. 'Do you know what happened that year? Two decades ago and a thousand miles away?'

'A little, Augustus.'

'After the much-loved Marcus Aurelius came his much-less-loved son, Commodus. After him came Pertinax, but he was assassinated by the Praetorian Guard, who then auctioned the Empire to the highest bidder. It was bought by a Senator called Didius Julianus. But my father's troops declared him Emperor too. Why did he accept? Personal glory or duty to the Empire? Of course, he always claims it was duty, a sacrifice he was forced to accept. But I have never really known his heart.'

'Could it not be both, Augustus? Maybe he could see that he would be a better Emperor than that Julianus, and by becoming Emperor, he would enhance both the Empire and his own good name.'

'Maybe. A follower of Christos once told me that Christos had said you cannot serve two masters. I had him executed of course, since he felt he could not serve me as well as his god.'

Silus thought of Atius' beliefs, and his too-often-open mouth, and hoped that his friend had the sense never to say something that stupid to someone important.

'But I understand the principle. Can I serve two masters? The Empire and my own glory?'

'If you are Emperor, Augustus, then your own glory and the glory of your Empire are one and the same.'

287

'Not if I have to share the glory with another!' said Caracalla, his voice suddenly harsh.

Silus closed his mouth, eyes cast down.

'I don't trust Papinianus. He is my father's man, through and through. I cannot talk like this to him.'

'Why confide in me, then, Augustus?'

'You have served me well, Silus. But besides that, who would ever believe you if you relayed this conversation to anyone? And you know I would have you strangled instantly if you did.'

Silus bowed his head, clenching his buttocks so he didn't loosen his bowels.

'My brother is weak. He is cossetted by his mother. He has no military experience. He doesn't have the iron in him to wear the purple. And yet, when father is gone, I have to share the power with him. It doesn't sit well with me, Silus. And I'm not sure it is good for Rome.'

Caracalla stopped speaking. Silus was unsure whether he should just sit quietly. Feeling more uncomfortable as the silence stretched, he asked, 'Why are you considering all this now, Augustus?'

Caracalla sighed. 'Because right now we are at one of those crossroads that we reach on life's road sometimes. It is in my power to save my brother, and my father too. It is also in my power to leave them to their fate. If Maglorix's army descends on Eboracum, my father and brother may die in the slaughter, and I would be sole ruler.'

Silus swallowed, shocked, not daring to speak.

'So, where is my duty, Silus? Which master should I serve? My own glory, or Rome's?'

Silus said nothing. His heart pounded. His face burned hot. He wished nothing more than to be out of this place, safe with his comrades.

Caracalla sighed. 'Leave me with my thoughts, Silus. I hope the revenge you seek brings you peace. I wish I knew where to look for peace for myself.'

Silus stood, bowed deeply, and left as fast as he thought was dignified.

-

Silus and Atius spent the night in Valentius' tent. Atius pressed Silus for details of his cosy chat with Caracalla, but Silus thought of Atius' big mouth, and he could feel the garrotte around his neck. He told Atius that Caracalla wanted some extra military details, and though his friend looked at Silus like he thought he was lying, Atius did not press him further.

Despite his unease, Silus slept soundly, and was woken at dawn by the sound of trumpets summoning the men to ready themselves to march. Valentius was already up and about, but he poked his head back in the tent to check on his guests.

'Get moving, you two,' he said. 'We leave in half an hour.'

'Where are we going?' asked Silus.

'You should know,' said Valentius. 'We are marching on your intelligence to Pinnata Castra. We are going to catch the barbarians in the field. No more of these ambushes, the kidnap and torture of stragglers, the raids on supply lines. This time, we are going to make them fight.'

He ducked back out of the tent.

Silus took a deep breath and let it out slowly. Caracalla had put Rome before himself.

Atius looked at Silus through bleary sleep-encrusted eyes.

'So the army marches to war? What are we supposed to do? We don't have any further orders, and our commanding officer is a couple of hundred miles away.'

'Well, I was an Explorator before I was inducted into the Arcani. I guess we report to the commander of the Exploratores.'

They quickly dressed and armed themselves, bow and quiver, short dagger and a gladius. Silus then went looking for orders.

Chapter Fifteen

Pinnata Castra was not so intimidating in the daylight with half a dozen Speculatores under his command, and the co-Emperor of Rome and the best part of three Roman legions close behind. It was even less intimidating completely empty of barbarians. Maglorix had already departed.

Silus had guessed they would be gone. When Maglorix learned that Silus had escaped, he would have hastened to depart before Caracalla's army could reach them. The barbarians had made no attempt to conceal the recent occupation. Why would they? Either Caracalla was miles away to the north, or if Silus had reached Caracalla with news of their plans, then their whereabouts would have been known anyway.

The ash in the camp fires had not yet washed away. Tracks of chariots, hoofprints, and footprints were visible everywhere in the partly dried mud. The detritus of a large body of men was strewn about the old fortress: irreparably broken weapons and pottery, the bones of cooked animals, shells, and shards of metal and splinters of wood left behind by the blacksmiths and carpenters. Their mounts shifted and snorted, unsettled by the sights and smells. They tied their horses, and Silus sent the other scouts to scour the camp for any barbarian hangers-on or any resources or information that could be of use.

In the centre of the camp, where the old Praetorium stood, was an oak tree that had grown up to be tall and strong in the century or more since the Romans had abandoned the fortress.

From its broad branches, three naked corpses were suspended by their wrists. Silus and Atius walked forward for a closer look.

They were two men and one woman. The woman was young, similar in age and appearance to Enid. A Brigantian slave, Silus suspected. Her death had been recent enough that Silus could see the rope marks around her neck from the hanging that had killed her. Then he looked to the other two. They were men – he could tell that but not much more. One was charred black, limbs twisted into the position they had contracted in the heat, charcoal lips drawn black to reveal broken, ash-stained teeth. The odour of cooked meat still permeated the air, but was largely drowned by the other putrid scents of death.

The third corpse had had his skin removed. Silus stared at the revealed anatomy that he had only ever glimpsed in parts before, usually through the mortal wounds of comrades and enemies. The blood had congealed on the surface of muscles striped with tendons and veins. The abdomen had been cut and the guts spilled out. Wild animals, unable to reach the corpses, had feasted on the offal, and the stench of decaying guts was stupefying.

Atius was staring open-mouthed at the three victims.

'Come away,' said Silus, putting a hand out to touch his friend's arm.

'This? This was to be our fate?'

Silus nodded. 'Yes, and you can thank your god that fate fell on others.'

Silus tried to take his friend's elbow, but Atius pushed him away angrily. He bowed his head, and muttered a prayer.

'Christos, accept these poor souls into your kingdom, and give them the peace they didn't find on earth.'

Silus waited a respectful moment until he was sure Atius had finished his prayer.

'Come, we need to report back to Caracalla, and start to track Maglorix. We don't know how much of a head start he has on us.'

Atius looked like he would be sick, but turned on his heel and walked back towards the main entrance.

'Will we be able to catch him?'

'I'm not sure. He knows the country better and will be travelling lighter. But his army is barbarian, and comprised of many tribes. I suspect getting them all to follow his exact orders will be like herding cats.'

A whistle reached them from the other side of the fortress; a warning signal. Silus and Atius ran, swift and low, to where the scout was looking through a gap in the fortress wall. When they reached him, he pointed, and Silus looked out. Approaching, a few hundred feet off, were four riders, long-haired, carrying spears and shields. Silus recognised Caledonian tribe markings.

The other Speculatores converged on their position.

'What are your orders?' asked Atius.

Silus watched their approach for a short moment, gauging where they would enter the fortress. Although the main entrance was on the other side of the fort, on this side the ditch had partially filled over time, and there was a large breach big enough for two horses to enter side by side. The Caledonians seemed to be heading for the breech.

'Into cover, quickly,' said Silus. 'On my signal, we take them down. Make sure one is left alive.'

The Roman scouts flattened themselves against the inside of the fortress wall, with three on either side of the breach, while Silus and Atius concealed themselves behind a pile of rubble near the breach. Silus watched the Caledonians approach and ride through the breach. He waited, bow strung and arrow knocked, controlling his breathing, silent, until all four had entered the fortress. Then he stood, drew his bow string back, and sent an arrow straight into the chest of the leading barbarian.

As the struck barbarian toppled from his horse with a cry, the horse of the barbarian next to him reared and bolted. The Caledonian hung on desperately. Atius tracked the horse's flight with the tip of his arrow, and loosed, striking the horse behind the elbow. The horse went down, flinging its rider over its head. The Caledonian lay still, stunned. Atius ran towards him.

Silus turned to see the other barbarians were already dead, dragged off their horses by the scouts who had been hiding behind the wall, and dispatched efficiently with knife thrusts. Silus ran after Atius.

By the time he reached him, Atius already had the Caledonian's hands trussed behind his back. The barbarian had a head wound and was groaning, but he was conscious.

'Wake him up,' said Silus.

Atius slapped the barbarian around the face twice, hard, rocking his head from side to side. The Caledonian groaned, opened his eyes and grimaced at the sight of the two Roman scouts looking down at him. A series of expletives emerged from him in Brittonic that was heavily flavoured with an accent Silus didn't recognise.

'What's your name, Caledonian?'

The barbarian frowned, then said proudly, 'I am Guthor, son of Boisil, the Chief of the Cornovii.'

'We have captured a prince,' said Silus to Atius. 'The Augustus will want to speak to this one.'

Silus settled down on the damp earth, pulled out some cheese wrapped in cloth, and ate slowly.

The main Roman force was not long in arriving, and Silus dispatched one of the Speculatores to get word to Caracalla that they had captured a Caledonian noble.

Caracalla arrived promptly, dressed in full armour immaculately polished but flecked with splashes of mud from the journey, and accompanied by Papinianus and two Praetorians. Even being Emperor did not protect you from the grime gathered while travelling. Silus grabbed Guthor by his long hair and pushed him onto his knees before the Augustus.

'What have we got here, Silus?' asked Caracalla, dismounting from his finely muscled chestnut stallion. Papinianus dismounted and stood protectively behind his right shoulder.

'Augustus, we captured this one when his party arrived at the fortress just after us. The rest are dead. He says he is called Guthor, son of Boisil, who he claims is the Cornoviian Chief.'

Guthor looked defiantly up at Caracalla when he heard his name being spoken, even if he didn't understand the Latin words that were being used. But Silus could see the fear in his eyes, as he understood he was kneeling before Caracalla himself.

'Have you interrogated him yet?'

'No, Augustus. I thought you might want to do that yourself.'

'Like everything else around here,' sighed Caracalla, but Silus saw the trace of a smile through his tight-curled beard. 'Very well, ask him why he has come to Pinnata Castra.'

Silus relayed the question, translating into Brittonic. Guthor spat back his answer angrily.

'He says he was answering the call to war of Maglorix of the Maeatae. That he was sent by his father with five hundred men to cast the Roman invader out of Caledonia.'

'Ask him where the rest of his men are and where Maglorix has gone.'

Silus translated again. Guthor obviously felt he was offering nothing of value to the Romans, as he answered freely.

'He says that his men are a day's travel behind him, that he went on ahead to let Maglorix know he had more men coming to augment his host. He says that Maglorix was still supposed to be here and that he doesn't know where he has gone. I think, Augustus, that may explain why they approached the fortress so carelessly. Maglorix has departed ahead of schedule.'

'No doubt because he knew I would be on his tail after you brought me word of his plans.'

'Yes, Augustus.'

'So, Maglorix has bolted from his hole and we must pursue. Like a fox, hunting a hare, being in turn chased by a pack of hounds. The chase is on, Silus.'

'Yes, Augustus. What do you want to do with the Caledonian? I suppose he may fetch a handsome ransom.'

Caracalla drew his gladius and in one smooth motion thrust it downwards into the gap between shoulder and neck, deep into Guthor's chest. A gladiator's killing blow. Guthor died with barely a sound.

'My father gave orders,' said Caracalla. 'No one is to be left alive.'

He handed his sword to Papinianus, who handed it to a Praetorian, who cleaned it on his red cloak, and offered it back.

Caracalla remounted with an athletic leap. 'Papinianus, we need to stop these bastards before they cross the vallum Hadriani and start causing havoc in the Roman province. Give the order to assemble, Papinianus. Forced marching until we catch them.'

Maglorix's host was not hard to track. It was impossible to hide the passage of that many men, even in the woods and marshes, the valleys and hills of the inhospitable Caledonian countryside. Like the other scouts, Silus and Atius ranged ahead of Caracalla's legions, seeking out the quickest marching routes, alert for sites that would afford the enemy a good opportunity for ambush.

The Maeatae and Caledonians tried to make things hard for the pursing Roman forces, and the scouts had to be on their toes. Various traps were set on the main marching routes. In one place the path was sprinkled with caltrops – small ones for men and large ones for horses hidden beneath the mulch of the previous winter's leaf fall, and a small number of men and mounts were put out of action by the spikes, lacerating tendons or penetrating soles. At other points on the route, spiked pits covered with branches had been dug, and thin cords strung between trees at neck height to decapitate an incautiously fast rider, or at ankle height to break horses' legs.

One time, a group of scouts came across a small herd of cows wandering a short distance away. Mindful of the supply problems that always dogged an army in foreign fields, they rode off to round them up, straight into a Maeatae ambush. Four were killed in the initial hail of arrows, and three were captured. The screams as they were tortured taunted the marching Romans, who muttered curses and wards against evil, and complained to each other that they didn't belong in that accursed country anyway. Scouts were dispatched to rescue them, but only ever found the traces of a freshly vacated camp.

Caracalla heard the effect the haunting sounds were having on his men, and summoned Silus and Atius.

'Find those men and free them, or put an end to their suffering,' he commanded.

Silus and Atius tracked alongside the army on foot, waiting for the torture to start up again. When the piercing screams began again, they moved quickly, darting through the brush like a hare avoiding an eagle. The barbarians were encamped a half mile from the Roman advance, near enough that the tortured prisoners could be heard by the Roman soldiers.

Silus approached them to within a few feet without detection, and peered out between the branches of a holly bush. Atius crept up behind him. Silus counted five barbarians with their lean ponies tied up close to hand. He held up five fingers to Atius and pointed out their locations.

The three Roman prisoners were trussed like chickens ready for the oven. Two were gagged, lying motionless in the dirt, only their gently moving chests indicating life. Their weapons and armour were gone, their tunics torn and bloody, and gashes, lacerations and burns showed through the holes in their clothing. One was missing a hand, the stump unbandaged, kept alive by a tourniquet on his forearm, while the other had oozing red wounds where his ears should be.

The third Roman was being held upright by two of the barbarians, and another barbarian stood behind him, a strong arm clamped around his neck, his head pulled back by the hair. The apparent leader of the group held a dry stick before the prisoner's face. Then, as Silus and Atius watched in horror, he pushed the stick into the prisoner's eye.

Up close the screams were shrill and piercing, and Silus had to force himself not to look away. When the stick was withdrawn, blood and a clear liquid ran down the prisoner's face. The screams subsided into hacking sobs, and Atius whispered into Silus' ear, 'There are too many. We need to go for help.'

Silus shook his head. 'By the time we get back, these bastards will have disappeared again. They know they can't stay in one place for long. You heard our orders. We need to end this.'

He nocked an arrow to his bow, and indicated he would target the earless prisoner. Atius took aim at the one-handed one. In perfect synchronisation, they let fly. The prisoners cried out as the arrows flew true and pierced their chests, struggling in their bonds as they bled and wheezed and coughed up red fluid.

The barbarians looked around in alarm, reaching for their spears as they searched for the source of the attack. The prisoner who had just had his eye gouged out was let go, and he stumbled onto his knees, where he began to howl again.

With no need for verbal communication, they both nocked another arrow and loosed them into the miserable Roman. He tumbled over backwards, two shafts protruding from his chest and was still.

One of the barbarians spotted the movement of their release in the bushes, and pointed and shouted to his comrades. Silus and Atius shouldered their bows, turned and ran. They made no attempt at discretion, just put their heads down, ignoring the branches and thorns that ripped at their clothes and skin as they sprinted through the undergrowth.

For a while the pursuers seemed to grow closer. These barbarians were fit and fast. But the shouts of anger abruptly stopped. Silus knew that they would not chase them too near to the Roman army for fear of being captured in turn, and figured they had pursued them as far as they dared. He tugged Atius' elbow to slow him down. They stopped and put their hands on their knees, sucking air back into their lungs.

'Those bastards will get away to do this to some other poor sod,' said Atius.

'Maybe,' said Silus. 'Let's hope no one else is as stupid as the last lot of sods. But at least those sods aren't upsetting the lads any more.'

Atius scowled, then marched backwards to the camp. Silus watched his retreating back, then followed.

—

Ultimately the ambushes and traps and tortured prisoners had no effect on the fighting power of Caracalla's army. The numbers killed or incapacitated were a tiny proportion of the whole of that enormous force. But it slowed them down and sapped their morale. The veterans of the last campaign reminisced glumly about the toll taken by the underhand tactics of the barbarians on the army led by Severus the previous year, scaring the new recruits. And the frequent halts to clear traps or to scout areas of possible ambush reduced the marching speed.

They reached the wall of Antoninus at the site of the fort immediately west of Voltanio. There were signs of a battle, but it had been short and bloody. The Roman auxiliaries left behind as a garrison were too few in number and had had too little time to repair the defences to provide much resistance to Maglorix's horde. What new defences had been raised, or what had not been set on fire on Maglorix's previous assault on the wall, had been reduced to charred timber and ash.

A pyre had been made in the centre of the fort, around which shields and swords had been placed, and some pots of honey and oil. Skeletons were visible amongst the still smouldering cinders, but they were few. Silus could picture the druids giving their honoured dead their funerary rites, waving his carved aspen rod and chanting instructions on how to reach the next world.

The Roman corpses had been left where they had fallen, for the carrion feeders.

Silus glumly watched the party detailed to collect the Roman fallen and give them an honourable cremation. At least they hadn't passed back through Voltanio. He didn't know if he could have borne to see his old base destroyed again, the garrison slaughtered.

They didn't tarry. As soon as the bodies had been dealt with, respectfully but efficiently, Caracalla ordered the army to march once more. From this point on it was easy to pick up the broad Roman road that ran from the wall of Antoninus to the wall of Hadrianus and beyond to Eboracum. No longer on rough terrain, no longer as vulnerable to Maglorix's surprises, their marching speed increased considerably.

Even after leaving the supply wagons behind, with a sizeable guard of course, and being able to march faster and for longer each day by reusing the marching camps they had made on their outward-bound journey, it became clear as days went by that they were gaining on Maglorix's host too slowly, if at all.

One evening, Caracalla summoned Silus and Atius to his Praetorium. When the Praetorian guard that had fetched them escorted them into the Imperial presence, they found Caracalla and Papinianus poring over a map. Silus and Atius stood at attention, ignored for the time being.

'We have one days' food left, Augustus,' Papinianus was saying. 'The men could carry no more on their backs. We should wait for the wagons to catch up.'

'We will halve the rations.'

'Augustus, the men cannot maintain a forced march on empty stomachs.'

Caracalla banged his fist on the table.

'Prefect, do not presume to question me!'

Papinianus' tone became conciliatory.

'Augustus, I do not question, I merely point out the difficulty.'

'The difficulty, dear Prefect, is that Maglorix will reach the vallum Hadriani in two days, and we will reach it in three. If they are not held there long enough for us to overtake them, they will be into the Roman province proper, wreaking havoc among the Roman towns and marching on my Imperial father and brother in Eboracum while we sit on our hairy arses waiting for the wagons to catch up.'

Papinianus bowed his head, saying nothing. Caracalla looked up, seeming to notice Silus and Atius for the first time. He glared at them, and for a moment, Silus felt as if the co-Emperor was thinking that all this was Silus' fault.

'You two, we need you to get word to the vallum Hadriani. We have been discussing the route Maglorix is likely to take. Will the barbarians attempt to cross the wall at Cilurnum, so they can use the bridge across the River Vedra?'

Silus hesitated. Was the ruler of the world really asking for his opinion?

'Yes, Augustus,' said Atius, and Silus groaned inwardly at the temerity of his outspoken friend. 'They know they are being pursued. Their goal is to strike Eboracum and end the invasion by killing your father. Speed is of the essence to them. Cilurnum and its bridge offer them the quickest route into the province.'

Caracalla smiled. 'It was a rhetorical question, soldier, but your reasoning accords with my own. You two are to get word to Cilurnum that the enemy will be upon them. You will need to bypass Maglorix's army, or ride through the enemy lines. Cilurnum is to gather what forces it can from along the wall. Its orders are to hold the barbarians in the field until I arrive with the legions. They are to stand fast, no matter what the cost, until the last man falls, should it come to that. Do you understand?'

'Yes, Augustus.'

Caracalla handed Silus a scroll, closed with the Imperial seal. 'My orders in writing. Put them in the hands of the cavalry commander at Cilurnum.'

'Yes, Augustus.'

'Take the swiftest horses we have. The more warning you can give Cilurnum, the more prepared they will be. Dismissed.'

Silus and Atius bowed deep, and the Praetorian guard escorted them back out.

Silus took a deep breath of the cool evening air.

'Haven't we already done our duty?' muttered Atius.

'I think the Emperor likes us,' said Silus. 'Unfortunately.'

–

Cilurnum fort was primarily a cavalry fort, garrisoned by the 500-strong Ala II Asturum, a cavalry wing originally recruited from the Astures tribe in Hispania. It was designed to protect the important bridge over the River Vedra, a useful natural defence against barbarian armies and raiding parties. Built in the usual rectangular shape, the fort had been continually occupied since it was first constructed around ninety years earlier at the same time as the vallum Hadriani. Compared to the forts and the wall of Antoninus, which were only occupied for about eight years after the completion of the wall before being abandoned during the reign of the Emperor Marcus Aurelius, and only recently having been reoccupied by Severus, the forts and vallum Hadriani felt more solid and substantial. The vallum Hadriani itself was stone, unlike the turf wall of Antoninus.

The fort had benefited from decades of improvements from its successive occupants.

The fort protruded north of the wall, with three gates on the north side and one to the south. The gates were double-portalled to allow two wheeled vehicles through at once, with a central spine separating the two portals. They were flanked by two stone towers on which were situated ballistae capable of firing huge bolts up to five hundred yards, far enough to reach halfway to the nearest milecastle fortlet, and so provide continuous cover along the whole length of the wall. The stones used to construct the gates were much larger than those used in the walls of the fort, resistant to most forms of attack employed by the barbarians.

But, despite the awe-inspiring sight of the massive fortification, which stretched from one coast to another, the vallum Hadriani was not actually designed as a defensive structure. Partly political – a way of cowing the natives with a display of Roman might – and partly offensive, the wall made incursions into the Roman province difficult but not impossible. The mutually reinforcing forts and milecastles were designed more for counterattacks. Assailants would be trapped against the wall and held by the defenders while reinforcements from the adjacent milecastles attacked from the flanks. For this reason, too, the garrisons were proportionately heavy in cavalry, fast and mobile for swift retaliation. The legionaries and auxiliaries of the vallum Hadriani could hit back at any invaders so hard that they would never dare attack in the first place.

That was the theory anyway.

Standing on the walkway at the top of the wall abutting the northern gate, the rising sun bathing the right side of his face, Silus looked out across thousands of barbarians yelling and screaming for Roman blood, and worried that the whole principle was a load of bollocks.

The headlong race to catch up with and bypass Maglorix's army had taken all of Silus' extensive stealth skills and all of his limited riding skills. On three occasions as they skirted the barbarian horde, they were detected and chased. The barbarian warriors rode short wiry ponies, which were suited to cold winters and were easily manoeuvrable in battlefield skirmishes, but were not as fast as the Roman horses used by the messenger services, which Silus and Atius had taken from a cavalry wing. Although arrows had whistled past them and even grazed Atius' upper arm once, they had managed to outrun their pursuit largely unscathed.

They had reached Cilurnum the night before, half a day ahead of the barbarians. The fort prefect, an Italian aristocrat called Gaius Sicinius, had paled on reading the message from Caracalla, and Silus wondered if the man had the mettle to deal with this crisis. But Sicinius had responded promptly and decisively. He had dispatched fast messengers to neighbouring forts and milecastles to send reinforcements to concentrate their force in Cilurnum. He had his troops gathering and stockpiling ammunition and anti-siege materials, making last minute repairs to armour and weapons. And though initially he did not want to divert the resources for this, at Silus' urging he sent word to warn the local civilians to flee south.

The result was that Cilurnum, while still woefully unprepared for a prolonged siege, was in much better shape than the garrison at Voltanio had been at the time of Maglorix's surprise attack.

But the force confronting them was vastly larger, some ten times the size. Conventional military wisdom was that an attacking force needed to be only three times the size of a defending force to overcome the defenders. Given time it would easily overwhelm the defences, raze the fort and burst through into Britannia province.

Time. That was the critical factor here. Maglorix needed to defeat the defenders quickly, before Caracalla's army arrived. The defenders of Cilurnum had to hold the barbarians for the same length of time.

Maglorix could have changed the location of his attack, probing for weaknesses further along the wall, or attempting to cross the wall itself at a position halfway between two forts. But crossing the wall using ladders would be very time consuming for such a large horde and risked him being caught with his force split on either side of the wall. Probing defences would take time and would lead them away from the broad Roman road and the bridge over the river Vedra that would take them rapidly down to Eboracum, their goal.

So it all came down to Cilurnum. The defenders here had to hold the barbarians for one day. If they failed, not only would they be slaughtered, but the whole province would pay for it.

Atius stood by Silus' side, bow slung loosely over his shoulder, a score of arrows at his feet. On the other side was another auxiliary archer – smooth-chinned, pale and sweating. Few of the defenders would have seen large scale battles such as this. Most would have plenty of experience of patrols in enemy territory, skirmishes and raids, but this was on a totally different scale.

'What's your name?' said Silus to the man on his right.

'Julius Vitalis,' said the young man.

'How many winters have you?'

'Nineteen.' He jutted his chin forward defiantly, inviting a comment about his youth. Silus didn't bite.

'We are going to get through this, Vitalis. For the Emperor, and the people of the province of Britannia.'

'Yes, sir.'

'I'm not your commander. Are you any good with that thing?'

'I can hit a moving hare at two hundred yards.'

Silus doubted that, but he nodded encouragingly.

'Make sure each arrow counts. And if you see anyone who looks like they are bossing the others around, take him out.'

'Yes, sir.'

'Boy, I'm really not your commanding officer. Just another poor sap out here trying to do his duty.'

'Yes, sir.'

Silus sighed and turned his gaze back to the barbarians.

'How do you think they will play it?' asked Atius.

'It's got to be a rush job. They are getting their battle lust up. Once Maglorix judges the time is right, he will send them on a suicidal dash to scale the walls and breach the gates. He needs to use his numbers to overwhelm us.'

'And? Do you think he can?'

Silus shrugged. 'We'll know soon.'

'Soldiers of Cilurnum.' Sicinius' voice reached them from below, and they turned to see the fort commander standing before the arrayed reserve of mounted and dismounted cavalry that stood behind the northern gates. His accent was Italian and rather high class, but it carried well enough. 'We face formidable odds. But we have been given a task by the Emperor Antoninus himself to hold here at all costs. The province of Britannia, our Emperors, our comrades, our civilian families and friends are all relying on us. We are soldiers of Rome. We will not fail!'

A huge roar echoed up from the courtyard and down from the walls and towers. Atius and Vitalis roared too, and Silus found himself joining in. It was not only the barbarians whose blood was up. He hoped the attack would not be too long in coming. Waiting was the worst.

Maglorix did not disappoint him. The answering roar from the Maeatae and Caledonian horde was blood-curdling. They beat their spears on their shields, screamed curses, thumped their chests and tore their hair in fury. Then, at an unseen command, they charged.

'Remember,' said Silus. 'Don't waste them. You may be able to hit a hare at two hundred yards, but these bastards will be a lot closer. Speed is what counts. Wait for it.'

Silus, Atius and Vitalis, like the rest of the archers along the wall, nocked arrows and half drew, waiting for the charging barbarians to come into range.

Vitalis loosed first. Silus was about to admonish him, but saw that his first shot had taken down a giant barbarian who had got ahead of his fellows. A neat shot, dead centre in the chest. Silus picked a target, pulled back and let fly. He took his man in the eye. Silus couldn't help but look across at Vitalis, a little smug at his accuracy. The young soldier paid no attention, though, taking aim again and shooting another warrior through the neck.

Atius held fire. He had the range but not the accuracy of his colleagues. As soon as he was confident though, he added his own missiles to the hail.

From the towers on either side of the gate, ballistae shot enormous bolts into the melee, spearing one, two or even three warriors at once. More ballista bolts fired into the flanks from the adjacent milecastles, shooting at the extremities of their range, but not needing accuracy against the tightly packed barbarians.

Too many made it to the walls. Some carried ladders, roughly constructed from tall saplings with the branches hacked off and tied on cross ways to make the rungs, and some carried poles which could simply be rested against the wall and shinned up as if climbing a tree.

The archers directed their aim at those carrying the ladders and poles, but as quickly as they were shot down, their comrades picked up the climbing equipment and continued. Soon the ladders and poles were slamming against the walls. The archers continued firing as the first barbarians started their ascent. Some auxiliaries and legionaries manning the walls used long poles of their own to push the ladders backwards, while others hurled rocks, masonry and burning pieces of wood onto the heads of the attackers.

The effect was tremendous. Maeatae and Caledonian warriors screamed as they fell off their ladders from a great height, breaking their backs and skulls on impact with the ground. Others crumpled, broken, under the solid stone landing on them from above, or ran screaming with their hair on fire.

Silus heard a commotion to his right. The barbarians had brought up a ram. Again, it was not constructed to Roman standards; it was just a hefty tree trunk with the branches cut short to make hand holds. A dozen warriors held it at waist height and charged the main gates at full tilt. One or two went down to arrow and sling shots, but the ram impacted the gates with an enormous thud that Silus could feel through his feet as much as hear.

The gates shifted inward a little, then recoiled back. The barbarians backed up to charge again, with more warriors taking the positions of their fallen comrades. Once again they crashed into the gate, and Silus winced as the sound of splintering wood cracked through the air. This time, however, the defenders on the gates poured boiling oil onto the ram and those holding it. All those who were touched by the oil screamed at the excruciating heat and abandoned the attack. Then archers sent fire arrows down onto the oil-drenched ram which promptly ignited, making it unusable.

A horn sounded from the enemy lines, and reluctantly and with ill-discipline, the barbarians slowly withdrew beyond arrow range. The ballistae could have continued to make a nuisance of themselves, but Sicinius had obviously ordered them to conserve their ammunition for when the targets were near enough to ensure accuracy, as well as to help break the charge of the next wave.

Silus took a long drink of water from his bottle and passed it to Atius and Vitalis. He called down for more ammunition, and a young auxiliary ran up the steps to the wall with some bundles of arrows, which he dumped at their feet. Silus watched the barbarians, squinting into their ranks. The druids were at the back, chanting to the sky and screaming at the warriors, no doubt issuing threats and promises of curses or glory from the gods for the cowards and heroes of the day. Silus wondered how many attacks they would have to endure before Caracalla arrived. Would the Emperor march his men through the night, or would he camp once the sun fell, as centuries of Roman military doctrine dictated? It could mean the difference between the Emperor arriving at a fort still being defended, or finding one destroyed, with a barbarian horde loose in Britannia.

The next attack came after the flames on the ram had died down. It started in the same way: the banging of spears on shields, war cries, horns – everything that could make a noise to intimidate the defenders. Silus glanced sidelong at Vitalis, and saw the tip of the arrow on the young man's half drawn bow was trembling. Silus put a reassuring hand on his shoulder.

'You're doing well, boy. The Emperor would be proud. Keep it up.'

The charge came, but this time accompanied by slingshots and arrows from the attackers. Silus felt a stone zing past here and ducked instinctively, even though he knew that by the time he had heard it, it was too late. A dozen yards to Silus' left, a defender took a slingshot in the mouth and toppled backwards into the courtyard below, where he lay, crying wordlessly, limbs at unnatural angles, until a medicus and his assistant dragged him off to the valetudinarium. More projectiles whizzed past them, and all around the walls, defenders fell, back into the fort where, if not already dead, they stood a chance of survival, or outwards where they were quickly killed by the spears of the barbarians as they reached the walls.

Fire arrows arced out from the barbarian archers, the tips wrapped in ignited oil-soaked cloth. The sun was high in the sky now, so the visual effect was not as profound as it would have been in twilight. The physical effect was the same, though, as they impacted the wooden gates and started to burn.

The defenders were prepared though. The gates had already been soaked before the barbarians arrived, and although they were drying out as the day warmed up, there were plenty of buckets of water in reserve to douse the flames. Some of the defenders fell to slingshots as they leaned over to slosh water down the gates, and one was struck by a fire arrow and fell dramatically, the flaming oil igniting his clothes. His cries were cut short as he hit the ground, where his corpse lay burning.

Another ram was brought up, as well as more ladders. Maeatae and Caledonians swarmed up the ladders as the ram thudded into the gates. The archers split their fire between those scaling the walls and those trying to smash in the gates. The loss of either would be disastrous. A breach in the gates would allow the attackers to pour in and use their over-whelming numbers. If they gained the walls, they could fire slingshots and arrows down into the ranks of defending soldiers and slaughter them without trading blows.

The division of focus of the archers between the two sets of attackers reduced the effectiveness of the defence. For every ram bearer struck down, another was swift to take his place, and for every ladder pushed over backwards, or barbarian trying to climb up felled with a rock or arrow, replacements came instantaneously. Maglorix was clearly throwing everything into this assault, doubtlessly casting fearful glances behind him to see if Caracalla was upon them yet.

A wild-haired, tattooed Caledonian tribesman suddenly appeared over the wall in front of Silus as he was taking aim at one of the ram-bearers. The barbarian carried an axe in one hand, and as he hauled himself up over the parapet, he swung at Silus' head. Silus ducked and his arrow flew wild. The barbarian vaulted onto the walkway, and charged at Silus, axe swinging wildly, forcing Silus to jump backwards. Behind the barbarian, another head poked over the wall at the top of the ladder. Vitalis shot him point blank in the face, but another appeared even before the previous attacker's screams were cut short by the fall to the ground. As he drew his sword, Silus backed into Atius, who likewise had his sword out, and was confronting a barbarian who had ascended another ladder to Silus' right. Wordlessly, with just grunts and exhalations, the two friends fought back to back, ducking blows and thrusting with short swords into exposed body parts.

The attackers had not been able to carry shields and weapons up the walls, and eschewing armour, they were sorely exposed. Silus killed one with a thrust to the guts. Stab, twist, pull, kick. He fell into the courtyard below. The narrow walkway at the top of the wall only allowed the invaders to attack single file, and so Silus engaged each attacker in single-handed combat, one on one. He had the advantage: armour, shield, and low cunning honed in a hundred skirmishes while fighting for his life in enemy territory. One barbarian went down to a sword thrust to the neck, while another crumpled under a kick to the knee from Silus' hob-nailed boot that caused him to topple into the fort, where he was swiftly dispatched with a long cavalry sword.

But it was tiring, and more were coming up the two ladders that had not yet been pushed back. Then he saw a relief force, a score of dismounted cavalry, racing up the steps on the inside of the wall. He traded sword blows with a chunky red-haired Caledonian, chest inked with tribal tattoos. A blow grazed his upper thigh, slicing into flesh but failing to penetrate. Silus grunted, his shield dropping for a moment. He locked eyes with his opponent and saw a momentary gleam of triumph there. Then a spatha spitted him from behind.

The cavalry auxiliaries swiftly cleared the walls. It was not a form of fighting they were used to, but at the end of the day, killing was killing, and they had enough of a local superiority in numbers to push the barbarians back and thrust the ladders away.

The defenders had been neglecting the ram as they fought the barbarians who had reached the parapet at multiple points around the fort. The walls shuddered under each crashing impact of the ram, and the gates bent. Silus saw that some parts of the gate were buckling inwards, split by great cracks. But they held, for now.

Silus ignored the pain in his thigh and returned his fire on the barbarians smashing the ram forwards. The attack on the walls petered out, and with the full fire of arrows, slings, rock and ballistae turned onto the enemies assaulting the gates, it soon became impossible for enough barbarians to hold onto the ram, and they dropped it and ran back to their own lines, out of range.

As the noise of battle died down, except for the jeers from the Roman side at the failed attack and the answering curses from the Maeatae and Caledonians, Silus took a few deep breaths to slow his heart. His hands trembled from fatigue and fear, and he clenched his fists so it didn't show.

Vitalis was unharmed but pale, legs trembling and teeth chattering. Atius looked tired, but had a satisfied smile on his face, like he had just won a sporting contest. Silus shook his head.

Atius noted the blood flowing freely from Silus' leg, and made a tutting noise.

'Bit careless, friend.' He looked around, and shouted, 'Anyone got a spare bandage?'

A nearby auxiliary tossed him a rolled-up cloth bandage. Without asking permission, Atius pulled Silus' mail vest up around his waist, and bandaged the wound tight.

'Make sure you see a medicus after the battle and get some cobwebs, honey and vinegar on that,' he said. 'If you die of gangrene, I'll kill you.'

Silus smiled weakly, and looked out from the walls. The sun was well past its zenith now. The base of the walls was scattered with dead, mainly Maeatae and Caledonian, but also many

Romans. Beyond, though, out of range of slings and arrows, was still a vast number of barbarian warriors, angry now as a provoked swarm of wasps.

The low twang of a firing ballista could be heard sporadically, but the missiles were more of an irritant than a cause of serious attrition. The rate of fire, and the accuracy at that distance, were both too low.

Maglorix clearly had little experience with siege warfare. The previous raid on Voltanio and the scuffles with rival hill-forts were completely different in scale from a full-frontal attack on a well-defended, well-prepared fort on the wall of Hadrianus.

But he was a quick learner and he still had numbers on his side, if not time. However, he couldn't afford to waste men needlessly. He needed a big army to pour into Britannia to wreak the havoc he craved. He could continue these assaults and wait for the inevitable but risk being caught by Caracalla. Or he could try something else.

Silus squinted into the distance, trying to make out the nature of the activity that was taking place in the barbarian camp. A large number of trees had been felled and were being dragged together. They were tall, at least twenty to thirty feet, thick-trunked and still covered in branches and leaves. Silus thought at first that they were just making more rams, but Maglorix had more imagination. The trees were trimmed and lashed together with thick ropes, making a broad platform like a raft. But the fort and wall were still between the barbarians and the river, so that couldn't be its purpose. Then it struck him.

'It's a ramp. To reach to the top of the walls.'

Atius looked at his friend quizzically. 'Is it tall enough?'

Silus remembered his father trying to teach him mathematics. There was an old Greek called Pythagoras or something similar. Silus frowned, trying to recall the details, doing the calculation in his head. The square on the hypotenuse something something. If the walls were sixteen feet high and they were going to put a ramp against them with a one-to-one incline...

'Yes,' he said, with more confidence than his maths justified. He was sure that was what they had in mind. 'I have to tell the Prefect.'

Silus pushed past Atius and ran down the steps, ignoring the curious looks he drew. Sicinius was talking to his second in command, directing the resupply of ammunition and organising a small group of engineers to reinforce the damaged gates with crosswise planks of wood and propped beams.

'Sir,' said Silus, a little breathless. Sicinius ignored him, yelling instead at a soldier who was taking a break from carrying rocks up the gates, leaning against a wall and breathing heavily.

'Sir,' said Silus insistently.

'What is it, Silus? I'm busy.'

'I know what they are planning.'

'Oh, really. Listen, you did a good job warning us in time. And you fought well today. I've noticed. But that doesn't make you an expert in siege tactics.'

'Sir, they are making a ramp. I'm sure of it. They are gathering trees and tying them together.'

'A ramp? Nonsense. They are just making more rams. We need to concentrate our efforts on reinforcing the gates.'

'No, we need to reinforce the walls. They are going to throw a broad ramp up, clamber up en masse and storm them.'

'These barbarians are stupid. They know nothing about taking a fortified position. It will be brute force attacks over and over until they wear us down.'

'No, sir.' Sicinius glared at Silus, angry at being contradicted, but Silus stood his ground and carried on. 'I know Maglorix. I have met him and fought with him. He is not stupid. He won't keep trying the same thing. He is in a hurry, but he can't just throw men away.'

Sicinius looked doubtful.

'Please, sir. We need to stop them on the walls.'

Sicinius considered then shook his head. 'No, the gates are the priority. That's where they will concentrate their next attack. Now get back to your post.'

Silus opened his mouth to protest further, then gave up and trudged back up the steps to his position on the wall. He leaned against the stonework, and retrieved some hard biscuit from his pack. He took a large bite, then offered the rest to Vitalis and Atius. Vitalis looked nauseous and shook his head, but Atius took the offering and wolfed it down.

Silus chewed his biscuit unenthusiastically, not hungry but knowing he would need the energy for the rest of the long day. He looked back out at the barbarians, watching the structure slowly being assembled. He was in no doubt; it was an enormous ramp that could be the basis for a massed assault on the walls. He sighed. Sicinius would realise and would have time to move men around when the assault started. It was just a shame he was wasting preparation time now on reinforcing the gates when he should be strengthening the defences on the walls.

Silus noticed a figure moving around in front of the wooden construction, waving his arms, seeming to direct things. A nobleman? Clan leader? He squinted and strained his eyes. Something about the way he moved...

Fucking Mars, Mithras and Isis. It was Maglorix.

Silus thumped Atius on the shoulder and pointed. Atius followed the direction he was indicating.

'Mother of Christos. Isn't that him?'

Silus nodded, gauging the distance through narrowed eyes. He pulled his bow off his shoulder, nocked an arrow, and drew experimentally. He estimated the strength of the wind, calculated the trajectory the arrow would need to arc up and back down into the barbarian leader. He drew the string back fully.

Then he let the tension out of the string, the tip of the arrow drooping down to the floor. Atius looked at him questioningly.

'It's too far. Fuck!'

Vitalis nodded. 'Even I couldn't hit him from here.'

Silus looked at him, half bemused at the scared young man's arrogance, but half appreciative of him now that he had seen him fight.

'What?' said Vitalis. 'You would need a ballista to reach him from here.'

Silus and Atius looked at each other, eyes widening as they both thought the same thing.

'Follow me,' said Silus to Atius. They hustled along the wall past a few archers and slingers who swore as their precious respite was disturbed.

They entered the side door of the tower next to the gate and climbed up to the platform at the top. Three auxiliaries were leaning against their ballista, taking it in turn to swig water from a skin. They looked at the two newcomers with suspicion.

'What do you want?' said the most senior, an optio.

'You busy, boys?' asked Silus. Their current state of inactivity suggested they weren't.

'We got orders to take pot shots when we like. Just to keep them stirred up. Don't want to waste ammunition at this range.'

Silus sized up the ballista. The machine was like a bow, but rotated ninety degrees so the angle the drawn bowstring made was parallel to the ground rather than perpendicular. On top of a stand sat a slider into which bolts were loaded. The bowstring was winched back, the strain taken by springs made of sinew ropes. Iron caps secured the springs, and these could be adjusted with pins for accuracy. The bolts were five feet long and weighed eight pounds and a direct hit could make a hole through the thickest armour and leave the victim a bloody wreck, no matter where on the body it hit.

'I've heard the ballista boys at Banna reckon they are the best in the whole of Britannia. They say they can put a bolt through a cat's eye at a hundred yards.'

The optio scoffed. 'The Banna lot couldn't hit an elephant at five feet.'

'So you guys are good with this thing?'

'We do alright.'

Silus looked over the parapet. Maglorix was still there, waving his hands. His heart pounded. These guys were not under his command; he couldn't order them to do anything. He could try to threaten them with a sword in their backs, but that wouldn't get the best out of them, and besides, there were three of them against only himself and Atius.

Feigning nonchalance, he indicated the distant figure of Maglorix.

'Reckon you could slot him?'

The optio narrowed his eyes as he weighed up the shot.

'Piece of piss. But why should I?'

'He looks important.'

The optio shrugged.

Silus let out a humourless laugh. 'Thought as much. You're all mouth.'

'If I say I can hit him, I can hit him.'

'Care to put some hard cash on that? A week's pay says you can't.'

'You're on.' The optio spat on his hand, Silus did likewise and they shook.

'You might want to hurry up about that. If he moves out of range before you get your act together, I still win.'

The optio gave Silus an angry glance, and gestured to his men to help. They placed the heavy bolt into the slider, then winched the bowstring back, the torsion coils taking up the strain, storing the immense energy that the men loaded into the machine. The ballista swivelled on a base, and its elevation could be altered by tilting the whole device. The optio carefully took aim, calculating distance and wind speed. Then he waited for the right moment to present itself.

Silus could feel his heart beating in his throat. Was this the moment he was finally revenged? He had hoped to be the one to end Maglorix personally, to look into his enemy's eyes as he slid a blade between his ribs. But this would do just fine. And if Maglorix died, and then the fort was overrun and Silus was killed in the assault, then that was fine too. Maybe he would join Sergia and Velua in Hades or the Elysian Fields or heaven or wherever the fuck you went after you died.

Maglorix stopped pacing, his back to the fort, bending over to inspect some part of the structure the barbarians were building.

The optio loosed the bolt.

There was an enormous twang as the torsion springs unwound, and the mechanism rattled loudly as the arms sprang forward and came to an abrupt halt.

The bolt was in the air for a heartbeat, two, three, arcing up and then down, eating up the distance to Maglorix at frightening speed. Silus held his breath.

-

Maglorix maintained an outward air of calm authority, while inwardly he raged. What he wouldn't give for a single Roman legion, with all their discipline and respect for orders. Trying to manage this confederation of unruly belligerent tribes, who had warred against each other for centuries, was like trying to herd a pack of wildcats.

He knew how short time was. In part, he blamed himself. He shouldn't have been so careless with the Roman prisoners. He knew that Silus could be wily, and he had been too confident that they would receive no aid from within the Maeatae camp, forgetting that there were some who had no reason to love him and his men. Their escape had meant word of their plans getting out sooner than he expected. But it would not matter if they could just breach these defences. Once through, there would be no fortification and no significant army to stop them from devastating the Roman province.

Many civilians would die as his warriors were set loose on the farms and villas and towns. He took satisfaction from this. The British tribes who had surrendered to the Romans and now lived softly with their baths and their imported wine and olives deserved no mercy. And when he reached Eboracum, the Emperor who had commanded the man who killed his father would kneel at his feet in abject surrender before Maglorix had him brutally murdered. He hadn't decided on the manner of his execution yet, but it would be both painful and humiliating.

But first he needed to get past this fort, which had proved surprisingly tough. Again, he had been complacent, his previous victories making him believe that the fort would be quickly crushed. He guessed that they had lost the element of surprise, and the fort had been reinforced. Even so, he had been dismayed to see his warriors beaten back, and the failure of the assaults on the walls and the gates had shaken him.

This would not fail though. It was time-consuming, and the Maeatae and Caledonians quarrelled about the division of labour, about the best wood to use, even about the best way to tie the ramp together. But once it was built, it would be unstoppable. The ramp itself would provide protection against arrows and slingshots, the freshly cut wood it was made from would retard any attempt to set it alight, and once it was thrown against the wall, his men could swarm up and overwhelm the numerically inferior defenders.

As long as it was all over before Caracalla arrived with the Roman army.

He stopped to talk to one of his men who was overseeing the construction. Taximagulus, his loyal lieutenant, stood in his accustomed position, behind him and to one side. Buan, his bodyguard, was a short distance away, talking to a warrior. Maglorix bent forward and took a grip of the rope holding the tree trunks together and pulled on it hard, testing the strength of the binding.

He heard a whistling sound. He started to straighten, to turn.

A huge force hit him in his back and he tumbled forward, sprawling against the wood, his bearded face scraping against the bark.

For a moment he lay still, winded. All around was stunned silence. Slowly he regained his feet.

Taximagulus lay face down in the dirt. A javelin-sized bolt pinned him to the ground, through his back and out the front of his chest. It still quivered with the vast energy it had contained before expending it in the Damnonian warrior.

Taximagulus made no movement. He had died instantly, thrusting his chief out of the way of the missile and taking the bolt instead. Maglorix stared at his friend and ally. Then he looked over to the fort. A man was looking out from the gate tower. Across the distance they locked eyes.

It was too far to make out detail. But Maglorix knew. It was Silus.

He threw his head back and let out a roar of rage and grief and anger. Then he picked up a spear and hurled it towards the fort.

It was a futile gesture, his projectile travelling only a fraction of the distance to his enemy. He howled again and raged at his men to redouble their efforts, then stalked further away from the fort, out of range.

–

The sun was below the horizon by the time the next attack finally began. A spectacular cloud pattern was lit from beneath, making the sky in the west look like molten iron in a black-smith's forge, ready to be poured out into the mould to cast a sword.

The die is cast, thought Silus as the wide wooden structure was hoisted upright by a score of warriors. Slowly, it advanced towards the walls. Two ballista bolts in succession fired into it, but the first passed straight through harmlessly, and the second simply hung there, buried in a trunk. The barbarians had given the ramp a flat base when held vertically, which allowed them to use a roller system to move it. This involved placing rounded logs in front, then retrieving them from behind when the structure had passed over, to replace them once more at the front. When the structure came into range, the archers and slingers joined in, but they had no effect on the integrity of the ramp itself, and fire arrows did not make the freshly cut wood catch fire. The warriors given the risky job of moving the rollers were exposed to fire, and several fell to missiles, but there was a seemingly endless supply of replacements.

Sicinius joined Silus on the wall to watch the approach, and grunted a grudging apology for his doubts. Ultimately, though, repositioning his forces was just a matter of inconvenience. The progress of the ramp was so slow it gave the prefect plenty of time to prepare. But how did you actually prepare against an assault like this?

The sky darkened. The final battle was at hand. They could only hold for so long. Now everything depended on Caracalla, and whether he had broken with military tradition and continued to march through the night. And if so, whether he would reach them in time. Silus had no doubt the battle would be over long before dawn.

Darkness had fallen by the time the ramp reached the walls. Its progress slowed as the range for the archers closed and they were able to pick off the men moving the rollers at will. But it never stopped, and eventually the warriors who had been standing behind the ramp, keeping it upright with long ropes, were given the order to release.

Like a score of trees being felled simultaneously, the ramp toppled forwards, slowly at first, then gathering momentum. Maglorix's maths had been up to the job. The ramp crashed down onto the top of the walls with a few feet to spare. Those defenders too slow or too unlucky were crushed under the impact.

A huge roar rose from the ranks of the Maeatae and Caledonian confederacy, and the waves of barbarians surged forward.

The first to clamber up the ramp were struck by a volley of arrows and slingshots, and most went down, rolling back down the slope or toppling off the sides. The few who made it to the top were quickly dispatched by the concentrated force of defenders. But wave after wave followed behind, and soon the Romans on the wall were engaged in vicious hand to hand combat. Axes and spears crashed into shields. Short swords plunged forward: stab, twist, pull back. The air was full of shouts of anger and screams of fear and pain.

Silus, Atius and Vitalis were stationed on the tower by the gates, and so were able to continue to rain fire down onto the barbarians climbing the ramp. Space on the parapet was limited, and there was a queue of defenders further round the walls and on the internal staircase, waiting to take the place of the fallen. But they were pitifully few compared to the overwhelming numbers of the attackers.

Slowly, the attackers gained the wall. First a foothold, with a small body of warriors fighting back to back. Then a larger group that the defenders desperately tried to force back over the walls.

Silus paused his firing. His drawing arm was become fatigued and his aim was suffering. Vitalis kept up a constant rate of fire, hitting more often than he missed, his youth giving him energy and endurance. Atius' strength also allowed him to keep firing, albeit with lower accuracy and rapidity.

Despite the darkness, Silus could see the hordes of attackers lining up to mount the ramp. The structure remained sturdy, the wood impervious to fire arrows. But it had to be destroyed, or they would all be soon overwhelmed.

He stared, thinking hard. The wood was non-flammable. But what about the horse-hair ropes that held it all together?

'Vitalis. Nock a fire arrow.'

Vitalis looked questioningly, but did as he was told.

'Can you see the ropes? Think you can hit them?'

In answer, Vitalis loosed the arrow. It struck the middle of a rope, severing a few strands, though not enough to weaken its tensile strength significantly. But then the rope started to smoulder, to catch. As Silus watched in hope, the rope ignited, then split apart.

It made no difference to the integrity of the ramp. It was lashed together by scores of the horse-hair bindings. But there were a lot of archers, and they had not yet found a use for the fire arrows that they had stored.

'Pass the word,' yelled Silus to all who could hear. 'Archers, the ropes are flammable. Aim for the ropes.'

Silus and Atius grabbed fire arrows – their cloth tips soaked in oil – ignited them, and fired.

At first the effect was negligible. But as word spread, as the archers began to realise the effect, more fire arrows were shot at the vulnerable bindings. Most missed. But a sufficient number were close enough that soon ropes were burning across the ramp.

The first trunk at the periphery of the ramp separated. It rolled sideways, spilling half a dozen warriors off the edge. The next trunk came loose soon afterwards, then another, and suddenly the whole structure fell apart.

It didn't collapse, as the individual trunks still rested against the wall. But they rolled wildly as warriors tried to climb, with many tumbling off. Those making it to the top slowed from a flood to a trickle. Sicinius, seeing the opportunity, threw his reserves against the pocket of warriors that still held part of the wall.

The archers and slingers continued to pick off warriors attempting to ascend the trunks. Silus took his time. Pick a

326

target, nock, close one eye, draw, let the string roll off your fingers. Repeat. His chest and arm muscles burnt, but he kept going.

Over the noise of the battle, he heard cries from far to his right. He looked over. The sentries stationed there were frantically waving to attract attention. He frowned, puzzled at what had worried them.

Then he saw the tops of ladders thumping against the wall.

Maglorix hadn't gambled all on one throw of the dice after all. While the defenders were fully occupied, he had sent another force around to take the wall on the opposite side of the fort. As Silus watched, barbarians began to swarm up the ladders and over the top of the parapet.

Silus looked around desperately. Sicinius was fully occupied with directing the defence against the ramp, and had not noticed the danger.

'Vitalis. Go to Sicinius and tell him the barbarians are coming over the east wall. Everyone else, follow me.'

Silus held no position of command here, but his authoritative voice and his actions held sway. A dozen auxiliaries, some bowmen and slingers, some infantry, followed him around the wall. They charged into the attacking barbarians with shields out, and several tribesmen were tipped backwards over the wall by the force of the impact.

Then it was the hard work of hand-to-hand combat. Advance, parry, thrust, withdraw. The barbarians here were fighting on two fronts, assailed from the north and south along the east wall. Compared to the melee still raging on the north wall, the combatants here were few in number, and the battle, real as it was to those in its midst, almost seemed a sideshow.

Almost. Because on the south section of the east wall were internal stairs leading down into the courtyard. Right next to the east gate. And when Silus glanced to his left, he could see tribesmen massing, readying themselves to swarm into the fort. He cried to the men around to redouble their efforts to force the invaders back, over the walls, off the ladders. And they succeeded. The barbarians gave ground, step by step, some retreating along the wall, some tossed over the side.

But to the south, the defenders were less numerous, and they were also being forced back. For each step forward Silus and his comrades took from the north, the Romans to the south were taking one back. Then suddenly, they broke.

A handful of Maeatae warriors charged down the steps towards the east gate while the rest held the Romans to the north back. Silus looked around to the north wall to see where Sicinius was. He could make out Vitalis talking to him urgently, pointing, and Sicinius turning to see the threat, dispatching men.

It was way too late.

The Maeatae reached the gate and engaged the half a dozen Roman defenders stationed before it. Silus disengaged from the battle and looked around desperately. The barbarians blocked access along the walkway to the stairs, and it was too high to jump down without serious injury. But there were no more attackers coming up the ladders.

'Atius, help me with this.' He indicated an abandoned ladder, and together they hauled it up the outside of the wall, then dropped it down the inside. With Atius following closely, he threw himself down the ladder, two rungs at a time. They hit the ground and sprinted for the gates. Four defenders were already down, dead or incapacitated. Three barbarians were lying supine or prone too, two of them unmoving. But six attackers still confronted just two defenders, who fought

328

desperately for their lives. As Silus and Atius arrived, one more defender fell to a spear thrust through the guts.

The two friends barrelled into two of the attackers from behind, sending them flying. Before they could rise, Silus and Atius had thrust daggers through their necks, and pulled them out with a sawing motion. The barbarians coughed out blood through the gaping wounds. Instantly, Silus and Atius were on their feet, short swords drawn. Two barbarians turned to confront them, one hefting an axe, one with a spear. Silus sized them up. They were typically large, dirty, with long straggly hair and beards, and blood was spattered across their bare torsos. They took a step forwards, then the spearman abruptly lunged at Atius, while the axeman swung at Silus' head.

Atius dodged, Silus ducked. They both counter-attacked, but the men they faced were competent fighters, maybe even hand-picked for their mission to open the gates while the main attack was ongoing. It was unconventional combat – none of them carrying shields, with mismatched weapons, like gladiators. Silus saw over the shoulder of his assailant the last defender of the gate being forced back. He thrust, thrust again, leapt backwards as the axe swung at his midriff, then caught his opponent with a stab through his side.

It wasn't a killing blow, just slicing the skin and muscles on the side of the barbarian's abdomen. It slowed him, but still he held Silus at bay, swinging his axe one-handed while clutching his side with the other hand. Next to him, Atius was struggling against the superior reach of the spear.

Then a spear found the upper thigh of the last defender of the gate. It buckled, he fell, and a second spear thrust through his chest pinned him to the ground. Desperately, Silus redoubled his efforts against the axeman, and a further thrust to the barbarian's armpit left his non-weapon arm hanging limp, blood streaming in rivulets down the inside and dripping from his fingertips. Still the man would not fall, fending him off with the shaft of his axe, displaying incredible endurance.

The blood loss told, though, and he dropped to his knees. Silus looked his opponent in the eyes, nodded, then thrust his sword downwards behind the collar bone into the chest. The barbarian died wordlessly. Silus raised his head to the barbarians at the gates, and watched helplessly as they lifted the cross bar that held the gates locked. He ran forwards, aware that Atius had finally defeated the spearman and was close behind him. The barbarians grunted with the effort of lifting the heavy wooden bar.

They reached the gates just as the bar toppled out of its seating and crashed to the floor. For a moment, the Romans and the barbarians stared at it, both sides as amazed as each other that it had actually happened.

Then the gates crashed open, and with a roar, the barbarians flooded in.

Silus and Atius stood their ground, lightly armoured, no shields, their short swords held forwards to fend off two score of charging, screaming warriors.

They might as well have tried to hold back an avalanche. The impact of the charge knocked Silus off his feet, and he fell onto his back winded. A tattooed warrior leered over him, lifted his spear and thrust down.

Just before the spear went through his guts, a figure hit the warrior in his midriff, arms outstretched, and the tip of the spear went through the muscle of his inner thigh. Silus let out a scream at the intense pain. A roar filled his ears, and for a moment he thought it came from within. Then he saw hob-nailed boots and Roman armour above him, the counter-attack pushing the barbarians back.

Atius finished off the warrior who had speared Silus, then came over to him, looking down on his friend with a face full of concern. He tried to draw the spear, but Silus shrieked and grabbed his arm. Instead, he pulled the spear out of the ground, leaving it buried in Silus' leg. Then he lifted his friend, threw him over his soldier, and retreated inwards away from the battle.

Silus fought to retain consciousness as his friend sawed away the spear on either side of the leg, then packed the wound with bandages. Weakly he tried to stop him.

'It's pointless,' he whispered. 'There are too many.'

The Roman counter-attack had pushed the barbarians back temporarily, but as Maglorix allocated more and more of his men to holding the gates they had gained, they were forced back, step by grudging step. Roman soldiers were masters of defence, interlocking shields to form barriers that the barbarians struggled to penetrate, but numbers told.

'They will be on us soon,' whispered Silus. 'It's over. Leave me.'

'Fuck you, Silus. What do you think I am? I ran once, because I was ordered to, and all my friends died. I'm not running again.'

Silus clutched his friend's arm and closed his eyes. He could feel himself nodding, like he was fighting to stay awake, despite the noise and the agony shooting up from his leg. Atius slapped his face.

'Stay awake, friend. This is no time for naps.'

Silus smiled weakly. 'It seems like the perfect time for a nap.'

Silus lay back, body relaxing. The sounds of battle came nearer and nearer, and Silus felt at peace. He would soon join Sergia and Velua. Wherever they were now, they would all be together. And that was fine.

Then he frowned. Something was different. The noise of the battle had changed. The Romans were cheering about something.

'Atius, what's going on?' Silus tried to sit up, groaned, but pushed himself upright nevertheless. There was commotion beyond the gates, beyond the fight. The barbarians were trying to fall back, but something was stopping them.

Atius got to his feet, drew up to his full height and stood on tiptoe. He let out a long whistle. 'Christos.'

'Atius, what the fuck is it?'

'The Emperor's here.'

The words sunk in slowly.

'Thank your God for me,' said Silus. And then he drifted away.

Chapter Sixteen

A shooting, excruciating pain in his leg brought him round, screaming hoarsely. He tried to sit up, but a heavy weight was pinning his chest down, and he couldn't move his arms and legs. His eyes flew wide open, and he found himself staring into Atius' grimacing face.

'Graaaagh,' he roared as he felt a wrenching in his thigh. 'Atius, what the... aaargh.'

Then there was a slipping, tearing feeling, and the pain changed in character to an agonising throb, his whole leg pulsing in time with his heartbeat. He felt firm pressure on his thigh, something being poked into a hole that shouldn't be there. Atius' face grew dim...

When he woke again, he was on his back in a cart, jolting painfully as the wheels hit potholes. His upper thigh was a steady, powerful ache, but below that he could feel nothing. He propped himself up onto one elbow and looked down at himself in a sudden panic. A feeling of relief flooded over him as he saw he still had both legs. He gripped his lower leg and was pleased that he could feel the pressure. The tight bandage around his wound must be restricting the blood supply to his lower leg, partially but not completely numbing it.

He looked to the soldier lying by his side. He was missing an arm, the stump wrapped in a carmine bandage. His muddy, stubbled face was blank, staring into the middle distance. Contemplating his future begging on the streets of Eboracum no doubt. He turned to his other side. The soldier had his midriff firmly wrapped in layers of stained cloth. He was pale, eyes closed, his breathing shallow. A gut wound, Silus surmised. He wondered why they were bothering to treat him. It would have been kinder to let him die on the battlefield than suffer the slow, agonising death that inevitably awaited him.

'Back with us, Silus?' came a voice from the front of the cart.

Silus looked over his shoulder to see Atius, seated by the driver, grinning down at him.

'Can't I ever be rid of you?'

Atius' smile broadened. 'Nope. Unfortunately for us both, we're stuck with each other, friend.' Atius clapped the driver on the shoulder. 'Time for a piss stop.'

The driver reined in the mules pulling the cart, and Atius hopped into the back to help Silus down. The one-armed man manoeuvred himself down. The gut-wounded soldier didn't stir.

Atius passed Silus a crutch. Silus waved it away, put his weight on his injured leg, and promptly collapsed. Atius grabbed him and held him upright, then reoffered the crutch. Silus took it grudgingly and positioned it under his shoulder. He limped a few yards from the cart, and fiddled around to prepare himself to urinate.

'Need any help there? Want me to hold something?'

'Fuck off, Atius. We aren't that good friends.'

Silus managed, sighing as he produced a strong stream. He shook, put himself away, then looked at Atius, frowning.

'Tell me then, friend. How fucked up am I?'

'Well there's good news and bad news.'

'Go on,' said Silus, guts clenching.

'The bad news is you are going to live, so I still have to put up with you. The good news is that you are going to be out of action for a couple of months at least. Lots of rest, beer and whores, and no hanging around in enemy territory in the pouring rain, freezing your bits off.'

'Will I heal fully?'

Atius' grin faltered. 'The medicus wouldn't commit. It's pretty bad. The muscle in your thigh is quite mashed. He was amazed the spear hadn't severed the big vessel near there – that would have killed you pretty quick. And of course, a couple of inches higher and we would be worrying about a different body part.'

Silus nodded. Atius was right. It could have been much worse. And now that his job was done, he could rest and recover with an easy mind. Then he frowned. His job was done, wasn't it?

'What happened, Atius? After Caracalla arrived?'

'It was a massacre. The defenders had all but collapsed, but once Caracalla's cavalry crashed into the barbarians from the rear, they broke and tried to run. The legions slaughtered almost every last one of them.'

'Almost?'

Atius opened his mouth, hesitated.

Silus lurched forward, grabbed his shoulder.

'Atius, fucking tell me. Is he dead?'

Silus shook his head. 'He was seen fleeing the battlefield with his bodyguard, heading back north into the depths of Caledonia.'

Silus grabbed Atius, two fists clutching his tunic, and yelled at him.

'How could you let him escape?' he yelled. 'How could you do it?' His head dropped. He buried his face in his friend's shoulder and wept. All the despair and loss, the pain and exhaustion, the misery and suffering he had endured poured out of him in an unstoppable flood. Atius held him, saying nothing, just letting the flood peak, then ebb away. Silus pulled back, breathing heavily, and roughly wiped the tears and snot from his face with his sleeve.

'It's not over,' he said. 'I will not rest until he is dead.'

'That's not your choice,' said Atius. 'We are to report to Oclatinius in Eboracum. Then you are to recuperate. After that, maybe—'

'Fuck maybe. That bastard will not live to breathe the air of the same land as me. I will end him.'

'Hey,' the cart driver shouted over at them. 'Hurry it up there.'

Atius helped Silus back into the cart. He sat, staring out at the road disappearing in the distance, his mind whirling.

By his side, the gut-wounded soldier had stopped breathing.

–

'I'll say when you are fit for duty, soldier,' said Oclatinius calmly.

'Sir, my leg is healed. The medicus said so himself.' Two months had passed since the injury in the battle of Cilurnum.

'Healed as good as it will get maybe. As good as before?' Oclatinius shook his head.

'Sir, I can walk ten miles with a fully loaded backpack. I can run a hundred yards in fifteen heartbeats. What more do you want of me?'

'What I want, soldier, is for you to obey orders.'

336

'Sir, I am sitting here on my arse while Caracalla leads the army around Caledonia, slaughtering every barbarian he meets, man, woman or child. The enemy are utterly defeated. And yet Maglorix, the one who has done us the most damage, remains alive, laughing at us.'

'I'm sure he isn't laughing, Silus.'

'Please, sir. Let me go and find him. Being confined to Eboracum is driving me insane.'

'Your friend Atius seems to be enjoying himself.'

Silus grimaced. 'Anywhere there is beer, gambling and fighting, he is happy. Besides, he is getting on rather well with Menenia.'

'I've noticed. Listen, it's out of my hands. I can't send you on some insane mission into the depths of enemy territory to chase a beaten cur who has had his teeth pulled. You will have more important work in the near future, mark my words.'

Silus considered asking about this important work, but decided Oclatinius was probably just trying to distract him.

'I'll appeal to the Emperor.'

Oclatinius barked a humourless laugh.

'Please, Silus. You're not thinking straight. Even if Severus would deign to see the likes of you, he is sick right now and is taking very few visitors. Caracalla is away, Papinianus with him. And Geta has no interest in military expeditions. Go back to your quarters. Continue to recover. Get fitter. Wait for Caracalla to return.'

'Sir—'

'Dismissed.'

Oclatinius looked down at his paperwork.

'Sir, please.'

Oclatinius did not look up.

337

Silus stood before him for a moment, tempted to reach across his desk and shake him. But arrest, trial and maybe execution for assaulting his commanding officer would not help him achieve his goal. He saluted, overly formal, whirled and left.

–

A month later, Caracalla rode back into Eboracum at the head of his triumphant army. A good proportion of his forces remained in Caledonia, garrisoning forts, repairing defences on both walls, mopping up any areas of resistance in the conquered regions, and devastating any settlements they found. Nevertheless, it was an impressive display of manpower that marched behind their Augustus back into the city that the Imperial family had chosen as their temporary capital.

Severus received his returning son, who was mounted on a fine black stallion, as a conquering hero inside the gates of the city, and lauded him to the cheering soldiers and civilians that had come to see the spectacle. Caracalla basked in the glow of the praise, sneaking glances at Domna who was mounted on Severus' right side. Geta, mounted to Severus' left, glowered, unable to disguise his resentment at his elder brother's success. Caracalla ignored him. This moment was his.

'Thank you, father,' said Caracalla, facing the old Emperor's throne. 'Your praise is welcome. And it is a blessing to see you looking better.'

Severus inclined his head. 'I do indeed feel much better. My gout still troubles me, but my chest is much eased. I have been sacrificing dutifully to Serapis, and the lord of the sun and of healing has seen fit to restore my health. I therefore thank you for your duty, and inform you that I am ready to retake my position as commander of the legions.'

Geta leaned forward, a smirk spreading across his face.

Caracalla's mouth dropped open. 'Father, the legions are mine.'

Severus frowned. 'My son, the legions are Rome's. And while we are co-Emperors, I am senior by length of service and age. And I am your paterfamilias.'

'But your health. Your gout—'

'I have been borne on campaign in a litter before. I can do so again. This is not a matter for debate. Now, let us return to the palace.'

Severus wheeled his horse, turning his back on his armed son. The crowd collectively held its breath, knowing the rumours that abounded about the apparent attempt on the old Emperor's life by his son at the Caledonian surrender the year before. But Caracalla simply bowed his head and followed in his father's wake.

-

'Damn him,' raged Caracalla, pacing the bedchamber. 'Damn him to Hades. He can't do this. He isn't strong enough. The army won't respect him. Why can't he retire gracefully? His dignitas, his auctoritas, they are so strong, but they will be hugely diminished if he persists in this plan.'

'He is a proud man,' said Julia Domna placatingly. She sat on the silk sheets, knees tucked up and to one side, leaning forward as she watched her furious lover and stepson with concern. 'You know this. He has been strong his entire life, and he has taken everything he wanted, whenever he wanted. Including the Empire. Including me.'

Caracalla grimaced. 'Don't remind me about the old man pawing at you.'

'It's nothing you don't know, Antoninus. I had a son with the man. How do you think Geta was produced?'

'I don't want to think about it. Nor of that weakling of a half-brother of mine.'

'Come here.' Domna patted the bed invitingly. 'Let me take your mind off everything.'

Caracalla continued to pace.

'So now we all sit around on our backsides, with the job nearly done. And if we don't finish it, it will be as if we were never here. They are like weeds these barbarians. Chop them down, and they grow back stronger. We need to uproot them so they are finished for generations to come.'

'Your father will lead the army, like he did last year. He may be infirm of body, but not of mind. The army will respect that.'

'So why aren't we marching out? We have been back a fortnight and there is no sign he is readying for war. We have defeated the Maeatae and their Caledonian allies, but Caledonia is full of unconquered tribes to the north and west who will rebel if given a moment's breathing space. We have seen their treachery already.'

Domna grabbed his wrist as he strode past the bed and pulled him off balance to lie beside her. Before he could protest, she pushed him onto his back and kissed him hard on the lips. He was tense for a moment, his hand on her chest between her breasts, pushing. Then he relaxed into the kiss, arms enveloping.

She held the kiss a long moment, her mouth and tongue moving against his, then her lips sliding to his ear. She whispered, no more than a breath.

'Make love to me, Antoninus.' He moved his bearded face to her neck, and she tilted her head to the side to give him access. One hand grasped her breast, feeling the nipple hard in

340

his palm. But his father's disapproving face swam before him, and he felt his nascent erection wilt. He rolled onto his back.

'Oh, to be Oedipus for a day.'

'You're halfway there.' She giggled, a light laugh that made his stomach lurch, and traced a fingertip through his hairy chest, showing no judgement or disappointment at his failure.

'Don't say that. You aren't my mother. You know what I am referring to. But I do love the old bastard. I wish him no harm, despite what people say.'

'He is an old man. You have seen and heard the omens. Patience. Soon everything will be yours. Including me.'

'Is that so? I thought I had to share everything with your son. Including your affections, albeit of a different nature.'

'Geta is my only son, and I love him unconditionally. But he is not a leader like you. At least not yet. He is young and impetuous, and his father hasn't trained him in the arts of war, like he did with you. Yes, you must share power with him, for that is your father's wish, and you must also share my affections, for what mother does not love her son? But you will be first. In everything.'

Her hand stroked over his belly, lower, lightly teasing his manhood, smiling as it hardened at her touch. She gripped it and pulled him on top of her, guiding him inside her. He groaned as she enveloped him, and for a while, all his frustrations were forgotten.

–

'I'm sitting here on my arse, Oclatinius, while that reptile sits somewhere safe in the depths of Caledonia, laughing at us.'

'I heard the same words from another recently, Augustus, and I will say to you what I said to him: I doubt very much that he is laughing.'

Caracalla stood and began to pace, his light breakfast of the finest Italian olives, shelled pistachio nuts and cold water lying untouched on the table.

'Maybe not laughing. But not being strangled to death in the arena for my revenge and the entertainment of the masses either.'

'No, Augustus,' acknowledged Oclatinius.

Caracalla grabbed some nuts, chewed angrily, then took a deep swig from his cup to wash them down.

'Who was this other, anyway?'

'Augustus?'

'The one that said Maglorix was laughing at us.'

'That was Gaius Sergius Silus, Augustus.'

Caracalla frowned. 'Him? Why does this man keep crossing my path?'

'Maybe because you have a mutual obsession with Maglorix. Or maybe because he is the most talented of the Arcani.'

Caracalla turned abruptly.

'Summon him.'

'Yes, Augustus.'

Oclatinius poked his head out of the door and snapped a command to one of the Praetorians on guard duty.

–

Silus stood, back straight as a pilum, teeth clenched to stop them chattering, knees pressed together so the tremble in his legs wouldn't be obvious. He didn't think he would ever get used to being in the presence of one of the co-Emperors – arguably the Augustus that the army looked up to the most.

Caracalla looked him up and down.

'You've had an eventful year.'

'Yes, Augustus.'

342

'You've assassinated a barbarian chief, provoked a war, survived an assault on the vallum Antonini, lost your family, joined the Arcani and assassinated a Caledonian spy, been captured by the Maeatae, escaped, warned me of the barbarian confederacy plan to invade Britannia province, then taken a leading part in the defence of the vallum Hadriani to delay the raid long enough for my forces to annihilate the enemy, during which you were badly wounded.'

Silus looked at his caligae. When he put it like that, it had been quite a year. He wondered how he would have coped with the loss of his family if his duty and his lust for revenge had not driven him to such lengths.

'Yes, Augustus. That's a fair summary.'

'Silus, most soldiers would feel they had earned an honourable discharge with a hefty pension for all their good work. You have done more in a few months than most will ever do in a lifetime. Yet despite all this, you are still unsatisfied?'

'Yes, Augustus.'

'And why is that?'

'Because the man who killed my family still lives.'

Caracalla nodded. 'The same fact causes me grief as well. I would like to be out there, hunting for him right now. Oclatinius has a network of Frumentarii, Exploratores, Speculatores, and Caledonian and Maeatae spies looking for him. We think we know where he is. But my father has me cooped up here, waiting for him to gather his strength and wits to lead the army out again.'

Oclatinius shot Caracalla a warning look for his unguarded words, but Caracalla was unrepentant.

'But Oclatinius here has a large degree of autonomy in his actions. I like it that way. It may be that Oclatinius will give you a mission to go into enemy territory once more to find and kill Maglorix and end his threat to the province forever.'

Oclatinius nodded. 'That is a definite possibility.'

Hope rose in Silus' heart. He looked from the Emperor to the spymaster, trying to read their expressions.

'This would be an unofficial mission. We are taking no action against the barbarians until my father is ready to march. If you returned, successful or unsuccessful, I cannot guarantee what your reception would be like.'

'When do I leave?'

Caracalla laughed and turned to Oclatinius.

'I can see why you have a soft spot for this one.'

'With respect, Augustus, I do not have a soft spot for him. But he is a useful asset, whether it is skill or luck.'

'Talk to Oclatinius, soldier, find out the latest intelligence, then go and kill that piece of shit.'

'With the greatest pleasure, Augustus.'

-

The old man looked up at them through watery, glaucomatous eyes, toothless gums working wordlessly. Atius grabbed him by the sparse hair at the back of his scalp, lifted him up, and punched him in the face again. The Caledonian elder fell backwards, his head thumping into the damp earth, and his eyes rolled up. Blood and snot dribbled from his nose, and his breathing was wet and bubbly.

Silus sighed. 'And now we question him?'

Atius looked abashed. 'He was pissing me off.'

'Maybe he genuinely doesn't know where Maglorix is.'

'Bollocks. I could see the look in his eyes. He was lying to us. I don't see what he has to gain though. Why doesn't he give up the bastard who brought all this down on them?'

Silus looked down at the old man. His ribs were prominent, arms and legs thin as javelins. Silus and Atius were getting used to seeing that look.

When Silus had told Atius about his mission, his friend had gone straight to Oclatinius and demanded to be allowed to join him. Oclatinius had agreed, amused at Atius' insistence at looking after his friend. He had provided them with all the information he had about Maglorix's movements and whereabouts. His network of spies, scouts and traitors had tracked the Maeatae chief's flight north and west from the vallum Hadriani, through the territory of the Votadini, who were allied with Rome, to the Selgovae, where he had sought sanctuary. Their chief, Sellic, knowing the war was a lost cause, had refused Maglorix shelter and sent him on his way, dispatching messengers to Rome to inform them of their enemy's flight, although he at least did him the small favour of not taking him prisoner to hand him over to the Romans.

From there, Maglorix had fled through the territory of the Damnonii and up the west coast to the Caledonii, where Argentocoxus, Chief of the Caledonian confederacy, had escorted him from his territories at the point of a spear. Finally, the grand alliance split into factions which were already fighting among themselves, Maglorix had retreated to his home, the only place where he could find any sort of welcome.

Silus and Atius had travelled a much more direct route, knowing roughly where Maglorix had ended up. Their journey had been quick. Once they left Britannia province, although the roads and tracks became less reliable and they had to make their way through forests and marshes, they rode without fear of attack. The Maeatae and Caledonians were well and truly broken, the cream of their warriors slaughtered at the vallum Hadriani, their people massacred, and their crops, livestock and stores destroyed. With winter coming, they were already starving. As they travelled, they heard stories, rumours, and solid leads about Maglorix's location. And as they narrowed their search, Silus began to believe he knew where his enemy was.

Atius dragged the old man to a nearby puddle and dunked his face into the cold muddy water. He came round, spluttering. Atius threw him onto his back, and the man propped himself on his elbow and spat.

'Let's try again,' said Atius. 'Silus, ask him once more.'

Silus sighed. 'Where is Maglorix?' he said in Brittonic.

The man shook his head. Atius drew his knife, and the man's eyes grew wide. He shuffled backwards as Atius advanced.

'Tell me, old man. Is Maglorix in Dùn Mhèad?'

The man stared at him, and his mouth fell open.

Atius looked at Silus suspiciously. 'What did you say to him?'

'I asked him if Maglorix was in Dùn Mhèad.'

'Well, it looks like the answer is yes. How did you know?'

Silus looked at his friend, and thought back to a time when he was a simple auxiliary scout and his family was still alive.

'Because that is where it all began.'

Chapter Seventeen

Maglorix stared at the bowl of soup in his hands. There was no meat, just some leaves and roots. It tasted of muddy water. The smoke from a cooking fire reached his nose. From somewhere behind him, a baby cried incessantly. No one made any attempt to succour it. It would die soon. Most of the young mothers' milk had dried up, and malnourished babies were beginning to fade. A wave of dysentery had swept through several families when a dead deer had been discovered and consumed. The flesh had been so rotten that even roasting it on a spit had not saved them from the illness that everyone knew accompanied eating decayed flesh.

Winter wasn't far. The leaves were turning. The sun did not reach as high into the sky any more. There was a chill in the air at dusk and dawn. He pulled his hooded cloak tighter around himself. He always seemed to feel cold these days, no matter with what strength the sun shone.

There was no food. The Romans had burnt their stocks of grain, slaughtered their cattle, ploughed up their crops, and burnt their homes. The countryside had been scoured of game and forest fruits. Now people were eating grass and roots, and even broken twigs. Anything to fill the painful emptiness of their bellies. Few in Caledonia would survive to see the spring thaw.

How had it come to this? Was it all his fault? Had he been full of righteous anger and pride, so determined to make the

Romans pay for their outrages that it had cost his people everything? Maybe it went back even further, to when Maglorix had been a boy and his people under his father had raided freely and frequently into the Roman province, stealing gold, cattle and slaves.

Or had the gods turned against them, sending Severus and Caracalla and their armies, letting them loose in their lands? Doing to the peoples of Caledonia what the peoples of Caledonia had done to the Romans, but on a much vaster scale?

'I curse you,' said Maglorix, out loud, his voice quiet but firm. 'Each and every god who has turned their back on me and my people. The hag, I curse you. The Aos-sídhe, I curse you. Esus, Teutates, Taranis, you abandoned me and your people. I curse you all.'

A few people turned to look at him. Lon the druid made a sour face. But none spoke up, and they all turned back to whatever it was they were doing to keep their mind off the hunger pangs. Some whittled sticks. A local elder sharpened his sword on a whetstone, a weapon it was unlikely he had wielded in anger for many years. Mothers held infants against them. No children played; they had no energy. No chickens clucked, no dogs barked, no cattle lowed. They were long gone.

He turned back to stare into his bowl. He didn't feel hungry, despite the length of time that had passed since he had consumed a proper meal. All he felt in his guts was a dull sickness.

Silus. That traitor to his countrymen. British, yet fighting for the Romans. If there was one man on whom he could lay the blame for everything, it was him. If he hadn't murdered his father, provoking him into rash actions in the name of revenge, they might have avoided this and made peace with the enemy. He clenched his jaw, gripping the bowl tight. Then sighed.

He could not summon the energy for anger. He took a sip from his bowl and swallowed with difficulty. Then he let the bowl slip from his fingers. It hit the floor, cracked, tipped. The watery broth pooled on the ground.

A murmur reached him, not loud – no energy for real interest or fear, just an acknowledgment of something happening. He looked up.

Two men, armed, fit, well fed and healthy, were striding into the village.

One spoke, in a loud clear voice, Brittonic, but tinged with a Roman accent.

'Where is Maglorix?'

—

Approaching Dùn Mhèad had brought back memories that provoked a flurry of emotions in Silus. This was where it had all started, that scouting mission that now seemed so long ago. When he was a simple explorator, when he had never met Oclatinius or Caracalla, when he still had a family...

They walked through the woods which Silus had previously fled through, carrying Maglorix's father's head. This time, he was careless about hiding their presence. He knew they had nothing to fear. Silus pointed out landmarks he recognised to Atius. Here was where he had camped, soaking wet, freezing and scared. Over there was where he had been hiding when he had first encountered Voteporix, Maglorix and Buan. And this was the spot where he had ambushed Voteporix and cut his head off.

Atius nodded in silent acknowledgement of each point of interest. His face was grim. The starvation and devastation of the civilians were affecting him, and his fierce loyalty to the Emperor was conflicting with his religious beliefs.

They strode up the slope to the hill fort. The palisade was gone, pulled down after a previous Roman assault. Some stakes still lay flat, broken or uprooted. Most had been taken for firewood. The civilians who had escaped the slaughter, with nowhere else to go, had returned to their ruined homes, to sit and wait for the approach of winter and death.

Just inside the boundary where the palisade had been, a young girl was sitting cross-legged, staring up at them. She had likely seen no more than six summers. Her red hair was long and straggly, with leaves and small twigs entwined. Her face was dirty, but there were no tear streaks through the grime. She must have finished all her crying. She looked up at them, eyes wide above hollow cheeks. Is this how I meet my end? she seemed to Silus to be thinking, with no fear, just a dim curiosity.

Silus turned his face from her, walked purposefully past her and into the settlement. A murmur of mild interest and concern went around the subdued Maeatae.

'Where is Maglorix?' he said in loud clear Brittonic Celtic.

A few more heads turned in his direction, but no one spoke. Then a large, bald-headed warrior, wearing a tattered tunic and bearing recently healed scars on arms and face, slowly, painfully stood. Silus recognised Buan and knew that Maglorix wouldn't be far. The chief's guard and friend limped towards them, spear held forwards, the tip trembling with the effort of presenting it.

Atius took two swift steps forward, brushed the outstretched spear aside with the outside of his arm, and thrust his dagger into Buan's belly. The huge barbarian gripped the hilt, pulling it from Atius' hands, and rolled forwards to lay still.

Another figure came towards them, waving his hands. High shaven forehead, long white hair, pointed nose. He no longer wore the flamboyant cloak and gaudy jewellery and he had become thinner, but it was easy to recognise Lon the druid.

'Curse you, Romans,' he hissed. 'Cailleach Bhéara, the hag, I call on you. Let these evil men never know peace.'

'Druid, you had some plans for us, as I recall.'

'The hag will make your eyeballs rot. She will make your testicles fill with pus and burst. She will make your cock—'

Atius drew his sword and in one smooth motion swept it horizontally. Lon fell to his knees, clutching his throat, blood spurting between his fingers. Atius watched dispassionately as he collapsed to one side.

Silus looked around. The barbarian people, all hope long ago leeched out of them, just watched.

'Maglorix!' roared Silus. 'Come and face us. Don't make us hunt you down like a scared weasel.'

For a moment, all was still. Then a figure in a hooded cloak looked up. He made no move to stand, but he gripped his hood at either side of his face, and after a moment's hesitation, pulled it back.

Silus let out a breath. Atius made to approach him, but Silus put a restraining hand on his chest.

'Wait here.'

'The man is a snake. Do not trust him.'

'Not any more,' said Silus. 'His poison has been milked out. His fangs pulled. Look at him. He's done.'

Silus approached him, his hands empty, arms swinging loose. He reached Maglorix, and looked down at him. Maybe it was his seated posture, but he no longer seemed to Silus to be as tall as he once was. Maglorix's long, curly red hair, magnificent when Silus had first met the Veniconian prince and smashed his hilt down upon his head, was now matted, the locks twisted into tangles of leaf and grit. His finely-toned body

351

had atrophied. The tattoos on his chest had become distorted as the skin had loosened when his pectoral muscles had shrunk.

But it was his eyes that captured Silus' gaze. They were empty, with no spark of fear or anger, capitulation or defiance. They just regarded Silus with no more interest than that of an old man sitting in his doorway watching the world go by as he waited to die.

They stayed like that for a long moment. Then Silus spoke.

'I'm sorry.'

Maglorix's eyes narrowed slightly. He tilted his head questioningly.

Silus gestured around him. 'All this. Your people. Your father.'

Maglorix shook his head. 'You are victorious. You are a true warrior. But the gods, yours and mine, decreed we must fight on opposite sides. Together, we could have been truly formidable.'

Silus nodded. 'You are a true warrior, too. You defied Rome, though you must have known deep down that it was hopeless.'

'Hope is too highly valued.' His voice sounded so pitiful that for a moment Silus wondered if, despite everything, he would shirk from what needed to be done. But Velua and Sergia dictated his actions.

'Stand up,' said Silus.

Maglorix took a breath, then let it out slowly. He put his hands on his knees, and levered himself upright. Silus looked around. Nearby were the Maeatae chief's spear and shield. He fetched them and handed them to Maglorix.

Maglorix slid his wrist through the shield straps. He grasped the shaft of the spear at the balance-point, about one third of the way back from the iron tip, and hefted it speculatively. Then he turned face on to Silus and let the shield and spear hang loose at his sides.

'Nooo!' The cry came from Buan. Still alive, he had drawn the dagger from his abdomen, and his arm was pulled back to hurl it at Silus. Silus turned, completely exposed.

Atius was there in a flash. He kicked the knife away from Buan's weak hand, then whirled and thrust his sword down through the barbarian's heart. He held it in place until the bodyguard had stopped convulsing, then withdrew it and wiped it on Buan's tunic.

Silus turned back to Maglorix. He hadn't moved. Hadn't even reacted to the death of his most trusted friend.

They locked eyes and Silus saw profound sadness and acceptance.

Maglorix inclined his head.

Silus took one step forward, drawing his dagger as he did so. He put an arm around Maglorix's shoulders.

Silus slid his dagger between Maglorix's ribs, halfway down his chest, just to the left of his sternum.

Heart blood blossomed around the wound. A widening of Maglorix's eyes was his only reaction. Then his legs became weak. He dropped his spear and shield and clutched at Silus for support. Silus gently lowered him to the ground. He lay by his side for the brief moments it took for life to leave him.

Then he lowered his head onto his enemy's chest and wept out his grief, his loss, and his emptiness.

-

The saddle bag thumped rhythmically against the flank of Atius' horse as they rode south, its solid load making a dull sound. Atius had insisted on taking Maglorix's head as proof of the success of their mission. Silus refused to carry the burden.

Atius seemed perplexed by Silus' reaction to his victory. In truth, Silus didn't understand it himself. He had pictured the moment so many times in his fantasies and dreams. The day when he finally had his revenge on the man who had taken everything from him. So why did it feel so hollow?

Maybe because nothing had changed. He still had nothing. In fact, he had less than before. At least then he had had a goal. Now what?

They would return to Eboracum. There they may be treated as heroes for slaying the barbarian chief who had caused so much damage. Or they may be treated as deserters and stoned to death by their comrades.

He didn't much care either way.

He looked over to Atius, who was whistling cheerfully, no doubt looking forward to being reunited with Menenia. For a moment he felt a surge of pleasure at the thought of seeing little Issa again. But then it was gone. Even his beloved little dog could not soothe the pain in his core.

Ahead of them lay days of riding through settlements of the starving, the diseased, the dying. He would harden his heart to their plight.

Atius leaned across and gripped his shoulder in a show of support. Silus gave him a half smile. Maybe the Augustus and the master of the Arcani would find a role for him, to give his life some meaning. Maybe.

He fixed his gaze on the path ahead and rode towards whatever it was Fortuna had ordained for him.

Epilogue

The elderly Greek physician leaned over Severus' chest and listened carefully as the Emperor inhaled and exhaled. He grasped his shoulders, lifted him up and shook him, cocking his head on one side to pick up any tell-tale signs of pleurisy. He eased him back onto his bed, and looked at the colour of his tongue and sclera. The he examined his joints, swollen from years of gout.

'Well?' demanded Julia Domna.

Galen shook his head. 'I am not Aesclepius. I cannot tell you if he will live or die.'

Domna turned to Caracalla and Geta waiting dutifully at the foot of the bed.

'Why do you listen to this charlatan?' demanded Geta. 'You know that most disagree with his methods. He refuses to use divination and the truth in the stars.'

Domna was hesitant. Caracalla knew that she shared his father and his half-brother's respect for astrology and eastern mysticism. Caracalla himself was ambivalent to the supernatural, largely accepting that he could change some things and not others. And yet Galen was Domna's friend, part of the cultured Empress' inner circle of philosophers and other intellectuals, and he could see she was torn between her respect for Galen and her natural desire to do the best for her husband.

'Augusta,' said Galen. 'You know my skills. I treated people dying of the Antonine plague. I was physician to the Emperor

Commodus, as well as to your family. I treated the philosopher Eudemus when he was sick with the quartan fever and all others had given up. I was the first to understand the way the differences between the arteries and veins function, the fact that there are two separate circulations in the body, and that venous blood is formed in the liver.

'Nevertheless, the Emperor's life still hangs in the balance and I cannot tell you whether he will live or die. What I can tell you, though, is that this is now the eighth day of his current attack, and most sufferers of pneumonia die by the seventh day.'

'So he will live?'

'Forgive me, Augusta, but you aren't listening to me. I cannot tell for sure. Only the gods know the future. My prediction though, is yes, he will survive this attack. Continue to use the linctus of galbanum and pine fruit in Attic honey, and apply the bladder of hot water to his chest regularly. I think he will recover. This time.'

'This time?'

'Augusta, winter is nearly upon us. His attacks grow ever more severe. You should prepare yourself that the time is coming when...' He let his gaze drop to the floor, knowing it was unnecessary to complete the sentence, and indeed may even be dangerous to do so.

'Mother,' said Geta, his voice a whine. 'Call my physician. He will consult the stars, make sacrifices—'

'Enough, Geta,' snapped Domna. 'It shall be as you say, Galen. Make him well. If his time on earth is soon drawing to a conclusion, then we can be consoled that he has lived a magnificent life.'

She swept from the room, her maidservant in close attendance.

Caracalla watched her go with mixed emotions. He was jealous of her obvious love for her husband, even though Caracalla shared that love for the old man. On the other hand, Severus was a shadow of what he once was. Should he give fate a helping hand, take the opportunity to hasten Severus' passing? For the sake of the Empire, and to preserve the dignified memory of the great Emperor. Not for his own advancement, of course.

He noticed Geta was watching him closely. What did his half-brother know? Or suspect? If his sibling found out about Domna and Caracalla, he would use the information to destroy him. That must never be allowed to happen. Because when Severus was gone, Caracalla had no intention of sharing power.

The easiest thing would be to end the relationship with Julia. But he loved her in a way he had never loved his wife, or a mistress, or a favoured slave. And she loved him back, he was sure, for all her distress at the enmity between the two siblings. No, it must remain secret. At any cost.

When the old Emperor finally passed, a reckoning would come. As he often did, Caracalla ran through in his mind the allies he could count on, and the enemies he could not, in the forthcoming power struggle. The court was split roughly down cultural lines, with the African faction, relatives and favourites of Severus supporting Geta, while the Syrian factions from Julia Domna's circle tended to support Caracalla. The Africans had never forgiven Caracalla for his part in the downfall of the former Praetorian Prefect, Plautianus. Papinianus, one of the Praetorian prefects and a close confidante of Severus, was related to Julia Domna and would likely try to remain neutral, as would the Augusta herself. Maecius Laetus, the other prefect who was still in Rome, was highly suspect in Caracalla's eyes. Valerius Patruinus tended towards Caracalla's viewpoint on military matters and the ruling of the Empire. Sextus Varius Marcellus and Quintus Marcius Dioga were supporting Caracalla in the hope of personal advancement. And of course, Oclatinius was Caracalla's man through and through.

At the thought of Oclatinius, Caracalla's thoughts drifted to the old man's protégé, Silus. He wondered if he had been successful in his mission to finish off the barbarian chief. If he made it back alive and Caracalla could protect him without losing too much political capital, he might find that resourceful man useful.

He returned Geta's gaze steadily and smiled with anticipation at what was to come.

Author's Notes

My other Roman series is set in the early Empire, and the sources, archaeological, epigraphic and literary are rich. By contrast, the sources for the period of the Severan dynasty are much sparser. This is a blessing and a curse. One the one hand, it means that research is difficult, and much is open to opinion and speculation. On the other hand, this is fiction, and speculation is what historical authors are all about.

Below is the entirety of the text from Herodian and Cassius Dio that pertains to the Expeditio Felicissima Britannica. Cassius Dio was a contemporary of Severus, who in his career was a senator, a governor and a proconsul, and knew Severus personally. However, he was hostile to Severus, and even more so to Caracalla, which means that while not guilty of sycophancy, he has a tendency to pick the worst interpretation of Caracalla's actions. This bias allows me to explore a less black and white demonic view of Caracalla's character in this book and the following ones in the series.

Herodian wrote a little later than Cassius Dio and is prone to inaccuracy. He is also thought to be somewhat hostile to Severus and Caracalla.

The other main text regarding the period is the *Historia Augusta* mentioned above, which is notoriously unreliable. It provides no information on the Expeditio Felicissima Britannica, except to note Severus' death in Eboracum. A few other ancient texts mention the expedition, but these were written much later.

My usual approach to historical fiction is to try not to write stories that are clearly in conflict with the historical record. However, I am quite happy to fill in the gaps with an entertaining and hopefully plausible story. I am also happy to choose between the less likely of two possibilities if it makes a good story, and this book has a notable example of this: the relationship between Caracalla and his mother/stepmother.

It is generally believed that Caracalla was born in AD 188, the child of Julia Domna and Septimius Severus, and full brother to Geta. However, Dr Ilkka Syvänne, Associate Professor at the University of Haifa and the author of the only full-length text on Caracalla, contends both in his book and in personal correspondence to me that it is possible that Caracalla was born to Severus' first wife, Paccia Marcian, in AD 186 or 174, and that the date attested in the Historia Augusta, AD 174, is the more likely. The affair between Julia Domna and Caracalla is also not my invention. Herodian claimed that the Alexandrians called Julia Domna 'Jocasta,' the name of Oedipus' mother, possibly in reference to rumours about an affair between Caracalla and his stepmother. The arguments are given more detail in Dr Syvänne's book, but the fact that it is possible is enough licence for me (in my personal rulebook) to play with this story.

Another liberty that I have taken with the known history is the unattested (i.e. made up!) battle at Cilurnum. However, the evidence of the exact nature of Caracalla's campaign are very limited, to the extent that even the chronology of the campaigns of those years is disputed. It seems that there were few pitched battles in the Expeditio Felicissima Britannica, the Caledonians and Maeatae having learned both from historical encounters such as Mons Graupius, and probably from initial encounters in the Severan invasion, that guerilla warfare and raiding was a safer strategy. That does not mean that large scale confrontations were completely absent, especially if unintended: I suggested in my narrative that Maglorix's intention was to avoid Caracalla's legions and raid deep into Britannia province instead.

Oclatinius, on the other hand, is a real historical character, albeit one about whom little is known. Marcus Oclatinius Adventus was a procurator in the service of Severus, but he seemed to have had an extraordinary career, starting in the ranks as a common soldier, being promoted to the Speculatores, the scouts, like Silus, and moving on to the Frumentarii, the spies that formed the Imperial intelligence service, probably as a centurion, then a camp commander. After the period covered in this book, under the sponsorship of Caracalla, his career rose to even greater heights despite his advancing age. In my book, though, I have placed Oclatinius as the head of the Arcani.

Only a tantalising glimpse of the Arcani or Areani is found in the sources. Areani, the term recorded in the extant copies of Ammianus Marcellinus, means 'people of the sheep-folds', and may relate to the fact that many of the members of this secret order were recruited from the rural dwellers of the lands between the walls. The term Areani is in fact a hapax legomenon, meaning that the word is only recorded once in the entire existing literature of a language. Ammianus Marcellinus relates how the Areani were involved in the Great Conspiracy of AD 367, taking bribes to provide intelligence to the invading Picts. Due to their role in this betrayal, the order was disbanded by Theodosius the Elder, father of Theodosius the Great.

Arcani is Latin for 'secret ones', and I have chosen this term over the Areani for two reasons. Firstly, the term Arcanus is found written in good hand in one of the Vindolanda scrolls. Secondly, the fact that this order is not mentioned anywhere until it was finally brought out of the shadows by its ill-deeds after it had existed for centuries suggest that it was indeed extraordinarily secret. The scarcity of information about the Arcani therefore gives the historical author considerable latitude to invent the society in more detail, which I have taken shameless advantage of.

I'll say only a few words on the Celts, as the subject can and does fill volumes. The Celtic people did not have a written language, and so were generally seen through the eyes of their enemies, particularly the Romans. The Celts were often held up by the Romans as ideals of how things used to be better in the olden days, while simultaneously condemning them as uncivilised and uncultured illiterates. I have referred to the Celts in this book as barbarians, since barbarian was the word the Romans used for all non-Romans, although ironically the Romans themselves would have been considered barbarians by the Greeks who invented the term (the Greek word *barbaros* was onomatopoeic, referring to the fact that all non-Greek speakers sounded like they were speaking nonsense, 'bar, bar, bar.') The term barbarian should not be taken to infer any value judgement on the respective societies, but this novel is written largely from the perspective of the Romans and reflects their viewpoint. However, the Celtic culture which once encompassed large swathes of Europe and extended into Asia was rich and sophisticated.

Religion played an important role in the lives of the ancients, both barbarian and Roman. At this time period, a number of Eastern mystery religions were vying for prominence in the Empire, including the cults of Christ, Mithras, Isis and Serapis, with Severus being a devotee of the latter. Various local gods were also worshipped, some merged with Graeco-Roman equivalents such as Sulis-Minerva in Bath (this combining of different beliefs is called syncretism). I've mentioned a few pre-Christian Celtic gods. Teutates, Esus and Taranis are Celtic gods mentioned by Lucan (Teutates being a variant spelling of the God mentioned frequently in the Asterix books, though I have resisted the temptation of putting the words 'By Toutatis!' in any of my characters' mouths). The Aos-sídhe are fairies which were worshipped in pre-Christian Scotland. Cailleach Bhéara, the divine hag, was a creator, an ancestor and a weather goddess.

Christianity at this stage was still finding its identity. Some persecutions against Christians are likely to have been carried out around this time, and the martyrdom of St Alban may have happened under Geta's watch when he was governing Britain. Many Christians will have viewed the Christian God and Christ as one of many in the pantheon who should be respected to be on the safe side, though clearly many will have followed the Christian teaching that there is only one God.

So ends Silus' origin story. The next instalment in the Imperial Assassin series, *Emperor's Knife*, sees Silus embroiled in the vicious sibling rivalry of Caracalla and Geta. The coming year will bring chaos, murder, scandal, divided loyalties and impossible choices. Silus' skills and morals will be severely tested.

Bibliography and Further Reading

I have consulted too many texts in the research for this novel to list here, but the following are some of the principal books I have relied on:

Sylvänne, I., (2017) *Caracalla, A Military Biography*, Pen & Sword Military, Barnsley

Elliot, S., (2018) *Septimius Severus in Scotland*, Pen & Sword Books Limited, Barnsley

Grant, M., (1996) *The Severans, the Changed Roman Empire*, Routledge, Abingdon

Levick, B., (2007) *Julia Domna, Syrian Empress*, Routledge, Abingdon

De La Bédoyère, G., (2003), *Defying Rome, the Rebels of Roman Britain*, Tempus, Stroud

De La Bédoyère, G., (2006) *Roman Britain, A New History*, Thames & Hudson, London

De La Bédoyère, G., (2015) *The Real Livrs of Roman Britain*, Yale University Press, London

Fraser, J. E. (2009) *From Caledonia to Pictland Scotland to 795*, Edinburgh University Press, Edinburgh

Fields, N. (2005) *Rome's Northern Frontier AD 70-235: Beyond Hadrian's wall*, Osprey Publishing, Oxford

Wilcox, P. (1985) *Rome's Enemies (2) Gallic & British Celts*, Osprey Publishing, Oxford

Breeze, D. J. (2008) *Edge of Empire, the Antonine Wall*, Birlinn Ltd, Edinburgh

Keppie, L. (2004) *The Legacy of Rome, Scotland's Remains*, Birlinn Ltd, Edinburgh

Shotter, D. (1996) *The Roman Frontier in Britain*, Carnegie Publishing, Preston

Historical Texts

Herodian on Septimius Severus and the Expedition to Britain

Adapted from Herodian's History of His Own Times, original transl. J. Hart 1749

While the Emperor was upset with his sons' immoral behaviour such as their fondness for games and shows, the Governor of Britain sent a message to say that the barbarians of that island had rebelled and were running amok in the country, looting and plundering. He requested the Emperor's presence, or at the least a strong reinforcement. Severus was delighted with this news, for he was naturally inclined to wish for glory, and wanted to add the victory over the Britons to the other victories he had achieved in the East and North. But he was also glad to find an excuse to take his sons away from the softness and luxury of city life and get them used to the discipline and labour of war. Without delay, he therefore gave orders for an Expedition to Britain. Even though he was old and afflicted with gout, he was still sound of mind even more than the most robust youth. He marched briskly, never resting long in any one place, but he had to be carried most of the way in a litter due to his infirmity. He arrived at the coast and embarked with his sons, landing in Britannia faster than the enemies expected. By levying soldiers from far and wide, he assembled a mighty army and readied it for war.

The Britons were frightened by the sudden appearance of the Emperor, and hearing tales of the size of the Emperor's force, sent emissaries to discuss peace terms and to offer reparation for their past offences. Severus was in no hurry to return to Rome, and still wished a victory over the Britons, so that he might add the title Britannicus to his other honorifics, so he sent the emissaries away, having refused their terms, and he continued to prepare for battle. His first job was to put bridges across the marshes so that his soldiers might be able to pursue the enemy over the treacherous terrain and fight on firmer ground. The majority of the island is often flooded by tides, making the country full of lakes and marshes. The barbarians swim or wade through these, not caring about the mud and dirt as they are always almost naked, for they don't understand the use of clothes, and only cover their necks and bellies with plate iron, which they hold as an ornament and a sign of wealth, and are as proud of iron as other barbarians are of gold. They dye their skins with pictures of various kinds of animals, which is one of the main reasons they don't wear clothes, as they don't want to hide the fine artwork on their bodies. They are a very warlike and fierce people, and arm themselves only with a narrow shield and spear and a sword hanging by their naked bodies. They do not use breastplates or helmets, as they think this would weigh them down when crossing the ponds and marshes of their country, which continually send up thick vapours, condense the air and make it foggy. Severus collected everything he thought might help the Romans and annoy and harass the barbarians.

When Severus considered that everything was ready, he left his youngest son, Geta, in the part of the island that was under Roman rule, to administer justice and manage all other political affairs, with the help of some of his father's older and more experienced friends. Accompanied by Caracalla, he advanced against the barbarians. After passing the ditches and parapets which protected the Roman territory, several short battles and skirmishes were fought, and the barbarians were always beaten. However, being well-acquainted with the countryside, they easily escaped and hid themselves in woods and marshes. The unfamiliarity of the Romans with the terrain served to protract a dull and tedious war.

Severus, now being old and infirm, was seized by a lingering illness that prevented him from leaving his quarters, and obliged him to give the command of the campaign and the army to Caracalla. But Caracalla showed little interest in the barbarians, and gave his attention to gaining the loyalty of the army. He made use of every means possible to concentrate the whole power into his own hands, while slandering his brother, Geta. He was annoyed at the slow progression of his father's illness and thought the old man a burden because he had lived so long. To rid himself of his father, he tried to persuade the physicians to give him a fatal dose of medicine. Eventually, Severus died, mainly from grief, after having achieved more glory in war than any other Emperor before him, none of whom could boast of so many victories, both in civil wars against rivals and in foreign expeditions against the barbarians. He reigned for eighteen years and was succeeded by his sons, to whom he left more treasure than any father had ever bequeathed before, and a military power so formidable that nothing could resist it.

Dio Cassius on Septimius Severus and the Expedition to Britain

Adapted from an English translation of Dio's Roman History, Book 77, by Earnest Cary PhD, 1914

Severus, seeing that his sons were changing their way of life, and that the legions were losing their vigour through idleness, decided to campaign against Britain, although he knew he would not return. He knew this mainly from the stars he had been born under, for he had them painted on the ceilings of the rooms in his palace where he held court so that they were visible to all, except for that portion of the sky which, as astrologers put it, "observed the hour," when he first saw the light – for this portion was not painted in the same way in both rooms. He also knew his fate because he had heard from the seers that a thunderbolt had struck a statue of his which stood near the gates through which he intended to march, and which looked out on the road leading to his destination, and the lightning had erased three letters from his name. For this reason, he did not return, but died in the third year of his expedition. He took with him an immense amount of money.

There are two main races of Britons, the Caledonians and the Maeatae, and the names of other tribes have been merged with these two. The Maeatae live next to the wall which cuts the island in half, and the Caledonians beyond them. Both tribes inhabit wild, arid mountains and desolate, swampy plains. They have no walls or cities and no tilled fields, but live off their flocks, wild game, and certain fruits, for they do not touch fish even though it is found in immense and inexhaustible supplies. They live in tents, naked with no shoes, and their women are shared, and they rear all their offspring together. Generally their rule is democratic, and as they are very fond of plundering they choose their boldest men as rulers. They ride into battle in

369

chariots, and their horses are small and swift. They also have infantry, who can run fast, and stand their ground firmly. They arm themselves with a shield and a short spear, and have a bronze apple attached to the end of the shaft of the spear, so that when shaken it makes a clashing noise to terrify the enemy. They also have daggers. They can endure hunger, cold and any form of hardship. They plunge into swamps and live there for days with only their heads above water. In the forests they live on bark and roots, and in emergencies can prepare a kind of food which eating even a bean-sized portion will prevent hunger or thirst.

The general character of the island of Britain however, is such that the inhabitants are the least hostile part. For it is an island, and this fact, as I have already stated, was proven beyond doubt at the time. It is 951 miles long and 308 miles wide at its greatest width, 40 miles at its least width. Out of all this territory, we hold slightly less than a half.

Severus therefore wished to subjugate the entire island and invaded Caledonia. But as he advanced through the country, he experienced countless hardships such as cutting down the forests, levelling the heights, filling up the swamps and bridging rivers. But he did not fight a battle and did not come across the enemy equipped for battle. The enemy put sheep and cattle in front of the soldiers for them to seize, so that they would be lured on further until they were exhausted, as the water caused great suffering to the Romans, and when they became scattered, they were attacked. Unable to walk, they were killed by their own men to avoid capture, and fifty thousand died. But Severus did not stop until he reached the furthest extremity of the island. From here he accurately observed the variation of the sun's movement and the length of days and nights in the summer and winter. Having thus been carried through practically all of this hostile country (as he was actually carried in a covered litter most of the way due to his illness), he returned to friendly territory after he had forced the Britons to come to terms on the condition that they should abandon a large part of their territory.

Caracalla was causing Severus alarm and anxiety by his intemperate life, and by his apparent intention to murder his brother at the first chance, and even by plotting against the Emperor himself. Once he charged out of his quarters, yelling that he was being wronged by Castor. Castor was the best of the freedmen who attended Severus, and he held the offices of both secretary and chamberlain. Some soldiers that had been got ready before this, got together and joined in the shouting, but they were quickly stopped when Severus appeared among them and punished the worst offenders. On another occasion, when Severus and Caracalla were riding forward to meet the Caledonians in order to receive their arms and discuss the details of the truce, Caracalla attempted to kill his father with his own hand. They were riding forward, Severus also being mounted despite injury to his feet from his illness, and the rest of the army were following behind. The enemy's force was also so far behind as to be mere spectators. While all were proceeding in silence in good order, Caracalla suddenly reined in his horse and drew his sword as if he were going to strike his father in the back. But the others who were riding with them saw this and cried out, so Caracalla in fright abandoned the attempt. Severus turned at the shouting and saw his son with his sword drawn. Despite this he didn't say a word, but ascended the tribunal, finished his business and returned to headquarters. Once there he summoned Caracalla, together with Papinianus and Castor, and ordered that a sword was placed within easy reach. He then rebuked his son for having dared to do such a thing, especially in plain sight of both allies and enemy. Then he said, "Now if you really want to kill me, do it now, for you are strong, and I am an old man and prostrate. And if you wish me dead but don't want to kill me with your own hands, there is Papinianus, the prefect, standing beside you, whom you can order to slay me, for he will do anything you command as you are virtually Emperor." Despite speaking like this, he did Caracalla no harm, even though he often blamed Marcus (Aurelius) for not quietly doing away with Commodus and had often himself threatened to do this to his own son. He only ever uttered these threats when he was angry though, whereas on this occasion he allowed his love for his son to outweigh his love for his country, and in doing so betrayed his other son, as he well knew what would happen.

When the inhabitants of the island revolted again, he summoned the army and ordered them to invade the rebels' country, killing everyone they met, and he quoted these words:

"Let no one escape sheer destruction,

No one our hands, not even the babe in the womb of the mother,

If it be male, let it nevertheless not escape sheer destruction."

After this, the Caledonians joined the revolt of the Maeatae, and he began to prepare to make war upon them in person. While doing this, he died from his illness on the fourth of February, some say with help from Caracalla. Whatever the case, before Severus died, he is said to have told his sons (I give his exact words without embellishment): "Be harmonious, enrich the soldiers and scorn all other men." His body, dressed in military apparel, was then placed upon a pyre, and the soldiers and his sons ran around it as a mark of honour. The soldiers who had items they could offer as gifts to hand threw them onto the pyre and the sons applied the flame. After the cremation, the bones were placed into an urn of purple stone, taken to Rome and placed in the tomb of the Antonines. It is said that Severus asked for the urn shortly before his death, and after feeling it, said, "You shall hold a man that the world could not."

Severus was small in height, but powerful, though he was eventually weakened by gout. He was keen and vigorous of mind. For education, he was eager for more than he obtained, and for this reason he was a man of few words, but many ideas. He was not forgetful to his friends, but to his enemies he was oppressive. He took great care over everything he desired to achieve, but was careless of what was said about him. He therefore raised money from every possible source, with the exception of killing to receive it, and he met all necessary expenditures with good grace. He restored a large number of ancient buildings and inscribed his own name upon them as if it was he that had erected them in the first place from his private funds. He spent a great deal uselessly repairing other buildings or constructing new ones. For instance, he built a huge temple to Bacchus and Hercules. But though his expenditures were enormous, he nevertheless left behind him many tens of thousands. He rebuked unchaste persons, and enacted some laws on adultery. As a consequence, there were many indictments for that offence (for example, when I was consul, I found three thousand entered on the docket!), but since very few people prosecuted these cases, he stopped troubling himself about them. Regarding this, a witty remark is reported to have been made by the wife of Argentocoxus, a Caledonian, to Julia Augusta. When the empress was jesting with her, after the treaty, about the free sexual relations women in Britain had with men, she replied, "We fulfil the demands of nature in a much better way than do you Roman women; for we consort openly with the best men, whereas you let yourselves be debauched in secret by the vilest." This was the answer of the British woman.

The following is the routine that Severus followed in peacetime. He was sure to be doing something before dawn, and afterwards he would take a walk while telling and hearing of things of importance to the empire. He would then hold court, unless there was a great festival. He used to do this very well, for he allowed the litigants plenty of time and he gave us, his advisors, full liberty to speak. He would hear cases until noon, then he would rise, as far as his strength permitted, and then perform some gymnastic exercise and take a bath. After this he ate a big lunch, either by himself or with his sons. Then he would take a nap, and after this attend to his remaining duties. He would then walk about, while engaging in discussion in Greek and Latin. Towards evening he would bathe again and dine with his associates, for he rarely invited guests to dinner. He only indulged in expensive banquets when it was unavoidable. He lived sixty-five years, nine months and twenty-five days, as he was born on the eleventh of April. He ruled for seventeen years, eight months and three days. He showed himself so active, then even when he was expiring, he gasped, "Come, give it here, if we have anything to do."